BLOOD
RED
SUMMER

ALSO BY ERYK PRUITT

PRAISE FOR ERYK PRUITT

"There are storytellers who seem to come to us fully formed. Bards who create worlds and characters that captivate us instantaneously. Eryk Pruitt is such a storyteller, and *Something Bad Wrong* is such a book. A kaleidoscope of Southern Gothic traditions seamlessly combined with an incredible murder mystery, all told with Pruitt's unique, indomitable style. *Something Bad Wrong* is some very, very good writing."

—S. A. Cosby, bestselling author of *Razorblade Tears* and *Blacktop Wasteland*

"*Something Bad Wrong* hits on every cylinder—expertly plotted, deliberately paced, deeply human, incredibly relevant, and just utterly absorbing. This is a golden example of the genre."

—Rob Hart, author of *The Paradox Hotel* and *The Warehouse*

"I still can't believe *Something Bad Wrong* wasn't written specifically for me. A gripping page-turner about a cold case murder with a gutsy true-crime podcaster as a main character. It's the most devourable mystery novel I've read in years."

—Brooke Cain, *Raleigh News & Observer*

"*Something Bad Wrong* is more proof that Eryk Pruitt is one of the most original, dynamic, and powerful voices writing today. While his uncanny flair for language and acute observation set him apart from his contemporaries, it's never lost that, foremost, Pruitt is a natural storyteller—the kind of person quietly telling a story to a group of people at a table in a restaurant, and by the end of the evening, the entire restaurant is listening, rapt. At a time when contemporary crime fiction is putting out outstanding title after title, *Something Bad Wrong* belongs on a bookshelf among the best of the best."

—E. A. Aymar, author of *No Home for Killers*

BLOOD RED SUMMER

A THRILLER

ERYK PRUITT

THOMAS & MERCER

Text copyright © 2024 by Eryk Pruitt
All rights reserved.

Published by Thomas & Mercer, Seattle

www.apub.com

Amazon, the Amazon logo, and Thomas & Mercer are trademarks of Amazon.com, Inc., or its affiliates.

ISBN-13: 9781662514562 (paperback)
ISBN-13: 9781662514579 (digital)

Cover design by Caroline Teagle Johnson
Cover image: © Cavan Images / plainpicture; © Olga Siletskaya / Getty Images

Printed in the United States of America

For Alexis, Jackie,
and, of course,
Lana

Where justice is denied, where poverty is enforced, where ignorance prevails, and where any one class is made to feel that society is an organized conspiracy to oppress, rob, and degrade them, neither persons nor property will be safe.
—Frederick Douglass

Journalism is printing what someone else doesn't want to be printed. Everything else is public relations.
—George Orwell

Where's the beef?
—Clara Peller

PART ONE

CHAPTER ONE

JESS KEELER

Present Day

Looking back, Jess Keeler reckoned she should have seen it coming. She'd stopped by Deeton's only cocktail lounge and found herself talking to the bartender about the ingredients of the latest special, when in walked a tall Black stranger. A handsome one at that, dressed in an impeccable suit. Chestnut-colored eyes, which scanned the room, looking for a place to sit. He settled on a seat two stools away from her. She tried not to pay attention—*did she mention that he was handsome?*—so she pretended to fuss over her cocktail so that it might offer the perfect photograph. She snapped a picture of it with her phone.

"It's a very pretty drink," he said.

"It better be"—she smiled—"for what they charge for it."

He looked over the menu. "Which one is it?"

"It's not on the menu. It's something special. You tell the bartenders what kind of flavors you like, and they'll make something for you."

The bartender wiped a towel across the bar in front of the man. "Good to see you again, Martin."

Jess's cheeks flushed hot. "My apologies. I had no idea you were a regular."

"I wouldn't say that. Until the past two weeks, I had never been here before. But I stopped in one day on a whim and had their margarita, the one with the . . . oh, what is it?"

"Hibiscus. It's amazing."

"Yes, the hibiscus. After that, I've made it a point to stop by for a cocktail after work. To treat myself."

"If you want to treat yourself, you should definitely get this one. I don't know what it's called, but it's got mezcal and carrot juice and a bunch of other stuff I can hardly pronounce. It's good. Here, try mine."

"Oh, I don't know . . ."

"It's fine. I've had my shots. Here. Try it."

Martin did. He lifted an eyebrow. "Wow. I would never have thought to put carrot juice in a drink, but . . ."

"She's good at what she does."

Martin motioned to the bartender that he would like another, then nodded at the empty stool between them. "Do you mind?"

"Not in the slightest."

He sat. "You know, please forgive me, but there's something familiar about you. I can't put my finger on it . . ."

Jess smiled. "Let me guess: You recognize my voice?"

"Is that even possible? To recognize someone for their voice?"

She sipped from her drink and playfully shrugged.

"Don't tell me. Let me guess. You do play-by-play for the Tucker Crawdads?"

"Is that a real thing?"

"They won the Double-A championship last year. They are very much a real thing."

"Obviously that's not it."

"Okay . . . you call bingo at the civic center?"

"No, but that sounds like fun. Keep trying."

"Are you the lady who robocalls me once a week to tell me about my credit score?"

"Getting colder."

His drink arrived. He watched the dehydrated lime wheel float inside the pinkish-orange pool before he poked at it.

"I give up."

"Are you a fan of true-crime podcasts?"

"Who isn't?" His chestnut-colored eyes lit up as it occurred to him. "Wait a second . . . no . . . Are you . . ." He slapped his hand on the bar. "You're the lady who did the podcast about the Christmas Eve Murders."

"Jess Keeler." She lifted her coupe to his. "Pleased to meet you."

Their glasses clinked. "Wow. I'm having a drink with a bona fide celebrity."

"Hardly."

"How can that be true? You helped catch the killer of a fifty-year-old murder."

"We didn't catch him. He's still out there."

"Really? Well, still . . . it was a good story, though. My mother and I listened to the whole thing driving to the beach and back."

"Nice. It took me two years to make it."

They laughed.

"So," he said, after another sip, "what are you working on next?"

She held her glass to her lips and pretended to find interest in the whiskeys on the shelf behind the bar. The ornate light fixtures. A painting on the wall.

"Oh, come on," he groaned. "Don't play coy with me. I'm your biggest fan."

Jess could barely swallow without laughing. "Are you now? Thirty seconds ago you thought I called play-by-play for the Tucker Crabapples."

"Crawdads." He squared his broad shoulders and leaned close enough for her to smell his aftershave. "Jess Keeler, from the hit podcast

3

Something Bad Wrong, surely isn't the type to lie low for long. Tell me what you've got cooking."

"I'm not really supposed to be talking about it . . ."

"I can keep a secret."

". . . and there's nothing really set in stone yet . . ."

"I'm all ears."

Jess looked over both shoulders before finally whispering, "I've been working with a television crew."

"Holy sh—" Martin realized how loud he was and immediately dropped his volume. "Wow. So, like, are we talking true-crime docuseries?"

"Something like that," she said. "But it's far from *official*. Just something in the works."

"What's the case this time?"

She plucked the edible flower from her glass and popped it into her mouth.

Martin mimed zipping shut his lips. "I won't tell a soul."

"That's the problem," she said. "We haven't found a story that interests us just yet."

"How can that be? Lake Castor has no shortage of sensational crimes."

"Oh, tell me about it."

"In fact, I was reading just the other day about the Bonnie Mills case."

"A little light reading before bed?"

Martin smiled, and she felt her knees weaken. "Are you familiar with it?"

"I am. Eleven years old. She went missing after walking home from church. Her body was found three weeks later in the woods just behind her house."

"It's horrible."

"It is. To think that her parents and police scoured the town, questioned all these people, and their poor little daughter's body was wasting away just outside her own house."

"What about the murder of Jessi Spangler in 1985?" he asked. "That's a good one."

"No killer was ever identified."

"But there were a ton of suspects." He ticked them off each of his slender fingers. "The drug dealer, the football player, those high school kids who—"

"Still . . ."

"I know . . ." Martin's face lit up. "The disappearance of Tonya Sue Sawyer. They never found her body."

"No, but they found her car, and in the trunk, there was a leather jacket from a well-known motorcycle gang."

Martin took another drink. "What about Marsha Reames? That would make a good story. I bet you could get several episodes out of that one. All the characters . . . the father, the ex-boyfriend . . . that *mother* of hers . . ."

"Sure." Jess shrugged, then returned to her drink. "There are all kinds of crimes in Lake Castor that would make for great stories, but none of them have piqued the Germans' interest."

Martin cocked his head. "The Germans?"

"Friedrich and Felix Schafer," Jess said. "They're the executives for the production company that hired me: Story Time Productions." She used air quotes. *"Where story matters."*

"That's their slogan?"

She rolled her eyes. "Tell me about it."

"What piques their interest?" Martin employed air quotes.

"They said they'll know it when they see it." Jess dabbed the side of her glass with a cocktail napkin. "I'm sure there's a German word for this special brand of frustration."

"What if you found a story that is so different from all the other stories and when you tell it, the way only *you* could, it forces them to open their eyes and look at you?"

"What kind of story is that?"

"One that doesn't revolve around another dead white girl."

Jess set her drink down on the bar top. She reconsidered him, taking him in a whole new light. "I'm guessing you might have one in mind."

"It's highly likely." He finished his cocktail, then nodded toward her empty glass. "Would you like another?"

"I'm not so sure."

"Come on. I'd tell you to try the pear martini, but you had that one last week. How about the habanero margarita?"

"Why do I get the feeling this isn't exactly a chance meeting?"

"Your Instagram feed."

Jess narrowed her eyes.

"You post your cocktails on your social media. So I knew you come here. I've been stopping by every night for the past two weeks."

"To what end?"

"To get your attention."

"You have it. Although there are less creepy and time-consuming ways. Like email."

"I've emailed you several times."

"I don't check it much anymore."

This was true. Ever since *Something Bad Wrong*, she'd received so many messages from people with murdered loved ones who wanted her to look into their cases. For the first several weeks, she'd responded to them. She'd even poked her nose into a couple of them. It was heartbreaking, but she couldn't investigate them all. After a while, she'd quit opening her emails.

Martin didn't waver. "So shall I buy you another drink or what?"

"Actually . . ." She began to gather her things. She felt like a fool. She was graduating from shamefaced to moderately angry.

"Wait. Hear me out."

"I don't think that's such a good idea. I've known you for all of ten minutes, and I haven't exactly enjoyed the last couple of them."

"We started off so nice."

"Then careened straight downhill."

"One drink."

Her eyes sadly ran over his broad shoulders, that wide chest. *He was so tall . . .*

"Please, Jess. I went to a lot of trouble to speak with you. A lot. Why don't you let me buy you a drink and tell you what all the trouble's about?"

She sighed. "One drink."

"Thank you." He motioned for the bartender. He ordered for them. She was slightly bothered by how well he seemed to anticipate her tastes, but only slightly. She wanted to be angry with him for playing her in such a fashion, but another, larger part of her admired his initiative.

It was like something you might have done long ago.

The drinks landed. She took a quick taste. "You better hurry," she said. "The second drink never lasts as long as the first one."

"Have you ever heard of the Lake Castor Sniper?"

She nearly choked on her cocktail. "Lake Castor had a *sniper*? When was this?"

"1984."

"How many victims?"

"Five were killed. One was injured."

Jess set down her drink. She racked her brain, but still came up empty. "Why have I never heard of this?"

"The killings took place in the Back Back."

"I'm sorry. The what?"

"It's an area now known as the South Side, but back in the old days, folks called it the Back Back. It's the historically Black part of town."

"Oh." Jess felt her cheeks heat up again. "That's horrible."

"There are worse indignities. Trust me."

"And I'm guessing they caught the man responsible?"

"There was an arrest, yes." Martin's smile tightened. "A confession. A conviction."

"Wow. That's great."

"Except a lot of people believe they arrested the wrong man."

"I have to admit, you have stoked my curiosity. Your surreptitious approach notwithstanding, the whole . . ." She motioned toward his handsome figure. "Yeah. That whole bit. I'll read up on it. But I have to ask, What's your interest in this case?"

"Besides the fact that it's an interesting story about a tragic period among my people?"

Jess said nothing.

"The man they arrested," Martin said, "was my uncle."

CHAPTER TWO

Jess Keeler

Present Day

[*EXT. LAKE CASTOR—DRONE SHOT*

The drone flies high above Lake Castor, giving the viewer an overhead view of the former mill town. We see the old June River Fabrics mill building, which only six years ago was renovated into upscale condominiums with a beautiful view of the lazy June River. We see downtown, recently revitalized with cupcake shops, boutiques, restaurants. We see the green spaces and the happy, vibrant people enjoying them.]

JESS KEELER: Lake Castor, Virginia, suffers a troubled history. For decades in the twentieth century, it was home to the largest textile mill east of the Mississippi. In the late seventies, however, that mill was shuttered, plunging the population into desperation and despair. Overnight, nearly sixty percent of the population lost their main source of income. Within six months, nearly half of the people who called Lake Castor home had relocated.

[*The drone sweeps wide, showing off schools, shopping centers, parks. Lake Castor could be Anywhere, USA. Its stories are shared by Americans across the country.*]

JESS KEELER: For decades after the closure, Lake Castor residents put up a brave front. They struggled mightily in the face of adversity, growing new businesses where they could. Finding new streams of revenue. But like any southern town during that era, there were divisions within the community. There were separations by class. By religion.

And by race.

[The camera continues its movement south of downtown. It crosses the highway, and the viewer sees signs of blight. Disrepair. Neglect. Many of the buildings have not been updated since the halcyon days of June River Fabrics. Several storefronts stand abandoned. The streets are less maintained.]

JESS KEELER: While the majority of Lake Castor citizens found life trying in the years following the abandonment of June River Fabrics, some communities found it remarkably more difficult.

Fears fueled by racism combined with the insidious practice of redlining resulted in the Black population of Lake Castor being directed to live in neighborhoods south of the city center. While the poorer white class was said to live in the neighborhood "in the back of town," the Blacks were pushed to what was called "the back back of town," or simply the Back Back.

[The drone draws itself lower, bringing the audience in closer. The streets become wider, the homes larger. We are no longer taking in Lake Castor as a whole, but are fully focused on the Back Back. We tighten the frame around a smaller cross section of streets within the Back Back.]

JESS KEELER: It was here, in Lake Castor's Back Back, during the dog days of summer in 1984, that the unthinkable happened. An unseen gunman embarked upon a calculated and deadly rampage that lasted four weeks, plunging the residents of Lake Castor's most afflicted neighborhood into abject terror. His victims appeared to be chosen at random. There was no rhyme or reason. People drew their curtains. They feared the daylight. They walked in zigzag patterns when out in the open. They prayed to their God that they might be spared.

In the end, five innocent victims lay dead, one wounded. A manhunt pillaged the once quiet streets of Lake Castor's Back Back. Law enforcement

questioned anyone and everyone, in search of the evil madman who terror-
ized the community.

[The camera tightens on a single street, then finally comes to rest in
front of a single home. It's modest, well manicured. A three-bedroom home,
its trim recently painted Carolina blue. The yard freshly mowed and the
hedges neatly trimmed. A two-door Kia sits in the driveway; a pickup truck
is parked in the street, near the mailbox.]

JESS KEELER: After a frantic three-day search, authorities finally
identified one man, twenty-three-year-old Ricky Lee Patience, as the assail-
ant, who had come to be known as the Lake Castor Sniper. Patience was
arrested, taken before a judge, and then placed in the Virginia state prison
system.

But before he was incarcerated, he resided here, in Lake Castor's Back
Back, the very neighborhood he would later terrorize. What happened
to Ricky Lee Patience? What could transform someone from a sweet boy
from the neighborhood into a cold-blooded monster who targets his own
community?

Or perhaps the question is, Did he actually commit these crimes?

We plan to answer these questions and more as we delve deep into the
horr—

"To be honest, I saw a much better house two blocks east of here."

Jess pulled her dictation device away from her mouth and turned to
face the source of the interruption. Aaron Blaine pushed a sandy-blond
lock out of his eyes and readjusted the camera on his shoulder. He
pointed with his free hand into the distance to his right.

"What do you mean *a better house?*" Jess asked.

"This one . . ." He shrugged and exaggerated a frown. "It's *okay*, I
guess, but if you're trying to tell a story about an impoverished community, it's not exactly going to sell it."

"Lake Castor has come a long way since the eighties," Jess reminded
him. "The last ten years or so, the town has undergone a bit of a renais-
sance. New restaurants, great rent for tech start-ups . . . there's been an

overall improvement in people's attitudes, as well. They don't even call this neighborhood the Back Back anymore. It's *South Side*."

Aaron wasn't swayed. "Still," he said, "it's important to provide the viewer with images of poverty. Challenge. The desperation associated with the area that is the setting of our story. This"—he motioned to the house and lawn in front of them—"ain't it. This is too suburban. It's too . . ."

"White?" Buffy Solomon, the sound engineer, had only removed her headset in time to catch the end of Aaron's complaint. Still, Jess noted, her timing was impeccable.

Aaron blew her off and turned to Jess. "I'm just saying. The other house is more clapboard. It reeks of despair. We film it for the sizzle reel. I know what Friedrich and Felix like. We need footage that will make people *feel*."

"We can't film a different house, Aaron," Jess explained. "We film *this* house. It's the home where Ricky Lee Patience was born."

"Actually, he wasn't *born* here." It was the researcher's turn to pipe up. Sandy Newman had been hired by Story Time Productions as their researcher for three reasons. As a twenty-four-year-old intern, she came cheap. She was also very hungry to learn the business. But most importantly, the Germans hoped her vibrant social media following would help sell the project to potential investors and distributors. She pushed her fashionable reading glasses farther up her perfect little nose and read her notes from her phone. "Ricky Lee Patience was born in Durham, North Carolina, in 1962 to Rosalie and Davis Patience. They moved to Lake Castor in 1974 after Davis took a job at June River Fabrics, only to have him lose the job three years later when the mill closed. After that, the father left to find work elsewhere—supposedly in Detroit—only to never be heard from again."

It was taking time for Jess to acclimate herself to working with a team. When she'd investigated and produced her podcast, *Something Bad Wrong*, she had most often worked alone, gathering all the research, analyzing it, and cobbling it together into a cohesive script. Her only assistance had come from an early partner, who would later quit the project, and Buffy, who had edited the sound files and uploaded the episodes.

Despite having most of her duties delegated to different members of the team, Jess found the television-crew experience to be more demanding. While Aaron scouted locations and Sandy dove into the research, Jess's main responsibilities were to organize interviews with subjects and to help shape the narrative of the story. However, without first immersing herself in the facts of the case, without those days-long sessions in the library in front of a microfiche machine or road trips to the courthouse for official documentation, Jess feared the story might forever remain just beyond her grasp. This was not how she was used to working.

After her initial meeting with Martin Potts, she'd pitched her story to the crew. Her first suggestion had been to head to the library and bury herself in old newspapers.

"How long will that take?" Aaron asked.

"Two weeks would be optimal," she answered, "but I'll settle for one."

"The best we can do is tomorrow," he countered. "Send Sandy to the library. She'll report back with all the important stuff. In the meantime, you set up the interview with the killer's sister."

"How will Sandy know what is the *important stuff?*"

Aaron had barely looked up from his computer, where he was editing footage for another project. "That's her job. She's the researcher. You're a producer now. You produce."

Still, she couldn't help but think that the biggest mistake the production was making was to rush the process without first grounding themselves in the facts.

Facts, she feared, as she watched Aaron grouse about the lack of poverty in his shot, were far from Story Time's main objective.

"Just get exteriors of the house, Aaron," Jess said.

"Fine," he sighed. "I suppose we can add some despair in post with VFX or something."

The front door of the house opened. Martin stood in the doorway, filling it with his broad shoulders. Jess had promised herself not to get taken in by his powerful chest or his smoky-brown eyes, but as soon as she saw him smile, she realized she was powerless.

"Wow," he called. "You brought the whole crew?"

Jess marched up the sidewalk to greet him, the others falling in line behind her. "There's no point having your mother tell her story twice," Jess said. "It's best if we capture it raw and unrehearsed."

"You're the expert," said Martin. He held out his hand as Jess approached, and it took her a moment to realize she was supposed to shake it.

Get your head together, Keeler, she told herself. Still, she counted backward the days since she and her husband had divorced. She took his hand and shook it firmly.

"Everyone come on inside," he said, opening the door wider. "I'll let Mom know to make some extra tea."

CHAPTER THREE

Jess Keeler

Present Day

The inside of the house smelled of recently brewed tea. The front door opened into a small living room, which was made smaller as the television crew squeezed in. It was tastefully decorated, but Jess found herself immediately drawn to the framed family photographs.

"Those are my sister's kids," said Martin.

"How old are they?"

"That young man, Noah, is five. Trina is nine."

"They look like a handful." She motioned toward a handsome man in the photograph with a younger, happy Martin. "Who is that? Her husband?"

"No." Martin let that word hang a moment before he eased out the next ones. "That's mine."

Jess might have slapped her own forehead. She felt her cheeks rush hot. "Of course he is."

He started to make a haphazard comment to apologize, but she wouldn't allow it. Instead, she distracted herself with another photograph. It was of the family. Mom, Dad, girl, boy. In black and white and older than the others. "Aaron," she said, motioning for her cameraman, "come push in on this."

Aaron steadied the camera on his shoulder and, with one eye through the viewfinder, grabbed footage of the framed photographs. He slowly tracked one end of the mantelpiece to the other.

Without making eye contact with Martin, Jess pointed to one of the pictures. "Is this your mother?"

"That's her. My grandmother died not long after I was born. I still have some memories of her, but not clear ones."

"And this?" she pointed at the young boy in the picture.

"My mother's older brother." Then he added, "My uncle."

Aaron blew a low whistle and zoomed in the camera lens on the photograph. "So that's him?"

"Ricky Lee Patience," said a voice behind them.

Jess spun to face a kindly older woman dressed smart in a pantsuit. She carried a tea tray, complete with six cups, a teapot, and an assortment of cookies. She placed this tray in the center of a coffee table sitting before a divan.

"Some newspapers tried to name him Richard, but he was born Ricky Lee. It says so on his birth certificate. Ricky wasn't short for nothing—Daddy used to say—except Ricky Lee Patience." The woman wiped her hands on the backs of her thighs and extended one. "My name, on the other hand, is Wilhelmina Potts. Everybody's always called me Willie. I hope you will."

Jess accepted her hand and shook it. "I'm Jess Keeler. Thank you for meeting with me."

"I apologize for taking so long with the tea." Willie looked around the room. "I wasn't expecting so many people. I don't suppose I imagined it took so many people to make one of your podcasts."

"About that," said Jess, "we are actually working on a true-crime docuseries."

"A docu-*what*?"

"It's for TV, Mom," said Martin. "Like that stuff you watch on Netflix."

Willie's face lit up. "Oh, so this is going to be on Netflix?"

"We don't know for sure," said Jess. "We pitch the show, and they decide where to try and sell it." Jess motioned to the rest of the crew. "This is Buffy, our sound tech. Sandy is our researcher. Aaron, here, runs the camera."

"I also edit, create graphics, produce, design theme music . . . ," Aaron grumped from behind his camera, ". . . but who's keeping track?"

Willie smiled at each of them and motioned to the tea tray. "I made enough tea for everyone."

Jess hitched a thumb at the photograph of young Ricky Lee. "He looks like a happy kid."

"He was, until he wasn't." Willie poured the tea.

Aaron peeked an eye out from his viewfinder. "Do you have a picture where he wasn't?"

Willie's face darkened. "I don't like to look at those."

"Understandably," Aaron said, "but the audience certainly might."

Jess shot him a glance, then smiled tightly at Willie. "I'm sorry. Go on."

"You know, when Martin told me that you had agreed to take our case, I can't tell you how happy that made me."

An immediate silence seized the room. Willie glanced at each person. Both Aaron and Buffy busied themselves with their equipment while Sandy opened her mouth, then closed it.

"What is it?" Willie asked. "What did I say?"

"We don't exactly take *cases*," Jess said. "We tell *stories*. Unlike law enforcement, our goal isn't to *solve* a crime, but rather to communicate to the public what happened, and to translate for them your experiences."

"I see."

"And furthermore," she continued, "we haven't really *agreed* to anything. This meeting here is very informal, as they say. We wanted to get to know you and hear your story, in hopes of finding out some of the particulars, to see what the story is, exactly."

Willie's eyes cut toward the cameraman panning across her family photos. The sound engineer loading the mic onto her boom pole.

"Yet you are going to be filming?" she asked.

"It's for our sizzle reel," Aaron explained.

"Sizzle reel?"

Jess stepped in. "This docuseries is produced by Story Time Productions, and they ultimately decide what story they are going to finance. Today, we'll record a short interview with you about Ricky Lee, about your experiences, and then we'll edit a short concept video for our producers to watch so they can determine if they think it's something they will choose to invest in."

"I see." Willie thought this over some. "So there's a chance they won't tell our story?"

"There is," Jess said.

"If Ricky Lee's story isn't *interesting* enough to them, they will finance another story instead?"

"I'm afraid so."

"Like a missing white girl?"

Jess fought every instinct to break eye contact with Willie while she searched for something to say. Before she could find it, Sandy stepped in.

"That's not going to happen, Willie," said the young researcher. "Because today you're going to tell a very powerful story—*your* story— and our kick-ass crew is going to cut together a reel that will tug at everyone's heartstrings and open all their wallets. Trust me."

Jess's first instinct at Sandy's intrusion was anger, but that quickly dissolved when she saw Willie's expression relax. The older woman seemed to consider every possible angle, then finally settled into an acceptance of her role and duty. Eventually, she relented.

"Okay," Willie said. "Let's make it sizzle."

◆ ◆ ◆

One thing Jess realized after producing her podcast, *Something Bad Wrong*, about the murders of Steven Hicks and Linda Harris—known locally as the Lake Castor Christmas Eve Murders—was that everybody felt they had a story to share. Jess would get emails, letters, and phone calls or even be stopped on the street by people who had some family history involving murder. An event that profoundly affected their bloodline, and all they wanted to do was share it with *someone*. Something that happened that they had only apocryphal information about, because no one would talk about it growing up, and they had done some amateur sleuthing, so wouldn't Jess Keeler find this exciting?

Sometimes, late at night, she might find herself bored and alone, and after a glass of wine, she might power up the laptop and perform a quick Google search or scroll through old newspaper articles to discover if there was any *there* there. A vast majority of the time, the crimes in question were hardly interesting outside family lore. The cheating husband killed his wife for the insurance money. An aunt turned up missing, and everyone suspected the uncle. Someone's son, fueled by his drug addiction, killed his parents.

Upon meeting Willie Potts and her son, Martin, Jess had no inclination this would be any different, but the allure of chasing a crime that wasn't a simple *missing white girl* or *marital discord gone wrong* had her juices flowing. Furthermore, the fact that she had never even *heard* of the Lake Castor Sniper, or an event in which six people had been randomly attacked by an unseen assailant, was too enticing for her to ignore.

She had to know more.

Aaron positioned his camera over her shoulder, so that Jess— the interviewer—could be seen at the edge of the frame. Willie Potts remained fast in the middle, the sole focus. Just above them and out of the viewer's range, Buffy hovered the boom pole with the mic pointed down at them.

"Let's start with Ricky Lee Patience," said Jess. "Tell us about growing up with him."

"He was my older brother," she said, "by about twelve years. They came and took him when I was about ten or so." Willie's eyes drifted toward the ceiling as she recalled. "Yes, that's right. I was ten years old."

"You were young," said Jess.

"I don't remember a whole lot about my brother growing up, I'm afraid." Willie turned her gaze back to Jess. "I have memories of him playing with me. I have a very distinct memory of a time when my teddy bear got torn and he filled it with new stuffing and sewed it up for me. I remember that being very sweet of him."

Aaron asked, from behind his viewfinder, "What are the chances that it was Ricky Lee who tore up your little doll?"

"What's that now?" asked Willie.

Jess shook her head tersely at Aaron, then turned back to Willie. "What can you tell us about when the shootings started?"

"Again, I was young." Willie sipped her tea, then replaced the cup on its saucer. "There were things that my mother kept hidden from me. She never told me why my daddy left us so early. She never told me why Ricky Lee had to go away for a couple weeks that last year he lived with us. And she definitely didn't tell me why I wasn't allowed to leave the house—not even to go to school—during the weeks of all the problems."

"You weren't even allowed to go to school?" Jess asked.

Willie shook her head. "No, and she refused to tell me why. I suppose it was to keep me from worrying. She was so protective of me, more so than she was of Ricky Lee. But I ended up hearing from some of the other girls from school that there were shootings and didn't nobody know what was going on."

"Did you ever suspect your brother?"

"Definitely not." Willie's eyes were stern. "Never once then, and never once since. I still don't think he did it."

Jess asked, "So why do you think the police targeted him?"

"Why do you think they target *any* poor Black man?" Willie's eyes tightened at the corners. "A lot of things have changed for folks in this end of Lake Castor, but a lot of things haven't."

"You never heard of anything that linked him to the crime?" asked Jess.

"Nothing that I was ever told about."

Sandy, the researcher, spoke from the back of the room. "According to my research, the assailant used an M40A1-style sniper rifle."

Jess's eyes widened at the intern's intrusion during her interview, but she kept her emotions in check. Before she could react, Willie shook her head.

"I'm not too familiar with guns, I'm afraid."

"That style of rifle was common with marine snipers in the Vietnam War," Sandy said, before anyone could stop her. "I didn't see any military record for Ricky Lee. Am I missing something?"

"No," she said. "He didn't serve."

"Did you ever see him in possession of—"

Jess spun to offer an angry expression toward Sandy, but noticed that Buffy had already silenced her by placing a hand on her shoulder. For a moment, Jess and Sandy shared eye contact that seemed to speak volumes.

Jess regained her composure, then turned to Willie.

"I don't remember Ricky Lee to have ever owned a gun," Willie answered. "Especially not any kind of military rifle."

"They were never able to tie him to a rifle of any sort?"

Willie shook her head, but Jess could feel Sandy stirring in her seat behind her, as if she were dying to say something. Jess took pleasure in denying her the opportunity and moved on instead with the interview.

"There was"—Willie appeared pained—"*one* thing."

Buffy cleared her throat. "I'm sorry," she said, "but can we turn off that ceiling fan? That hum is reading on my monitor, and it—"

Jess leaned over and flipped the switch, then returned her attention to Willie. "What is it, Willie?"

"The police . . . ," she said. "When they came for Ricky Lee, they didn't knock on the door. They kicked it in. I remember it clear as day because I was sitting right there, doing my homework, when they stormed the house. They showed Momma some papers, then went upstairs to tear apart his bedroom."

"Did they find anything?"

Willie lowered her head. "They said they did."

"What was it?"

"A rifle cartridge."

Jess cocked her head. "That's it? A single rifle cartridge?"

"That's all."

"Did they ever discuss the discovery of this evidence in the trial?"

Willie fell silent. Jess could feel Sandy's fidgeting reach a fever pitch behind her. She turned to face her.

"There was no trial," Sandy said.

"How can that be?"

"Because Ricky Lee Patience pleaded guilty."

Jess whipped her head back around to face Willie. Again, she silently rebuked herself for not doing more research before the interview. She felt a blaze in her cheeks and knew Aaron would have filmed her reaction.

"He *what*?"

"None of that matters," said Willie, "because he didn't do it. Those police forced him to confess, and they planted that rifle cartridge in his room."

"Why would the police frame your brother for the murder of five people?"

"For years," Willie said, "I've had half a mind to go down to Deeton County and ask that man that very question. Why he targeted Ricky Lee the way he did."

Jess sat forward. "Wait a minute," she said. "What do you mean *Deeton County*? I thought all the murders happened in Lake Castor."

"They did," Sandy said from behind her. "The arresting officer was a Deeton County deputy."

Jess closed her eyes. She knew the answer before she asked the question.

"What was this deputy's name?"

"Ennis Worthy. The first Black sheriff of Deeton County. He only retired last year."

When Jess opened her eyes, she saw that Aaron had the camera pointed directly at her, and Buffy had lowered the boom mic nearer to her lips.

"Ennis Worthy was the man who helped me with the first season of my podcast," Jess said.

"Ah," Willie said. "So you know him?"

Jess shook her head. "Not as well as I thought I did."

But, she thought to herself as she began planning the rest of her day, perhaps it was time for them to get reacquainted.

CHAPTER FOUR

HAL BROADSTREET

1984

Hal Broadstreet awoke to a pounding in his head. That came as no surprise after a night of drinking two jars of Uncle Meaney's corn liquor. What did come as a surprise, however, was that the pounding actually came from his front door. He sat up in bed only to realize he wasn't in his bed, but rather on his living room floor. He'd managed to undress himself only so far as to unbuckle his belt, so there would be no problem making himself decent.

But for whom? he wondered. The ruckus at the door continued as he peeked out the front window. A tan Dodge four-door idled in his drive. He shuffled to the bathroom to relieve himself.

When finally he'd gathered himself, he opened the door. Two plain-clothes cops stood on his porch. Neither of their faces reflected a happy home life.

"Hal Broadstreet," said the one most in need of a shave. "What do you say we go for a little drive?"

"I'm not going anywhere just because somebody asks me."

The second one cracked a smile. "That's where you're wrong. Ain't nobody asking you."

"I know you," Hal told him. "You're the dick who pulled desk duty back in January for beating on his wife. Detective Smolinski, is it?"

"You still digging through trash cans, Broadstreet?" Smolinski kept both hands deep in his own pockets. "What do you think that's going to get you?"

"Oh, I don't know. A rank and file like you? I doubt I could fetch more than an inch on the back page, I'm sure." Broadstreet pointed to his partner. "Now a *sergeant*, on the other hand . . . especially one with a hankering for prostitutes . . . I bet I could whip up a seven-hundred-word article in no time that might land on the front page of the local section. What do you think are the odds for syndication on the wire with a story like that, Sergeant Bravos?"

"How do you want me to do this, Sarge?" Smolinski asked his partner.

"With kid gloves, Jack," came the answer. "Avondale said to bring him in one piece."

Avondale. Hal sighed. As the ranking official in the Crimes Against Persons division of the Lake Castor Police Department, Lieutenant Kip Avondale tended to get whatever he wanted.

Hal wondered if the two suits would give him time to fetch a couple of aspirins. The day, he realized, was going to be a long one.

Smolinski and Bravos escorted him to the back seat. They didn't bother with the formality of handcuffs. They also didn't bother with a smooth ride, as they chose roads that challenged the Dodge four-door's suspension.

"You know there are fewer potholes if you take Barron Road to Lucas Avenue," Hal informed them.

Smolinski laughed. Kept his eyes on the road. "Will you listen to the reporter back there? Little Jimmy Olsen is filled with all sorts of news we can use."

"You want to tell us something we don't know?" Bravos asked from the passenger seat. "Tell us where you were last night."

"On the phone with your sister," said Hal. "Don't worry; I let her down easy."

Bravos said nothing. Turned his face toward the city passing by the window. Outside, the old mill crumbled from within, and its cancer seemed to infect everything around it.

"It ain't that long a drive," Smolinski said, "but we can make a stop, if you like."

"No need," said Hal. "I hit the jakes while you boys were knocking at my door."

"Big night last night?"

"No bigger than usual."

"You sure about that?"

Hal didn't like the tone in Smolinski's voice. Cops liked to hide their cards. He knew from years writing the news that some people liked to talk, while others preferred to listen. His job was getting them to talk.

"I may have had a drink or two," Hal said. "Makes my memory foggy."

Bravos turned around in his seat to face him. "Those drinks wouldn't be from illegal liquor, would they?"

"Is that why you picked me up?" Hal laughed. "Moonshine?"

Bravos turned back around in his seat. The car turned right on Fitzpatrick, and a bad feeling settled into the bottom of Hal's belly. Since waking, each moment only seemed to unsettle the ones previous.

"Something tells me this isn't about moonshine," Hal said. "I bet this has more to do with Lieutenant Avondale disliking that article I wrote about him last weekend."

"Wrong again," said Smolinski. "The L. T. hung it up on the bulletin board in the locker room. Maybe he likes the picture."

"Let me guess," said Hal. "It's right next to a picture of me?"

"Nah," said Bravos. "We hang your picture somewhere else."

"If he doesn't like me writing about him," Hal said, "then maybe he ought not to break the law in the name of upholding it. I only listed six times that Crimes Against Persons was caught planting evidence to make a case. That doesn't count the number of times they were *accused* of doing so."

"Somebody breaks the law," Bravos chuckled, "they always want to blame the police. That ain't news."

"Here's an idea," Hal said, feeling his oats. "It's revolutionary, so you'll have to bear with me. Maybe—just *maybe*—if your boss wants to keep his picture out of my newspaper, he ought to chase cases he can make stick with real police work. Maybe do his job for once. He ever think of that?"

Smolinski turned the wheel and parked between two Lake Castor police cars. Hal took in his surroundings. Through the windshield, he saw the front facade of Jem Fosskey's auto garage. He needn't any introduction. Over the years, his El Camino had consistently required service. Furthermore, Fosskey hosted one of the best card games in town.

He realized the cops knew *exactly* where he had been last night.

Hal watched Lieutenant Kip Avondale step out the front door of Fosskey's garage to light up a cigarette. He'd removed his jacket, loosed his tie, and rolled up his shirtsleeves. It wasn't even eight in the morning yet, but Avondale looked to have had a long day.

"Do his job for once, huh?" Smolinski said as he killed the engine. "I got an idea, paperboy. Why don't you ask him yourself?"

The previous Sunday, the *Times* had featured Lieutenant Kip Avondale on the front page. In the article, Hal accused the Crimes Against Persons division of crimes ranging from—but not limited to—planting or with-holding evidence, coercing confessions, unwarranted searches and sur-veillance, and witness tampering. The vast majority of these infractions, Hal alleged, had taken place against persons in the Black community. For a brief moment, Hal's editor and publisher feared there might be protests, or even riots, in response to the exposé.

There were not.

A prison break at a nearby correctional facility's death row captured the public's attention span, and Hal's article was immediately forgot-ten. Instead of calling for Lieutenant Avondale's resignation, the *Times'* readers were anxious for any information on the escaped convicts. Hal's editor, Vince Fenelli, convinced him to comply.

If Avondale appreciated the relaxation in coverage, his expression certainly did not betray any gratitude.

"The free ride for a face-to-face meeting was totally unnecessary," Hal told the lieutenant. "If you wanted to talk to me, all you had to do was pick up the phone. I gave you plenty of opportunities before we ran that article, but all we kept getting from your office was *no comment.*"

"I gave you what I felt you were worth, Broadstreet." Avondale struck a match and lit his cigarette, cupping his hands to shield the flame from the wind. "I would have said more if I was worried about anybody reading it. I have no idea how that rag of yours can still afford to line the bottom of my kid's birdcage."

"We're supported by a healthy subscribership," Hal said, "and even healthier advertisements."

"Businesses like to have their logos printed next to the latest UFO sighting?" asked Bravos.

Avondale crossed his arms. "We'd have more to worry about if a real paper covered it. But that didn't happen. I didn't read about it anywhere in the *Herald,* and it wasn't syndicated in the national press.

Only the *Times*. I might never have heard about it, but my wife likes the horoscopes."

"I like the crossword puzzles," said Smolinski with a sneer. "They're a lot easier than the ones in the *Herald*."

"So you see"—Avondale shrugged—"my feelings aren't hurt. That's because I know your days are numbered, Broadstreet."

Hal stuffed both his hands in his pockets. "I guess it's good that I'm lousy at math."

Behind Avondale, Hal watched a uniformed cop reel out the front door of Fosskey's garage. He looked green. He clutched his stomach and staggered behind the hedges to retch.

"What's going on in there?" Hal asked, nodding toward the garage.

"I'll ask the questions, if you don't mind," Avondale snapped. "Like why don't you tell us where you were last night?"

"Do all you boys dance to the same music or something?"

Avondale blew smoke in Hal's face. "This is your last chance."

"Am I under arrest?"

"Not yet."

"Then I'm free to go?"

Avondale looked up the street, then back down it. "We don't need you to tell us where you were, because we already know. You were here."

"So what?" Hal asked. "I get my car serviced here. Since when is that a crime?"

"Jem Fosskey is one of the area's biggest bootleggers," Smolinski said. "But of course, you know that. What did you call him in that *Times* article a couple years back?"

"King of the Piedmont Bootleggers," said Bravos.

"Yeah," said Smolinski. "That's it."

"They also like to play cards up there," said Avondale. "Gambling is a big no-no."

"That why you boys rousted me this morning?" asked Hal. "You worried maybe I had too much to drink while playing cards?"

Avondale took his time sizing Hal up. Hal didn't like the look in the detective's eye. Something felt off.

"Why don't we take a look upstairs?" Avondale didn't wait for a reply. He opened the door to the garage and motioned for Hal to enter. Hal didn't need to be shown the way to the stairs. He was very familiar with the place. He walked across the garage, toward the back, and then up the stairs to where Jem kept an apartment over top of the garage. Less than twelve hours had passed since he'd descended those very stairs.

At the top of the steps, he stopped shy of Jem's door made of solid steel, six inches thick. There was a sliding window in the center of it, which Hal knew Jem would have used before allowing entry. Hal also knew that no matter what was on the other side of that door, he would keep his trap shut. He had no intention of telling the lieutenant anything about the night previous. Not without knowing what they knew first. His plan was to play dumb, to extract as much information as he could without giving any away.

That plan went straight to hell as soon as the door was open and Hal finally saw what was inside.

CHAPTER FIVE

HAL BROADSTREET

1984

Hal knew death. He'd covered the Lake Castor crime desk for two decades. He'd greased the palms of enough medical examiners to get unvarnished peeks at the results of violence, which had desensitized him to brutality and gore. He'd covered shootings. He'd covered stabbings. He knew death's smells. Its secrets.

Nothing could have prepared him for what he saw inside the apartment over top of Jem Fosskey's garage.

Hal recognized Jem Fosskey immediately. Aside from his status as the region's most prolific bootlegger, his lumbering, hulking frame could give him away in any crowd. Even with Fosskey lying face up in a pool of his own blood, his face beaten beyond recognition, and the front of him torn and tattered with bullet holes and what have you, Hal knew it was him.

Hal turned his face away. He held vain hopes that the sight of his old friend wouldn't forever scar his memory.

"Jesus Christ," Hal whispered into the back of his hand.

Hal could barely process what he had just seen before the detectives started in on him.

"What were you doing here last night, Broadstreet?" Bravos asked of him.

Smolinski followed up. "We know you were here. Tell us everything, and we'll take it easy on you."

There was a second corpse on a cot in the corner. Hal could make out only two details. One was that blood still dripped from it onto a spreading pool on the floor. Complete saturation. The second was that the body was equipped with a pair of black alligator boots. Hal recognized them as belonging to Mel Kemble. Kemble had driven for Fosskey's liquor ring for decades and never dressed worth a damn, but would never be caught dead without the black alligator boots he'd won with a straight flush back in 1979.

"Broadstreet . . ." Avondale snapped his fingers several times in front of Hal's face. Snap, snap, snap . . . "You in there? You listening to me?"

"Huh?" Hal focused. He didn't like the look on the lieutenant's face. "Like I said . . . I told you, I, uh . . . I was—"

Hal was interrupted by the sight of even more blood, not connected to the spatter and smears of the others. This—a great deal of it—leading back to the darkened bathroom in heavy concentration. Hal had used that bathroom several times the night before, his bladder stretched to its limits by Meaney's wicked whiskey. Now flashbulbs chased out the shadows as they snapped—pop, pop, pop—and his stomach turned. He felt a heat blanket his forehead. He grew dizzy and caught himself in time before he tumbled to the ground.

"Who is that?" he asked, pointing toward the bathroom. "Is it . . . is it Wilbur? Meaney?"

Bravos wrote something in his notepad. "Meaney? Who is *Meaney*?"

"Who's back there?" Hal asked again. "Are they . . ."

There was too much blood for him not to know the answer.

"We're asking the questions here, Broadstreet," said Smolinski. "We know you were here. That's without a doubt. We got you dead to rights on that."

"Yeah, Broadstreet," said Bravos. "We got you."

"Wait." Hal blinked furiously. "You don't think I . . . you don't think I *possibly* could have—"

"Eh, eh, eh," Smolinski said. "What did I tell you? *We* ask the questions."

Hal's attention drifted again to the details of the room. The easy chair in the corner. The card table, still ringed with chairs. The blood-soaked cot where he'd sneaked some winks during all-night poker games. He knew the room so intimately that its current state cast a violent perversion upon his memory of it. It wasn't *supposed* to be smattered with gore; it wasn't *supposed* to be occupied by lawmen.

Yet here they were . . .

"Hey, look . . ." Avondale, playing the good guy. "I know you and me have had our differences, Hal. You think that little article last weekend was the first that's ever been written about me? It's like the captain says, *Don't fuck up on a slow news day.* At the end of it all, you and me are still friends."

Hal, still in a daze. "Is that right?"

"Yeah. Sure."

"Is that what you would call this here? Yanking me out of my house in the morning and hauling me up these stairs?"

"What would you call it?"

"I think you and your squad have such massive hard-ons for me," said Hal, "it's starting to make your wives suspicious."

Hal could see behind the lieutenant's eyes that Avondale would love nothing better than to punch him. The other men saw it, too, and turned their attention elsewhere, in case their superior might like to clean his laundry in private. Avondale took a breath, then put some space between himself and Hal.

"Why don't you tell us who else was here?" Avondale's tone dropped all pretense.

Hal's eyes flitted again to the blood smear headed into the bathroom. "Can you at least tell me who that is?"

"Sure," said Avondale. "First, give us some names."

"We know it was a poker game," said Smolinski. "Who else was playing?"

There wasn't a world in existence where Hal Broadstreet would give up those names. Not a chance.

Still, he recognized *opportunity*.

After all, he had a job to do and realized he had been gifted with a front-row seat.

"Names, Broadstreet," said Bravos, losing patience. "I ain't asking you again."

"The sooner you tell us," Smolinski said, "the sooner this will all be over."

Hal stared at his shoes a minute. To look anywhere else would fill him too much with sadness.

"Come on, Hal," said Avondale. Still testing out the good-cop routine. "Take us home."

"You want names?" Hal asked.

"I want five minutes alone with you," Avondale said, smiling. "But for the sake of our union reps, I'll take names."

"Okay. I got some names for you." Hal looked up. His eyes met Avondale's. "Two of them."

"All right."

"Got a pen and paper?"

Avondale nodded to Bravos, who produced both.

"Sure, Hal," said Bravos. "Give it to me."

"Two names," he said. "James and Linwood Briley."

Smolinski's and Bravos's faces fell. Not Avondale. He was waiting for something like this. Oh, he was *waiting*.

"How's that for names?"

Avondale's eyebrows raised a whole inch.

"I got some news for *you*," he said to Hal. "You just bought yourself a pair of bracelets."

◆　◆　◆

Four days earlier, six violent inmates had staged an escape from Mecklenburg Correctional's death row facilities. Among those escapees were the notorious Briley brothers, James and Linwood, who committed a seven-month rampage through Richmond in 1979. At first, Hal had resisted chasing the story, as he hoped to maximize exposure to his article highlighting the Crimes Against Persons division. But as more and more people reported sightings of the terrible Briley brothers, Hal saw an opportunity to soak up those fears like a sponge by reporting each and every one of them in the *Times*. He'd gone so far as to maintain a map of the sightings across Virginia and North Carolina. He'd written lurid headlines like BRILEY RAMPAGE II: ELECTRIC BOOGALOO and JAMES AND LINWOOD STRIKE BACK.

This, of course, was another reason for Lieutenant Avondale to hate him.

Hal had harassed the police department's phone lines for tips and information regarding the Brileys and had haunted press briefings by peppering them with questions, wondering high and low if the Brileys might be behind the most benign of local crimes. Upon Hal's mention of them in Jem Fosskey's apartment, however, Avondale appeared to have blown a gasket.

Once Hal was cuffed, Bravos and Smolinski roughed him down the staircase. They bounced him off one wall, then another as they descended, but Hal made sure to notice details: a bloody boot print on one of the steps, an array of blood droplets near the landing.

"So I take your brutality as confirmation," Hal panted, "that the Briley brothers are suspects?"

They answered by shoving him through the front door of Fosskey's garage, then parking him, his hands still cuffed behind him, on the stoop in the parking lot.

"Keep an eye on him," Bravos shouted to one of the uniformed officers manning the perimeter. "If he moves, shoot him."

The policeman watched him with very little interest once Bravos and Smolinski had returned up the steps. After a while, his attention drifted elsewhere, as did Hal's as he tried to process what he had just seen upstairs. He was careful to commit as much as he could to memory. His hands, being cuffed, could not take notes, but he did not think the image of the bloody carnage inside Fosskey's garage would escape his head anytime soon.

Hal saw movement to his left and turned his head to find Jem's brother, Wilbur Fosskey, lighting one cigarette off another while standing beneath a sycamore.

"Hey, Wil," said Hal.

"Hey, Hal," said Wilbur.

"Bum me one of those, will you?"

Wilbur looked like a man who'd spent the past hour or so with terrible grief. Still, he tapped a cigarette from his pack and placed it between Hal's lips, then lit it for him. Hal sucked at it until the cigarette was burning good and maneuvered it to the corner of his mouth.

"I'm real sorry about what happened to Jem," Hal said.

Wilbur remained on the brink of tears. "He always liked you, Hal."

"I liked him too."

"He always said you do right by us. So many of them newspapers want to run us through the wringer after a liquor bust or something, but you were always real fair."

"I sure tried." Hal wasn't much of a smoker, but he would do it to establish a bond with anyone he was interviewing. "Can you tell me what happened up there?"

"I got no idea. There was a phone call this morning."

"What time?"

"Oh, I don't know . . ." Wilbur's eyes went up and to the left. "About five thirty or so? They said there was something wrong with Jem and maybe I should go check on him."

"Who was the caller?"

Wilbur shook his head. "I didn't recognize her voice."

"Her?"

Wilbur nodded.

The cuffs rubbed against Hal's wrists, and he cursed his inability to take notes. "So you went upstairs to check on him?"

"I did."

The silence that settled between them was more pertinent than anything either could have said.

"You know what it was that I saw," said Wilbur.

"Yeah, Wil," said Hal. "I know."

Wilbur reached over and removed the cigarette from Hal's lips. It was only half-smoked, but Hal hadn't sucked a drag since the first one, and Wilbur no longer seemed inclined to continue the charade. He tapped off the long finger of ash, then stuck it into his own mouth.

"Answer me a question," Hal said. "There was somebody who'd been dragged into the back bathroom. I saw the blood but couldn't see who it belonged to. What can you tell me?"

Wilbur's eyes were elsewhere. "It was Felton."

"Felton?" Hal hadn't expected that. "Dammit. He didn't deserve that."

"None of them did, Hal."

True, but especially not Felton Loe. Where Jem and Mel were considered old-timers, Felton Loe was just a kid. Barely twenty years old, but could fix anything that ran on an engine. He kept Fosskey's cars running smooth, which was handy for a bootlegger as well as someone who owned a garage. The night previous, Felton had smiled big and wide after winning a pot with a pair of kings.

"He'd been shot at least once," Wilbur said. "They'd beat on him some, then stabbed him I don't know how many times."

"Overkill," Hal whispered.

"That about sums it up."

Hal considered that a moment. There was no excuse for what had been done to Jem Fosskey and the others. That level of brutality was unprecedented, in his experience. It was the stuff he'd read about only in articles covering the Manson family, atrocities in Vietnam, and . . .

. . . *the Briley brothers.*

"Hey, Hal?"

"Yeah, Wil."

"You mind me asking you something?"

Hal shrugged.

"Why they got you in handcuffs?"

Hal ignored that question and asked one of his own. "Who do you think done this, Wil?"

Wilbur's eyes hardened. "Hell, Hal. Who do you think?"

"I don't know. That's why I'm asking you."

"Jem didn't do nothing to call the likes of this, and you know it. He helped anybody looking for a drink, and that's all he did. He never was cross with nobody, and he damned sure wasn't violent."

"I know it. So help me out here. Who would have done it? The Briley brothers?"

Something flashed behind Wilbur's eyes. "Come off it, Hal. Jem ain't having nothing to do with no escaped convicts."

"Then who?"

Wilbur shook his head. "I got a family, man. I can't go around getting quoted in no newspapers."

"What about Jem?" Hal nodded over his shoulder, back toward the garage behind them. "Jem's your family."

"*Was*, man. And I ain't doing him or nobody else a lick of good by getting myself further into trouble."

Hal saw the sense in that. "Let's try it another way. I left here around midnight. That's when everything was a little foggy for me. The only people still in the game was you, your brother, Ralph Sparrow, Felton, Mel, and Uncle Meaney."

Uncle Meaney was the Black man Jem used to still his liquor.

"There was some more that come around after, and some that left long before," said Wilbur. "I, myself, checked out about an hour later and went home." He pointed across the street to the house where he lived.

Hal nodded. "Anything happen out of the ordinary after you left for the night?"

"Not really."

Hal leaned in. "You don't sound so sure."

"Well . . ."

"Lay it on me, Wilbur."

"Somewhere around five, five thirty," Wilbur said, his eyes swimming, "I heard a noise. Sounded loud, like somebody dropped something up at Jem's place. I come to the window to look out."

"What did you see?"

"Car. Backed up to the door."

"What kind of car?"

"A white one."

"Make? Model?"

"Hell, Hal. You know I don't want to—"

Hal's cuffs clinked together. "It didn't come from you, Wilbur. An unnamed source close to the investigation."

"One of them damn Pintos."

"You recognize it?"

Wilbur shrugged.

"Anybody in it?"

Wilbur shook his head.

"You know anybody who drives one?"

39

Wilbur turned his head to face the distance. "I couldn't say off the top of my head."

"Think about it."

Wilbur shook it off. "You've always given Jem a fair shake. Not like the other newspapers. He always liked you."

"I liked him too. Your brother was a decent, honest man."

"Some folks didn't see him that way."

"We all got to drink," said Hal. "Jem found a way to make that easy on folks. I'm the last person to judge."

"All I'm saying is that he always said you were solid." Wilbur cut eyes toward yonder garage. "Those cops, though. They're going to take one look at that mess upstairs and say it weren't nothing but criminals who got what was coming to them."

Hal wished he could tell Wilbur he was wrong, but he couldn't. He knew better. Those trains never ran on time in Lawles County.

"Make me a promise, Hal."

"Lay it on me."

Wilbur met Hal's eye. "Don't let them write off my brother. Treat him solid in the paper, like you always did. And don't let them talk down on him."

"You know I will."

"I'm serious." Wilbur threw his cigarette to the ground and stubbed it with the toe of his work boot. "My brother never set out to hurt no other man. All he ever did was trade in bootlegged liquor and look out for his friends. He didn't deserve to be killed like that. Them cops aren't going to do nothing about it. I need to know that somebody is going to pay."

"I'm just a reporter, Wilbur," said Hal. "There's only so much I can do."

"You said your job was to find the truth."

"Something like that."

Wilbur narrowed his eyes. "Then make sure to find it for my brother."

CHAPTER SIX

HAL BROADSTREET

1984

Hal, still cuffed and propped on the stoop outside Jem Fosskey's garage, was unable to take notes, so he concentrated to congeal them in his head. He allowed himself brief glimpses into his memory of the carnage upstairs. He did so without focusing on the fact that it was a man he'd known for quite some time up there, ravaged and mutilated. That it had been his friend.

He'd been measuring the angles he might approach when finally free to write about it, trying to ignore the light gathering of lookie-loos who'd arrived—curious about what might have happened inside, why there were so many police, why Hal was handcuffed on the stoop—when a bright-yellow Volkswagen rolled onto the street abutting the garage.

He knew the driver well. Olivia Crane, his rival, had worked the crime desk at the *Lake Castor Herald* for over twelve years. She stepped close to the crime scene tape and tucked a brown cigarette between her lips. One of the uniforms offered a flame from his Zippo while another blocked the wind.

"Thank you, boys." Olivia fixed her gaze on Hal. "What do we have up there?"

"Triple murder," said Hal.

Olivia raised an eyebrow. Impressed. "Well, well, well. And who, may I ask, were today's winners?"

"It was Jem Fosskey," Hal said. "Fosskey, Kemble, and Loe."

"All bootleggers?" She pursed her lips. Disappointed. "No civilians?"

"Jesus, Liv."

Olivia looked him over. "Why are you wearing bracelets?"

"You read my article last Sunday?"

Her expression reflected that she had but would rather die than admit to it.

She waved over one of the officers. "Sweetheart, let's get these hand-cuffs off of Mr. Broadstreet, will you?"

"I'm afraid I can't do that, Mrs. Crane."

"They're hardly necessary." She employed a demeanor geared to generate results. "Mr. Broadstreet is harmless as a pussycat."

"I wish I could, ma'am, but I have my orders."

She pouted her lip. "Sweetie, who is the ranking investigator who might have given you those orders?"

"It's Avondale, ma'am."

"Would you be a dear and let him know that Liv Crane has arrived?"

The two officers exchanged glances before one of them disappeared into the doorway leading him to the crime scene. Olivia tossed Hal a smile, one that hinted honey was much more effective than vinegar. That smile disappeared at the sight of the black town car parked between two squad cars.

Captain Henry Dorritt had made a career in Lake Castor's Crimes Against Persons division. Hal was accustomed to seeing him well put together, day or night, complete in suit and tie, one of the last men to abandon the fashion of wearing a hat. The morning of the Fosskey murders was no exception. His shirt had been starched crisp enough to draw blood. His necktie was severely knotted at his throat. His sharp, although weary, eyes took in the scene from the outer perimeters, then—in a series of blinks—moved to the finer details.

Details such as Hal Broadstreet, shackled at the stoop.

Or Lieutenant Kip Avondale, emerging from the garage door. He caught sight of his superior, and his eyes bugged wide, and he suddenly appeared to wish to be anywhere else but in Dorritt's crosshairs.

Dorritt nodded toward Hal. "What the hell is he doing here?"

"Sir," said Avondale, "I should brief you on the matter upstairs."

Dorritt's impatience wafted off him in waves. "What I need to know right now is why this man is anywhere near your crime scene."

"We had information, sir, of Broadstreet's involvement with . . ." Avondale nodded with his eyes to the apartment over the garage.

"*His* involvement?" Dorritt's distaste was so profound he could barely turn his gaze toward Hal.

"He admits he was here last night," said Avondale, "and when we brought him upstairs, he—"

"You brought him *where?*"

Avondale's discomfort intensified. "We brought him upstairs so that we could—"

"You granted him access to *the crime scene?*"

"Not *granted*, sir, we . . ." Avondale didn't bother chasing after the thought.

Dorritt motioned for one of the uniformed officers. "Release him. Now."

◆ ◆ ◆

By the time Captain Dorritt emerged from Jem Fosskey's garage, several more print and television reporters had gathered at the perimeter tape. He gave everyone a moment to assemble and settle down, then addressed the crowd.

"For those of you who don't know me," he began, "I'm Captain Hank Dorritt with the Lake Castor Police Department. I have commanded the Crimes Against Persons division for nearly ten years. I've seen it all, but what we have in that garage behind me is something beyond comprehension."

Flashbulbs popped as photojournalists snapped shots of the first body bag being wheeled out of the garage on a gurney toward the waiting medical examiner's van. It was followed by two more.

"At nearly six thirty this morning," Dorritt continued, "we were alerted by Mr. Wilbur Fosskey that there was no answer to his brother's apartment, which is located on the top floor of this garage. He discovered three men, deceased, then quickly notified authorities. Those men have been identified as Jem Fosskey, Felton Loe, and Melvin Kemble."

More flashbulbs popped. The WLCR cameraman shifted his video camera from one shoulder to another. More than a dozen microphones moved closer to Dorritt.

"Have you determined the cause of death?" asked a reporter for the *Whitfill Beacon*.

"You know that we'll have to wait for the medical examiner's report," Dorritt said, "but I can say right now that there were multiple wounds on the victims, from multiple potential weapons."

A collective gasp rose up from the press.

Hal, who already had this information, raised his hand in the air. "Captain Dorritt," he said, "is there any indication of who might have wanted Mr. Fosskey and his associates dead?"

If Dorritt heard him, he did not acknowledge him. "This investigation is underway, so you'll understand if I don't answer any questions at this time."

"Have you ruled out the involvement of the Briley brothers?" asked Liv Crane.

Dorritt seemed to anticipate this question. "I know we're all on edge ever since James and Linwood Briley broke out of prison. Trust me, when I heard that six convicts escaped from Mecklenburg's death row last week, I said to myself, *Please don't let it be the Briley brothers*. However, we believe they are headed north and are nowhere near Lawles County, and that this incident might be something altogether unrelated."

"Are there any details of the crime scene that you would be willing to share?" asked Liv Crane.

Dorritt arched an eyebrow. "I've seen everything Lake Castor has to offer," he said. "From the average Saturday-night shooting to the double suicides, to bodies found after rotting for weeks, or even months. I'll tell you this: I've never seen anything like what we have upstairs. It's more like something you'd see done by one of those Manson girls than something you'd find here in Lake Castor."

Hal raised his hand again. "Captain Dorritt, do you think this has anything to do with—"

"Like I said," Dorritt interrupted, "there will be no more questions at this time. If you're looking for a quote to help sell your papers, I'll give you one. We will investigate this heinous crime to the full extent of our highly trained detectives' abilities, and the person or persons responsible will be apprehended, arrested, and arraigned. The citizens of Lake Castor will be kept safe. Thank you."

Dorritt ducked back beneath the crime scene tape to confer with the other investigators. Hal clicked his pen shut and returned it to his pocket, then caught sight of Liv finishing her notes.

"Did he give you anything?" Hal asked her.

"Who, me?" A twinkle hit her eye.

"Come on, Liv."

Liv smiled. "How about I tell you all about it tomorrow?"

"Tomorrow?"

"Yeah," she said. "You can find it on the front page of the *Herald*, baby."

Hal rolled his eyes. "I'm going to write this story, and unlike you, I don't need the police to write it for me."

"Good." She slapped him playfully on his cheek. "I'm looking forward to your article in the morning, sweetheart."

I bet you are, he thought to himself as he watched her saunter toward the parking lot. He didn't wait for long, but rather rushed off into the early summer morning so he could start writing it.

CHAPTER SEVEN

JESS KEELER

Present Day

Since retiring as Deeton County sheriff, Ennis Worthy had spent most of his days on a nice patch of land he had up near the state line. He'd bought himself eight chickens and a rooster, so that he might have something to occupy himself with his uptick in free time. Nine months later, he had nearly a hundred birds.

"Can't blame me," he said, "given the price of eggs these days."

Jess couldn't argue there. She stuffed both hands in her pockets and watched as Ennis stroked an Ameraucana chicken's brown feathers. She'd made a casual habit of stopping in to talk with the former sheriff over the past couple of months. They'd become friends after he'd been instrumental in helping her produce the first season of her podcast. Their mutual friendship hinged on the fact that he liked having someone to tell stories to and that she loved to listen to them.

"That chicken there," he said, pointing at a gray silkie, "dances like Nancy Sinatra. That's why I named her *Nancy*."

There was a warmth to the old man, and she never doubted why he'd been elected to so many terms as a North Carolina lawman. Still, as she looked around the well-manicured farmland and tidy house, she wondered why he'd never found a woman with whom he could settle down.

"How's your mother doing?" he asked.

"She has good days and not-so-good days, but my son, Benny, watches her while I'm working." Jess would rather talk about nearly anything than her mother's worsening Alzheimer's. "Benny spends less time at his father's these days because Philip has taken up with a yoga instructor."

Worthy chuckled to himself. "Boy howdy, I bet that's got you rankled."

"Have you ever heard of anything more cliché?"

Worthy knew better than to comment. "I hear you travel with a tribe these days."

"It's a television crew," she said. "Where did you hear that?"

Never one to lay down all his cards, Worthy shrugged. "Just things I hear, is all."

"Did you also hear we've been looking into another story?"

"Is that right?"

"Yes sir."

Worthy slipped a slender blade of grass between his teeth and chewed it, his eyes fixed on the horizon before him. "Got one in mind?"

"I do, as a matter of fact."

Worthy said nothing as he poured chicken feed from a bag into a small metal feeder. The chickens whirred and squawked at his feet until he finished and hunched over to roll up the bag.

"It's actually a case you worked on," she said.

He didn't look up. "I worked on a great many of them. I reckon it's a bit difficult to remember them all."

"This one was pretty sensational. I doubt you'd have much trouble calling it to mind."

Worthy hefted the bag and walked toward the small shed where he kept his tools. She followed after him.

"Do you remember Lake Castor's sniper in 1984?"

Even a trained eye might have missed the small stutter in Worthy's step, but not Jess. Worthy hid his tells better than most poker players, but Jess had made it her business to study when he was lying and when he was telling the truth.

Worthy placed the bag of feed high on a shelf so no rodents could get after it. Then he dusted off his hands and turned to face her.

"I recall some of it, yes ma'am."

"Based on what I've learned so far," she said, "you were the man who arrested him. Nearly a month of terror, all ended by you."

Worthy wiped the bottom half of his face with the palm of his hand. "I just happened to be in the right place at the right time. The arrest of that man was the culmination of hundreds of man-hours of good police work. I'm just glad I was able to help in some way."

"Ennis, it's me." She smiled. "This isn't an interview for the eleven o'clock news. You've told me all kinds of stories from your time behind the badge. How come I've never heard you talk about this one?"

Worthy picked up a shovel, then put it down. He searched the small shed for something to do with his hands, but couldn't settle on anything.

"I just never reckoned it was all that interesting," he said. "It was another day on the job for me."

"I don't believe that for a minute," she said, but let it go. "One thing I'm curious about, Why were you arresting a man in Lake Castor? You were a Deeton County deputy at the time, weren't you?"

"I was." Worthy fished his hand into a bag of cracked corn and walked out of the shed. He sprinkled it along the grass, much to the delight of his gathering chickens.

Jess followed after him. "So I don't get it. If you were a North Carolina lawman, what were you doing pursuing a suspect up in Virginia?"

The flesh around his eyes tightened, and he glanced at the road behind her, which led to his home. "I'm surprised you don't have your camera crew with you, to get all this on tape."

"They don't know I'm here," she said. "I thought I would talk to you first."

A slight smile creased his face. "I was there," he said, "because I was doing a favor for a friend."

"What kind of friend?"

"An influential one."

Jess scratched her head and tried to make sense of what little she'd been given. "I still don't understand."

"There's nothing to understand," Worthy said. "South Side now is nothing compared to the Back Back then. It was 1984. Crack cocaine was just beginning to stretch its nasty fingers into the urban Black community, and nobody knew what to do when somebody started acting out, like Ricky Lee did."

Jess whipped her head around. "Wait a second . . . *Crack*? Willie didn't say anything about *crack*."

"Willie?" Worthy's face registered comprehension. "Aah . . . So that's who you've been talking to? Miss Wilhelmina Potts? The sister? Yes, I've heard from her a fair share over the years. She can be . . . *persistent*."

"Her brother is in prison, perhaps unjustifiably so. I can't say I blame her."

"What she can also be is *in denial*. She was too young to remember what her brother was like."

"Why don't you tell *me* what he was like?"

Worthy's tone deepened. "Angry. He was very angry."

"Was he dangerous?"

"His mother seemed to think so. Honestly, though, I don't feel comfortable talking about all of this."

Jess wouldn't let him off so easy. "Why was he arrested? What evidence did you have to link him to the sniper murders?"

"For one thing," said Worthy, "Ricky Lee Patience confessed to them."

"You know as well as I do that doesn't mean a thing. People in custody—Black men *especially*—have a tendency to confess to all sorts of things they never did."

"I'm the one who took his confession."

Jess had already queued up something to say, but quickly abandoned it in favor of a dumbstruck expression.

"I wish I had better news for you," Worthy said, "but I was standing right there in the room when he told us what all he did, then signed the paper attesting to it. There was no coercion; there were no dirty tricks."

Jess didn't know what to think. Worthy's account differed drastically from Willie Potts's recounting. She had said nothing about her mother regarding Ricky Lee as dangerous, or anything about a crack addiction. Jess's experience with Ennis Worthy showed he could be a trustworthy source, but still her visit with him had far from produced any answers, and had instead yielded only more questions.

"I'd like to talk with Ricky Lee Patience," she said.

"I don't think that would be a good idea," said Worthy.

"Why not?"

"This case was solved," he told her. "That man caused a lot of people a lot of harm a long time ago. Those wounds have scabbed over and don't need anybody picking at them."

"But—"

"There ain't nobody in the world who'd like to hear you record another podcast or whatever you're doing with the television crew more than I would." Worthy locked the door of his woodshed and slipped the keys into the pocket of his jeans. "But this story is one you ought to leave be."

"You know I can't do that. Not until I've dug around a little more. I've already placed a call to Sheriff Lorne Axel up in Lake Castor. I'm due to meet with him this weekend. I just assumed you would want to help me."

Worthy nodded. "I understand your position. Now please understand mine. I think it's a bad idea to go digging that up again and don't want to be party to it. You can talk all you want with Lorne, but I'd appreciate being left away from it."

Jess nodded, shook his hand, and then followed him into the house for a glass of iced tea. She allowed the subject to be changed and continued on for another hour with genial conversation about her family or his chickens and other general whatnot. However, she couldn't shake the feeling that Worthy seemed to be actively trying to keep her from finding out the truth about Ricky Lee Patience.

Fine, she told herself. *It's not the first time I've had to work a story without his help.*

CHAPTER EIGHT

ENNIS WORTHY

1984

That morning, when Deputy Ennis Worthy dressed for work, he had no idea he'd be spending half his day in Lake Castor's Back Back, in an entirely different county north of his jurisdiction, in an entirely different state. If he had, he reckoned he might have dressed different. The muted-brown Deeton County deputy's uniform didn't carry the same amount of gravitas north of the state line as it did back home in North Carolina. He might also have packed a lunch, as he didn't like the looks he'd get from white waiters up in the Virginia restaurants. However, when he'd buttoned his crisp, clean uniform to the top and tightly tucked the knot of his necktie beneath his chin, he assumed he would be crossing into Lawles County for only a quick visit, then would be back home to spend the day where he normally might: the Deeton County jailhouse.

"You dress mighty fine for a man who gets himself posted at the jail for twelve hours a day," his girlfriend, Shirley, told him. "I thought you said it was the *new guy* who gets stuck with guard duty. Didn't they hire another deputy?"

"They did," said Worthy as he inspected his cheeks for any errant stubble.

"And let me guess," said Shirley. "Would this new deputy be white?"

"They haven't found a permanent spot for me yet, is all."

"You seem to have plenty of permanent spots in the campaign literature that Sheriff McCoy posts in the Black neighborhoods."

Worthy said nothing.

"I'm serious, baby." Shirley sat up in bed. She wore only his T-shirt, and it took every ounce of self-control for him not to undress himself and climb back between the sheets with her. "Why don't they put the new boy in the jailhouse and send you out on patrol, where an experienced deputy is supposed to be?"

Ennis didn't want to tell her the truth. He'd rather she not know about the letters sent to the sheriff's office. About how some folks said they wouldn't stop if they were pulled over by a Black deputy. How other folks spelled out their fears in more deliberate terms.

"Bobby McCoy ain't the same kind of sheriff as Red Carter was," said Worthy, referring to the late lawman who had hired him as a deputy twelve years earlier. "Red could stand up to any of the social pressures that hiring a Black deputy can create. Bobby can't. He says they'd run him out of town on a rail if he put a Black deputy on patrol."

"Even in the Black parts of town?"

"They don't seem to like it any better," Worthy explained. "Most of them call me Uncle Tom or the houseboy."

"And what do the other deputies call you?"

Worthy smiled sideways. "They call me Mr. Tibbs."

Shirley waited a moment to laugh. Ennis loved her laugh. He checked himself once more in the mirror and picked some fluff from the side of his head.

"Back in the day, it was all Red would let them call me."

"I'm sure that's not what they were thinking."

"They could think whatever they wanted. But Red wouldn't tolerate any other talk."

Shirley wrapped herself in the Carolina-blue bedsheet. "But here it is, twelve years gone by, and they still won't let you out of that jail."

"It's my job."

She rose from the bed. Glided across the bedroom floor to press herself against him.

"You don't owe this county anything," she whispered into his neck.

"Maybe not," he said, "but I owe Reverend Elijah Stallings. He wants me to drive up to Lake Castor today to talk to a parishioner of his who says her son is in trouble."

"Lake Castor? Honey, what can a Deeton deputy do with some troubled boy in Virginia?"

Worthy shrugged. "That's what the reverend wants me to find out."

"And you're going to drop what you're doing and do it?"

"He put in the good word for me way back when, and I'd rather jump in the June than let him down."

"Because he's reverend to the largest Black congregation in North Carolina?"

"No." Worthy kissed her forehead. He let his lips linger to collect her heat. "Because he's daddy to the woman who means more to me than anyone else in the entire world."

Shirley kissed him the way she knew would leave her fingerprints on his brain throughout the rest of his day.

"Besides," he told her, "jail duty gives me plenty of time to study."

She pushed away from him. She stepped to the bureau on her toes, then dropped the sheet. Rifled through her drawers bare bottomed until she found underwear that suited her. Made sure Worthy got a good look at everything.

"Good," she said. "You'll need the extra studying if you have any hope of earning your JD. You can't miss any more classes, En."

"I know. I know. It's just that—"

"I've already heard it. *The job.* I get it. Sheriff McCoy needs you to stay late because some crime halfway across the county calls the attention of the other deputies, and that's another couple hours you got to sit in the jailhouse. It's bullshit, Ennis. You and me have our lives laid out in front of us. We get our JDs, then we move to DC. We leave this backward county behind."

"Yes, babe." He reached for her, but she shrank from his touch.

"Then you can't miss any more classes." She burned him with the look that said she was *serious*. "Tell Sheriff McCoy today. You are out of that jail by six o'clock."

"I will."

And, that morning, he damn well meant it. By noon, however, the day began to take different shapes. He'd driven into Lake Castor, through downtown, and then out the other side to the neighborhood known as the Back Back. He'd been given an address on Newton Street, and it took him a good piece to find it, as the Back Back's labyrinthine thoroughfares were crisscrossed with one-way and dead-end streets, and some of the street signs had been vandalized or stolen. The home he found, however, was a modest wood-paneled house that had been well maintained.

Worthy was greeted at the door by Rosalie Patience, a woman who carried herself much older than he reckoned she might be. She smiled, hugged him, and then invited him inside. She poured him a glass of sweet tea and asked him to join her in the living room, where she might keep an eye on her ten-year-old daughter, who was coloring in a kid's activity book.

"I thank the Lord on high for Reverend Stallings to send you here," said Ms. Patience. "I am at my wit's end with that boy."

"Can you tell me what's the problem?"

Ms. Patience peeked her head around the corner at her distracted daughter, then lowered her voice. "I'd rather the child not hear any of this," she said. "My little Wilhelmina loves her brother something fierce, but it's because of her that I reached out to Reverend Stallings."

"I understand, ma'am."

"My son has been taken by the Devil."

Ennis let out a slow breath and fought the urge to check his watch.

"He used to be the sweetest thing." Ms. Patience fussed with the paper doily upon which she had set her glass. "He would help me with the groceries and hold open the door for strangers, white or Black. That was before the Devil took hold of him, and, Deputy Worthy, I swear before God to you that I have prayed and prayed for my son's salvation, but I am no match for Satan. Cut out my tongue for saying so, but he has hold of my Ricky Lee, and I am but a woman alone."

Worthy placed his hat in his lap. Silently, he cursed Reverend Stallings for not tending to this woman himself, but reckoned the least he could lend was his ear.

"You are far from alone, ma'am," he told her. "Tell me, was there something that happened? Something that made him change?"

"The Devil must have come to him at night, because I keep a close watch during daylight."

"No," said Worthy, "I mean something *specific*. You seem convinced that there was a change in his behavior. Was it sudden, and if so, was there an event that might have spurred it along?"

She thought it over. "No . . . Ricky Lee was a good boy. Very trusting. I'd supposed that's why he fell in with that one white boy who weren't nothing but trouble."

"What white boy?"

"I don't remember his name," she said after thinking it over, "but they got caught messing around with a car. That boy was taken home to his parents and given a warning, but Ricky Lee was sent to a work camp for boys."

Worthy nodded. Such was the way of things. He'd seen it time and again, even down south in Deeton.

"How did he fare at the work camp?" he asked.

"Oh, not so fair at all." She brought the tea to her lips, but hesitated to drink. "While he was there, him and another boy walked across the street to fetch a pop from the store. They said he was trying to escape, although Ricky Lee denied it up and down. That little stunt earned him a stay at the jailhouse, and after that, he couldn't find a job anywhere in Lake Castor because didn't nobody want to hire anybody who'd been behind bars."

Worthy shook his head. He was well aware that a simple infraction could keep an employer from hiring someone who checked the box on an application. *Have you ever been convicted of a crime?* Manning the jailhouse down in Deeton, Worthy had watched a parade of young men who were forced to look for other means to feed their families, thanks to that damned question.

"I reckoned it a better idea to send him to my sister's up in New York State," Ms. Patience said, "but it weren't long before he found himself mixed up in something up there, and I don't turn around twice before he's on a bus bound for home. Ever since he come back, he hasn't been the same."

"How so?"

Ms. Patience's expression grew pained. "He don't leave his room much, but when he does, all he does is walk around the backyard or yonder woods and talk to himself. He grows angry and agitated at the smallest of things. He quit picking his hair, and no matter how often I wash his clothes, he prefers to wear the dirty ones. The other day . . ."

Worthy heard the strain in her voice. "What happened, Ms. Patience?"

"The other day . . ." She collected herself, seemed to prepare for the worst. "He was sitting on that couch right there talking to someone who wasn't there. It's like there was a conversation happening with somebody I couldn't see. When I asked him who he was talking to, he flew into a rage. Bless me, Jesus, but I spent the entire night praying that somebody might come and take him from me because I would rather die than see my little Willie hurt."

Worthy let that settle for a few breaths. "Have you spoken to the police?"

"Oh, Lord, no," she said. "I trust Lake Castor police to do one thing and one thing only. That's hurt Colored boys. No sir. I can tell when I'm doing well with the Lord because I ain't had no run-ins with Lake Castor police."

"Ms. Patience, I'm a Deeton deputy down in North Carolina. I have absolutely zero say-so in anything up here. I doubt there's very much I could do, even if I knew what that might be."

"My son has been taken by the Devil, Deputy Worthy," she said. "I asked God for help, and he sent you to me. I don't question him; I simply trust in his will."

"Ms. Patience, I—"

"I spoke with Reverend Stallings. He and I are of the belief that if Ricky Lee saw a Black man like you, one who is proud and walks with the Lord and helped his community the way you do . . . maybe it might be inspiring for him." She placed her hand on his arm. "Just let the Lord shine through you."

Although Worthy didn't subscribe to that school of thought, he couldn't help but feel humbled. All the stress and worry he'd suffered over his endless stint on jail duty seemed trivial. Perhaps the old lady was right: maybe God *did* put him in the right place to do something worthwhile.

"Okay, Ms. Patience," Worthy said, finishing his tea. "Why don't you introduce me to Ricky Lee?"

◆　◆　◆

Ricky Lee Patience's bedroom was up a short flight of stairs, and with each step, Ennis Worthy prepared himself for the absolute worst. *The Devil,*

Rosalie Patience had warned him, *has taken hold of my boy.* Ennis was no stranger to religion among the older folks in the South—particularly the Southern Baptists—and how quick they were to blame the Devil. Still, his years of training whispered that where church folk saw the Devil, most likely the culprit was manufactured by man.

For that reason, he kept his eyes peeled for evidence of drug use. That, he believed, might explain the sudden change in behavior from sweet and good natured to odd and erratic. However, when he pushed open the door, he was momentarily taken aback that he found himself unable to differentiate Ricky Lee's bedroom from one belonging to any other young man. The walls were festooned with posters of Carl Lewis and Eddie Murphy, the Washington Redskins, O. J. Simpson, and Magic Johnson. Upon a closer look, he found signs of distressing behavior: a book with the pages torn out. Two cassettes with the tape unspooled. Pencils that had been stabbed through the walls.

Ricky Lee lay on the bed, wearing a pair of oversize headphones that were connected to a speaker. He didn't see Worthy enter, which gave the deputy the opportunity to size him up. The kid's hair had grown out unevenly. His clothes were unkempt and wrinkled. He wore sneakers with holes in them. When Ricky Lee finally took notice of Worthy entering his room, his expression remained disaffected, and he seemed to take more interest in the music pumping from his stereo.

That is, until Ricky Lee caught sight of the badge pinned to Worthy's chest. That brought on a wild-eyed panic.

"Easy, brother," said Worthy. He displayed his empty palms. "I come in peace."

Knowing Ricky Lee couldn't hear over the headphones, Worthy motioned with both hands for the boy to remove them. Ricky Lee could barely peel his eyes off the badge, but eventually complied. Slowly. Worthy recognized "When Doves Cry," by Prince, playing through the headset.

"Is that the new one?" he asked, pointing toward Ricky Lee's cassette deck. "My girlfriend, Shirley, she loved his last album. She's one who can party like it's 1999. Me, on the other hand . . . that's too much screeching guitar for me. I'm more of a Teddy Pendergrass or Luther Van—"

Worthy noticed the boy transfixed by something over his shoulder. Whatever it was caused Ricky Lee to laugh, then nod. Worthy turned to look. Nothing was there. He turned back to the boy, whose pupils had dilated.

"What is it?" Worthy asked.

Ricky Lee cocked his head at the deputy. "Did you hear that?"

"Hear what?" Worthy checked over his shoulder again.

Ricky Lee's eyes drifted away, as if he no longer had any interest in anything in the room. Worthy sized him up again. There were no telltale signs of drug use. The boy seemed almost childlike in his manner. Disheveled, oddly dressed. A strange thought struck Worthy, and he reached for the badge on his chest and angled it so that it caught the sunlight peeking in through the curtains. Ricky Lee's attention was once again spurred, and his eyes fixed on the badge.

"You don't hear it?" Ricky Lee asked him.

Worthy spoke slowly. "Tell me what you hear."

Ricky Lee opened his mouth, but the only sounds that came out were mumbles. Incoherent ramblings that he seemed to give up hope communicating with. His only concentration and focus seemed to come by staring at Worthy's badge, as if it were dispatching a coded message to him.

"Would you like me to take it off, son?" Worthy asked.

Ricky Lee didn't take his eyes from it.

"It's really no bother," Worthy said. "I can just unpin it from my shirt. I'm happy to do it, if it means you and me can have a little man-to-man. How about it?"

Worthy unpinned the badge from his shirt. He started to slip it into his pocket, but noted the wonderment in Ricky Lee's gaze.

"Would you like to hold it?" Worthy asked.

He could tell by Ricky Lee's expression that he wanted to. Worthy reached out his hand, the tin star resting in his palm.

"Go on, son. It ain't going to bite you. It's just a piece of metal. Not a damned thing more."

Ricky Lee glanced up from it. Again, his eyes went to somewhere over Worthy's shoulder. He moved his lips, as if he were speaking inaudibly to someone, but Worthy couldn't make any of it out. An idea began formulating in Worthy's head, pieces fitting into place, but before he could make sense of any larger picture, Ricky Lee reached out, quick as a copperhead, and snatched the badge from Worthy's palm. He turned it every which way in his hand, studying its every angle. Ricky Lee ran his fingers across the badge number and admired the impression of Deeton's official emblem, which was modeled after the courthouse's clock tower.

"You see?" Worthy said. "That old thing can't hurt you."

Worthy's voice seemed to break the spell. Ricky Lee glanced up at the deputy. Slowly, his eyes narrowed to slits. He returned his focus to the badge in his hand, and a rage simmered up from within him. Without any warning, he balled his fingers into a fist around the badge and thrust it as hard as he could against the far wall. Worthy's shield bounced off it and skittered across the floor.

Worthy let out a long sigh. He shifted his gaze from the badge to Ricky Lee, who tugged his headphones back down over his ears.

"I hear you, son," Worthy said to him. "I feel the same damned way sometimes."

After closing the bedroom door behind him, Worthy trod slowly down the staircase to where Ms. Patience awaited. Her face brimmed with expectations, those Worthy knew he'd never have the power to meet.

"Well?" she asked. "Is there hope to cast the Devil from my boy, Deputy?"

"Ms. Patience, have you ever taken that boy to a doctor?" he asked.

"Oh . . ." She looked away, as if trying to remember. "It's been a while, I suppose. Truth be told, we can't rightly afford any doctor."

"So he's never been diagnosed with anything?"

"Not to my . . . Diagnosed with *what*?"

"I'm the furthest thing from a medical professional," Worthy said, "but when my uncle Charlie came home from the war years ago, he brought something back with him."

"Something *evil*?"

"No, Ms. Patience." Worthy realized he was going to have difficulty explaining things to her. He rubbed his face with the palm of his hand. "I'm afraid we're dealing with something a bit more troubling than the Devil."

"So you'll be able to help us?" she asked. "You'll be able to give comfort to my Ricky Lee?"

Worthy thought briefly of a hundred things. He thought of his duties at the jailhouse. He thought of Shirley and the mountains of disappointment she might have in him if he did anything besides study for his JD. He thought of Reverend Stallings. He thought of that look in the boy's eye as he threw Worthy's badge across the room.

But mostly, Deputy Ennis Worthy thought about his uncle Charlie and how nobody was able to help him because they didn't know what they were dealing with when he returned home from Vietnam. That, at the time, everyone thought he was just shell shocked or having problems readjusting. That he might be coming off heroin, which was so prevalent among platoons in Southeast Asia. How if they had known then what they would later come to discover about Charlie's mental health and a diagnosis that came far too late, they might have prevented an unspeakable tragedy.

Worthy knew he couldn't go back in time, so there was little use in fantasizing about it. Instead, he would have to deal with the here and now. He turned to Ms. Patience.

"I'll see what I can do."

CHAPTER NINE

HAL BROADSTREET

1984

Driving from Fosskey's garage, Hal imagined his mind like a cave that, the deeper he went, only grew darker. Without the gift of sight, he could only place one foot in front of the other. To keep walking forward. Ignore temptations to venture off the path. Grief was one of those temptations, and it would only lead him to a dead end.

Fosskey had been a friend. For the immediate future, however, Hal needed him to be a *story*.

Hal burst through the doors of the *Times* offices like a dynamo. The offices were small, but after the latest round of layoffs and cutbacks, they had become even smaller. One person who remained on the payroll was Peg, a former proofreader who now answered the telephones.

"Sweetheart," Hal said to her, "I need every single article ever written about Jem Fosskey and his bootlegging operation. This will run you back to the thirties, but it's important. Nothing is too small or insignificant. Every court case, every conviction, every marriage and divorce announcement. Not just what we've written, but scour the clips from the *Herald* as well."

"You're going to have to do that yourself, hon." Peg's expression was flat. "These phones have been ringing off the hook ever since you started milking that prison break over in—"

"I can't do it myself," Hal said. "I have a monster story to write, one that's going to be much bigger than anything anybody is going to call in on that prison break. I got a *scoop*, and for all I know, the Briley brothers' fingerprints could be all over it." He pressed both his palms together like he might be begging. "Help me out, please, and while you're at it, would you mind collecting last night's police blotter for me?"

Hal didn't wait for her answer. Instead, he went to another desk, where he found one of the remaining advertising salesmen. Grant was a man with a habit of smiling. Hal was about to disabuse him of that.

"Do me a favor, buddy," Hal said. "Get me everything you can find on Mel Kemble and Felton Loe. They never earned the same amount of ink as Fosskey, but I guarantee there's paper on them at the courthouse. Birth certificates, marriage licenses, convictions, dismissals . . . our readers are going to want to know the men who were found dead in that apartment. Let's introduce them."

Grant's smile never wavered. "I sell ads, Hal. You tell me how rooting around the courthouse is going to do that?"

"This article is going to be all the advertising we need, baby. Hop to it."

Hal made his way to the layout room, where a feisty fellow named Scott rarely had time for him.

"I know you and Phil are deep in layout," Hal said, "but the layoffs have left me with slim pickings. Fosskey had him a Negro running his stills that everybody called Uncle Meaney. I don't know his given name, but I know he's been stilling that corn since longer than anybody can remember. I hear he's got a sister living somewhere in the Back Back. I need somebody to find him and put him in front of me."

Scott's answer was lost to Hal, as he'd already barreled toward his own desk, which was cluttered with articles of the recent prison break and all the misdeeds associated with the Briley brothers' 1979 Richmond reign of terror, which got them sentenced to death in the first place. *Yesterday's news,* he thought as he shoved it all aside. He looked around at his desk, at the stapler, the pens, the geegaws from the 1980 RNC convention he'd collected while on assignment in Detroit. He wondered where to go next . . . felt like it was right there in front of him. *Think, Hal. Think.*

It hit him. He stood and flagged down the last available *Times* employee, a printer named Russ. "I want you to get me a list of every white Ford Pinto in Lawles County." Before Russ could get away, Hal added, "Scratch that. *All* the surrounding counties."

"I don't take orders from you, Hal," Russ said.

"You want me to find someone you *do* take orders from?"

"Eat shit, Hal."

Tired of it, Hal stormed into the office of his editor, Vince Fenelli. Vince was in the middle of his sandwich, but lowered it upon sight of his last remaining full-time reporter.

"You said you had an article cooking on the Briley brothers," said Vince. "Please tell me that's where you've been all morning."

"Forget the Briley brothers," said Hal. "I'm on to something bigger."

"It's the only time in American history that inmates have escaped from death row," Vince reminded him. "It's only the largest manhunt Virginia has seen since John Wilkes Booth's final exit from a theater. You really want to tell me to *forget the Briley brothers?*"

"They're long gone," Hal said. "They're likely headed north, not some forgotten mill town like Lake Castor. I got something way bigger than them."

"They're *long gone?*" Vince was apoplectic. "That's not the song you were singing yesterday."

"I don't write for yesterday," Hal said. "I write for tomorrow. Besides, I've known they headed north for two days. I've just been fanning the flames because that's all anybody wants to read about. Until now."

Vince closed his eyes and shook his head. "What do you got?"

"Triple murder," Hal answered. "The King of the Piedmont Bootleggers and two of his crew—brutally beaten, stabbed, and shot to death in their apartment overnight. This is big press, Vince."

"Any suspects?"

"Cops haven't named any."

"Not even off the record?"

"Hell, Vince. Cops won't even talk to me on the record. Dorritt crashed the scene, and after last Sunday, he ain't tossing me any treats. He'd rather wait for me to watch it on the evening news."

"Or read about it in the *Herald*."

Hal heard the disdain in his editor's voice and did his best to deflect it. "I'm on it, Vince. I've got several advantages on this story that Liv Crane never dreamed of."

"Like what?"

"For one, I was close with Fosskey. I've sat in on enough poker games that I'll be able to transport the reader directly inside the crime scene."

Vince mocked a yawn.

"That ain't all," said Hal. "I was inside the crime scene."

Vince's face fell. "When?"

"Last night, before it happened." Hal paused for dramatic effect. "Then again today, after."

"The cops let you access the crime scene?"

"They practically dragged me upstairs for a firsthand look."

Vince was skeptical. "And you didn't get a quote?"

"It's a long story."

"Readers want quotes from cops, Hal. It's what gives us gravitas. You know that."

"You knew the price I was going to pay for writing that article on the Crimes Against Persons squad last Sunday."

"If only you were the one paying it." Vince ran his fingers through his hair. "Look, they're talking about another round of layoffs."

"There's nobody left to lay off, Vince."

"Speak for yourself, pal."

Hal tried to smile. "They can't kill you, Vince. You're the *editor*."

"When I first came on," said Vince, "we ran neck and neck with the *Herald*. But the mill closed, and the paper sold to that outfit in Baltimore. When the cuts came and the advertising cooled off, I agreed with you that instead of competing with the *Herald*, we should offer an alternative with these sensational, lurid stories, but we also need to adhere to certain journalistic standards. I don't think we can afford to sink any lower." He took a bite from his sandwich. "I want your story by six, and I want you to have talked to a badge."

Hal closed the door behind him and sat down at his desk. He set the margins on his typewriter and slipped on his bifocals. He'd penned more articles about Jem Fosskey than anyone else in the area. The old man had been arrested for damn near anything liquor related running all the way back to the thirties. Stilling liquor, running liquor, possession of tax stamps, illegal booze . . . he'd been arrested many times, stood up in court, and even served time. He was a family man with no history of violence. In an article Hal had written, he'd christened Fosskey the "King of the Piedmont Bootleggers," a name that stuck. Although Fosskey had been a humble man, folks said he wore that moniker with pride.

Fosskey was more than a story to Hal. He was more, even, than a source. Of course, Hal bought liquor from the old man, and even called him for quotes when the trials went down. Hal had little interest in what the police had to say on those matters and found Fosskey and his ilk provided much more color. Fosskey was somewhat of a friend. Hal was no stranger to the poker games in his apartment over top of the garage. He knew Fosskey's daughter, Jennie, and had been in attendance at her wedding the year previous.

"He always liked you," Wilbur had said to him. *"He always said you do right by us. The cops aren't going to do nothing about it. I need to know that somebody is going to pay."*

Words that haunted Hal as he struggled to remain objective. Employing his trademark descriptive flair, he detailed the crime scene. He sketched the scant details offered by Dorritt's press briefing. He offered an overview of Fosskey's history of run-ins with the law, preparing for a more in-depth sidebar to come. He painted the portraits of Felton Loe and Mel Kemble, two men with dwindling options who—

A knock at the door whipped him out of his fervor. He looked up from his typewriter to find the receptionist in the doorway.

"I'm still collecting the clips on Fosskey," she said, "but I got the police blotter from last night that you asked for."

"Thanks, Pam," he said, accepting it.

"It's *Peg*, asshole."

Hal scanned it. There wasn't much to see. A break-in at Liberty grocery downtown. Two kids picked up and brought home to their parents after toilet papering the high school. A drunk driver.

Hal's eyes perked up near the bottom. Three men had been picked up in a white Ford Pinto after three in the morning. Arrested for possession of narcotics and illegal weapons, including a firearm. Hal scanned the names.

CROWE, EDWARD

WILCOX, CHARLES

DICKERSON, WILLIAM WAYNE

He thought back to Vince's parting words. *"I want you to have talked to a badge."*

Hal checked his watch. *Good idea, Vince,* Hal thought to himself. He grabbed his jacket and a fresh pen and hustled for the door.

CHAPTER TEN

JESS KEELER

Present Day

Jess disengaged her call, then stuffed her phone into her pocket. The look on her face must have said it all, because Buffy removed her headset and turned away from the monitor.

"What is it?" she asked.

"Bad news." Jess waited for Aaron's and Sandy's attention, so that she wouldn't have to tell the story twice. "I still can't get approval for visitation with Ricky Lee Patience at Stormgate State Prison. I've been calling and emailing, but I don't think we'll be able to get him on camera for the sizzle reel unless we—"

"Tell it to the Germans." Aaron positioned the monitor so that he filled the camera feed, the rest of the crew falling in behind him. "They're about to sign on."

Everyone huddled tighter around the laptop, behind which had been positioned the ring lights and camera. Sandy took the time to check her makeup in the mirror. The screen came alive, and there, in two different panels, were the faces of Felix and Friedrich Schafer.

Felix's face lit up, and he ran his hand through his boyish long curly locks that Jess always thought made him look like a young American surfer.

"Hello, team!" he said in a cheery voice. "I have been reading your reports about this sniper, and I have to say I am very excited. A sniper! Is there nothing more sexy?"

Friedrich Shafer was much more subdued than his brother in both speech and appearance. "We noted that your sniper only killed six victims. In terms of American violence, this is quite a low casualty count, no?"

"The Lake Castor Sniper actually killed only *five* people," Sandy interrupted. "One of the victims was only wounded."

Friedrich frowned. "Still, this is a very low body count."

"Yes," Felix agreed. "I read that there was a Virginia serial killer named Calvin Cantrell who they estimate murdered twenty-two victims. Is it true that he carved numbers into each of their—"

"Unfortunately," Jess said, "there are not many people peripheral to that story left to interview. We looked at it, sure, but the amount of content we could draw for a visual medium would be very low."

"Ah." Felix's disappointment only dented his demeanor. "So tell me what you have to draw from here?"

"For one," Jess said, "we've conducted a preliminary interview with the sister of the accused."

"Wonderful!" Felix cheered. "Did she describe what it must have been like growing up in a house with a monster?"

"It's a little early to call him a—"

"What about the accused himself?" Friedrich asked. "Can you interview him?"

"Not without approval," Jess said. "I've applied online, but none of my calls so far have borne any fruit."

"We can handle the procedures with the prison if we decide the story merits further investigation," said Friedrich. "What else have you got?"

"There are the families of the victims," Jess offered.

"What about collaboration with law enforcement?"

"We've got a meeting with the Lawles County sheriff this weekend, who was a patrolman in Lake Castor at the time," Jess reported. "Furthermore, I have history with the arresting officer. He's resisted cooperating in the past, but eventually came around. I have no reason to think this time would be different."

"And the families of the victims?" Felix asked. "With six victims, that would make a splendid number of interviews, don't you find?"

"Sandy and I have been compiling a list of living relatives of the sniper victims and any possible witnesses," said Jess. "Our next step will be to dig into them."

"Perfect," said Felix. "We will want the most detailed and heart-wrenching descriptions of this madman's reign of terror."

"What about other members of the community who grew up with the man accused of the crime?" asked Friedrich. "Have you found any that will go on record about early signs of this man's behavior that were missed? Viewers always respond to that."

"No . . ." Jess blinked a handful of times. "Actually, Friedrich, I think I should be clear that there is a chance Ricky Lee might be—"

Felix leaned closer to the camera so that his face filled the entire frame. "It's no matter, Friedrich. Aaron can cut together what they have gathered so far to make one of his uberamazing sizzle reels. No?"

"Absolutely, *mein* main man," Aaron said. "We still need a bit of footage, but I bet I can produce something within the week. Maybe I can throw together a couple reenactments?"

"Ooh," Felix exclaimed. "I love those."

Jess couldn't believe her ears. "Wait," she said. "What?"

"Reenactments are the hallmark of the docu-biz," Aaron informed her. "Trust me: they can be a lot of fun."

"We can't reenact something we know nothing about," Jess protested. "First we'll need to interview the surviving family members of the victims, or potential witnesses."

"Of course," said Friedrich. "That will be top priority if we choose to move forward with this, and the deciding factor will be how potential distributors react to our sizzle reel."

"In the meantime," said Felix, "you'll want to start booking actors. Aaron, you still have the contact information for Burt Robertson, don't you? He and Kara DeMoray live in that area and have been wonderful in the past."

Aaron made a face. "Um . . ."

"What?" Felix asked.

"I don't know if Burt would be appropriate for this role."

"He's British," Felix countered. "They can play anything."

"Not this."

"Do you care to expand?"

"The relatives of the shooting victims were Black."

Friedrich filled his frame on the monitor by leaning closer to his camera. "I'm sorry," he said, "but it sounded like you said the victims' relatives were Black."

"I did."

Felix's grin broke wider. "How is it that the sniper victims had Black relatives?"

"Because"—Aaron drew out his words like molasses—"the *sniper victims* were Black."

This information was met with silence.

Jess grew confused. "Is this going to be some kind of problem?"

"No, not a *problem*, per se . . ." Felix left the thought for Friedrich to complete.

"Our test markets have indicated that American audiences respond to shows about crimes against the white population," Friedrich explained. "Particularly white *women*."

"How many shows are there about crimes against the Black population?" Jess asked.

Both Schafer brothers answered with the same empty expression.

"The good news, then," Jess offered, "is that we have the opportunity to be pioneers."

Those empty expressions did not change.

"Look, it makes sense." Jess tried a pivot. "If everybody zigs, then it's highly logical that we should zag. Why is it that whenever someone in the entertainment industry catches lightning in a bottle, all the producers start ordering the construction of more bottles?"

Friedrich muted his microphone and spoke to his brother. Jess could feel panic—or what could be confused for panic—beginning to settle into the rest of her crew in the room. She felt like she might be disappointing not only the crew, but also Willie Potts, who wanted so desperately for her brother's story to be told, or Ricky Lee himself, languishing in prison with a life sentence for a series of crimes that he might not have committed. She knew she had to talk fast, to say something that might save the project.

"If nothing else," she said, grasping at straws, "we could critique racial relations in the United States. Our documentary series could be an indictment against those very demographics. We could hold a mirror up to that very system and—"

Friedrich unmuted his microphone. "Okay, gang," he said, "Felix and I have conferred, and we believe perhaps—"

"What if I told you," Sandy interrupted, "that the sniper's last victim was white?"

This time, those blank expressions were contagious.

Aaron turned to Jess. "Is this true?"

Jess's cheeks blazed hot. She opened her mouth, but could only suffer from the shame associated with saying those three words no investigator ever wants to admit: *I don't know.*

Luckily, Sandy was there to pick up the ball that had been dropped. "It's absolutely true, and it's a compelling story. Apparently, he was a well-known journalist in the community."

"Aah," said Felix. "This is magnificent. Please, continue."

Jess felt herself shrinking. It was her fault that she hadn't had all the information before the call with the Germans. When working on *Something Bad Wrong*, she had ravenously chased and consumed all the information. If her partner had uncovered something before she had—which would have been rare—she had insisted on seeing his work, then tracing his steps so that she, too, might arrive at the same conclusion on her own. The use of a dedicated researcher on her staff was making her lazy, complacent. She had no one to blame but herself.

She swore to do better.

"There doesn't seem to have been much attention paid to the first five shootings," Sandy added. "However, once the white journalist was murdered, a *lot* of ink was spilled, and the perpetrator was apprehended within days."

Even Friedrich couldn't hide his enjoyment. "This is quite a development," he said. "If we were looking to make a comment on the complacency of American media due to racism, this could possibly be a foothold in such an argument, no?"

Jess fought the urge to leave the room, get in her car, and drive until she ran out of gas. Instead, she sat still in her chair and accepted the punishment.

"Start on the sizzle reel," Felix instructed. "Cobble together some actors . . . perhaps Burt could play the reporter in the reenactment. What did you say was the name of this murdered journalist?"

Sandy consulted her notes. "Harold Broadstreet," she said. "His colleagues all called him *Hal*."

CHAPTER ELEVEN

HAL BROADSTREET

1984

The desk sergeant on duty was a thick fellow named Baxter Cummings. Hal walked up to the desk and waited to be acknowledged. That did not happen immediately.

"What do you want, Broadstreet?" asked the sergeant without looking up.

"You hear about the murders at Fosskey's?"

"I did. I got nothing to say to you about that."

Hal tried a different approach. "I know you busted him once. What was that, back in sixty-nine?"

"Seventy-one, you son of a bitch." Cummings softened his edges. "Me and Dom Gibbons picked him up carrying two hundred liters of tax-stamped booze. Of course, the stamps were counterfeit, and he'd taxed nary a drop of it. But old Jem was never one to argue if you had him dead to rights. Which we did. He raised both his hands to the sky, stepped out of the truck, and positioned himself in the back of the cruiser."

"I've covered him for years now and never once heard a story of him being violent."

"And you won't neither. As far as I'm concerned, he had his side of the law, and we had ours. For him, it was just a way to make a living. Like a game, even. Sometimes you win, sometimes you lose. But the point is to stay alive so you can play again tomorrow." Cummings shrugged with his face. "I guess it's *game over* for that poor bastard."

"They pick anybody up for it yet?"

Cummings wised up. "I ain't talking to you about nothing, Broadstreet. You want a scoop for your dirty little rag, you'll get it from the captain, same as everybody else."

"What about those bikers who were brought in this morning?"

"What bikers?" Cummings asked, but his face had already given him away.

"Oh come on, Baxter," said Hal. "I saw y'all picked up Billy Wayne Dickerson and two of his buddies. It's no secret Billy Wayne rides with that biker outfit . . . What do they call themselves these days, the Vandals?"

Cummings knew better than to say anything.

"It's on the blotter," Hal said, "so I know they were brought in. You have to tell me when they are being arraigned."

"Is that right? Says who?"

"Says my First Amendment and the Freedom of Information Act." Hal was bluffing. "I could have you and the entire department tied up in court if you don't—"

"Okay, okay . . ." Cummings was over it. He hefted the crime log onto the desk in front of him. "Anything to shut you up and move you along." Cummings moved his finger down the logbook. He twisted his face in confusion. "Hmm . . . that's weird."

"What is it?"

"We ain't got them."

Hal leaned over the desk to see for himself. "What do you mean *you ain't got them?*"

"I mean we ain't got them." Cummings turned the book around and pointed to the information. "Says right here we had them picked up—looks like possession of narcotics and an illegal firearm, illegal knife, illegal weapons—but they were kicked loose a couple of hours ago."

"*Kicked loose?* By who?"

Cummings checked the log. "It don't say."

"It don't say?"

"It don't say." Cummings crossed his arms. "Anything else, Broadstreet?"

"Just so I get this right . . ." Hal pointed at the logbook. "You're telling me that on the morning three bootleggers get brutally massacred, a couple of bikers get picked up with weapons and drugs and then are let go the next morning?"

"What do you want me to tell you?"

Hal studied the sergeant's face, but found no sign of relenting. "Can you tell me who was the arresting officer?"

"Will it get you out of my face?"

"Double time," said Hal. He readied his pen.

Noon meant lunch for most people, but for cops who worked third shift, it meant sleeping. Hal knew what he was walking into when he entered the apartment complex and knocked on the door.

The man who answered looked none too pleased. "What do you want?"

"Are you Lorne Axel?" Hal asked. "*Officer* Lorne Axel of the Lake Castor Police Department?"

Axel rubbed his eyes. "Yeah. What's it to you?"

"My name is Hal Broadstreet, sir, and I work for the *Lake Cas*—"

Axel made to slam the door. Hal caught it with his foot.

"I just have a couple questions," Hal said.

Axel groaned. "You know I work third shift?"

"It's why I'm here, sir."

Axel leaned his head out the door. He looked up the hallway, then down the other side. "You know what will happen if anybody finds out I talked to you?"

"They won't," said Hal.

"Says you."

"I talk to all kinds of people. If I say I won't quote them, then I don't quote them. My reputation is very important to me."

Axel rubbed sleep from his eyes. "Can you make it quick?"

Thinking of his deadline, Hal nodded enthusiastically. "Last night, you arrested three men."

"That's right."

"What can you tell me about that?"

Axel thought it over. "My partner and I, we—"

"Who's your partner?" Hal opened his notepad. He clicked his pen.

"Tommy Stokes. He ain't going to talk to you. Trust me."

"Fine. So you and Stokes . . ."

"Yeah. We're on patrol. It's quiet. We see a white Ford Pinto roll through a stop sign. No big deal, but I recognize the driver. It's Billy Wayne Dickerson."

"Ah," said Hal, scribbling. "Billy Wayne."

"You know him?"

"Sure, I do. Baseball player in high school. Enlisted in the military, was stationed overseas. Saw some action. Came back with a *Born to Lose* tattoo on his forehead."

"Pretty much. Billy Wayne rides with the Vandals, and if he's out past three in the morning, then the chances are pretty high that he's up to no good. So we flip the lights, sound the siren, and pull him over."

"For rolling through a stop sign?"

"Sure," said Axel. "Then came the fireworks. There's three of them. Two other guys. The one in the back seat is someone I don't know. ID says Charles Wilcox. The one riding shotgun was Digger Crowe."

"I don't know him."

"You don't want to. He's part of that crew that rode in from Omaha last year."

"Bad dude?"

"Let's just say his momma and daddy didn't teach him the best of manners."

"These three guys"—Hal jotted notes in his notebook—"were they wearing Vandal colors?"

"Not in the car," said Axel. "It's against club rules to wear their cuts in the cage."

"I'm sorry?"

"Cuts are what they call their patched-up jackets," Axel explained. "Cages are how they refer to their cars. I found their cuts in the trunk."

"What else did you find?"

"A couple of grams of speed," said Axel. "Some weed. A pair of brass knuckles, which are illegal. A knife with a blade bigger than my hand, also illegal. Wilcox had a .38."

"Did they give you any explanation for the arsenal?"

Axel shook his head. "Nor did they have an explanation for the blood trace I found on the knife."

"You found *blood*?"

"I did. Digger had some on his pants. Some on Billy Wayne's boots. They said they'd been out hunting, but who goes hunting with just a .38? I didn't buy it. We hauled them in and booked them."

"Just charged them with the weapons and the drugs?" Hal asked. "Nobody thought to charge them with the murders?"

"Murders?" Axel looked lost. "I haven't heard anything about any murders?"

Hal reckoned it best to play it safe, for the moment. "The car," Hal said. "Did you tow it to impound?"

"No. We left it where we found it. Corner of Fitzpatrick and Striegler."

Hal wrote that down.

"You said *murders*." Axel seemed more awake. "What murders are you talking about?"

"Something tells me that roll call is going to be very enlightening for you this evening."

"Come on, Broadstreet," said Axel. "Spill it."

"Jem Fosskey and two of his boys were murdered in the apartment he kept over his garage," said Hal. "Right now, my number one suspects are the bikers you arrested."

Axel hid a yawn behind his hand. "Good thing we know where to find them then."

"If only that were true." Hal clicked his pen shut and turned to leave. "For some reason, they were released this morning."

"*Released?* By who?"

Hal handed over his business card. "Give me a call if you find that out, will you?"

"Keep my name out of this," said Axel. "I didn't never talk to you."

Hal winked at him. "Thank you very much, Officer Axel."

Hal headed for the stairs, checking one last detail before he pocketed his notebook.

Fitzpatrick and Striegler, he thought to himself.

He wanted a look at that Pinto.

CHAPTER TWELVE

HAL BROADSTREET

1984

The car was still parked where it had been pulled over, yards beyond a stop sign marking the corner of Fitzpatrick and Striegler. A white Ford Pinto, badly in need of a wash. Hal cupped his hands against the glass to better see through the window. He tried the door, found it unlocked.

Once inside, he poked around. Traces of blood on the floor mats, the seats. A couple of marijuana roaches the cops had missed in an overflowing ashtray. More blood in the back seat.

Fosskey's garage, a mere three blocks away.

How could they have simply been released?

Hal popped open the glove compartment. He rifled through the papers inside until finally finding the registration and proof of insurance. There was nothing in any of the documents that mentioned the three men who had been arrested for driving the car. Instead, Hal found the car registered to MCNAUGHTON, CALEB.

His address was also included.

Hal slammed the door shut and headed back to his own car. Fifteen minutes later, he was on the other side of town, knocking on the door of another apartment. Hal could hear a baby crying inside. He knocked again. A young woman, about nineteen, blocked the door when she opened it. Hal could judge by the disarray over her shoulder that she wasn't the maid.

"Hello, Mrs. McNaughton?"

The young woman found that funny. "Not even close," she said. "If you're looking for Delilah, you ain't going to find her here. And when you do find her, I'd keep running, if I were you."

"I'm sorry," said Hal. "I'm looking for Caleb McNaughton."

"He's at work."

The baby kicked up another round of wails, and the woman partially closed the door. From behind it, Hal could hear her pleading with the child to shush.

"I'm dreadfully sorry for bothering you," he said, "but could you tell me where Mr. McNaughton works? It's crucial that I speak to him. And fast."

She looked him up and down, then scrunched her face. "Are you a cop?"

"Me?" Hal could barely contain his laughter. "Not by a mile. I'm trying to get to Mr. McNaughton *before* the cops do, if that helps."

She appeared to think it over some, interrupted by the baby again.

"I won't tell him that you told me," Hal promised.

Three minutes later, Hal's El Camino was on the road into Deeton, the neighboring county to the south, just over the North Carolina state line. Deeton was far more rural than Lawles County, and didn't enjoy the larger city centers like Lake Castor. While that may have been a disadvantage during the boom times of the June River Fabrics textile mill, Deeton was spared the devastation from the mill's closure only years earlier.

After traveling two miles of highway bisecting vast timberlands, Hal arrived at a small shop next to a modest sawmill. The sign on the front said FORRESTER'S FINE FACTORY FURNITURE. He stepped out of his truck and was immediately beset by the sound of power saws and the scent of fresh-cut pine.

The lady inside the front office was halfway through a sloppy joe sandwich and did not appreciate the intrusion. "How may I help you?"

"I'm looking for Caleb McNaughton."

"And you are . . . ?"

"Someone with a couple questions for him."

Her expression didn't change. "He's working."

"I won't be more than five minutes."

She sighed, took a long look at the man interrupting her lunch, and then realized she would be quicker getting back to it if she gave Hal what he wanted. She pressed a button on the phone, and suddenly the entire premises were alive with her voice.

"Caleb, you're wanted up front. Caleb to the front."

When finished, she stared at Hal with a flat expression until finally he took several steps away from her desk so she could eat in peace.

About a minute and a half later, Caleb entered the lobby. He was about six-three, was very muscular, and wore a scraggly beard nearly down to his chest. His long black hair was tied back in a tail, which he kept under an orange reflector jacket. He was covered in sawdust, except for a small ring around his eyes from where he had recently removed a pair of safety goggles. He looked around the lobby for who might have paged him, only realizing at the last minute that it was Hal.

"Who the hell are you?" he asked.

"I just want to ask you a couple of questions."

"Did Delilah hire a lawyer?" he asked. "Because if she did, you can scurry right back to her and tell her that she already took enough from me. She ain't getting one shitting thing more, and if she wants to send Digger or anybody else down here, then I'll—"

"Whoa, whoa, buddy." Hal raised both his hands, palms out, to show he meant no harm. "No use getting riled up. I don't know any Delilah, and I'm a pretty far cry from a lawyer." Hal then offered one of those hands to Caleb. "My name's Hal Broadstreet. I'm a reporter with the *Lake Castor Times*."

Caleb did not shake his hand, but instead stared at it as if it were a two-headed cottonmouth. "I . . . I don't think there's much I want to say to any reporter neither."

"Just a couple quick questions and I'll be long gone." Hal motioned toward the door. "How about we have a word outside?"

The receptionist watched them over the tops of her bifocals, then returned to her sandwich. Caleb, perhaps more out of curiosity than anything else, followed Hal out the front door. Outside, the air was thick with the smells of woodworking. Hal pulled out his pen and paper, and got to work.

"Caleb, do you own a white Ford Pinto?"

Caleb shrugged and looked anywhere but at the reporter. "I used to. I don't have it no more."

"It was stolen?"

"Something like that."

"Did you *report* it stolen?"

A shadow crossed Caleb's face, darkening his demeanor. The big man blinked it away, then said, "No. It wasn't like that. Can you tell me what the hell this is about?"

"When is the last time you had possession of this white Ford Pinto?"

"Man . . ." Caleb's patience appeared to fray. "I haven't had that car since—man, tell me what you want. I got to get back to work."

Hal took a breath, then tried a different approach. "Is it true that you are a member of the Vandals motorcycle club?"

"I've never rode as a Vandal. Not a single day of my life." Caleb's hands clenched to fists. "After all I've been through, you better at least get *that* right. Do you understand?"

"Not really," said Hal. "Explain it to me."

"I rode as a *Blood Raven*," said Caleb. "When I joined the club, that was our patch. About a year ago, all these other crews from everywhere started sniffing around, asking us to patch over into their club. Our president held out for the longest time, but things started heating up with another crew, the Rare Breed, from down the coast, and we needed more protection than we had."

"So the Vandals made an offer . . ."

"Exactly." Caleb eased out some of the tension. Talking seemed to calm him. "Those Vandals came down from Omaha and changed everything the Blood Ravens stood for. Brotherhood. Family. All those things meant something to me as a Blood Raven. Not so much for the Vandals. Once they took over, brotherhood got abandoned real fast. The Blood Ravens sold out so that they could be lapdogs for those drug-dealing pimps. I had a family. A *real* family. I got a baby boy and my wife . . ." His eyes narrowed, and Hal could see a tiny vein bubbling near Caleb's temple.

"So what happened when you told them you didn't want to go along with the Vandals?"

"They gave me a choice: I'm in or I'm out. I chose out. And there's only one way *out*."

In all Hal's days writing crime, he had heard the rumors. A man couldn't simply walk away from a motorcycle club after he had joined. They would take his jacket with the patches heralding his chapter. Sometimes they even took his bike. But the worst of it all . . .

"Did you have any Blood Raven ink? Tattoos?" Hal asked.

Caleb offered a twisted smile. He turned his back to Hal and dropped the top half of his coveralls. Hal gasped at the sight. Large swaths of skin had been burned from the big man's back, presumably where the tattoos had once been, leaving scarred and twisted flesh.

"That ain't all they took," Caleb said as he readjusted his work clothes. "They got my bike, my car. They even took my wife."

"What?"

Caleb nodded. "She was given a choice too."

Hal thought back to his encounter at the apartment, less than an hour earlier. *If you're looking for Delilah,* the woman who answered the door had said, *you're not going to find her here.* The baby crying couldn't have been more than two years old.

"What kind of mother would do that?" Caleb asked in a hollow whisper. "What kind of mother would choose those animals over her own child?"

Suddenly, Caleb didn't seem so big anymore. His shoulders hunched, and the skin on his face seemed to have gone gray. Hal knew from experience that this kind of defeat would kill any desire to answer more questions. He kept his foot on the gas.

"What do you know about Charlie Wilcox?" he asked. "Or Billy Wayne Dickerson?"

"I knew Billy Wayne, sure," said Caleb. "I grew up with him. Not the sharpest tool in the shed, but . . . anyway, yeah. I knew him."

"And Wilcox?"

"I don't think I know anybody named Wilcox." Caleb swatted away a fly that wasn't there. "I don't think I want to neither. Look, I've been out here long enough, and my boss is going to—"

"How about Ed Crowe?" Hal asked. "I believe he's from Omaha. He's one of the Vandals, and I hear—"

Caleb cut the distance between him and Hal in two steps. He towered over him and jammed a finger just shy of his face.

"I got nothing to say about that piece of shit," he growled. "You asked me about my wife. You want to know about her? You want to know what kind of choice she made? Go ask that son of a bitch, because that's where you'll find her."

"Hey, Caleb, I didn't mean to—"

Caleb was heated now. "If I so much as see Digger Crowe anywhere near me or my baby boy, I'm going to put two rounds of double-aught buckshot in his goddamn face. Put *that* in your fucking newspaper. You hear me?"

Hal's pulse was off the charts. He could barely still his hand long enough to close his notebook and slip it back into the pocket of his jacket. He took two steps back, but Caleb kept up with him.

"Now I don't want to ever talk about the Blood Ravens no more," Caleb thundered. "I don't want to ever hear about the Vandals or Digger Crowe. And I damn sure don't want to talk about Baby Doll. Do you understand me? Make sure that's clear. When they burned them tats off my back, they cut any ties I have between me and them. You print anything with my name on it, make sure it's that. Or else I'll be paying a visit to your little newspaper, and trust me, this ain't the face you want to see ever again."

Hal got the picture. He wasted no time returning to his car, but before he started the engine, he watched six-foot-three Caleb McNaughton shrink again as he walked back up the steps to his job at the furniture store.

Caleb had nothing to do with the Pinto, thought Hal, *but I am driving away from here far from empty handed.*

He turned the key and pointed the car back to Lake Castor.

CHAPTER THIRTEEN

Jess Keeler

Present Day

Sandy pleaded for the opportunity to give the presentation. Jess saw no harm in it and agreed. After all, the young intern had put in the hours, done the research, mucked through the microfiche. Sandy had toiled in the trenches—much like Jess had done on *Something Bad Wrong*—and Jess felt like she should reap the rewards. They worked together to assemble informative slides; then Jess settled in with everyone else to watch the presentation.

Aaron took a seat up front and activated a phone camera so that the presentation might be recorded. Buffy switched on her mic. Sandy thanked Jess, then took her place at the front of the room.

"As we all know by now," Sandy began, "the Lake Castor Sniper targeted six victims over a period of a month, during the summer of 1984."

Sandy clicked her first slide, and the screen at the front of the room showed a serious older Black man wearing a tan jacket and hip gold-framed sunglasses.

"The first victim was Ronald 'Ronnie' Daye, sixty-one years old. On July sixth, he was killed by a single gunshot wound while walking on Barclay Street in Lake Castor's Back Back community. The shooting was never reported in any newspapers until after August seventh, although an obituary was printed in the *Herald* two days after his death."

Sandy clicked to the following slide, a photograph taken from a college yearbook of a younger man wearing a letter jacket and a fashionable Afro.

"The second victim was Quincy Williams, a sophomore at North Carolina Central University who had returned home for the summer to visit his family. He was playing basketball with friends at a neighborhood park when a single gunshot claimed his life on July tenth, only four days after the death of Ronnie Daye. Again, he was memorialized in the *Herald* with a one-hundred-word obituary, but not a single word mentioned his murder until August seventh."

The third slide offered a Black man in his fifties with white hair on the sides of his head and clean bald on top. He wore his beard scruffy and gray, like a wizened sage, but one with great appetites. The photograph had been chosen for his obituary, and Jess thought that whoever selected it had been fond of the mischievous character in his eyes and smile.

"Our third victim," Sandy continued, "is Clarence Moulton. On July eighteenth, Mr. Moulton was returning from an S&P on the corner of Loftin and McCorkle when he was the recipient of a single gunshot wound, like all the others. Also like all the others, it would be weeks before his murder was mentioned in the local newspapers, not until the day when—"

The door opened. Jess turned and was surprised to see her mother, Samantha Bowen, carrying a tray of sandwiches. Samantha made an effort to steer clear of the projection screen showing the pictures and slides.

"Don't mind me," Samantha said. "Keep going on about your business. I won't disturb anyone."

But her fussing with the table while she set out the snacks caused enough of a disturbance. Jess motioned for Sandy to pause while she hit the lights.

"Mom," she groused, "what are you doing here?"

"I thought I would bring some snacks for you and your friends." Samantha continued unpacking the food and spreading it across the table. "You don't think I'm too far gone to notice that you've been too busy to eat? You're a shadow of yourself. Just look at you."

"Mom . . . Where's Benjamin?"

Samantha looked around as if she might have misplaced something. Not finding it, she threw up her hands. "Oh, I'm sure he's fine. When I left, he was doing whatever on his computer."

"Wait . . ." Jess's eyes bugged. "You *drove* here? Yourself? Mom, I told you I don't like you driving in your condition."

Samantha waved her away with her hand. Just like that, she had dismissed her daughter's concerns, much as she always had. Jess measured her exasperation; their entire lives had been a series of one of them showing concern and the other blowing it off. Instead of pursuing it, she silently mouthed an apology to Sandy. Aaron and Buffy, on the other hand, took advantage of the offering and pounced upon the free food.

"My name is Samantha Bowen," she said. "I promise I raised Jessica not to be so rude. I'm her mother."

"She told us all about you," said Aaron as he introduced himself with a mouth full of croissant. "So happy to finally meet you."

"You can imagine my reaction when I heard Jessica was working on another one of these little crime stories," Samantha said. "However, I've always tried to be supportive of my daughter's passions, in hopes that she might one day find her true calling."

Jess rolled her eyes, knowing full well that her mother spoke the furthest thing from the truth. Throughout Jess's life, Samantha had been anything *but* supportive. When Jess had wanted to quit the cheerleading squad in high school so she could focus more on her role with the student newspaper, her mother had thrown an absolute fit. Same as she had when Jess had announced she would be studying journalism at Virginia State instead of enrolling at UNC at Chapel Hill. And when Jess had informed Samantha that she would be producing *Something Bad Wrong* using the notebook she'd discovered belonging to her own grandfather—the deputy who'd investigated the original unsolved mystery—her mother had literally lost her mind.

Still, Jess saw no reason to bring the crew into their own interpersonal drama.

"Mother," she said, "you remember Buffy?"

Buffy stopped loading her free hand with mini sandwiches and glanced up with eyes wide, as if she'd been caught shoplifting.

"Ah, yes," Samantha said, extending her hand. "You helped Jessica with her podcast."

"That's right, Ms. Bowen," said Buffy. "It's wonderful to see you again. I see you're looking well."

While everyone busied themselves with snacks, Jess clapped her hands to try and keep everyone on track.

"Okay, okay, everyone," she said. "I want to thank my mom for dropping in unexpectedly like this, but we've only got a few days before our meeting with Sheriff Axel. It's very important that we're all brought up to speed on the sniper case so that we know what to ask him during the interview."

"Thank you, Jess." Sandy powered up her next slide, which showed an athletic man in his late thirties. Again, the photo appeared to be cribbed from an obituary. "On July twenty-second, Dwight Fontenot was filling up a car at the Esso where he worked. Again, an unseen assailant struck him with a fatal bullet, and the crime remained unreported until August seventh."

The only sound that followed was the crew unwrapping their sandwiches or digging into bags of potato chips.

"The pattern breaks with the fifth victim." Sandy clicked to the next slide, which showed a man in his late twenties, grinning ear to ear. "On July twenty-sixth, just four days after the latest victim was killed, Gary

Mock was loading groceries when a single bullet tore through his upper left arm. Previous to this attack, every shooting had been fatal, so we are left to believe that the sniper missed his target, therefore allowing our first survivor. Once again, this attack—"

"Let me guess," Aaron said, his mouth full of potato chips. "It wasn't reported in the local papers until August seventh."

"You would be correct," Sandy said.

"What happened on August the seventh?" Samantha asked.

Jess shushed Samantha and patted her lightly on her forearm. She motioned for Sandy to continue.

Sandy clicked to the next frame, and the screen was filled with the image of a ruggedly handsome white man in need of a shave and a haircut. He had a boyish charm, despite his age. His clothes were rumpled and the style of a man much older than he.

"I remember him," said Samantha.

Jess turned to her, surprised. "You do?"

"Most certainly. He was a newspaperman, and it was just awful when he was murdered. Oh, what was his name?"

"Hal Broadstreet," replied Sandy. "He was a journalist for the *Lake Castor Times*."

"That's right," said Samantha. "After he was killed, we couldn't go anywhere. We had to draw our curtains closed and could only go shopping after the sun had gone down. It was horrible."

"You didn't hear anything about the other shootings?" Jess asked.

"What other shootings?"

Jess pointed to the screen, where Sandy's presentation had shown the previous five victims. "The ones in South Side."

"Where, dear?"

Jess shifted uncomfortably. "I believe you called it the Back Back then."

"Oh, dear," said Samantha. "Of course, we weren't told of those. There was always somebody getting killed down there. It was hardly news at the time."

"Mother . . ."

"It's true," Samantha said. "They don't like us to say things like that these days, but that doesn't mean it wasn't true. It's just the way of things, I'm afraid. I'm hardly to blame."

"Don't you dare record that," Jess hissed at Aaron, who had adjusted the camera so that it pointed toward them.

Aaron repositioned the camera, and the room fell silent for an uncomfortable moment.

Once it passed, Sandy cleared her throat and resumed her presentation. "The sixth and final victim was, of course, Harold Broadstreet, known to his colleagues as Hal. There were several deviations from the sniper's normal patterns with this shooting. For one, the victim was inside a house, instead of out on the street."

Sandy clicked a slide, and a present-day picture of a nice brick home filled the screen. A red arrow indicated the window where the fatal bullet had entered.

"Secondly," Sandy continued, "the target was not inside the confines of Lake Castor's Back Back."

The next image was an aerial map of Lake Castor. The Back Back neighborhood was highlighted; two miles away, an arrow pointed toward Hal Broadstreet's house.

"Also of note," Sandy pointed out, "this victim was white. It is that fact that we are left to deduce led to the greatest deviation of all: the following day, the shooting was front-page news and the police were mobilized."

While the rest of the crew were left to simmer with that information, Samantha leaned closer to her daughter's ear.

"She's a very good presenter. Very well spoken and knowledgeable."

Jess whispered back, "She's quite a find. We definitely got lucky."

"She wasn't always like that," said her mother.

Jess cocked her head. "What do you mean?"

"When she was younger," Samantha answered. "She wasn't always as presentable."

"Mom, what are you talking about?"

"I feared the worst when her husband left her, but when I see her up there now, I think maybe she can finally make something of herself."

Jess stared at her mother until the confusion melted away. She realized that Samantha was having another of her fugues, and had confused Sandy for Jess.

"Mom . . ." Unsure how to proceed, Jess rested a shaking hand on her mother's arm. "Mom, I—"

"But let's see how far she gets this time without her grandfather's notebook."

Jess retrieved her hand and used it to flick away the single tear welling in her eye. Once again, her mother had confounded her. Only this time, it was something else operating that was far crueler than Samantha Bowen. A heaviness settled over Jess, and in that moment, she envied her mother's deteriorating mind and its ability to shrug off painful moments such as those.

CHAPTER FOURTEEN

ENNIS WORTHY

1984

It was all eyes on Ennis Worthy as he walked through the front doors of the Lake Castor police station. He told himself it was because it had been a while since someone had worn a brown Deeton County deputy's uniform inside that building. The two jurisdictions had enjoyed a deep, historic rivalry over the years, albeit one that had lessened considerably since the death of Worthy's mentor, Sheriff Red Carter.

However, Worthy respected that it was more likely that the officers weren't used to seeing a Black man entering the front door.

"My name is Deputy Worthy," he explained to the sergeant at the front desk. "I have an appointment with Captain Henry Dorritt."

The sergeant appeared skeptical until he had confirmed it, then just plain bored. He motioned to a bank of seats for Worthy to wait.

Nearly twenty minutes later, Worthy was escorted to the fifth floor, where Dorritt's office was located. Dorritt, dressed in his blues, invited Worthy to enter and sit before a desk larger than the deputy had ever seen. Dorritt removed his jacket and sat across from him.

"Ennis, my boy," said Dorritt, "it's been too long. How's Bobby and the gang doing?"

"The sheriff is well," said Worthy. "He's gearing up for another election this November. I don't reckon anyone is going to run against him, so it shouldn't be too difficult."

"If anybody can lose an uncontested election," said the captain, "it would certainly be Bobby McCoy. How many deputies does he have under his command right now?"

"Sixteen, sir."

Dorritt cracked a wry grin. "Old Red Carter used to run that county with just seven. Then again, Bobby McCoy is a far cry from Red Carter."

Worthy knew better than to respond. "Captain Dorritt, I am sure you are familiar with Reverend Elijah Stallings."

"Of course," said Dorritt. "The good reverend is instrumental with outreach to our Negro communities."

Worthy took a breath. "Yes sir. Reverend Stallings is a friend, of course, and he asked that I look in on a parishioner of his who lives in the South Side community."

"The South Side community of Lake Castor?"

"Yes sir."

"You mean the Back Back?"

Worthy nodded. "That's correct, sir. Her name is—"

"We've worked with the reverend for many years. Do you have any idea why he thought it prudent to ask a Deeton deputy to cross the state line instead of one of my men?"

"It wasn't an official visit, sir," said Worthy. "Reverend Stallings simply wanted me to pay a call is all."

"In uniform?"

"I believe I chose the uniform, sir. I meant no disrespect."

Dorritt let that sink in, then dismissed it with a wave of his hand. "At any rate," he said, "how can I help you and the reverend?"

"The woman's name is Rosalie Patience," Worthy proceeded. "She's communicated with the reverend that she was worried for her boy,

Ricky Lee. He'd come across some trouble with the law, and she wanted to help him find a more narrow path."

"What kind of trouble?" asked Dorritt.

"I don't remember the details," Worthy lied. "So far as I could tell, it was trouble that had come and gone and was well in the rearview. She was more concerned with the state of his here and now."

Dorritt nodded for Worthy to proceed.

"While interviewing the boy," Worthy continued, "I came to realize there was something deeper affecting him than resentment."

"Aah, yes," said Dorritt. "I'm afraid it's epidemic in that community. It's not like it is down in Deeton. The culture in our Back Back is such that a few rotten apples can bring everybody down with them."

"Beg pardon, sir?"

"It's cocaine," Dorritt explained. "It's grabbed hold of folks down there, and they've synthesized it now so that it's cheaper and much, much more addictive. They're calling it *crack*, and you'll be seeing it soon down in Deeton. I fear now that it's gotten its hooks in your boy, Ronnie Lee, that it may not let go."

Worthy bit his tongue. "*Ricky* Lee Patience exhibited no signs of drug use. I'm fairly well trained to spot them, as I'm sure are you and your officers, but I assure you that he was clean."

"Even so," said Dorritt, but he added nothing to it.

"What I observed," said Worthy, "is that the boy may be suffering from a type of mental illness."

Dorritt wiped a smug grin from his face with his hand. "Mental illness? I didn't know Sheriff Bobby trained his men to diagnose such a thing."

"No sir." Worthy's cheeks burned hot. "I have personal experience with it."

"Tell me about that."

"My uncle Charlie—er, *Charles*." Worthy struggled to maintain eye contact. "He came home from the war and wasn't the same as when he went in."

"A lot of boys weren't, son."

"Yes sir. But Charlie . . . his behavior was *radically* different." The memory of it added a strain to Worthy's voice. "He thought the army was blocking his thoughts, making it hard for him to concentrate. He said we were all in danger. Couldn't never tell us from who. Sometimes he would sleep for three days straight, then other times . . ."

"Sounds like he was shell shocked."

"That's what some of the old-timers said, sure." Worthy regretted the words as soon as they were spilled. "Lucky for us, Charlie had veteran's benefits. He got special care, and they were able to diagnose him."

"With what?"

"Schizophrenia."

Dorritt frowned. His eyes wandered to his desk.

"The same look I used to see in my uncle's eyes," said Worthy, "I see it in the boy's."

"I don't remember you telling me that Ricky Lee served."

"No sir. He didn't. But they say it can be brought on by sustained trauma."

Dorritt's eyes returned to the deputy. He appeared amused. "What possible *sustained trauma* could Ricky Lee be experiencing stateside, son?"

"Some would argue"—Worthy chose his words carefully—"that being Black in a systemically racist society is plenty trauma enough."

Dorritt studied him for a long, uncomfortable moment. Worthy immediately realized that he had overstepped. Still, he kept a stony expression. He willed himself not to blink, not to look away from the captain's oppressive gaze.

Finally, Dorritt rested his forehead into the palm of his hand. "And what, pray tell, are you asking from me, Deputy Worthy?"

"The boy needs help, sir," he said. "My uncle could get what he needed because of his service to our nation. That boy and his family, though, they can't hardly rub two pennies together. There's no way they can get the level of care he's going to need. And without it . . . well, it's likely that something will happen in which your men are going to be dispatched down to South Si—er, the *Back Back*, and they might mistake his behavior for something more nefarious."

"*What?*"

"Nefarious, sir," said Worthy. "It means evil and mali—"

"I know what *nefarious* means." Dorritt's tone held an edge. "Listen, I suppose you think my men on this side of the state line aren't as sophisticated as Bobby McCoy's men down in Deeton County, but if you are trying to insinuate that we—"

"No, no sir. I promise you, I didn't mean anything by it. I just mean in the heat of the moment, Ricky Lee's symptoms may appear that he is unpredictable and—"

Dorritt held up a hand. Worthy's lips snapped shut. He waited for Dorritt to collect himself, take a breath, and say, "Deputy Worthy, I was very impressed with the way you approached the Christmas Eve Murders down in Deeton way back when. We all thought Red was pulling a publicity stunt when he pinned that badge on you, and you proved every single one of us wrong. You're a smart investigator, and quite honestly, you're being wasted down there in that podunk, one-horse county's jailhouse. That being said, if you think you have earned the right to step into my jurisdiction and challenge the judgment of my law enforcement officials, then maybe you aren't half as smart as I gave you credit for."

"Sir, I didn't—"

"I'm going to do you a favor by explaining things to you slowly, so that you might understand. For one, this isn't Deeton County Sheriff's, where the law is encouraged to get in the business of every Tom, Dick, and Joe Bob. We're a modern police agency, and we uphold the laws governed by the commonwealth of Virginia. We're not community outreach. We're not prevention. We are in the business of law and order. This kid—while his situation is unfortunate—is not breaking the law.

Therefore, we are unable to do anything, *even if we wanted to*. However, I assure you, that if he were to step one toe over the line, my men will be there. Because it is not our job to babysit. That task falls to the family unit and the churches. Our job, son, is to clean up the mess after it happens. Now, if there's nothing else . . ."

It took Worthy a beat to realize that he'd been dismissed. Once he did, he grabbed his hat with both hands and stood quickly from the chair. He had so much more to say, but his training and his experience had taught him to keep it to himself. Instead, he thanked the captain and headed for the door.

Before he could quit the office, he heard Dorritt call to him one last time.

"Thank you for your concern, Deputy," he said. "And if there's ever anything else you need on my side of the line, I trust that you'll call and make it known."

CHAPTER FIFTEEN

ENNIS WORTHY

Present Day

Ennis Worthy slid into the booth across from where Sheriff Lorne Axel had just taken the first bite from his barbecue sandwich. The lawman set his lunch back on the tray in front of him and reached for his glass of sweet tea. His smile could not be concealed.

"You look out of place," said Lorne.

"Because I'm on your side of the state line?" Worthy asked. "Or is it because I'm an eastern Carolina man when it comes to barbecue and the fact that Whitman puts tomato in his sauce would keep any stick-burning purist from walking through that door?"

Lorne's grin widened. "No, it's because I'm still not used to seeing you in civilian clothes."

The waitress appeared table side. "Well, lookie here," she said. "I got me a booth with two sheriffs in it."

"I'm not sheriff anymore," Worthy said with a soft smile.

"You'll always be sheriff to my people," said the waitress. "What can I get you?"

Worthy waved his hand. "I'll just have an iced tea. I'm afraid my appetite isn't what it used to be when I was working all the time."

"I'll have that right out," she said.

"She's right about one thing," Lorne said after she'd disappeared to fetch the tea. "You'll always be sheriff to some folks. That's on both sides of the line. You made a lot of friends in your twenty-some-odd years down there. Lots of goodwill. I hope to do the same."

"You ain't running again?" Worthy asked.

"I haven't decided yet," he said, "but I had me a little scare a while back." He tapped his chest, about where his heart was. "Mindy's got me watching what I eat, which explains the vegetables."

Worthy eyed the pile of coleslaw and fried okra skirting alongside his pulled-pork sandwich, but held his tongue. "Mindy is a good woman. No one would blame you for wanting to spend as much time with her as you could."

"But don't you miss it?"

Worthy nodded. "Every damned day."

The tea was delivered, and Worthy took a big gulp of it. They sat there a moment, two men who'd served their counties as sheriffs longer than many of their successors. Folks in the restaurant continued on with their conversations, eating their lunches, carrying on as if neither of them were there.

Worthy finally broke the silence. "Jess Keeler came to see me yesterday," he said. "She wants to dig up a story about another one of our old cases. This time she's got herself an entire TV crew."

"We're due to meet this weekend," said Lorne.

"That's what she told me." After a silent moment, Worthy asked, "Did she tell you what her story was about?"

"No. But after watching how she handled herself with those Christmas Eve Murders, I owe it to her to hear her out. I thought she treated law enforcement fair, which is pretty rare with journalists these days."

"They want to tell the story of the sniper from 1984."

Lorne's expression immediately wiped away any remnants of a smile. "That would be a bad idea."

"I told her as much."

"And I suppose she didn't appreciate your advice."

"What do you think?"

Lorne set down his sandwich, appearing to have lost his appetite. He sucked sweet tea through a straw until he'd cooled himself down.

"The last thing we need," Lorne said, "is some TV crew digging up dirt from that mess. I'd think you, of all people, would know that."

"And you, of all people, would know that she isn't liable to let it go just because I tell her to."

Lorne nodded. "You think I should cancel our meeting?"

"That's what I did when she first came around asking about those Christmas Eve Murders," said Worthy. "It only made her work harder to kick over more stones. No, I'm afraid that won't cool her off."

"So what then?"

"I've been thinking about that," said Worthy. "I say we find her another story. Another unsolved homicide—something sensational, something curious—that will make her forget all about the sniper."

"Like what?"

"I don't know, but I'm sure if you take a minute to reflect on it, there's something on the books that's rankled you for some time. Something that you might have had a stake in, but you were told nothing could be done, so you did nothing, but now, now that you sit behind the big desk, maybe you can clean up your side of the street a little bit. Leave the job a little more dignified than it was when you first slipped on the tin. You and me, we got old. How much longer you think you got in that chair?"

"Is that what you did?" Lorne asked. "Clean up your side of the street?"

"It's an awful lot more clean than it was when I took over for Bobby McCoy, that's for damned sure." Worthy rattled his ice cubes, then sucked what tea he could from the bottom of his glass. "But no, I left plenty dirty."

"You talking about Ricky Lee Patience?"

Worthy turned his face to the door. "Yeah," he said. "I'm talking about Ricky Lee."

The silence between the two old men spoke louder than any words they'd said their entire careers. They were of two different backgrounds. From two different cultures. Different races and different sides of the state line. Still, they had each served the highest office of their county and shared the responsibility it had. They each thought highly of the other and respected their words as bond, but they also knew what it took to defend that office. They shared a kinship that not many other men outside wartime might share.

After a moment, Worthy spoke up. "It's best if we keep her off that story," he said. "For all of our sakes."

Lorne didn't say anything. Instead, he picked up his sandwich, took an angry bite of it, and then chewed while staring at the far wall, lost in thought.

"Besides, for all we know, her TV show might actually solve whatever crime you put her on."

Lorne tossed his half-eaten sandwich to his plate, then stood from the table. He fished a couple of dollars from his pocket and set them near his empty glass.

"Everything okay, Lorne?" asked Worthy.

"I think so," Lorne answered. "I just might have the perfect case for Ms. Keeler's television program."

"Is that right?" Worthy cocked his head. "Which one?"

Lorne plucked his hat from the empty chair beside him and slipped it onto his head.

"The Jem Fosskey murders."

CHAPTER SIXTEEN

JESS KEELER

Present Day

Jess arrived at the set, and the first thing she noticed was that everything was completely wrong. To call it a *set* would be a gross exaggeration, as it was a quick bump-and-run setup by Aaron, Sandy, and two bored actors who spent time between takes scrolling through their phones.

"Where is Buffy?" Jess asked as she approached.

Aaron didn't take his eye from his viewfinder as he carefully set up his next shot. Sandy stepped forward and offered Jess a cup of coffee from a makeshift craft-services table she had assembled on the tailgate of Aaron's pickup truck.

"Buffy took off when she heard we wouldn't be using any sound from the shoot," Sandy reported. "The plan was to Foley in the gunshots in post."

Jess disapproved, primarily because Buffy's presence comforted her. Lately, she had felt more and more divisions between her and Aaron regarding the direction of the story. Buffy often took Jess's side, and Sandy's vote appeared still up for grabs.

Jess became aware of another such division as she noted the actors' costumes.

"What on earth are they wearing?" Jess wanted to know.

"Period clothing," Sandy explained.

Jess took in both actors. Despite the noonday's summer sun, the man wore a tan leather jacket, checkered bell-bottoms, and a comically large Afro. He'd also bedecked himself with gold chains, rings, and sunglasses.

"This is supposed to take place in 1984," Jess reminded them, "not 1974."

Sandy consulted the Notes app on her phone. "According to our research, Ronnie Daye was a flashy dresser."

Jess placed both hands on her hips. "Okay, but Ronnie Daye was killed on Barclay Street. That's six blocks east of here."

"He was, but . . ." Sandy nodded toward Aaron, almost as an apology.

Aaron didn't look up from his viewfinder. "Barclay Street is over-run with boutique shops and manicured midcentury moderns. For this shot, we need something a little more run down. I want *despair*. I need *squalor*."

Jess mouthed an apology toward two women in Lycra who jogged past with dogs on a leash and an unkind glance toward the film crew.

Aaron, unfazed, continued with his scene. "Okay," he called to the actors, "let's take this from the top. Real simple shot here, guys. Let's get the energy *up*. Everybody take your places . . ."

The actor with the flashy gear was joined by a second actor, a woman, wearing bell-bottoms and a tie-dye shirt.

"Did anybody google *the eighties* before they assigned costumes?" Jess asked.

"Quiet on the set!" Aaron called. He raised his hand high. *"Action!"*

The two actors walked casually toward the camera. They mimed polite conversation, but the male actor walked with exaggerated bravado. The woman feigned adoration of him.

"Keep walking," Aaron directed. "Forward, forward . . . keep it coming . . . and now . . . *gunshot!*"

Aaron dropped his arm, and the male actor dramatically recoiled, then stumbled backward, clutching his chest. He waved his other arm wild, as if reaching for something that might save him. The woman beside him stared at him with incredulity, which quickly gave way to terror.

"Baby?" she cried. "Baby, what happened?"

The man gasped for air, wheeled around in a wide circle, and then collapsed to the ground. The woman dropped to her knees beside him; then upon discovery of the fatal wound, she turned her head to the sky and let fly a terrible wail.

"Aaaand . . . *cut*," Aaron called. "That was perfect! Absolutely perfect! Let's take another one!"

The actors rose to their feet, dusted themselves off, and returned to their original marks. People in passing cars craned their necks to better see what was going on, but didn't so much as slow down.

"I didn't see anything about Ronnie Daye being accompanied by a woman when he was shot," Jess pointed out.

Aaron fired back, "I didn't see anything that said he *wasn't*."

Sandy moved between them, as if to mediate.

"We have very little information to go on regarding Mr. Daye's murder," she explained. She consulted her Notes app again. "According to the newspaper, it said, 'On July sixth, Ronald Daye, sixty-one, Negro, was shot while walking on Barclay Street.' That same sentence is repeated several times over the next several weeks during the coverage of the manhunt, as well as in syndicated papers. That's *literally* all we have to go on."

"That doesn't mean we simply *make up* what happened," Jess said.

"True," said Sandy, "but it gives us room to move between the lines. Just for the sizzle reel."

Jess was getting tired of hearing that untruths were to stand *just for the sizzle reel*. Before she could communicate as much, Aaron called out to his actors.

"Let's take this next one from the top. This time, let's try something different. Eddie, why don't you fall a little more quickly, and Belinda, I want your anguish to really read on camera."

Jess's frustrations were becoming more palpable. Sandy must have registered them, because she stepped in tight and gently placed her hand on Jess's back.

"You said you were trying to establish contact with the victims' families?" she whispered. "How is that going?"

"Not well at all," Jess said. "I've called everyone on the list that you and I made, but I'm getting no response. The one time someone picked up the phone, they hung up after I told them why I was calling."

A coy expression passed over Sandy's face. "It's not exactly like Jess Keeler to give up so easy."

"I'm not giving up." Jess watched the two actors rehearse their scene and wanted to throw up her hands. "This is precisely why I said we shouldn't start production until we have all the facts. It takes *time* to tell a good story. You can't rush the truth."

"We give the Germans something shiny and dramatic for their pitch; then we'll strive for accuracy once we get the budget." Sandy rubbed her hand up and down Jess's back in an attempt to comfort her. "Trust me. We're just doing this for the siz—"

"I'm tired of hearing about the *sizzle reel*. I'm not prostituting my integrity for a *sizzle reel*."

Behind them, the actor, Eddie, dropped to the ground, as if shot. Belinda raced in wide circles, pantomiming panic.

"Dear Jesus," Jess sighed. "This may actually be the lowest point in my career."

Sandy blinked in disbelief. "Are you kidding me?" she asked. "You're the producer of a true-crime documentary that—with any luck—will be the number one streaming show."

"I wanted to tell the truth. I wanted to find justice."

"And you will," Sandy said. "Let's just get that money, and you can do all of those things."

Jess sighed again. "Why do you do this?"

"Honestly?" Sandy's eyes blazed bright blue. "It's because of you."

"What?"

"It's true," Sandy said. "I read an article about you after *Something Bad Wrong* came out. You were talking about how you rediscovered yourself during the COVID lockdowns and that inspired you to start investigating an unsolved murder. That was, like, so *amazing*. There I was, trying to be an influencer on social media, playing video games that I didn't care about and dressing up like sexy cartoon characters at conventions, all so some horny nerds might give me likes and follows. Reading about you inspired me to take charge of my life and try and refocus my energy toward something *good*. You taught me that I could do so much more than what I was doing."

Jess didn't know what to say. She thought of her own son, Benjamin, and how she might feel if she let him down. Or the failure she felt every time she looked in the mirror because she had been unable to bring the killer to justice after her podcast. Or the words spoken by her mother only days previous, when her dementia had confused Sandy for Jess.

Still, the thought she might have actually touched someone's life in a positive way reinvigorated her.

"Thank you for saying that," Jess whispered. "Those words couldn't have come at a better time."

"I'm sorry you feel down," Sandy said. "But us girls need to stick together."

Jess threw an arm around Sandy and drew her tighter. "I'm going to go personally to each of the victims' relatives' houses and knock on their doors. Sometimes all it takes is a little face to face to convince them we're the right ones to tell their story."

Sandy nodded. "That's a great idea."

A thought struck Jess. She shot it down twice before finally giving in. "Hey, Sandy?"

"Yeah?"

"Would you like to go with me?"

The smile spreading across Sandy's face was all the answer Jess needed.

"We're going to do great work," Jess said.

And then, as if to answer, Aaron broke the moment by calling for his actors to give him a take with the drama "turned up to eleven."

CHAPTER SEVENTEEN

HAL BROADSTREET

1984

Hal Broadstreet had always felt more comfortable around criminals than he did around police. Sometimes, he believed, it was impossible to draw a line between them. The only difference was that one side wore a badge and could legally carry a firearm. He resented Liv Crane's style of journalism, which sometimes acted as a conduit for the police. Why be a mouthpiece for that side of the law when he could just as easily work a little closer to the dirt in order to chase a story?

These methods brought him notoriously close to some of the most unsavory locations for quotes or background information. He knew every road in and out of the Back Back. He could provide intimate details of the apartment over top of Jem Fosskey's garage. He could maneuver the forest beyond the old service road blindfolded and still locate Peck Holleman's secret field of marijuana.

However, one door he had yet to darken was that of Club 809, situated on a red clay drive just off the farm-to-market road leading out of downtown. Once upon a time, it had been a double-wide trailer home, but Harker Green, who owned it, had converted it into a local watering hole. Due to its remote location near the outskirts of the county, it was a favorite pit stop for the Vandals motorcycle club to have a few beers, shoot a game of pool, and let off some steam.

Hal realized he'd come to the right place. He noted the long row of Harley-Davidson motorcycles that stretched along the outside of the building. The burly tattooed men who congregated outside the front door with longnecks and surly stares. The angry death metal music throbbing from inside the walls.

None of that would dissuade Hal. Not when there was a story on the line.

Based on what he'd gathered from Caleb McNaughton, the ex–Blood Raven had lost everything—including his white Ford Pinto and wife, Delilah—to the Vandal from Omaha, Digger Crowe. If that same Pinto was involved in the murders of Jem Fosskey and his boys, then it made logical sense he should have a word with Digger, to possibly quote his side of the story. According to Officer Axel, the police had no interest in following up this angle with the Pinto, especially if they pulled it over and didn't pursue questioning.

But why?

It was a question he would have to shelve until a moment he could garner a face to face with Captain Dorritt himself. Until then, he had plans to try and find someone who would talk to him about the Pinto and its occupants.

He parked his El Camino on the far side of the red clay parking lot. To enter, he had to walk a gauntlet of inked-up felons eye-fucking him like he was a new guy in the prison yard. He kept his head high, his chest forward, and one foot in front of the other until he'd entered the front door of the converted double-wide trailer home. Immediately, his senses were assaulted. The air was thick with cigarette smoke and the piercing screams of heavy metal. There were maybe thirty people inside a room designed to hold fifteen. Men and women wearing colors or patches on their leather jackets that associated them with the Vandals motorcycle club. Hal squeezed his way through them and approached a bar top that had been hastily constructed from plywood and particle-board. It took a minute, but he finally got a bartender's attention and ordered a beer.

He didn't get two sips before a woman bumped into him, sloshing his beer across the wooden bar top. She had dyed her hair jet black and wore more makeup than was necessary and less clothing than she probably should. Hal imagined she had been pretty once, and those days weren't too far in the rearview.

"Goddamn, I'm sorry." She looked him up and down, then exploded into a fit of giggles. "What's your deal, man? Are you, like, a professor or something?"

"Or something." He smiled. "I'm a journalist."

"A what?"

"A reporter."

She teased the word around in her mouth before spitting it back out. "A *reporter*. La-di-da, then."

"I'm looking for someone."

"Keep looking, pal," she said. "I don't think you're going to find her here. Not dressed like that, anyway."

"Her name is Delilah McNaughton."

"Who?"

"I heard she goes by Baby Doll."

That seemed to sober her up. Her eyes canvassed the room, but never made their way back to his.

"I don't know anybody by that name," she said.

Hal knew she was lying, but dropped it. "What about Digger?"

"Who?"

"Ed Crowe. He goes by Dig—"

"I don't need you to repeat it, man." She still couldn't look him in the eye. "Look, man . . . maybe you ought to find some other place to drink."

"Why's that?"

"Because," she said, "right now you're healthy. That's a good thing to be, but it can be awfully short lived if you got bad habits."

"Like what kind of bad habits?"

She finally made eye contact, underlining how serious she was. "Like the kind where you ask around about people you ought not to be asking around about."

The juke changed the song to something with pulsing guitars and meth-soaked drums. Hal held up a twenty-dollar bill.

"Maybe you can make an introduction for me," he said.

"I'll do you one better." She snatched the twenty out of his fingers. "I'll keep you out of the hospital. Get lost."

"Hey, listen—"

"I said *fuck off!*" The last two words were said over the hideous wailing guitars, so loud that they caught the ears of the two barbarians next to her. To accentuate her position, she slapped him hard across the face. "Do I need to tell you again, *creep?*"

The barbarians moved in. "Is this guy bothering you, Duchess?" asked the bigger of the two.

Duchess wadded up the twenty-dollar bill and tossed it into Hal's face.

"Not anymore, he ain't," she said.

The men erupted into laughter. Hal turned his back to them and reached for his longneck. Before he could grab it, the bartender removed it.

"Hey, I wasn't finished," Hal said.

The bartender shook his head. "Yeah, you are. I'm sick and tired of cleaning up blood in here."

"You think I'm going to make somebody bleed?"

The bartender's eyes did not smile. "No," he said. "I don't."

Hal got the picture. With all eyes on him, he elbowed his way to the door and made his way back to his car. He'd be lying to himself if he said he wasn't surprised to find Duchess waiting for him, sucking on a filterless cigarette.

"That was quite the performance in there," he said.

"I couldn't risk being seen talking with you, Hal. Not tonight." She nervously scanned the parking lot. "You got a lot of nerve coming out here tonight and asking questions."

"Come on, Duchess." Hal grinned. "I figured since you and me are old friends, it wouldn't hurt anything. I never once named you as my source on that bank job five years back."

"No, you didn't, and if you ever did, you know that peckerwood ex-husband of mine will make a beeline for me, and won't nobody ever see me again." She tapped the ash off her cigarette. "Serves him right for cheating on me."

"What's the deal?"

"I don't know," she said. "Everybody's acting weird."

"Weird?"

"Yeah. Like on *high alert* or something. Ever since that club back east—what are they called, Rare Breed?—started beefing, it's been real tense around here."

"What are they saying?"

Duchess choked back a laugh. "To me? They ain't saying a word. They don't tell us chicks nothing. And, brother, we don't want to know." She held out her hand. "I'll take my twenty bucks back now."

Hal handed her the money, still balled up. "I'm looking for Delilah. Baby Doll. I want to talk to her."

Duchess's expression darkened. "Good luck with that, man."

"Why do you say that?"

"She ain't around."

"What do you mean *she ain't around*?"

"I mean ain't nobody seen her. She's gone missing."

"Missing? You mean she's gone? Where?"

"I don't know, and I don't think I want to know." Duchess rubbed her bare arms to warm them, despite the summer's evening air. "Look, girls around here sometimes go missing. It didn't use to be this way, but ever since the Blood Ravens patched over, man . . . honestly, we're better off not thinking about it, and there's plenty around to help forget. But man . . . Baby Doll was my *girl*."

"When was the last time you've seen her?"

"Yesterday. She left with Cuckoo."

"Cuckoo?"

"That's what they call Billy Wayne. *Cuckoo.*"

"Where did they go?"

"Probably out to see her old man."

"Caleb McNaughton?"

Duchess's eyes went wide. "No, man. That's her *old* old man. She's with Digger now."

Hal nodded. He remembered the look in Caleb's eye when he'd mentioned Digger. The rage. A larger picture was taking shape.

"What can you tell me about Digger?"

"Digger is somebody I don't want to talk about."

Hal nodded. He could feel that she wanted to talk. He needed to show her the way to do it.

"Okay, listen up, because I don't want to repeat myself." Duchess scanned the horizon for anyone who might hear them. "I hear Digger was married twice back in Omaha. One wife just disappeared. A year later, he got another one. It wasn't long before she went missing too."

"You hear what happened to them?"

"No. And I didn't ask. Keeping my mouth shut is the only health-care plan I got right now."

A trash can lid clattered against the ground behind them, and Duchess panicked until she saw an alley cat race across the parking lot.

"I don't want to talk about Digger no more," she said. "Change the subject."

"Fine," said Hal. "What about a guy named Charlie Wilcox?"

She looked confused for a moment; then realization dawned on her. "I think you mean Charlie Chains. That's what everybody calls him. He's a prospect. Hangs around Billy Wayne a lot. Quiet dude. Keeps to himself. Not like the other guys. I ain't seen him chase after the women, and I ain't never seen him doing any drugs."

"You mentioned Billy Wayne."

"Cuckoo. Yeah."

"What's his deal?"

"Cuckoo's in over his head, man."

"What do you mean?"

Again, Duchess checked over her shoulder. "When they rode as Blood Ravens and it was about the motorcycles or kicking ass—man, that was one thing. But this shit with the Vandals, it's different. I don't think Billy Wayne has the stomach for it."

A thought tickled Hal's mind. He made a note: if there was a lever to which pressure might be applied, it might very well be Billy Wayne Dickerson. That information might be valuable to Axel.

Duchess didn't like the sight of him writing in his pad. "You better not write my name down nowhere," she warned him. "I ain't kidding. Not a single scrap of paper. Make me that promise."

"I promise."

"I'm serious."

Hal nodded. "So am I, Duchess. I've been in this game a long, long time, and I know the rules. Ninety percent of the people I talk to have plenty of reason not to talk to me. I've got the Constitution on my side, and there's nobody who can force me to reveal the name of my sources. I've had threats from people ten times more frightening than those meatheads back there."

"No, you haven't," said Duchess. She pocketed the twenty and turned back toward Club 809. Over her shoulder, she added, "You don't even know what frightening is until you've come face to face with Digger Crowe."

CHAPTER EIGHTEEN

HAL BROADSTREET

1984

Hal knew every entrance and exit to Lake Castor's police station. The five-story-tall stucco building in the middle of downtown was very familiar to him, due to the various perp walks he'd witnessed and ambush interviews he'd performed over the years. He thought more than once about waiting around for Lieutenant Avondale, but changed his mind upon sight of Captain Hank Dorritt quitting for the day. Hal made his move. The captain saw the reporter approaching and rolled his eyes.

"You got a pair of brass ones, I'll give you that," said Dorritt, dropping his briefcase to the asphalt. He used his free hand to light a cigarette. "I'll give you to the end of this cigarette; then I want you off this property. Deal?"

"I made a promise to a friend," said Hal.

"You got no friends, Broadstreet. Especially around here."

"Possibly. But I got one hell of a story."

Dorritt considered this as he sucked blue smoke into his lungs. Upon spitting it to the sky, he said, "I never understood, with all the economic challenges this town has suffered since the shuttering of the

June River mill, how on earth Lake Castor can sustain two newspapers. I could tolerate it back in the day, but don't you reckon that's kind of super . . . superflu . . . oh come on, college boy. What's the word I'm looking for?"

"Okay, you've got your licks in," Hal conceded. "Why don't you talk to me?"

"What do you want to know?"

"The white Ford Pinto that was pulled over the morning of the murders."

Dorritt's expression didn't change. "I don't know what you're talking about."

"The one that was registered to ex–Blood Raven Caleb McNaughton and was occupied by three current members of the Vandals motorcycle club."

"How did you come across that information?"

Hal considered mentioning his source, but wisely decided against it. "It was on the scanner," he said. "Public information. What *isn't* public is why y'all decided to let those boys go, instead of taking them in for further questioning."

Dorritt didn't blink.

"I've followed up on that lead," Hal told him. "I'm sure you are aware by now that McNaughton claims his car was stolen by the Vandals, along with his bike. His wife left him for another member of the club. Do you know which one?"

If Dorritt was interested in the slightest, he didn't let on.

"A man named Ed Crowe, who goes by Digger," Hal said. "He's a founding member of the Vandals in Omaha who has a very interesting history. Apparently women in his orbit tend to go missing. A similar situation may have happened here with McNaughton's ex-wife. Crowe was in that car that was pulled over, and I'm hearing that a knife with blood trace was found on his person."

Dorritt sucked harder on the cigarette, glowing the cherry a bright red.

"Come on, Captain. What can you tell me?" Hal's voice colored with frustration. "I'm working my ass off over here, and I want to know if you're even looking into these guys. Anybody with half a brain knows this was biker business, but for whatever reason, y'all aren't out there rousting the clubhouse and shaking guys down. At least give me *something* so I can poke a stick in the rattlesnake hole and see what comes out."

Dorritt leveled with him. "You want to know why? I'll give you something, but it's off the record."

Hal made a show of putting away his notebook.

"I know you like to mix with them bastards," Dorritt said. "The pushers and the pimps and the bootleggers and all that muck that crawls out of the sewer after a long, hard rain. I've read that shit you write in the newspaper, where you glorify scumbags like Jem Fosskey with your *King of the Piedmont Bootleggers* and all that shit. You want to know why we're not pursuing it? Because it's criminal versus criminal, and all of it—every bit—is coming out in the wash. Since that damned mill closed, this place has become a cesspool, and what am I but a lifeguard? All we do is try to make sure the innocents don't drown. We're all that stands between the good people of this town and the jungle, and if those animals want to thin their own herd, then who am I to stand against progress?"

"What about Jem?" Hal said. "He was innocent. He never hurt nobody his entire life. He was a good, decent man who just happened to work the liquor trade."

"You lie down with dogs," said Dorritt, "then you can't come crying when you catch fleas."

Hal couldn't believe his ears. He'd suspected such a level of cynicism from the older police like Dorritt, but had never heard it voiced in such a way. It took Hal a minute to process.

Still, Hal knew his own strength. He had a skill when it came to talking to criminals. He reckoned if you held the picture a certain way and squinted, that's exactly what cops like Dorritt were: criminals.

So he buckled down.

"So you've got these scumbags . . ." Hal leaned in, as if conspiring. "Dead to rights. The three of them, armed with a knife and blood trace. Why not take them off the street? Why did you let them go?"

Dorritt shrugged. "Sometimes we fuck up."

"That's it?"

"It's the truth. I hate to break it to you, Broadstreet, but not everything is some grand conspiracy. Police is just like any other bureaucracy. Mistakes get made."

"So why don't you beat the bushes, try to haul them back in?"

"And do what?" Dorritt asked, bemused. "Ask them if they killed the bootlegger and his crew? Do you think they would simply roll over and admit it? To convict them, we'd need one of three things: evidence, a witness, or a confession. Any evidence is probably gone. No witnesses have come forward. And I doubt anyone would give us a confession."

"I think you pick up Digger Crowe and you'll find plenty of reasons to keep him locked up. My sources say he's got quite a lot of bodies stacked up behind him. With him off the board, I can find you plenty of people who will be eager to help you put him away."

Dorritt appeared to think long and hard about his next course of action. "What if I told you I had Digger Crowe right now?"

"What?"

"How's that for an exclusive? We picked him up two hours ago."

Hal looked for a read on the captain, but could get nothing.

"You're serious?" Hal asked.

"As a heart attack. You want to see him?"

Hal felt icicles forming in his chest. "Yes. You'd facilitate that?"

"Let's call it a little makeup for freezing you out the other day at Fosskey's."

"Would you let me ask him some questions?"

Dorritt appeared to think it over. "Why not? Although I can't guarantee he'd answer them."

"Let's go."

Dorritt pitched his cigarette butt and led the way back toward the station. However, instead of taking him to the holding cells, Dorritt led him to the medical examiner's. There in the center of the cold, sterile room was a slab that had been covered by a sheet. Dorritt pulled back the sheet to reveal a muscular, tattooed man who had been inked up with Vandal tattoos. The front half of his head had been blown out by whatever had been fired through the back.

"What the . . ."

Where Hal had lost his ability to speak, Dorritt had no such problems.

"Hal Broadstreet," said the captain, "I'd like you to meet Digger Crowe. Digger, this is Hal Broadstreet."

Even in death, the biker appeared angry and stoic. Hal took two steps backward from the slab, still unable to process what he was looking at.

Dorritt, on the other hand, stayed right where he stood.

"Our friend Hal here has a couple of questions he'd like to ask you."

CHAPTER NINETEEN

ENNIS WORTHY

1984

Ennis Worthy received the call at eleven thirty, while he was down at the jailhouse. Within ten minutes, he'd raised his girlfriend, Shirley, on the phone.

"Babe," he said, out of breath, "it's that boy. Ricky Lee Patience. He's been arrested."

He could hear the strain in her voice through the line. "Where?"

"Lake Castor."

"It's not your jurisdiction, En." She sighed. "We've talked about this. *Everyone* has talked to you about this."

"I looked his mother in the eye," Worthy said. "I *promised* her. I said I'd help her. And now she's calling me . . . I can't just look away, Shirley. You wouldn't, either, if it was you that she was calling."

"Have you talked to my father?"

Worthy had. Just a week earlier, he'd sat down for dinner with the good, right Reverend Elijah Stallings and explained the plight of Rosalie Patience and her son, Ricky Lee. About how his mental illness was being confused for illicit drug use or, worse, demonic possession. Worthy detailed Captain Dorritt's refusal to commit resources to Ricky Lee and expressed his fear that an incident might lead to a disastrous outcome. Reverend Stallings, however, did not share the deputy's concern.

"God has put you in a position to help that boy, Ennis. You are his instrument, and he trusts you to do the right thing."

"Unfortunately, I'm going to need a little more help. The Patience family doesn't live in my jurisdiction, so my hands are effectively tied."

Reverend Stallings shook his head as he motioned for the waiter. "God doesn't recognize *jurisdiction*, son. His kingdom is where we serve, and we are duty bound to care for all his subjects." He picked up his menu as the waiter arrived. "Order whatever you want, Ennis. It's a refusal of God's gifts to not enjoy the finer perks of our positions of power."

Worthy finished that dinner with no better sense of resolution. He spent the rest of the week mired in studies for his looming JD exam, wondering why he worried for Ricky Lee when, clearly, no one else did. He might have allowed himself to forget about it altogether, were it not for the echoes of Rosalie Patience's words to him that first morning:

. . . if Ricky Lee saw a Black man like you, one who is proud and walks with the Lord and helped his community the way you do . . . maybe it might be inspiring for him.

So when Rosalie Patience called to tell him that her son had been arrested in Lake Castor, Worthy felt he was morally obligated to step in and help.

"Fine," sighed Shirley through the phone. "Tell me what happened, and I'll see what, if anything, I can do."

There were, of course, two versions to the story.

Rosalie Patience gave Ricky Lee's account. Best she could put together, her son had been minding his business on the streets of Lake Castor, when he had come upon a white man beating his daughter.

"You know my Ricky Lee has a big heart," she had told Worthy. "There's no way he could have stood idly by and let that happen."

He hadn't. Ricky Lee had approached the man and retrieved from his pocket a homemade badge and commanded the man to stop assaulting the woman.

"I don't know why in God's name he would have something like that," Rosalie moaned.

Worthy, on the other hand, did. He remembered Ricky Lee's wide eyes when Worthy had removed it from his own shirt and handed it to him. *Maybe he might be inspired that he could rise . . .*

"When that white man bucked," Rosalie continued, "Ricky Lee was left trying to defend himself and that poor girl."

Wilson Keats, the district attorney, communicated a different view.

"The initial charge is impersonating an officer," he explained. He met with Worthy, Shirley, and Ricky Lee's overworked court-appointed attorney between hearings out of professional courtesy. "He's also been charged with kidnapping and assault, but I think given the nature of the incident, those aren't likely to stick."

"The nature of the incident," Shirley said, "is that our client was defending a woman from assault."

"Your client struck a white man," said Keats.

"Who was abusing a woman."

"Who was disciplining his *daughter*." Keats turned to Worthy. "Again, the father can be convinced that he might not want his dirty laundry aired out in court. It's a slow news day, and this might attract some ink. The impersonation charge, however, is going to need an answer."

"He wasn't impersonating an officer," Worthy groaned. "When he and I were talking, he took a shine to my badge and must have made himself one. It's my fault as much as anything."

"I don't follow, son."

Shirley's face brightened the way it sometimes did when an idea struck her in class. She stepped in front of the court-appointed attorney.

"Ennis here has had some revealing conversations with Ricky Lee. You see, Ricky Lee is not in his right mind."

Keats cocked his head. "How do you mean?"

"I'm not a psychiatrist," she said, "but I'm sure you might find one who would be able to testify that he most likely suffers from something similar to schizophrenia."

Keats's eyes widened, and for a moment, he appeared to run through a list of options before turning to the court-appointed attorney. "Are you suggesting that you might plead insanity?"

"I'm suggesting," Shirley intervened, "that we might argue that Ricky Lee is unfit to stand trial."

Keats nodded. To Worthy: "Would you be prepared to testify that you observed behavior consistent with this?"

Worthy wasn't certain. Shirley must have read as much from his expression, because she tucked in tight to him. "En, honey," she said, "this is as close to a win-win as you are going to find. If Ricky Lee is found unfit to stand trial, he will be remanded to psychiatric care. This is care that he is unable to get on his own. The other option is that he is tried for the impersonation charge, and neither judge nor jury will be lenient on a Black man who struck a white man. He'll go to jail, and after that, it's anybody's guess how Ricky Lee's story plays out."

Worthy thought it over. He couldn't argue with the logic. If he took the witness stand and testified to his observations of Ricky Lee's state of mind, the worst-case scenario would see Ricky Lee admitted to Addams State Mental Hospital, where he might get good psychiatric care he would otherwise be denied.

Reverend Stallings's words rang in Worthy's ears. *You are God's instrument. He put you here because it's where he needed you to be.*

"I'll do it," Worthy said. Already, he was thinking about how he would explain it to Ms. Patience.

He only hoped it was the right thing.

CHAPTER TWENTY

JESS KEELER

Present Day

Henrietta Newton lived in Tucker, a township on the far side of Lawles County, which was known for two things: a high school football state championship in the nineties and its status as a safe haven for expatriates who fled Lake Castor after the crime rate soared. Newton was the ex-wife of Lake Castor Sniper victim Dwight Fontenot. Jess plucked her name from Dwight's obituary in a July twenty-fourth edition of the *Lake Castor Herald*. From there, she tracked her through a marriage to Andrew Newton in 1995 and his subsequent death from a COVID-related illness in 2021.

At approximately noon, Jess and Sandy arrived at the address they'd found. The woman who answered the door was in her midforties, Black, and wearing a polite expression. She asked how she might help them.

"We're looking for Henrietta Newton," Jess explained with a smile. "You must be her . . . daughter?"

"Mom's in the garden," said the woman. "May I tell her who is asking for her?"

"My name is Jess Keeler, and this is—"

The woman's face fell. "You wouldn't happen to be the people who have been calling her on the phone, would you?"

"We are. We thought we might—"

"Didn't my mother explain that she didn't feel like talking to you?" Any trace of her polite expression had left the premises.

"We apologize for the intrusion," Jess said. "We wanted to—"

"You wanted to exploit a woman's pain from an event that happened forty years ago."

"Ma'am, you've misunderstood our intentions. We—"

"No one cared when it happened. Why do you care now?"

Sandy stepped forward. "Ma'am, I respect your concerns. But this is Jess Keeler here, the host of the podcast *Something Bad Wrong*. Last year, she was able to shine a light on the tragedy of the Lake Castor Christmas Eve Murders. Now—with your mother's help—we would like to do the same for the victims of the Lake Castor Sniper."

"My mother doesn't need any lights shined on her tragedies." The woman's tone edged harsh. "Her story isn't *content* for some thirty-minute show for wine-drinking white women. This is her *life*, and it's unfair what that man did to her. It's *unfair* what he took from her."

"You said *that man* . . ." Jess reached in her bag for her recorder. "You are referring to Ricky Lee Patience?"

The woman scoffed. "Everyone in the Black community knows that boy didn't shoot those people."

"You're saying he was framed?" Jess's pulse quickened. "By whom?"

"I'm not saying a damned thing. And neither is my mother." The woman placed her hand on the door. "If you contact us again, I'll file trespassing charges."

The woman closed the door and locked it.

As they walked down the sidewalk toward the car, Jess deleted Henrietta Newton's name from her list.

"That was amazing," said Sandy. "Did you hear what she said? Nobody in the Black community thinks Ricky Lee was guilty."

"It was great, but I wish we had gotten it on tape."

Sandy's smile widened, and a spring appeared in her step.

"What?" Jess asked.

"Maybe somebody had their phone recording some video . . ."

"You didn't . . ."

Sandy produced her phone from the breast pocket in her jacket. She showed Jess the screen.

"It's not usable," Jess said, her face falling. "We need permission from everyone before we use their likeness."

Sandy winked. "We'll see what Aaron and the Germans have to say about that."

Instead of arguing, Jess consulted her notes. "Next up is Bradley Matthews. He lives in Whitfill, about twenty miles away."

Sandy scrolled through her Notes app. "Bradley Matthews—he was the cousin of Clarence Moulton, who was the sniper's third victim."

Jess got behind the wheel. Sandy fastened her seat belt in the passenger seat.

"I was so excited when we made this list," Sandy said. "So many names. I was sure we were bound to find *someone* who would talk to us on the record. But now we're halfway through, and everyone so far has told us to kick rocks. Is this what it was like when you worked on *Something Bad Wrong?*"

"Worse, almost." Jess started the engine, then watched through the side mirrors as she pulled onto the street. "Those murders took place in the seventies, so nearly everyone had died. Any remaining nurses refused to talk, and there were plenty of family members still living, and none of them had any interest in cooperating. Same with law enforcement. No one took us seriously until finally someone did. That's what it will take: we just need one person to crack, and then the rest will follow suit."

Sandy considered this a moment while Jess maneuvered them toward the highway. Once their speed kicked up to seventy miles per hour, she asked, "What keeps you going?"

"What do you mean?"

"I mean, I get why you were so driven during the podcast. Your grandfather was one of the detectives, and it was the case he could never solve. It was *unfinished business*. But this time . . . why are you putting yourself through all of this?"

"For Ricky Lee and his family," Jess said without hesitation. "Can you imagine what it must be like for them? To be accused of something, then spend most of your life paying penance for something you didn't do? It must be horrible. It's our job to get his story out there."

"Have you ever thought about the fact that he might not be innocent?"

"Of course. And it's not our job as investigative journalists to determine guilt or innocence. It's our job to tell the story and hope that it moves the needle closer toward justice."

"And you believe that?"

Jess nodded, her eyes fast on the road. "I do."

"We've got about thirty minutes until we get to Whitfill," Sandy said. "So if Ricky Lee Patience really *is* innocent, then who was the sniper?"

Jess let that question stew a moment. She'd spent plenty of time with it since first meeting Martin Potts and his mother, Wilhelmina. Lately, it had been the last thing she thought about before bed and the first thing upon waking. What kind of man, she often asked herself, would commit these kinds of crimes in the eighties? In modern times, explosions of rage and gun violence were more ubiquitous, but in the 1980s, these things were less commonplace. Instead, the times tended to favor serial killers. But, she wondered, what kind of serial killer would target the Black community? The dearth of Black serial killers seemed to lean the argument in favor of Ricky Lee's innocence, but did it point the finger instead toward a different motive?

"Perhaps a white supremacist?" Jess offered.

"That's certainly possible," Sandy agreed, "but how does that explain the fact that the highest-profile victim was a white man?"

Jess couldn't answer, but something tugged at her, and she made a mental note to revisit that.

"Furthermore," Sandy continued, "if Ricky Lee is not guilty, then why did the shootings stop upon his apprehension? The moment he was plucked off the streets, there were no more murders. Explain that."

Jess had no answer for that, and she'd never had an answer for it. She'd twisted herself each way morning, day, and night trying to square that and never could. Every single explanation she had for it sounded more and more like some paranoid conspiracy thriller. She could never, for the life of her, come up with a single sane reason and wasn't about to confess that to her young research intern and, thankfully, would not have to, because a notification on Sandy's phone distracted her from the conversation.

"It looks like Aaron sent us his rough edit of the sizzle reel," Sandy said.

Jess jerked the steering wheel and parked the car on the side of the road. "Let's see it."

Sandy turned her phone sideways for horizontal orientation. The thumbnail lit up with fonts that popped.

TITLE CARD: TERROR IN THE STREETS—THE LAKE CASTOR SNIPER

Produced by Story Time Productions

Executive Producers: Felix & Friedrich Schafer

Producer: Jess Keeler

Camera/Edit: Aaron Blaine

Sound: Buffy Solomon

[The screen fills with a colorful neon 1984.]

NARRATOR: July 1984.

[A montage of images flashes across the screen.

A Rubik's Cube.

Ronald and Nancy Reagan.
Kids playing Atari.
Michael Jackson and his glove.
Jane Fonda working out in tights.]
NARRATOR: *Ask anyone in Lake Castor, Virginia, what they remember about that era, and they will tell you the same thing.*
CUT TO:
Man-on-the-street interviews.
PERSON 1: *We couldn't leave the house.*
PERSON 2: *It was terrifying.*
PERSON 3: *We pulled shut our curtains and slept under our beds, just in case.*
NARRATOR: *The former mill town of Lake Castor had been plunged into a reign of terror. As the dog days of summer reared their ugly head, an unseen sniper began targeting innocent civilians.*
CUT TO:
RONNIE DAYE *and his* GIRLFRIEND *walk casually down the street. All is well on this summer day . . . until Ronnie seizes up and falls to the ground, where he dies in a gruesome puddle of his own blood. The girlfriend* SCREAMS.
CUT TO:
QUINCY WILLIAMS *and his* SISTER *sit on a park bench, enjoying ice cream cones, when suddenly blood splatters across her face. She* SCREAMS.
CUT TO:
DWIGHT FONTENOT *is helping his* MOTHER *to the car when suddenly he is struck by an unseen bullet that drops him to the ground in a fit of spasms. His mother* SCREAMS.
CUT TO:
Quotes from Sheriff Lorne Axel about how they had a killer on their hands and it was paramount that they stop him.
NARRATOR: *And stop him, they did.*

WILHELMINA POTTS: The police searched the house. They found a rifle cartridge in his bedroom.

[Image of Ricky Lee Patience on front page of the paper getting arrested.]

ACTOR PORTRAYING ROSALIE PATIENCE: Ricky Lee became aggressive. So angry. There seemed to be no bottom to his anger and despair. I was so afraid he might do something to me or my daughter. When the police came for him, I was relieved.

My son had been taken by the Devil.

NARRATOR: What drove twenty-two-year-old Ricky Lee Patience to violence? Why did he embark upon this reign of terror? Did he choose his targets, or were they merely random victims of his horrible psychosis? For the first time anywhere, Story Time Productions brings you the true story of the madman who preyed upon his own community. The manifestation of evil who plunged Lake Castor into a terrifying summer.

The Lake Castor Sniper.

Jess had seen enough. She turned away from Sandy's phone and placed both hands on the steering wheel.

"It's a rough cut," Sandy said.

If Jess wasn't at her wit's end, she was quickly approaching it. "I can't even think of the words to describe how I'm feeling right now."

"Directing is not Aaron's strong suit."

"Oh, I'm not even talking about Aaron's *directing*." Jess rested her head on the steering wheel. "It's a blatant bastardization of our project. They have practically convicted Ricky Lee in the court of public opinion. I thought our objective was to prove his innocence?"

Sandy began texting.

"Those quotes from the mother . . . Where the hell did they get those?"

Sandy fired off her text and awaited a reply.

"It's nowhere *near* factually correct," Jess continued. "Quincy Williams wasn't shot while swapping ice cream cones with his sister. He was playing basketball. And Dwight Fontenot wasn't with his mother.

He was manning the pumps at the gas station where he worked. Did they not bother to read any of our research?"

"It's just a sizzle reel. It doesn't mean—"

"If I hear *it's just a sizzle reel* one more time . . ." Jess let the words hang like a sinner. She took a deep breath. "I'm losing control of this story. It's nothing like the podcast was. When I was producing podcasts, it was just me and Buffy. I controlled what we included and what we left out. Every day, this story spins further and further away from me."

"We can get it back on track, Jess," said Sandy.

Jess turned to her. "Getting it back on track means we need to get all the facts. Every one of them. Because I'm not producing a documentary about a man's guilt if there's a fraction of a possibility that he might be innocent."

Sandy's phone chimed. She thumbed it open and read the screen.

"Aaron said he'll explain everything tomorrow," said Sandy. "What do you want to do?"

"Tomorrow is our meeting with Sheriff Axel," Jess said. "If he gives us the case file on the sniper murders, we'll have everything we need to tell the true story."

"And if everything points to his guilt?" Sandy asked.

"Then we'll show that too. But I want it to be based on facts." Jess cut her eyes at Sandy's phone. "Not whatever *that* was."

Jess got them back on the road, but a sinking feeling took hold of her. This wasn't Jess's first investigation. She had learned things the hard way. Sandy, on the other hand, had no idea how hard it would be to keep track of the truth.

CHAPTER TWENTY-ONE

HAL BROADSTREET

1984

They met in the train yard at midnight, parked between two rusted, dormant railcars. The echo of the last engine rang through the still night. Hal sat on the hood of his El Camino. Axel remained in the front seat of his patrol car.

"I shouldn't be talking to you," Axel told him. "If the captain finds out, there will be no requests for transfer, no being placed on leave. The next time anyone will see me, I'll be flipping burgers."

"As far as anyone is concerned, you aren't here." Hal tugged his notebook from his pocket. "Tell me what you got."

"Digger Crowe's murder was an execution," Axel reported. "Someone got him with a single bullet in the back of the head. I don't think he saw it coming. His body was found in the back of a seventy-six Ford pickup in the Tillotson tobacco fields, which are up near—"

"Houlihan Road, I know it." Hal scribbled in the notebook. "You run the truck?"

"It came back stolen." A cat yowled from beneath an empty coal car, and Axel paused a moment, then said, "There was a belt buckle in the truck with him. It bore the emblem of the Rare Breed."

Hal played dumb. "Who are they?"

"A gang of bikers from the Virginia coast. Real bad dudes. Natural rivals to the Vandals over who controls the drug routes from Miami to New York."

"Don't you think that's kind of sloppy to leave evidence at the scene of a murder which would point to your organization's involvement?"

Axel shrugged. "Unless it was intentional."

Hal stopped writing.

Axel explained, "Like it was their way of taking credit for it. Bragging."

"Why would they do that?"

"I have no idea. Why don't you tell me? You're the one who's fluent in dirtbag."

Hal raised his hands in mock surrender. Eased up a little. "So what's our next step?"

"There is no next step," Axel said. "And there is no *we*."

"You're not investigating?"

"Investigating?" Axel's hackles raised even higher. "I'm a patrolman, dammit. Not Jim goddamn Rockford."

"I don't think I can let this go as easily as everyone else can."

"Face it, Hal," said Axel, exhausted. "Nobody gives a shitting damn what happens to a bootlegger."

Hal sensed the tension. He knew Axel could, at any minute, decide to start the engine and drive away. His life would be much easier if he did. But for some reason, Axel didn't. Hal had enough to write the story, but something told him there was *more*.

"You okay?"

Axel massaged the bridge of his nose with his thumb and forefinger. "It's the stress. This job . . . it's getting to me."

"I get it." Hal changed his tone. "Want to tell me about it?"

Axel blinked, seeming suddenly aware. "I should have my head examined talking to you."

Hal laid his pen down on the hood of his car and closed his notebook. "You know why I stay at the *Times*?"

Axel did not appear to possibly give a damn.

"For real," Hal continued. "When they started laying folks off and cutting departments. Hell, they cut the *copyediting*, and as a writer, you know you're in trouble when the editors go. I could have jumped ship at the first sign of the iceberg, joined up with the *Herald*, or hell, I got family in New Orleans and could have strung wire at the *Picayune* no problem, but I stayed put. You know why?"

Axel raised an eyebrow, but said nothing.

"Because that's what my daddy would have done." Hal's eyes drifted up and to the right, taking note of the bats hunting moths in the lamplight. "Old Henry Broadstreet was a man always in search of greener pastures. When the going got tough, my momma used to say, Henry got going. He never saw anything through, not once. Not even when I got sick."

Hal could feel Axel's eyes on him. Hal turned to face him.

"It was while I was still in grade school," Hal said. "I got better, but how could Dad know? He was long gone by the time I got out of the hospital. I saw what it did to my momma, and I swore I would never be like him. I was going to see things through to the end. For that reason, I'm sticking with the *Times*. I'm sticking with my promise to Wilbur Fosskey. And I'm damn sure sticking to my story."

Axel said nothing. Both hands were still fixed fast to his steering wheel. Faraway, a train whistle moaned its lonely cry.

"Let me ask you a question, Lorne," said Hal. "Why did you become a cop?"

"For the same reason I vote Republican," Axel said. "Because it's what my daddy did, and his daddy before him. You know, I grew up thinking my daddy was a good man. A good *cop*. But now, as I get older and actually *see* . . . Broadstreet, I swear to God, if I read one word of this in your goddamn paper . . . Jesus, what the hell am I doing talking to you?"

"Lorne, no . . . wait." Hal hopped off the hood and approached Axel's car window. "You can still do some good. You can. I can help you."

"Yeah?" He wasn't so sure. "Is that right? How, by ratting out my fellow cops?"

Hal shrugged. "I don't know, but you're a good man. I can see it. Your compass is pointed in the right direction, so that means your daddy did something right. Maybe he was a good man and you got those best parts of him inside you. I think you'll know what to do and when the right time to do it will be."

Axel eyeballed him for a moment, seeming to look for a tell that may or may not be there.

"All I know," Axel finally said, "is that you print that bit about the belt buckle in your newspaper tomorrow, and you might spark the fuse that sets off a full-scale gang war."

CHAPTER TWENTY-TWO

JESS KEELER

Present Day

They sat in the lobby of the Lawles County Sheriff's Office, the four of them. While Buffy inspected her sound gear and Aaron dusted his assortment of camera lenses, Jess read every word of the documents Aaron had given her. Twice. Upon a third reading of each page, she handed it to Sandy so that she might inspect it as well. In many cases, Jess would read something and ask for yet another reading of a page she had already handed off.

It was a bombshell.

Since Ricky Lee Patience had pleaded guilty, there was no trial before a jury. Instead, a judge heard impact statements from witnesses before he delivered his sentence. To Jess's knowledge, the records of those proceedings had been sealed. One way or another, she held them in her hands while sitting in that lobby.

The most damning witness had been Rosalie Patience, Ricky Lee's own mother. She spoke in great detail about her son's spiraling mental state in the weeks before his arrest. "*He had been extremely agitated for years,*" she had testified. "*Quick to temper. Easily riled and provoked. In the spring of this year, he began talking to people who were not there.*

Laughing at jokes I could not hear. He would lash out, violently, never hitting myself or his sister, but I feared every night that would come. In the weeks of the shooting, he would be sullen, remaining in his room for days on end. Other days, he might leave the house and go God knows where, not returning for a couple of days. He would eat his dinner on the floor, like a dog. When I asked him about it, he said everyone treats him like a dog, so he may well eat his food like a dog. I feared for our lives. When the police came for him, I was relieved. I believe him to be capable of extre—"

"You didn't know about these?" Jess asked Sandy.

Sandy was taken aback. "No!"

Jess narrowed her eyes.

"No. Jess." Sandy grabbed her upper arm. "I would have told you."

Jess turned to Aaron. "How long have you had these? I was told they were sealed."

"The Germans are very resourceful," Aaron said, clearly proud of himself. "They acquired them, oh, three days ago? Maybe four."

Jess opened her mouth, but quickly closed it, for fear of the rage that might fly out of it. *Three days . . . maybe four . . .* while she had been out there canvassing for interviews with victims and shaping the argument for Ricky Lee's innocence, Aaron and the Germans had been sitting on a smoking gun.

"It's not personal, Jess," Aaron said. "We were occupied with editing the sizzle reel, and you were out on the road."

"You could have sent a text. A simple text."

"True, and that's my bad." Aaron showed both his palms, as if to say mea culpa. "Obviously, we were consumed by this discovery because it presented a huge shift in focus."

"No shit it did," hissed Sandy. "Come on, Aaron. Can we talk? Like, for real?"

"Honestly?" Aaron got down to it. "Okay, the two of you have been gung ho on this innocence narrative, and we felt, despite this new information, you might be reluctant to play ball."

"You withheld information." Jess struggled to control her tone. "*Crucial* information. If I'd have had it . . ."

"You would have played ball?"

Jess's immediate impulse was to say, *Yes, of course I would have,* but she wavered. Would she? She thought of the times while producing *Something Bad Wrong* when clues had kept pointing a certain direction and she had ignored them with bullheaded resolve, to her own detriment, to protect the narrative she had already preconceived in her head. If a witness's testimony didn't dissuade her—and a *mother's* witness testimony at that—what else would? They had a *confession,* for Christ's sake. She grew angry at herself for being so preternaturally stubborn, but would never, in a dozen lifetimes, admit that to Aaron.

"It's sensationalism," she said. "It's *manipulative.*"

"It's a gold mine"—Aaron's smile showed teeth—"and you know it."

Sandy leaned between them. "She'll play ball, Aaron. I know she will."

"Good." He glanced over them both a moment before reaching into his bag for a folder. "Here are the lines I want you to get Sheriff Axel to say on camera."

Jess's eyes bugged; then she scanned the paper. "There's no way I can coach him to say these lines."

"You just said you would *play ball.*"

"Sure, but this is a documentary. He says what he's going to say. There's not supposed to be a script."

"This is a *sizzle reel,*" Aaron reminded her. "This is what guarantees us the funds to make your documentary."

"A *true-crime* documentary." Jess handed back the notes. "You're suggesting that I *lead* him."

"He's old school," Aaron reminded her. "The newer guys, they know how to play the game. We use them, and they use us. It's symbiotic. These boomers, on the other hand, forget that when they want to eat supper, they need to sing for it."

Jess rolled her eyes and returned to her notes.

"Trust me," Aaron continued. "Did you see *Small Town Homicide*? Two seasons and we made an absolute *star* out of Detective John Pecor. He gets invited to all the film premieres and consults on nearly every movie and TV show with cold cases, but I can remember his first season when we had to feed him lines."

"You wrote scripts for Captain John Pecor?"

Aaron nodded. "We've had scripts written for almost all the TV cops you've heard of and none of the ones you haven't."

"How do you sleep at night?"

"With the fan on." Aaron ran his hand through his hair and flashed her a smile that he probably thought worked well on women half her age. "Jess, we're paid to do a job. You and me. We're *producers*. That means we *produce*."

"What about the truth?" Jess asked.

"The truth is fluid," he told her. "It's an imaginary line. Show me instead something that I can touch with my fingers, or that I can hold in my hands."

"Like a paycheck?" Jess resented the way Aaron looked at her, as if she were a little child learning that the tooth fairy wasn't real.

"You think I'm a mercenary."

Jess met his gaze. "I think this job has made you cynical."

"It's made me *comfortable*," he said. "What will it make you?"

Before she could answer, the door on the far wall opened, and a uniformed deputy filled the frame.

"If you'll follow me," he said in a low baritone voice, "the sheriff will see you now."

◆ ◆ ◆

The sheriff's actual office was in a location central to all the other offices, each one filled with investigators, administrators, and deputies who all hummed along busily to the matters of the day. His walls were made of glass, which offered him a clear line of sight to everyone who worked for him, and vice versa.

Aaron hoisted his camera onto his shoulders to film the spectacle. Axel noticed Jess admiring the walls. "It's for accountability," he explained. "Me to them, and them to me. If anyone needs me, I'll be able to spot it before they can stand up and ask. But it is also so that they can see what I am doing. My administration is a two-way street."

"That's very unusual," Jess told him. "How long have you been doing this?"

"Only the past four years," he said. "Law enforcement has come a long way. Especially here in Lake Castor. I think we have all read the recent news articles. Policing is under a lot of scrutiny. I have been blessed to serve as sheriff of this county for nearly thirty years, and I want to make sure that my staff—and by extension, the people of this county—have full and unfettered access to me."

Jess turned to Aaron and offered him a wink. In her mind, Axel had just dashed any hope Aaron might have had about coaching the man toward any lines from a script. The look on his face said something different.

Sandy stepped forward, eyes cast down at the screen of her phone. "Sheriff Axel," she said, "before we start filming, would you mind confirming some information for me?"

"I'd be happy to."

"You began your career in law enforcement with the Lake Castor Police Department in 1982," Sandy read aloud. "Three years later, you transferred to the Lawles County Sheriff's Office. In 1996, you ran for sheriff and have been successfully elected every four years since."

"That's correct."

"In fact," Sandy added, "the last three elections you have run unopposed."

Axel's face remained impassive. "I was a big fan of your podcast," he told Jess. "I thought you treated some potentially tender subjects in a fair light. I shared those episodes with several other sheriffs at our annual convention and even spoke on a panel regarding how cold case podcasters could actually be used as a tool to help assist on cold cases."

"I take that as high praise." Jess blushed.

Axel cut a discerning look toward the crew, particularly at Aaron's camera. "You think you might achieve the same thing with these documentary TV programs?"

"The jury is still out." Jess smiled.

"Why don't you tell me what you're working on next?"

"It's a very compelling case," Jess said. "One that happened right here on your side of the state line, in fact."

"Let's hear it."

"We're interested in doing a story about the 1984 sniper attacks."

Axel didn't blink. Jess had the unsettling feeling that perhaps he might have expected as much.

"That wasn't ours," he said. "That one was with the police department, which, as you know, was decommissioned twenty-some-odd years ago."

Jess nodded. "Of course, but like my colleague pointed out, you were with the department during that time."

"I was on patrol, yes. But I had no access to the case." He furrowed his brow. "I'm afraid if you look back at the LCPD, there was a reason they were found to be superfluous, and it wasn't just the decline in population after the June River mill closed. Things were done different back then. The people in charge felt a stronger police presence would deter the criminal element, which followed naturally after a shift in the community's economic situation."

"I'm glad you said that," Jess told him. "That's exactly the type of insight that would be interesting when talking about the difficulties surrounding the community which was terrorized by the sniper."

Axel cocked his head. "You know we caught the guy, don't you? That case is closed. The killer was sentenced to life, and to my knowledge, that's where he sits. I thought you liked to report on unsolved cases."

"His sister, Wilhelmina Potts, claims they convicted the wrong man."

"His confession, a lot of good police work, and even a liberal judge saw things a touch different." Axel stiffened his demeanor. "I'm not going to be too inclined to help overturn a conviction, Ms. Keeler. For all intents and purposes, that case is still closed."

"You sound like Ennis Worthy."

Axel smiled thoughtfully. "You know he was the man who brought Patience down?"

"Why won't either of you help us?" she asked.

"Because," said Axel, "Ricky Lee Patience confessed to the murders. After he was taken off the streets, the shootings stopped. In all of forty years, Patience has never so much as hinted at his own innocence."

Aaron rested his camera in his lap. "I can personally assure you, Sheriff Axel, that the goal of our production isn't to cast doubts on Mr. Patience's guilt. In fact, our current direction proves the value of promoting the horrific nature of his crimes, investigating his motives, and detailing the phenomenal work done by law enforcement to capture him and convict him. I think if you took a look at the sizzle reel I've edited, you'll see—"

"I'm certain that you mean well." Axel addressed the entire crew, but centered his gaze upon Jess. "However, if your intention is to dredge up these murders and exploit the trauma they inflicted upon the members of our community, then I'm afraid I'm going to have to decline to participate. This moment was a blight on our town's history, and I don't care to see it relived, especially during the tensions we've been experiencing as of late. Thank you for the courtesy of reaching out, but if you intend to continue investigating this story, you'll have to do so without the resources of my office."

"I respect your decision," Aaron said, "but is there any chance we can get you to fire off a couple of lines for us? For the sizzle reel?"

The flat expression Axel fired at him gave the cameraman his answer.

Jess's shoulders slumped. She'd expected this reaction from neither Axel nor Worthy, but had instead received it from both. She realized that without any representatives from law enforcement, their investigation would be made all the more difficult.

"Unless . . ." Axel's eyebrows arched. He let the moment breathe before interrupting it with the rest of his thought. "What if I told you I had another case? A sensational one? One that was unsolved and haunted the psyche of Lake Castor for decades?"

The stirring among the crew indicated their interest. Aaron kept the camera fast on the sheriff, and Buffy's boom pole didn't waver.

"We're listening . . . ," said Aaron.

Jess opened her mouth but had no idea what to say. She had even less of an idea what to *feel*. On one hand, she had already invested a significant amount of time in researching the sniper case and had fallen in love with the prospects. It was a forgotten and abandoned moment in Lake Castor's history, and the implications looked damning. On the other hand, she realized that without law enforcement talking to her, and without any access to or cooperation from Ricky Lee Patience, there wasn't much content to fuel the story.

"I'm committed to this sniper story," she said, unsure if she meant it.

"I'm sure you are," said Axel, already rising from his desk. "And you can always return to that whenever you want. But in the meantime, why don't you just look at what I have to offer and see if it might possibly interest you to look further."

She thought about it. She read the expressions on Aaron's face, then Sandy's. Both of them appeared to be holding their breath in anticipation.

"Okay," she said. "We'll just take a look . . ."

PART TWO

CHAPTER TWENTY-THREE

JESS KEELER

Present Day

TITLE CARD: MASSACRE IN LAKE CASTOR—SIZZLE REEL

[An older, eighties-era television set fills the frame. There is static for a moment, but it clears to show President Ronald Reagan addressing the crowd as the Olympic torch is carried into Los Angeles. The people around him cheer as the flame burns bright.

The channel changes, and we see children joyfully playing the Atari game Pitfall!, *guiding their pixelated hero over a lake with three alligators . . .*

The channel again changes, this time showing Clara Peller in the famous Wendy's commercial as she demands, "Where's the beef?"

The channel changes once again, as we see the scene in Ghostbusters *where the Stay Puft Marshmallow Man menaces New York City . . .*

The channel changes a final time, now showing a Reagan campaign ad, a soft yet affirming voice declaring, "It's morning again in America . . ."

The screen now fills with giant neon text reading: **1984**]

JESS KEELER: It's morning again in America, yes, but after one morning in the American small town of Lake Castor, Virginia . . .

[The camera pushes closer to the TV screen, which now shows an aerial image of the former mill town of Lake Castor, Virginia. The camera pushes

Eryk Pruitt

closer, closer, until the entire frame is now filled with that image. The camera lowers down, closer to the streets of Lake Castor, until we come to a stop where Jem Fosskey's garage used to stand.]

JESS KEELER: . . . the world would never again be the same.

[We see an older woman in her seventies.]

OLDER WOMAN: It was just the most awful thing to ever happen to our community. There weren't no sense in it.

[We see an older man in his eighties.]

OLDER MAN: You hear about things like this happening in big cities like New York or Philadelphia or whatnot. But nothing like that ever happens in Lake Castor, by God.

[We see Sheriff Lorne Axel, the quintessential square-jawed, broad-shouldered lawman. He stands at his desk in his office with a cardboard box in front of him marked FOSSKEY, J.]

LORNE AXEL: Sometime in the wee morning hours of June 4, 1984, someone entered the apartment over top of a garage and killed three local men in a brutal fashion. Jem Fosskey . . .

[The camera cuts to the grisly crime scene photo of Jem Fosskey's bloodied remains.]

LORNE AXEL: . . . Felton Loe . . .

[The camera cuts to the grisly crime scene photo of Felton Loe's bloodied remains.]

LORNE AXEL: . . . and Mel Kemble.

[The camera cuts to the grisly crime scene photo of Mel Kemble's bloodied remains.

The audience is treated to a close-up of Lorne Axel's grizzled face.]

LORNE AXEL: To this day, no one has been arrested for that crime.

[Cut to stylistic shots of Lake Castor. The rolling hills on the outskirts of town, the former June River Fabrics mill, which has been transformed into the June River Condominiums, the renewed downtown business district with light traffic. The historic courthouse. The scenic river walk.]

JESS KEELER: *Folks in Lake Castor have lived forty years without knowing who entered Jem Fosskey's garage and committed the city's greatest atrocity. News of the murders dominated the headlines for nearly six days . . .*

[The screen is filled with images of newspaper headlines that read: LAKE CASTOR MASSACRE and THREE FOUND SLAUGHTERED IN BOOTLEGGER'S GARAGE. Another one reading, POLICE SAY NO LEADS IN TRIPLE HOMICIDE. A final one: REWARD OFFERED FOR INFORMATION LEADING TO ARREST FOR TRIPLE SLAYING.]

JESS KEELER: *. . . then seemingly vanished from the newspapers altogether. But why? How could a community this small be affected by a tragedy so horrendous, then let it slip from memory after nothing was ever done?*

[The camera returns us to Lorne Axel's office. He now sits at his desk across from producer Jess Keeler. The box marked FOSSKEY, J still sits between them.]

JESS KEELER: *You're telling me that the police never had any leads? That they never had a single suspect in custody?*

LORNE AXEL: *I'm not necessarily saying that. There was a single lead that I feel has never been run down.*

JESS KEELER: *And what is that?*

LORNE AXEL: *The bodies weren't discovered until the morning of the fourth. A few hours previous to them being found, two officers pulled over a car that rolled through a stop sign.*

JESS KEELER: *A routine stop?*

LORNE AXEL: *I don't like that phrase. I been doing this over forty years, and I know there ain't never such a thing as a "routine stop." These officers observe three men in the car and, upon further inspection, discover a small amount of drugs, some weapons, and trace amounts of blood on their clothing. They were arrested, booked, and placed into a holding cell.*

JESS KEELER: *And the next morning, when the bodies were discovered, they were never considered suspects?*

LORNE AXEL: *By the next morning, they had already been released.*

JESS KEELER: Were there any reports that told you why they had been released?

LORNE AXEL: Not only were there none, but there were also no reports that said they had ever been arrested.

JESS KEELER: So you're telling me that the suspects were released and the documentation of their arrest was destroyed?

LORNE AXEL: To say they were destroyed implies malice. I am not implying anything of the sort. There were good men on the force back then. All I'm saying is that somehow they disappeared, like many records do over time, and today there is no record of the arrest ever happening.

JESS KEELER: If that's the case, then how do you know it happened?

LORNE AXEL: Because I was one of the officers who arrested them.

[CUE MUSIC

The camera now cuts to more thrilling images of Lorne Axel rifling through the evidence box. Profile shots of Sheriff Axel as he rides through the county in his patrol car. Axel, with his sidearm in his holster, knocking on the door of a potential suspect or witness. Axel, with that same sidearm, at the range, knocking the dust off his shooting skills, just in case he needs them. All the while, our intrepid producer narrates . . .]

JESS KEELER: The murders of Jem Fosskey, Felton Loe, and Mel Kemble may have been forgotten over time by the sleepy former mill community of Lake Castor, but they haven't been forgotten by the one man who once had the suspects in his grasp, only to see them escape.

I'm Jess Keeler, producer of the Something Bad Wrong *podcast. Join us as we follow Sheriff Lorne Axel as he seeks to finally obtain justice for the grisly crime that has gone unsolved for too long, but hopefully not for too much longer, on this season of* Massacre in Lake Castor.

◆ ◆ ◆

The screen displaying the sizzle reel minimized, then revealed the split screen showing Felix Schafer on the left side and Friedrich Schafer on the right. Jess, Aaron, and Sandy each held their breaths, their hearts pounding, until finally both Schafers erupted in wild smiles.

"Wunderbar!" Felix declared. "Aaron, you have outdone yourself once again."

Friedrich agreed. "This was very good work, team. What you have here is infinitely more exciting than the urban crime story you were pitching. What you have here is compelling, very—how you say?—visceral . . ."

"I am thrilled and can't wait to hear about more," Felix said. "And that *sheriff*. . . he is for real the sheriff, or did you find him from central casting?"

"He's for real," Aaron answered. "He's been sheriff for something like thirty years."

"Twenty-eight," Sandy corrected.

"He's like a modern-day John Wayne, isn't he?" said Friedrich.

"Much more manly than John Pecor," said Felix. "Think of the female demographic and the possibilities on social media."

"Is he attractive to women?" Friedrich asked.

Felix nodded. "He has sort of the *daddy* element that American wom—"

"I'm not asking you," snapped Friedrich. "I am asking the women. Sandy, Jess?"

Sandy struggled with it. "He's . . . uh . . . *rugged*, yes."

"But is he *sexy*?"

Sandy looked to Jess for help.

Jess, however, knew there was nothing she could do. When it came time for them to abandon the story of Ricky Lee Patience and the Lake Castor Sniper, in favor of the murders of the bootleggers in Fosskey's garage, she had done everything she could to fight it. All her efforts had proven fruitless. Sheriff Axel's presentation had been too persuasive. His story had everything that Ricky Lee's didn't: law enforcement's participation, the original case file, evidence (although scant), and plenty of press coverage.

"That goes to show," Jess had argued, "that the Fosskey case is already well-trodden ground. There's far less coverage on the sniper and his victims."

"Because far fewer people *cared*," Aaron had argued. "The extra press coverage of Fosskey gives the story more texture. People were curious about the bootlegger massacre. I mean, do we even *have* bootleggers anymore? Just think, we could spend an entire *episode* on that angle alone."

"What about Willie and Martin Potts?"

Aaron had appeared confused. "Who?"

"The sister of the accused sniper and her son."

"Ah, yes." Aaron couldn't have appeared less invested. "Just explain to them that, in the end, there was far less access to their story. The cops didn't want to participate, we couldn't get access to the inmate, and none of the victims' families wanted to speak with us."

"About that . . ." Jess had thought about that fact for a while. "Perhaps if we hired a Black producer, we might gain credibility in that community and they would be more inclined to open up to us."

That suggestion, like most previous, had been met with silence.

In the end, there was nothing she could do to sway them. Aaron had made up his mind and done a remarkable job convincing the Germans to invest in the bootlegger story. Even Sandy, it seemed, realized the value of it. She had thrown herself entirely into the project, lapping up details like a kitten at a saucer of milk.

"Jem Fosskey's brother died of lung cancer twenty years ago," Sandy reported to the Germans, "but he had a daughter that's still alive. We can interview her and hope she might add some color to her father's character."

"Splendid," said Friedrich. "And the other victims? Do they have family still local to the area as well?"

"They do," Sandy said. "I have made a list, and Jess and I will begin to attack it tomorrow."

"And we have full cooperation from this sheriff?" Felix asked.

"One hundred percent," Jess confirmed. "He's opened the case files and is willing to allow us to interview him as needed."

"This is excellent," said Felix. "Now, what about these three suspects that our sheriff is certain did the dirty deed?"

"Sandy and I are digging up more information about them," Jess said, "but Sheriff Axel has already informed us that the three primary suspects are dead."

Even Felix's face registered disappointment. "That is most unfortunate news. I would have much preferred an ending where we might prosecute. Audiences love a courtroom drama. But even still, Friedrich and I would love to commend you on an excellent job snatching victory from the jaws of defeat. I have a great feeling about this story. I believe we are looking at the next hot true-crime documentary on streaming!"

In a blink, the Germans had logged off. Aaron glanced at Jess briefly before switching the screen on his laptop back to the footage he had been editing. Jess excused herself and stepped outside. In moments like these, she almost wished she smoked cigarettes. She felt an oppressive need to punish herself. If she had been working alone, she told herself, she would have stayed focused on the original story. But, she reminded herself, she needed the money that Story Time was offering if she wanted to provide her mother the best care she could. Aaron had been right: she was a *producer*, and her job was to produce.

Before she could beat herself up too much about it, Sandy appeared in the doorway. She stepped outside and slipped an arm around Jess's neck.

"Don't worry," she said. "This story will be great, and we'll do a bang-up job."

"I know," Jess said, still feeling defeated.

"And when we're done"—Sandy let it hang a moment—"maybe we could take another peek together at that sniper."

CHAPTER TWENTY-FOUR

JESS KEELER

Present Day

The following day, Jess and Sandy hit the library. Jess had spent hours upon hours grinding through microfiche, but found it invigorating to teach the younger Sandy how to use the machines and the value of a seemingly antiquated tool. They posted up at both machines on the second floor and swallowed every article they could find relating to the three men that Sheriff Axel had named as his primary suspects in the Fosskey killings.

There weren't many.

They each scanned the *Herald* articles forward and backward from June 3, 1984, and still came up next to empty on each one.

There was not much written about Edward Crowe, a.k.a. Digger. His name was listed along with two other men in an assault charge in Omaha, Nebraska. Jess uncovered a marriage announcement to a woman named Gloria Tanner, then another article less than a year later where the Tanner family reported her missing. Sandy located a small article that stated he had been found in the back of a pickup truck with the belt buckle of a motorcycle gang known as the Rare Breed.

There was much more written about William Wayne Dickerson. He had been a local boy. He'd played well for the high school baseball team. Instead of enrolling in college, he enlisted in the marines and served two tours in Vietnam. An article detailed a homecoming at the depot when he returned. The next article written about him was about how he and a couple of men from a local biker gang had been arrested for stealing a car. Another time for assault. Another time for driving while intoxicated.

The last article about Billy Wayne Dickerson was a notice from the local funeral home. No one had written an obituary for him; they'd simply stated the times for his services and interment.

"That's two mentions of motorcycle gangs," Sandy said, making a note in her phone. "That might be something worth checking out."

Jess agreed, then showed what she had found on Charles Wilcox, the third man that Sheriff Axel had identified from the white Pinto on the night of the murders.

"Your notebook is blank," Sandy said.

Jess nodded. "That's right. I can't find anything."

They both took turns, scrolling, scrolling, until Sandy finally turned up an article.

> STATESVILLE, NC—A man found burned and buried in the woods has been identified by officials as Charles A. Wilcox, 36. Authorities say the victim was shot once in the head, then the evidence was set on fire and buried, so as to conceal the crime. Anyone with information about this crime is to report to the Iredell County Sheriff's Office.

"That's it?" Jess scratched her head. "The only piece of information on Charles Wilcox are those sixty words?"

Sandy was already scrolling farther. "Do we know his hometown? I've had luck tracking down relatives by using old obituaries that list people as survivors."

"Nothing so far," Jess reported. "I can check the issues of the Statesville newspapers, see if there's anything further there."

She gathered the microfiche to return to the librarian. Upon Jess's arrival, the librarian asked, "Would you also like to search the *Times* articles?"

"The *Lake Castor Times*?" Jess allowed a smirk to sneak across her face. "I remember those from when I was in high school. Local scandals and alien abductions, right? Those old things were fun to read sometimes, sure, but right now we're overloaded with research."

"You're researching the early eighties, right?"

Jess nodded.

"Back then," the librarian explained, "the *Times* was still semireputable. For decades, Lake Castor had two newspapers, but the *Herald* was better funded. The *Times* started chasing more sensational stories to stay afloat. When their last serious journalist died, they just started syndicating tabloid articles and puzzles, until they finally folded. But in eighty-four, you might still find some local interest."

Jess thanked her and retrieved the proper files. She was halfway back to the table with them when she was stopped by Martin, dressed sharp in a dark suit and no necktie.

"It's been a while since we heard from you," he said. "You never told us what happened in your meeting with Sheriff Axel. How did it go?"

Jess had been caught off guard by his appearance. She'd tried to prepare herself for a discussion with him, but so far had managed to only avoid his phone calls and ignore his emails. She realized an encounter was inevitable.

"Former sheriff Ennis Worthy wouldn't speak on the record about Ricky Lee," Jess told him. "The Germ—er . . . *Story* Time decided that with Ricky Lee refusing to speak with us from prison and none of the families of the sniper victims answering our calls . . . I'm afraid we don't have much to go on."

Martin eyeballed the microfiche in her hand and the stacks of notes on the table in front of Sandy. "It looks like y'all have found significantly more than a *little*."

Sandy averted her eyes while Jess cleared her throat. "We've decided to go in a different direction," Jess explained.

"Ah," said Martin. "You're investigating another story. Let me guess: some murdered white women?"

"That's not fair," said Jess. "Your mother wasn't exactly forthcoming about Ricky Lee when we initially spoke with her. Had she been, we wouldn't have entertained the story to the extent that we did."

"How do you figure?"

"For one," said Jess, "your uncle *confessed*."

That didn't seem to matter to Martin. "So what? Cops get confessions out of innocent people all of the time. If that was a sport, they'd be Super Bowl champions."

Sandy spoke up from her seat at the table. "Your mother also didn't tell us that he was prone to violence."

"Who told you that?" Martin demanded. "The police?"

"According to official court records," Sandy said, "your grandmother testified at his sentencing hearing about his temper and erratic behavior in the weeks leading up to the killings. His *own mother*."

Martin didn't bother to hide his disdain. "I expected more from you."

A heat flashed through Jess. "What else do we have to go on, Martin?" she asked. "Your grandmother can't refute it. Ricky Lee won't grant us access to an interview, and none of the victims' families will speak to us. There's nothing I'd like to do more than help free an innocent man from prison, but I can't do it with what we've been given, and what we've been given isn't exactly helping him look innocent. I'm trying, Martin, but I'm all alone here."

Behind them, the librarian shushed a harsh rebuke. Jess nodded toward her as a tacit promise to keep it down. Martin's expression was far less acquiescent.

"I thought you were different, Jess Keeler," he said.

She placed both hands on her hips. "I'm sorry to have let you down."

He lowered his head and backed out the door. Jess's blood was still riled, but she took a seat at the table next to Sandy.

"You okay?" Sandy asked.

Jess nodded, but kept her eyes fixed on the microfiche. "Let's get back to work."

They spooled the fiche from the *Times* into the machine, and when it came alive, they set their eyes on the prominent *Lake Castor Times* banner. It was just like she remembered it from when she was younger, only a little more subdued. The paper had not yet evolved (or *de*volved) into the tabloid fodder it would later become, although the front pages were still dipped in scandal. The first issue they loaded in was an exposé on a town councilman's DWI and an exposé on the former mayor's sexual escapades with various local women. It only took a couple of moments before they found the *Times*' sensational account of the Fosskey murders.

SENSELESS SUNRISE SLAYINGS LEAVE NO SURVIVORS

BOOTLEGGING BOYS BRUTALLY BLOODIED

AMONG THE DEAD: KING OF THE PIEDMONT BOOTLEGGERS

"These articles are written much different than those in the *Herald*," Sandy commented. "I mean . . . *wow*. Muckrake much?"

"They would get much crazier by the time I was in high school," Jess said. "This writer here, though, has the gift for alliteration."

Sandy peered over her shoulder. "Look at that byline: Harold Broadstreet . . ." She furrowed her brow. "Where have I heard that name before?"

Jess wasn't sure, at first. It did sound familiar, and the answer rested somewhere just out of reach, beyond the tip of her tongue, the edge of her mind. Like a landscape, slightly out of focus. The name . . . *Harold Broad—*

Then it hit her.

"That's the name," Jess said aloud, "of Ricky Lee's final victim."

CHAPTER TWENTY-FIVE

HAL BROADSTREET

1984

Everybody knew that if a dollar was spent on gambling, numbers, or lottery anywhere in Lake Castor, that money would pass through Ralph Sparrow's hands. The man was legendary in Lawles County crime, but his days had already begun to grow short. No more did he prowl the back alleys of downtown in search of action. No longer did he take bets on college ball games. His numbers racket had been scaled down to nearly nothing over the years. If you asked him once, he'd tell you it was age slowing him down. Ask him again, and he might blame the cops. Get a couple of drinks in him, and he'd tell you the truth: it's a much different game out there nowadays.

"It ain't like it used to be," Sparrow said to Hal Broadstreet over a pint of corn liquor. "There was a code, and everybody followed it. Cop and criminal alike. We did our thing, and the cops tried to stop you. Sometimes they did, but if you were good—and, brother, you know I was *good*—then the scales tipped in your favor more often than not. Now, however, folks are playing for keeps. Life ain't nowhere near as valuable as it once was."

"You were there that night," Hal said. "When I left that card game, you and Wilbur and Uncle Meaney were still at the table with Jem, Felton, and Mel."

"I don't want to talk about that night," said Sparrow.

"Nobody does. That, to me, is a big problem."

Sparrow swatted at Hal as if he were a fly. "Man, ain't you got some television to watch or something?"

"It's summer. Nothing but repeats."

"Every paper I open is talking about what Mondale and the Democrats are up to. Why you want to go digging up ancient history?"

"This ain't ancient history, Ralph. It happened four weeks ago. But everybody's acting like it never happened, which is interesting to me."

Sparrow wouldn't budge. "Seriously, man. We're running a pool on Mondale's pick for VP. Five-to-one odds says he's going with Lloyd Bentsen of Texas. I can get you ten to one on Fritz Hollings."

"Nah," said Hal. "He'll pick a woman."

"Not if he wants to win."

Hal rested both hands on the card table between them. "Level with me, Ralph. What the hell happened after I left the poker game?"

"What about basketball? You see the kid the Bulls drafted out of Carolina? I'll give good odds that he—"

"Ralph."

Sparrow sighed heavily. "Fine, Hal. Just don't write my name down on nothing. I never enjoyed the same levels of attention that Jem did. That's probably a good reason why me and him is on separate sides of the soil right now."

Hal raised three fingers, as if to say, *Scout's honor.*

"You left after eleven or so, if I remember correctly," said Sparrow. "We played among ourselves for a while, but then somebody came knocking on Jem's door shortly after."

"Who was it?"

"I'm getting to that, goddammit," Sparrow sassed. "You want me to tell the story or not?"

Hal bowed his head apologetically and motioned for him to proceed.

Sparrow did. "You know Obie Dickerson's boy? The one who played shortstop for the Tigers, then went off to Vietnam?"

"Billy Wayne."

"That's him. He showed up at the door with two other fellas, looking to score some hooch. One of them boys was real mean. You could tell he wasn't up to any good whatsoever. He had these coal black eyes that kind of looked through you. I forget what they called him—"

"Digger?"

"That sounds about right. It gets hard to keep up with all their silly nicknames." Sparrow took a sip from the jar of corn liquor, then passed it to Hal. "Anyway, that boy—Digger, you called him—saw the cards and chips, then the seat you had vacated and asked if he could take it. Jem said sure, but that boy put eyes on Uncle Meaney and said he didn't want to play cards at a table with a Black man. Jem told him in that case he wouldn't play cards at all. To further that, Jem informed the gentleman that the whiskey they were buying was cooked by that very Black man, as Uncle Meaney had been his master stiller going back several years."

"I bet he didn't like that none," said Hal.

"Oh no, he didn't." Sparrow's expression hardened. "Some of us have come a long way down here in the South, but there are those of us who can't never be reached. I reckon this fella was one of the latter."

"Racist peckerwood," said Hal.

"Mm-hmm. Anyway, that boy Digger said he didn't want nothing to do with a bunch of bootleggers who'd call a Black man *master*. Only he didn't say *Black man*—he used a word more common in my daddy's day, and Jem didn't cotton to it. Not one bit."

"What did he do?"

"He threw the son-bitch out."

Hal nodded and sipped from the corn. He'd always known Jem Fosskey was the stand-up sort, but never reckoned in a million years that it would be what got him killed.

"We knew when those boys showed up that *rough* was on the menu." Sparrow reached for the corn. "After they was gone, the fun was pretty much spoiled. Me and Wilbur decided we'd had enough and went our merry way."

"What about Uncle Meaney?"

"What about him?"

"Did he leave with you?"

Sparrow shook his head. "We didn't think that would be a good idea. We reckoned those boys might not have gone too far and if they saw him out and about, they might get the idea to hassle him some more. That door to Jem's apartment was about six inches of pure steel, so we thought it a good idea if he kept on the other side of it for the night."

Hal jotted into his notebook. "Uncle Meaney wasn't among the dead that morning, though."

"Thank God for small mercies."

"So where is he?"

Sparrow pulled from the corn. "Probably keeping scarce, which is what I'd do if I was him."

"I think Uncle Meaney knows what happened that night."

Sparrow nodded. "Which would lend to him keeping a low profile."

"Why don't you tell me where he is?"

"Boy," said Sparrow, "I ain't got no earthly idea."

"You're lying."

Sparrow turned his head to face the opposite wall. "I'm pretty good at minding my own business. You should try it sometime."

Hal picked up the mason jar of corn liquor as if he were going to drink it but instead held it just below his nose. "You know I've been to quite a few liquor houses lately. From Deeton to Lake Castor and beyond."

"That's a healthier hobby than poking sticks into snake nests, if you ask me."

"I've developed a taste for shine. I've had some stuff that was really fine, and I've drank some juice that would strip the paint off a claw-foot tub."

Sparrow crossed his arms and waited for the punch line.

"This here corn liquor," Hal said, motioning to the jars from which they drank, "was stilled by Uncle Meaney."

Sparrow knew better than to say anything else.

"Why don't you save us all a lot of time and tell me where I can find him?"

CHAPTER TWENTY-SIX

HAL BROADSTREET

1984

Hal followed the address given to him by Ralph Sparrow. It led him to a house in the Back Back that belonged to Uncle Meaney's sister. Soon after, he found himself at their kitchen table. Uncle Meaney stood at the counter, chopping onions and garlic while a dark roux simmered at the stove. His eleven-year-old niece colored pictures in a book at the opposite end of the dinner table from Hal.

"I got my love of cooking from my daddy," Uncle Meaney told him. "My daddy could whip up damn near anything. He could catch him a raccoon and make it taste like a fricassee. It was him that taught me how to still corn into liquor."

"If that's right," said Hal, "then they ought to build a statue of him and plant it in the town square."

"Last I heard they don't plant no statues of Black folk in Dixieland." Uncle Meaney agitated the roux, then dropped his onions and garlic into it. "My daddy had him a fish house when I was younger that was real popular. Made him some honest money for a bit."

"Which one?"

"Moulton's. Down on Washington Street."

"With the green roof?" Hal perked up. "I knew it real well. My daddy used to take the whole family there every Saturday night. That was some of the best fish I ever had."

"You hear that, Clarice?" Uncle Meaney said to his niece. "I told you my daddy's store was popular with the gentry."

If the little girl heard him, she gave no sign of it. Instead, she kept her head tucked into her coloring book.

"I didn't know you were a Moulton," Hal said. "Come to think of it, I've never known your given name."

"I don't reckon many people do."

"Why do they call you Uncle Meaney?"

"Because they named me after my daddy, and Momma didn't want to holler *Clarence* and have both of us come running." Uncle Meaney slowly added chicken broth to his vegetables, stirring as he did so. "They said I talked sass even when I was yea high, so they called me Little Meaney. By the time I was—I don't know—twenty or so, I wasn't so little anymore, but I was uncle to about a half dozen whippersnappers, so the name just stuck."

"How'd you get mixed in with Jem and his outfit?"

Uncle Meaney looked up from his pot. "Hey, little one," he said to his niece. "Stop pretending like you ain't listening. Look at me."

She stopped coloring and turned her eyes toward her uncle.

"I'm going to need some fresh okra for this stew," he told her. "Run on down to Aunt Mo's, and fetch some out of her garden for me."

"I don't want to go to Aunt Mo's," said the little girl. "Her new man is always trying to—"

"I ain't asking you, child." The bottom dropped out of Uncle Meaney's tone, and it was missed on nobody in the room, least of all the niece. She closed the coloring book and sloughed out of the kitchen, leaving the two men alone. "I don't want to talk about what happened at Jem Fosskey's."

"Nobody does, Uncle Meaney," said Hal, "but somebody needs to. From what I'm to understand, you were the last one in that apartment and the only one still alive."

"And I aim to stay that way." Uncle Meaney crossed the kitchen to the refrigerator, where he removed a bowl of shrimp and a bowl of andouille sausage. He stopped in the middle of his return trip to the stove. "They're taking over, man." Uncle Meaney's eyes were desperate. "They're cutting out all the competition. They're doing it right in front of everybody, and ain't nobody doing nothing about it."

"Who is?"

Uncle Meaney reached for his wooden spoon, but Hal grabbed him by the wrist. They locked eyes.

"I'm trying to do something about it," Hal said. "I need you to help me."

Uncle Meaney's shoulders slumped. His eyes danced from Hal's to the pot of bubbling stew. Finally, he sighed.

"Fine," he said. "I got to let this cook an hour. Let's sit at the table, but when that child returns with the okra, we're done. You hear me? I ain't talking about this no more."

"Deal."

Uncle Meaney shuffled over to the table and took a seat. "I should have listened to my daddy a long time ago."

"How's that?" Hal asked, taking the seat next to him.

"He told me don't ever get mixed up with white people. It will only get you killed."

CHAPTER TWENTY-SEVEN

HAL BROADSTREET

1984

There were parts of the story that Hal Broadstreet already knew. He had spent most of the evening of June 3 at the poker game in Jem Fosskey's apartment. Ralph Sparrow had filled in some of the details of what had happened after he'd left: three Vandals had shown up to buy liquor, then taken umbrage at drinking hooch stilled by a Black man. Jem had tossed the bikers; then shortly after, Ralph Sparrow and Wilbur Fosskey had taken their leave.

Jem Fosskey, Felton Loe, Mel Kemble, and Uncle Meaney had remained behind. Three of those men would be found dead the next morning. Only Uncle Meaney had survived to tell the tale, and he hadn't spoken a word to anyone.

Until that afternoon.

"Just after midnight, there was a knock at Mr. Jem's six-inch steel door," Uncle Meaney said. "I told them not to answer it. I warned them."

Hal looked up from scribbling in his notebook. The smells of the gumbo on the stove had intensified over the past ten minutes while Uncle Meaney recounted the events of that night, but in Hal's mind, he could see only Jem's apartment. The cot, where Mel Kemble would be sleeping. The card table, where Jem and Uncle Meaney might be flipping playing cards. The hall to the bathroom, where Felton Loe had just disappeared.

"Who was it?" he asked.

Uncle Meaney's eyes hit the floor. "It was Baby Doll."

"Delilah McNaughton?"

Uncle Meaney nodded.

"What did she want?" Hal asked.

"She asked could she buy some liquor."

"And Jem opened the door?"

Uncle Meaney nodded again. "He always did like that girl. He said her and Caleb were like children to him. There weren't nobody more heartbroken when they split up than Jem."

"So Jem opened the door for her."

"Yeah."

"Only Baby Doll wasn't alone."

"No." Uncle Meaney's voice grew sad. "She weren't alone."

Before Jem Fosskey opened the door, Uncle Meaney had already stepped into the closet. "I just had a bad feeling. I reckoned it better to be safe than sorry."

It started the moment Jem opened the door. There was no *Hello* or *How's it hanging?* or *What are you doing here?* Instead, all Uncle Meaney heard was Jem getting greeted with a Bowie knife to the stomach.

Then the chest.

Then again in the gut.

"I covered my ears," Uncle Meaney said, "but I could still hear it."

While hiding in the closet, Uncle Meaney listened to the voices from in the room expressing shock, anger, and revulsion.

"One of them was screaming," Uncle Meaney said, "saying they didn't have to do that. Saying he thought they was only going to *scare* him."

"Then what happened?" Hal asked, although he already knew.

"Then it was Mel Kemble's turn."

Hal caught flashes in his memory of the blood-soaked cot. Mel Kemble's leg hanging off the side of it. The sanguine pool spreading from beneath it.

"I could hear them stabbing on him." Uncle Meaney's voice, faraway. Intruding on Hal's visual memory. "And then they stopped."

"Did you recognize the voices?" Hal asked.

Uncle Meaney nodded.

"Who did they belong to?"

Uncle Meaney licked his lips. It was as if he knew that to cross this Rubicon, there would be no going back. If he said the words, they would be out there, and no amount of effort would ever return that toothpaste back into the tube.

"Come on, Uncle Meaney," Hal urged. "I know who they are. I just need to hear you say it."

Something flashed through Meaney's eyes, something akin to hate or anger or . . . Hal wasn't sure, but whatever it was only lasted briefly; then it was replaced by sadness.

"It was them boys," Uncle Meaney said. "It was them bikers."

"Digger Crowe?"

Uncle Meaney nodded.

"Billy Wayne Dickerson?"

Again, he nodded.

"And Charlie Chains?"

He nodded a final time.

Uncle Meaney proceeded to tell the rest of the story. About how it was Digger's voice, on the other side of the closet door, who implored the other two men to finish the job. How Jem wasn't dead yet. He'd lain on the floor, spilling out and pleading for help. How that's when the gunfire started. A coup de grâce to the head, most likely out of mercy and most likely from the barrel of a gun fired by Charlie Chains.

"Digger didn't like that," Uncle Meaney explained. "He was telling Billy Wayne that he needed to finish off Jem with his bare hands. Billy Wayne, all the while, crying and begging not to. Saying over and over that him and Jem were friends and it didn't have to be like that. I got the impression that when Charlie Chains finally ended things for Jem, that Digger was plenty pissed, because he wanted to drag it out."

"Sick son of a bitch," Hal muttered.

"And then some."

Then there was the matter of Felton Loe.

"He come out of the bathroom around then," said Uncle Meaney. "Everybody knows he got that ankle holster with a .38. He must have been feeling froggy, because there's a gunshot from the other side of the apartment, which I reckon must have been him. That gets answered by a much louder gunshot, same as the one that finished Jem off. That gets Digger all riled up, saying, *That's what I'm talking about* and telling Billy Wayne he's got to get in there and finish him off."

Hal looked up from his notebook. "That was Felton Loe getting killed?"

"I reckon it was."

"So Felton comes out of the bathroom, guns blazing. He misses, and Charlie Chains fires the same gun that was used to end Jem's misery. Only Felton doesn't die. He crawls back to the bathroom, wounded, and the three of them follow him back there to finish him off."

"Well," said Uncle Meaney, drawing out his words, "not *all* three of them."

Uncle Meaney had been hiding in a closet, listening in darkness as two of his friends and colleagues were brutally murdered. Then, as they tracked Felton Loe to the bathroom to similarly dispatch him, Uncle Meaney knew it was time to act. Rather than wait and possibly be discovered by the hideous band of outlaws, he decided to use the opportunity to make a run for it.

He could hear the violent attack on Felton Loe in the bathroom, so he slowly opened the door of the closet and stepped into the apartment. He tried his best not to look at the mangled corpse of his friend lying in the middle of the floor, which turned out not to be difficult, because something else commandeered his attention.

"One of them biker boys had remained behind." Even weeks later, the fear on Uncle Meaney's face as he recalled the moment was calculable. "It wasn't Digger or Billy Wayne, but the other one."

"Charlie Chains."

"That's the one," said Uncle Meaney. "He was having himself a moment. Seated with his back against the wall and his head in one of his bloody hands, the .38 in the other. You could tell he was in an awful state over what he done, but you could also tell he was just as drugged up as the rest of them."

"How so?"

"His eyes."

"You could see them?"

"I could," said Uncle Meaney, "when he looked up and saw me."

"He saw you?"

"Oh yeah, he did. We locked eyes and stared at each other like didn't neither of us know what to do. We just stood there, frozen, looking at each other. It was the longest moment of my life. All the while, you could hear them other two in the back, just killing on Mr. Felton with their bare hands."

"Then what happened?"

"After a minute of that, it hit me that if I didn't do something quick, them other two were going to finish with Mr. Felton and find me in there and my goose would be cooked. Or this fella on the floor would come to his senses and do something his own damned self. Either way, I was good and fucked, so I might as well try for the door."

Hal couldn't think of anything worth a damn to say. He realized he hadn't even written a word in his notebook for a long while.

"So," Uncle Meaney continued, "I just started inching my way to the door. I didn't take my eyes off that boy on the floor, because if he drew up that .38 and sent me to my reward, then he was going to do it while looking me in the eye. Hell, maybe it was my eyes that kept him from it. I don't reckon I'll ever know. What I do know is that once I got through that door, I was running. I ain't never run that fast in all my life. I reckon I will probably be running the rest of my life."

Hal let all that settle. Like Charlie Chains, Hal could not take his eyes off Uncle Meaney. He watched the old man stand from the table and walk to the stove, where he stirred the gumbo, the steam wafting up toward his grizzled face. Something tugged at his mind.

"You said it was Baby Doll who convinced Jem to open the door," Hal said.

"That's right."

"You're sure of it?"

Uncle Meaney nodded. "That little girl had the voice of a songbird. I'd know it anywhere."

"Did you see her when you came out of the closet?"

Uncle Meaney thought that over. "Come to think of it, I never heard her again after the door was opened."

Hal imagined she may have never entered the apartment. "What about when you left? Was she waiting outside?"

"If she was," Uncle Meaney said, "I didn't see her. My only thought was getting as far as I could away from there and as fast as I could do it."

"Fair enough." Hal made a note. "What about a car? Did you see it outside?"

Uncle Meaney's eyes drifted up and to the left. "Yeah," he said, after a moment. "I did."

"Do you remember what kind?"

"It was one of them Pintos," said Uncle Meaney. "A white one."

Hal slapped his notebook shut. "Thank you, Uncle Meaney." After a second thought: "Would you prefer I call you Clarence? Or Mr. Moulton, even?"

"No sir," he said. "I've been Uncle Meaney my whole life."

"Do you know what you are going to do?"

Uncle Meaney tasted the gumbo from the wooden spoon. "I got a cousin up in Baltimore. I might go stay with her for a bit."

"You won't stay here?"

Uncle Meaney heard the sound of his niece singing outside. Knowing she was home with the okra, he motioned for Hal to finish up. Hal stood and walked with him to the front door.

"I can't believe they're gone," he told Hal. "I knowed Jem most of my life. He always did right by me. But if they can up and kill him and those two boys, and won't nobody give a damn, then imagine how little anyone is going to care if they do it to me."

Hal wished he had a response to that, but anything he might have said would only have been lost to the sounds of Uncle Meaney's little niece singing as she skipped up the sidewalk with her sack of okra.

CHAPTER TWENTY-EIGHT

JESS KEELER

Present Day

Jess and Sandy spent the rest of that afternoon in the library, eyes glued to the microfiche while they scanned through every available issue of the *Lake Castor Times* and Harold "Hal" Broadstreet's articles. They were so caught up in the work that they didn't hear the librarian step up behind them and nearly leaped out of their seats when she tapped them on the shoulder.

"I'm afraid it's almost time for us to close for the night," the librarian apologized. "It's nearly seven o'clock."

"How much time do we have left?" Jess asked.

The librarian pointed at the clock on the far wall. "Ten minutes, max. I have to cook dinner for my husband, so . . ."

Jess thanked her, then barely waited for her to leave before turning to Sandy. "What do you make of all this?" She pointed to the notes, to the microfiche, to the index cards and nearly filled yellow lined tablet.

"All I know is that the *Herald* wrote very little about the murders at Jem Fosskey's garage," Sandy said, "but you could write an entire book with the material we've pulled from the *Times*."

"And not only that," Jess whispered. "Nowhere in the *Herald* does it mention that there were three bikers pulled over in a Pinto on the night of those murders. *Nowhere.* Broadstreet mentions that several times throughout June. While the *Herald* barely mentions Dickerson, Crowe, or Wilcox, save for any death notices or obituaries, Broadstreet goes into great detail about these men in the pages of the *Times*. He even credits the murder of Edward Crowe as the spark that lit the fire fueling a war of retaliation between two biker gangs that claimed so many lives. He christened the time period *Lake Castor's Blood Red Summer*, even going so far as to run a homicide count in the July issues."

"Yet," Sandy added, "no mention of this war or the subsequent deaths anywhere in the *Herald*."

"How can that be?" Jess asked. "How can an entire newspaper like the *Herald* completely ignore what Broadstreet went so far as to describe as a *holocaust*?"

Sandy snickered. "He certainly wasn't shy with the hyperbole."

Jess stared at the corner of the screen. Each issue of the *Times* during the month of July had a red box next to Broadstreet's articles that was labeled BLOOD RED SUMMER. The number inside reflected the number of homicides since the beginning of June, including the three at Fosskey's garage.

"Do you think the *Herald* didn't report them because they didn't know," Sandy asked, "or because they didn't care?"

An idea struck Jess. She reached for her clipboard with the yellow lined paper and leafed through the pages until she found what she was looking for.

"The lone article in the *Herald* about the death of Charles Wilcox," Jess said, "was written by the staff's top crime writer, a woman named Olivia Crane."

"That's right," Sandy concurred.

"I've met Olivia," said Jess. "We interviewed her for my podcast."

Sandy raised her eyebrows.

"What do you say we go ask her ourselves?"

Sandy was already gathering their notes while Jess grabbed her keys.

◆　◆　◆

Jess knew the deal with Olivia Crane. She had interviewed the veteran print journalist years earlier when working on the first season of her podcast. Olivia had been one of the only local reporters to cover the Lake Castor Christmas Eve Murders and had provided interesting background and audio content on the case. She had also been married to one of the lead investigators, which offered brilliant insight.

Twelve years after that tragedy, Olivia Crane had written about the murders at Fosskey's garage, which, therefore, inspired another lunch date with Jess Keeler. She invited the reporter to lunch at the steak house in Tucker where they had met before. There, Olivia held court at a table near the back, where the restaurant's house music would not interfere with Buffy's recording, and Aaron could get a decent shot of the two women. Sandy stood behind Jess, just out of the camera's frame, and fed her notes into an earpiece.

Olivia insisted that they wait to talk business until their food had been ordered. Once that was taken care of, she set her sights on Jess's notes.

"I apologize in advance," Olivia said while glancing over printouts of the three articles she had written about the Fosskey murders. "My memory isn't what it used to be, and this was so terribly long ago."

"I understand." Jess watched Buffy lower the boom pole so that the mic was positioned closer to Olivia's mouth. "Just tell me what you remember."

"Jem Fosskey was the ringleader of a large bootlegging outfit in the area. One morning, he and two of his henchmen were found murdered in their lair over top of a chop shop Fosskey owned just outside of downtown. I don't remember it ever being solved."

"It wasn't," said Jess, "but do you remember the police ever having any theories on who might have done it?"

"At first we thought it might have been some escaped inmates." Olivia placed a finger to her chin and turned up her eyes, as if trying to remember. "I think later they reckoned it was some sort of retaliation from a local gang. I can't rightly recall."

"I'm sure that had to frighten the local population, though."

"Anytime someone is found murdered and in such a brutal fashion, it can be terrible," she said. "But I believe everyone realized it was a targeted crime and no one was ever in any danger."

"The *Herald* only ever ran the article after the bodies were discovered, and then only two more very brief follow-ups later that week," Jess said, pointing to her printouts. "Why was there never any more attention brought to it?"

"Because there were never any more developments," she answered. "Our job was to record what happened, and if nothing happened, then that meant there was nothing left to report. I trust the police did their best to investigate it because why wouldn't they? Short of finding the culprits, there was never anything else to write about."

"I'm curious, really, why a triple murder wouldn't rate more ink from a newspaper with such stature as the *Herald* enjoyed."

Olivia's lips formed a tight line over her coffee cup. "Sweetheart, I interviewed Jesse Helms in 1984. I went toe to toe with him over some of his more vitriolic ideology and offered him no quarter. If I remember correctly, I was one of the first reporters in Virginia to cover the epidemic of crack cocaine, which had been flooding the streets of our inner cities for two years before I broke the story. I was writing about AIDS, the Russians, and saving the whales, which is what my newspaper's stature *enjoyed*. For that reason, you will have to forgive me if the unsolved murder of three Lake Castor criminals didn't manage to dent my priority list."

"I didn't mean to offend."

"And you didn't, dear." Olivia sipped her coffee, then set it onto the saucer in front of her. "At the time of those murders, the only prison break from death row occurred only a few miles from us. Six condemned inmates, led by the notoriously vicious Briley brothers, were on the loose somewhere nearby, and it was a far more encompassing story than the one you're researching. I think this was also around the time that the biker war between the Vandals and that other club from the coast broke out. So this wasn't exactly a slow news time in Lake Castor."

"You bring up that war between the biker gangs," Jess said, "but strangely it was hardly covered in your newspaper. You were the top crime-desk reporter, and the Vandals committed their fair share of crime. Shouldn't it have warranted more ink?"

"The only people those bikers ever took interest in hurting was each other," Olivia said. "Most of the time, those scumbags would huff and puff, but I never heard anything about them blowing anybody's house down. Most anything out of that world was chalked up to rumor and conjecture, which the *Herald* never saw fit to print."

"Harold Broadstreet, on the other hand, may have argued with that assumption."

The smile faded from Olivia's lips. She exhaled through her nose and appeared to be transported to a different place and time.

"Oh, Hal . . . ," she said. She brought herself back to the here and now. "Hal was a different kind of reporter. A throwback. Imagine some character from a sleazy film noir; then multiply it by ten. He wanted so badly for there to be a gangland conspiracy for him to report on, like there might have been in one of those old black-and-white movies. *Where, oh where,* he used to moan, *is our Saint Valentine's Day Massacre and our Al Capone?* He was a great guy—don't get me wrong—but he could be a bit . . . *sensational.* He used to refer to this period in Lake Castor as its '*Blood Red Summer.*'"

"He sounds like a lot of fun."

"He would get along famously in the media of this day and age."

"They committed far more ink to the murders in the *Times* than they did in the *Herald*."

Olivia's eyebrows inched higher. "They also reported more bigfoot sightings. The *Times* used to be a reputable news source and served as a competitor to the *Herald* for many years, but when it was sold in the early eighties, the editors were forced to make some decisions to chase a different readership. Hal was the last remaining holdover from its journalism days, but there was no one there to curb his sensational instincts."

"So you think his theories were equivalent to tabloid fodder?"

"Sweetheart, it didn't matter what I thought. What mattered is what I could confirm and who I could quote while doing it. At the time, there were no more reputable people to quote than those in law enforcement. Hal made a career of antagonizing those sources, which was a reason why his paper was subject to ridicule. I, on the other hand, made friends with police and detectives, and I enjoyed a long career of writing crime. When the police no longer had anything to report, there ceased to be anything to write about it, and in no time another story came along—usually soaked in blood—and the public would quickly forget."

"Another story like the sniper?"

Olivia answered that question with silence. Through her earpiece, Jess could hear Sandy's sharp rebuke.

"Jess," she whispered, "what the hell are you doing?"

Jess ignored her. "Your paper didn't cover the early sniper shootings, where five people were targeted—four were killed—in July. However, the only time their names were mentioned in the *Herald* was if the paper was paid for an obituary."

Jess could see Aaron fidgeting behind his camera and shoot a glance over to Sandy.

"It may sound callous," Olivia said, "but if we wrote a story about every murder that happened in that particular part of town—especially back in those days—our newspaper would have been three inches thicker. We printed a crime blotter. Was it far from complete? Sure. But we couldn't print *everything*. It just wasn't realistic, and our editor at the time chose what he felt was newsworthy."

"The sniper's last victim certainly turned out to be newsworthy."

"Jess," whispered Sandy's voice deep in Jess's ear, "stay on the topic. We need her talking about the Fosskey murders. We're not doing a story on—"

Jess popped the earpiece out of her ear and homed in on Olivia. There were too many unanswered questions, too many dangling loose ends. Jess could never let it go and would never forgive herself for getting this close and not at least asking.

"In fact," Jess said, going for it, "the sniper's last victim was on the front page for several days. From the time he was killed, through the manhunt, until they found a man upon whom they placed the blame for his murder. Now, why do you think his death was more newsworthy than the other ones?"

"I think you know why."

"I'd like to hear you say it," said Jess. "Part of the intrigue of these true-crime documentaries is watching the subject voice their opinions. It makes up for the instances where law enforcement refuses to contribute."

Olivia turned to the camera, as if it were the first time she acknowledged it, then shot her eyes back to Jess. "What happened to *my friend*, Hal, was a tragedy."

"There were five tragedies which preceded his."

"If we had any idea that was the handiwork of a madman, we might have brought more public awareness." Olivia fussed with the napkin in her lap and craned her neck in the direction of the kitchen, in search of their food. "Perhaps we might have even stopped him. It was a long time before I was able to forgive myself for not looking into it sooner, but we didn't know. We couldn't have known. We just reported the news."

Olivia offered an expression that seemed to ask, *Is this what you want to hear?*

Jess leaned forward on her elbows. "So you believe Ricky Lee Patience was the sniper?"

"Why wouldn't I?" Olivia furrowed her brow. "I have never heard anything to the contrary. He confessed. I never thought there was any argument about his involvement."

"There have been a lot of forced confessions."

"And there was not another sniper killing after his arrest. Hal was the last one."

"And why Hal?" Jess asked. "It certainly looks odd to see it now, but even back then, didn't it strike anyone as strange that the previous five victims were Black men in the Back Back, but Hal was a white man killed in his own home?"

"We believed everything about this tragedy was strange," snapped Olivia. "Every damned thing, including the senseless murder of my friend."

"But did it never occur to you that Hal might have been *targeted*?"

Sandy, who had been fidgeting in her seat, finally leaned closer to Jess. "Jess, stop it," she hissed.

Olivia stared cooly at Jess before turning to Aaron. She nodded toward the camera. "Turn that thing off," she said.

"Excuse me?" Aaron asked.

"I said to turn off that damned camera."

Aaron lowered it from his shoulder. The look he fired toward Jess could have fried eggs.

"I don't know what kind of story you people are trying to gin up," Olivia seethed, "but I won't be party to it. I agreed to come on camera and talk with you about that mess that happened to those bootleggers, but I won't have anything to do with you taking what happened to a dear, dear friend of mine and turning it into some twisted narrative which skewers law enforcement, or whatever the hell it is that you're trying to do for likes and subscribers."

"Fair enough," Jess said, "but maybe you can tell me why anytime I try to talk to someone about what happened down in the Back Back, everyone shuts me down. Law enforcement, victims' families, my own damn producers, and now you."

"Because what's done is done," Olivia said. "You can't change anything, and talking about it will only bring heartache and pain."

"For whom?"

The food arrived, and Olivia made room in front of herself for the plate. As the waitress fussed over her, Olivia laid her hand gently over top of Jess's.

"This isn't like your last podcast, sweetheart," she said. "You're not chasing some eighty-year-old doctor. The men who pulled the trigger may very well be dead, but the organization they belonged to is very much alive and has no interest in being talked about in public."

"Who are you talking about?" Jess asked, incredulous.

Instead of answering, Olivia thanked the waitstaff and collected her cutlery.

"Enjoy your dinner, child," Olivia said. "If I learned anything from Hal Broadstreet, it's that we never know when the next meal might be our last."

CHAPTER TWENTY-NINE

JESS KEELER

Present Day

No one said a word as the crew packed their equipment away in the van. Buffy drove. Aaron rode shotgun. In the back seat, Sandy scrolled through her phone, while Jess stared out the window. She watched the landscape pass, Tucker's quaint hometown charm quickly giving way to rural pastureland, then wide swaths of wilderness interrupted only by billboards and Dollar General stores.

The air in the car felt like a fuse had been lit, but no one had any idea when it would go off. The tension became so unbearable that when Aaron finally spoke, Jess felt like he was doing them all a favor.

"You told us all," he said, in a voice that started low but had no problem picking up steam, "that we had until the food was served to get the good stuff. You said to have the camera ready, because Olivia never liked to talk business while she was eating. *You said* time was of the essence with Olivia Crane. That's what you said."

"It's true," Jess agreed. "When we interviewed her for *Something Bad Wrong*, she—"

"You had a list of questions. You had an earpiece, so that—in the event you *forgot* those questions or got off track—Sandy could feed them to you."

"Look, it wasn't because I—"

"You *abandoned* that earpiece." Aaron's anger was palpable. Jess felt like she could reach out and touch it. "You *deviated* from the questions we had all decided on. There were marks we needed her to hit, things we needed her to say, in order to get the content we needed for our doc. You went in a completely different direction, and we blew it!"

"The story leads us, not the other way around," Jess told him. "An interview is a living, breathing thing. When it starts to take us in an interesting direction, I'm beholden to follow it."

"Bullshit." Aaron twisted himself so far in the passenger seat Jess thought he might strangle himself with the seat belt. "That approach might work for a podcast, where your overhead is so low you might trip over it, but not when you have a crew of professionals who are trying to feed their families. Not when you have producers who are—and I can't stress this enough—*paying you*."

"Aaron, this is *true crime*, and you can't simply—"

"Don't talk to me anymore about what the definition of *true crime* is, Jess Keeler. I know more about *true crime* than you will ever know. I've worked on seventy-two of these programs. I've shot film of men who have killed more people than were in your high school graduating class. You've done *one* podcast, and you think that makes you Nancy Drew. I've got news for you, sister: This isn't podcasting. It's a *business*. A multimillion-dollar *business*."

Jess turned to face the window again. Instead of the passing land-scape, all she could see was her reflection. She closed her eyes.

Aaron wasn't ready to let up. "In that little podcast of yours," he asked. "What was your budget?"

She didn't dignify the question with a response.

"Let me ask a different question: How much money did it earn?"

Again, Jess answered with silence.

"You spent how long making that podcast? A year? Two years?" Aaron's laugh dripped with cynicism. "So if you didn't make a single red penny, then how much does that mean you—"

"Aaron," Sandy snapped. "You've made your point."

"Have I?" His eyes bugged wide, and the flesh around his cheeks turned pink. "I don't think I have. We tried to do the story on the sniper. We gave it our best shot, and we were turned down. No one was interested in it. What they were interested in is this thing here, with the bootlegger massacre, or whatever we're calling it. We have been given a budget, and each of us were paid an advance. Did you cash your check yet, Keeler?"

Jess said nothing, only wished silently that the trip would mercifully end.

"Of course you did," Aaron continued. "You cashed it and have probably spent a fair chunk of it. So this means you don't pull another stunt like you did back at that restaurant. When our project needs valuable content and sound bites from our interview subjects, then you get them for me. If you don't, I'll see that you are found in breach."

The only sound that could be heard for several minutes was the tires on the asphalt. Jess's head was still swimming from the interview, and she could focus on very little else besides that look in Olivia Crane's eyes when she'd challenged her on the sniper coverage prior to Hal's death. Olivia knew something. Jess absolutely knew it. But how could she get her to open up?

"What if," Sandy said, her voice small and uncertain, "the two stories are connected?"

Jess wondered if her expression of incredulity might possibly match Aaron's. He twisted himself farther in the seat to get a better look at the researcher, to make sure she hadn't sprouted another head, or perhaps horns. He then switched his gaze from one woman to the other.

"Not you too" was all he could say.

"It makes sense to run it down," Sandy said.

Aaron turned again to face forward. "It makes more sense to fire you and hire another researcher. I bet I could find a college kid to intern for free."

Sandy took that comment as a rebuke and offered nothing more. Jess, on the other hand, was shocked at the show of solidarity.

"How about you?" Aaron asked Buffy. "You joining this piteous mutiny?"

Buffy cut him a look that told him to back off.

He did.

The rest of the drive to Lake Castor was spent in silence. Twice, Jess and Sandy made eye contact; both times a warmth passed between them that Jess thought had previously been absent.

The third time, they shared a quick grin.

CHAPTER THIRTY

Ennis Worthy

1984

To listen to them, it was a scourge. It had overtaken the streets of the urban centers, the schools. It had started up in New York, or Baltimore, infecting first the inner cities, then spreading, like a cancer down the east coast. Up from Miami. Atlanta.

Lake Castor.

"They call it crack." Deputy Michael Howard clicked the remote control, and the carousel continued to the next slide. An image of chalky white lines of cocaine appeared on the screen across the room. Several of the deputies grumbled in the dark. "Crack is the street name for synthesized cocaine, and it has overtaken the Black communities of our great nation."

Deputy Ennis Worthy shifted in his seat and checked his watch. On a normal day, he'd be studying for his law degree at the desk in the jailhouse, breaking occasionally to check on whatever inmates the county was accommodating. However, Sheriff Bobby McCoy insisted that all his deputies—new and old—should be brought up to date on current affairs.

"This cocaine is synthesized by adding baking soda, ammonia, or a handful of highly toxic cleaning products to the narcotic," Deputy Howard intoned, "then cooking it into a solid. Then it is broken into chunks, which are known as *rocks*."

Deputy Howard clicked the remote again, and a new slide clanked into place. The new image on the wall was of rocks of crack cocaine.

"The end result is a product that is fifty times more addictive than any other drug known to man."

The next slide showed a graph with text claiming that twenty-five million Americans had tried cocaine, one-third of all college students would try it, and five thousand Americans would try it each day.

"This new, synthesized cocaine is cheaper, more addictive, and easier to obtain." Deputy Howard clicked to the next slide, which showed several junkies hovering over a pipe in a dark alleyway. "Users are often spotted due to their lack of hygiene, humanity, and fear of consequence."

The next slide showed the famous actor Mr. T pointing at the camera, with bold and colorful text declaring that he "pities the fool who tries crack cocaine."

Worthy sighed. He counted the heads of the other lawmen present in the room and realized that no one was on patrol. No one was manning the jailhouse. No one was at the front desk answering any calls that might come in. Sheriff McCoy had demanded all present and accounted for—including Deputy David Gentry, who had been on sick leave due to a rolled ankle during a traffic stop—because the voters of Deeton County had been forced to fear this unseen scourge threatening their children.

"It's in Lake Castor and will come down to Deeton to take our babies away," a woman had declared at a public-safety meeting two weeks earlier. She had been in hysterics because of a special report aired on *Nightline*, followed by an article in the *Herald* that provided stats and quotes supporting the scare.

"If it ain't crack babies," Sheriff McCoy had muttered at the time, "then it will be AIDS or the nuclear bomb."

There was no illusion that Deputy Howard's research reflected the attitudes of his sheriff. "Addiction to crack cocaine will cause its users to enter a frenzy, which can often lead to unprovoked violent attacks. It will turn women into hookers, kids into killers, and plunge our population into poverty."

Worthy's mind, however, was preoccupied with another matter. He'd spent the majority of the presentation fidgeting in his seat. Not because of how Deputy Howard presented his material, which of course left plenty to be desired, but because of how other things in his life were playing out.

His girlfriend, Shirley, was growing impatient with him. She had already been looking for apartments in DC and no longer seemed interested in entertaining his desire to wait, wait, just a little bit longer, baby . . . no, she was leaving and had told Worthy it was up to him to decide if he was coming with her.

At present, however, that didn't occupy him the most. No, that distinction fell to the phone call he'd received from Rosalie Patience only two days earlier.

"They let him out, Deputy Worthy," she had told him.

"What do you mean they let him out?" Worthy had demanded. "He was sentenced."

"He was remanded to the state hospital," Rosalie answered. "Three weeks, they had him. Three weeks and then they said he was released. Oh, Deputy Worthy . . . it's gotten worse."

Worthy closed his eyes. "Tell me what's happening."

"He says the Devil lives inside him."

"It's the sickness," he had told her. "It's not the Devil. It's—"

"You can say that all you like, but my boy says the Devil is inside him. He talks to himself. When I ask who he is talking to, he tells me he speaks only to the Devil. He eats dog food off the floor."

"He does what?"

"He says if we're going to treat him like a dog, then he might as well eat like a dog."

Worthy was helpless. "Ms. Patience, you know there's very little I can do. I'm a Deeton deputy and—"

"I know," she sighed. "I've heard you say it over and over. It ain't your jurisdiction. But when I talk to Reverend Stallings, he says—"

"The Lord doesn't know anything about jurisdictions. I know, Ms. Patience. I'm afraid the Lord ever crossed through Lake Castor, he would have been crucified long before the Last Supper."

Worthy had reason for his concern. His great hope had been that the state hospital might provide Ricky Lee with the resources he'd need to get better. Barring that, he had neither the church nor the local law to help him. If he was escalating as Rosalie Patience had indicated, then it was only a matter of time before the inevitable run-in with law enforcement happened. As things were shaping up that summer, the timing would be profoundly inconvenient.

Worthy knew his choices were limited. Without Reverend Stallings, Captain Dorritt, or his own sheriff to turn to, and without the resources of the state hospital, Worthy feared he would have to consult the one institution he had been trained to avoid.

To do so, he rose from his chair and silently excused himself from the darkness of the room. Within minutes, he was in the lobby of the sheriff's office, standing at the pay phone. He dropped a shiny quarter into the slot and waited for the phone to pick up. Two rings . . . three.

"*Lake Castor Times*," answered the receptionist.

In a low whisper, Worthy said, "I'd like to speak to Harold Broadstreet."

CHAPTER THIRTY-ONE

HAL BROADSTREET

1984

If Hal were writing the story, he would describe his own grin as *shit eating*. He would forego such clichés as *ear to ear* and *toothy*. He would describe instead the jubilation he felt in every heartbeat. The *vindication* filling his lungs. The *validation* as he pushed open his editor's door and found Vince behind his desk, choking down a banana in one hand and holding a ragged copy of a Danielle Steel hardback in the other. He glanced up from the book at Hal, then took another bite from the banana.

"We got 'em, Vince," said Hal. "We got the story."

Vince raised an eyebrow. "Which story?"

"The murders at Fosskey's garage."

Vince rolled his eyes and took another bite from his fruit. "It's time to move on, pal. This story is colder than those bootleggers' bodies."

"Not anymore it ain't." Hal waited for Vince to set down his romance novel. "You said there's no gas in the tank unless I found someone significant to quote."

"Since when do you actually listen to me?"

"Guess what I got?"

Vince didn't bother to swallow his food. "The lead detective?"

"Better."

"The killer and a gift-wrapped confession?"

Hal winced. "Maybe dial it back a bit."

Vince had already grown bored, looking forlornly at his half-eaten banana. "Who is it, Hal?"

"I got an eyewitness."

Vince popped the last of the banana into his mouth and balled up the peel. He sailed it short of the wastebasket, but didn't bother to pick it up.

"Tell me more."

Which Hal was all too happy to do. He recounted his trips in and out of the area's liquor houses in search of Uncle Meaney. He told Vince how Jem Fosskey had defended his master distiller from racist slights delivered from the bikers who had shown up after Hal had left the poker game. He then read aloud his notes detailing the assault after Crowe, Dickerson, and Charlie Chains had breached the six-inch steel door.

"How did this Uncle Whatever manage to survive the ordeal?" Vince asked.

"He was hiding in the closet."

Vince scratched his head. "How can he be sure it was the three bikers who committed the murders if he was hiding in a closet?"

"For one," Hal explained, "he was there when they came in the first time and was able to lay eyes on them. Therefore, he would be able to recognize their voices."

Vince narrowed his eyes and shrugged, still unsure.

"For another," Hal continued, "he saw one of them."

"How did he *see* one of them?"

Hal explained the story as told to him by Uncle Meaney.

"The biker just let him go?" Vince asked.

"He didn't stop him."

Hal could see the wheels turning in his editor's head.

"If he's telling the truth," Vince countered, "then why didn't he go to the police?"

Hal's expression said that he expected more from his editor.

"Okay, fine," said Vince. "Why aren't *we* taking it to the cops?"

"Because," said Hal, "can you find me one within a hundred miles who gives half a damn about closing the Fosskey case? They seem to think that whoever iced Digger Crowe did all the heavy lifting for them. I don't think there's a single badge down on Carlton Street who's even looked at that case file since then."

"He said there was a woman who helped them gain entry?" Vince asked.

"Delilah 'Baby Doll' McNaughton," Hal reported.

"Has anyone spoken to her?"

"Negative. She's gone missing."

"What does that mean: *missing*?"

Hal explained that Baby Doll McNaughton had left her husband, Caleb, after he quit the Vandals motorcycle club. She'd chosen instead to go with Digger, one of the men who killed Fosskey, Kemble, and Loe. After which, she was never seen again. Since Digger had two missing ex-wives in Omaha, there was only one logical conclusion.

Vince pursed his lips. "We don't traffic in *logical conclusions*, Hal. We traffic in double confirmations. Can you get a separate confirmation of everything you got from this Black bootlegger? Can you get more information about what happened to this Baby Doll? If we can tie her to the scene of the—"

"We're not going to find her," Hal said. "When these guys want someone to disappear, they make them disappear. She's encased in cement at the bottom of some quarry or somewhere we'll never, ever see her again."

"Again," Vince said, "you're dealing in speculation. We need double conf—"

"Did you get double confirmation on that bigfoot story you ran last week?" Hal demanded.

"I can't, in good conscience, run this story without attribution from police."

"Fuck the police!" Hal shouted. "They don't care about it. They had these three guys after the murders, and they let them go. Billy Wayne Dickerson and Charlie Chains are out there walking the streets, and no one is looking for them. What's the point in getting quotes from them when they aren't involved in the story in the slightest?"

Vince tapped his pencil on top of his desk while he stared out the window, a movement Hal had seen him do several times when he was teetering on the edge of a decision. Hal knew Vince would present his idea seconds after the tapping stopped.

It did.

"How about this?" Vince said. "We call them and tell them we have a development, would they care to comment. They're not going to comment, because they're still miffed at you for the Avondale article. They're going to tell you to pound sand."

Vince stood up from his desk. He was on a roll. "That's fine, you see, because we can run the article the very next morning—*tomorrow* morning—quoting this previously unknown witness to the goriest and most gruesome crime in Lake Castor's history, and at the very end of this damning and intriguing article, we'll print, *Lake Castor police detectives refused to comment on this article.*"

Vince had nearly run himself out of breath, pacing the floor of his own office, yet he still had the energy to puff out his chest and place both his hands on his hips as if it were he who had conceived, researched, and written the damned thing himself.

All that bluster left his sails as Hal offered his own opinion.

"Actually, Vince," he said, "I got a better idea."

Vince's shoulders slumped. He slouched back to his chair and dropped himself into it.

"Of course you do," he sighed. "Well, spit it out, will you?"

"We saw what happened with the Avondale article," said Hal. "People read it, and they were outraged. They talked about it in the grocery store aisles and on the party lines, but by the time the next newspaper landed on their front lawns, they were on to the next hot topic. Here we stand in the middle of primary season and heading into the Summer Olympics . . . this article would be lost in the shuffle of daily life."

Vince leaned back in his seat and studied his star reporter. He made a tent of his fingers and licked his lips, wondering what savory proposal was about to be offered.

"How about this?" Hal teased. "We run a multiedition spread. Five days of articles about the Fosskey murders and the outlaw motorcycle activity in the area. Nobody at the *Herald* or the *Sun* or the *Dispatch* or any other Virginia paper has done anything like it, and we—the redheaded stepchildren at the *Lake Castor Times*—can be the first to dare. We run it in August, between the two presidential party conventions, and in the meantime, I can soak every bit of drama there is out of this baby. This full week of articles will have interviews with former gang members, people who have been affected by crimes, and so on and so forth."

"I like this," said Vince. "I like this a lot."

"So you're game?"

"Sure," said Vince. "Can you get law enforcement to go on the record?"

Hal winced. "Is it make or break?"

"It would round out the piece," said Vince. "Something this encompassing will look biased if we don't have someone talking. We can send some scotch up to the brass and see if that helps us make nice. Let's see"—Vince thumbed through his Rolodex—"what is Dorritt drinking these days?"

"I'll have no luck with Dorritt," said Hal. "I'm better off chasing a lead of my own."

Vince plucked a card from the Rolodex. "That's my boy. They give us hell, and we give them Hal. You follow your lead, and I'll have a word with the captain and see if we can't do each other some favors."

Hal winked at him, game for it all. Hal had pitched it well; now he had to deliver.

And he knew exactly where to find a cop that would talk with him.

CHAPTER THIRTY-TWO

HAL BROADSTREET

1984

The victim was long dead by the time Hal Broadstreet arrived on the scene, but no one had bothered yet to cover his body. He lay as he had fallen: face first upon the cracked sidewalk that lined Barclay Street. In death, as in life, he accumulated quite the crowd. Onlookers gathered at the perimeter of a crime scene hastily constructed by a pair of uniformed patrolmen and the three detectives that Hal knew better than most others.

"If Hal Broadstreet is here," greeted Detective Smolinski, still in need of a shave, "that must mean he's tracking down another Jimmy Hoffa lead."

"UFO went thataway, Broadstreet," cracked Sergeant Bravos.

"Good morning, Smolinski." Hal sniffed the air. "Is that vodka or gin I smell on your breath?"

"What kind of hack reporter don't know the difference?" Smolinski snarled.

They could have swapped barbs like that all day, but the voice of reason appeared as their lead detective, Lieutenant Kip Avondale. He approached with both palms showing, as a gesture of peace.

"Your momma didn't teach you to play nice, Broadstreet?" Avondale asked. "Not even when you're visiting someone else's crime scene?"

"Is that what we're doing here, Lieutenant? Playing nice?"

"I scratch your back," Avondale offered, "you stay off mine."

"I heard a call on the scanner. Murder in the Back Back."

"That's hardly news, Broadstreet."

"It is when half the Crimes Against Persons division shows up." Hal nodded with his chin toward the dead body. "Like the lady on TV says, *Where's the beef?*"

Avondale appeared thoughtful. "You'll never guess who is the guest star of this episode."

Hal narrowed his eyes, as if to say, *Surprise me.*

"Ronnie Daye."

One of the patrolmen whistled real low.

Everybody else on the street raised absolute hell.

According to anybody with eyeballs, the man had been walking down Barclay Street, arm in arm with a woman. The woman was dressed smart, in a floral-patterned sundress, one that showed off the shape of her legs. She'd recently straightened her hair. Everyone in the neighborhood knew she was not his wife, but nobody knew her name.

Everybody, on the other hand, knew his.

To use an outdated term, Ronnie Daye was the closest thing folks in Lake Castor had known as a *kingpin*. He'd been installed by the notorious drug lord Frank "Superfly" Lucas into the Black neighborhood known as the Back Back to control the heroin trade. Lucas's hold over the East Coast's drug routes evaporated upon his arrest in 1975, but Ronnie Daye still reigned supreme in the immediate area surrounding Lake Castor.

Police would arrest him, but no charges would stick. Rivals would come at him, but they would only miss. He'd survived a fruitful criminal career with what seemed to be more lives than a cat, walking between the raindrops, plucking bullets from the air and altering their course. No one could touch him. Ronnie Daye was invincible.

Until July 6.

Two days after hosting his annual Independence Day barbecue for his community, he'd called up one of his girls and made plans to stop at a chicken hut on the west side of Lake Castor's Back Back. They'd shared a dozen wings and a large order of fries, and were walking toward Mercy Park when a shot rang out on an otherwise still summer day.

The girl with Ronnie Daye didn't see anything. Lemmy Arvin, a thirty-five-year-old homeowner across the street, heard it. He, like many people in the Back Back, was no stranger to the sound of gunfire. He'd been watering his lawn, but dropped the hose and rolled to safety beneath his car.

If Ronnie Daye heard or saw anything, that mystery would follow him to the grave. A single bullet entered his back between both shoulder blades and perforated his heart in the left aorta. He fell immediately to the pavement and never uttered another sound.

While the detectives processed the scene, Hal canvassed the area in search of someone who might give him something. The girl walking with Ronnie Daye did not care to be named or quoted. Two kids playing at the corner argued whether they'd heard one shot or two, but swore they'd seen nothing. A woman walking out of the convenience store on the corner of Barclay and Hart said she'd seen Ronnie Daye fall, but thought he was pretending. She hadn't even heard the gunshot.

He was wrapping up his interviews when Olivia Crane's bright-yellow Volkswagen rolled onto the scene. She opened her door, but took her time gathering her things before she climbed out of the car. She took in her surroundings, seemed to make a mental note, and then approached the detectives for a summary.

Once finished with that, she caught up with Hal.

"I can't believe they finally got Ronnie Daye," she said. "I was beginning to think he was going to outlive us all."

"What did the cops tell you?" Hal asked her.

"Single gunshot. No suspects." The medical examiner's van arrived. "Didn't you speak with them already?"

"Sure," he said, "but maybe they tell you things different than what they tell me."

Olivia nodded toward the gathering lookie-loos. "What about them? What did they have to say about it?"

"Nobody saw nothing. Nobody heard nothing."

"Ah, life in the Back Back," said Olivia. "Same as it ever was."

CHAPTER THIRTY-THREE

JESS KEELER

Present Day

Jess had yet to forgive herself for derailing the interview with Olivia Crane. For the last couple of days, Aaron's rebuke continued to ring in her ears. She no longer felt confident in her decisions. He had a point: Yes, they were getting paid to do a job. If she were working alone on her podcast, she could follow the story where the interviews led them. However, the Germans were paying them to produce a documentary about Jem Fosskey, so alienating a source by asking questions about the sniper was detrimental to their work.

She wished she could go back in time and do things different.

But she couldn't.

Just as she couldn't get Aaron's words out of her mind, she also couldn't erase the image of Olivia's face when Jess confronted her with burying the sniper stories. It was the same expression she had seen on Ennis Worthy's when she said she was investigating Ricky Lee Patience's guilt.

What were they hiding?

Jess could hardly stand to look at herself in the mirror, so she spent no time brushing her hair, choosing instead to tie it back in a bun.

She applied minimal makeup, knowing that she was only spending the day at the sheriff's office, going over the case file for the Fosskey murders. Then she remembered that she would be joined by the much younger Sandy, so she took a little more time with herself, made sure to moisturize.

However angry she was at herself, she was ten times as angry with her son, Benjamin, who had yet to answer her when she had been calling for him. She walked up the stairs and pushed open the door to his room, then quickly discovered the reason he'd been ignoring her.

Benjamin lay in bed, beneath the blanket, with his phone up to his face while wearing earbuds.

"—then the man got angry, went home, and brutally murdered his wife," Benjamin said into a small microphone. "I guess he wanted to save on the divorce attorney's fees."

His laughter was cut short upon his mother's entrance. He quickly sat up in bed and covered his phone's mic with his hand.

"Mom," he groaned, "what are you doing in here?"

"What are *you* doing?" Jess demanded. "I've been calling for you the last five min—"

"Can't you see I'm in the middle of something?"

"I can, but I don't for the life of me know what it is."

Benjamin spoke with a low voice into his phone. "Hey, man, can we pause this? We can pick it up in a minute. Thanks, man." He disconnected the phone and glared at his mother. "Happy now?"

"Hardly," Jess said. "What was that? Pause *what*?"

Benjamin threw the blanket off him and climbed out of bed. He wore gym shorts and tube socks. He plucked a T-shirt off the floor, sniffed it, and then selected a different one.

"I'm doing a podcast," he said.

"A *what*?"

"A podcast." Benjamin slipped into his shirt and walked past her and exited the bedroom. "Surely you know what a *podcast* is."

"Don't get smart with me, buster." Jess followed him through the hallway and down the stairs. "What do you mean you're *doing a podcast*? A podcast about what?"

"True crime. Just like you."

Jess shook her head, as if to clear any cobwebs. She watched him walk into the kitchen, open the fridge, and take out a carton of orange juice.

"Explain to me how you are doing a true-crime podcast," she said.

Benjamin drank from the carton, then smiled after wiping his lips. "What, you think you're the only investigative journalist in this family?"

"As a matter of fact . . ." Jess canceled the rest of her thought. For two years, she had been trying to reignite Benjamin's interest in returning to college. What started as a "small break" had developed into a "gap year," which had then become a "gap *two* years." She realized she served as no shining example for her son, since she herself had dropped out of college when she'd become pregnant with him. However, she'd be damned if she let him make the same mistakes she did. She reckoned instead she should help nurture his interests and see if they couldn't serve as a launching pad to reenrolling in school. "Tell me about this podcast."

"Me and my friend K-Pop . . ." He meant his friend *Kevin*, who Jess had never much cared for. ". . . we investigate a crime, and then we tell people about it."

"How do you investigate?"

"We look it up on the internet."

Jess blinked. "Do you talk to law enforcement?"

"God, no," he said. "All cops are bastards, Mom."

"Don't talk like that." But she stayed on point. "So you two just google a murder, and then what?"

"We talk about it."

"You *talk* about it. Is that what you were doing when I walked in your room?"

"Yeah. Each episode is like twenty minutes."

"How many episodes do you spend on a particular murder?"

"One."

"So you google a murder, talk about it for twenty minutes, and then post it? No editing? Nothing?"

Benjamin rolled his eyes. "We don't have time for all that, Mom. We need to get ten episodes in the can so we can maximize the algorithms."

Jess sighed. She felt herself unable to resist unleashing the torrent of anguish she felt by watching her only son bastardize the passion she had put into her own work, but before she could get a word out, the doorbell rang.

"Oh shit," she said, "that would be my production assistant. Will you grab the door? I need to get my notebook and—"

"Oh my God," Benjamin gasped. "Is that Sandy C?"

Jess furrowed her brow and turned in the direction he was pointing. She could see Sandy waving outside the storm door, on the patio.

"Sandy?" Jess clarified.

"Sandy C is at *our* house?" Benjamin said.

"She's my production assistant."

"She has, like, eight hundred thousand followers on Howler, and she's *your* production assistant?"

"Get the door, Ben. She's waiting."

Benjamin bounded to the door like a puppy.

"You must be Benjamin," said Sandy after he opened it. "I've heard so much about you."

"You have?" He was dumbstruck. "Really?"

Sandy giggled, and a wave of resentment rippled through Jess. "Of course I have. Your mother talks about you all the time."

"Oh." Benjamin's face fell. "Sure."

Jess took the young woman in. There was no question that men would be attracted to Sandy. She was perfect in all the ways that Jess was not. However, she had hoped against all hope that her son might be immune to those charms. Her heart grew heavy with disappointment that he was not.

"Benjamin," she said, "I need you to keep an eye on your grand-mother while we're gone."

"But, Mom," he groaned, "I told you I got stuff to do."

"Your grandmother has Alzheimer's, Ben. She needs our help right now."

"She's been doing better," he said. "For all we know, she's got it licked."

The expression Jess offered her son warned him off that idea. "Nothing is more important than keeping an eye on Nana."

"I still have to finish my podcast."

Sandy brightened up. "You have a podcast?"

"That's right," he said. "We're investigating murders."

"Sweet. Like your mother?"

Benjamin's chest puffed. "Kind of. But with way more downloads, once it gets started."

"What's it called?"

"*Stoned Cold Murder*," he answered, "because right before we tape the episode, we light up a giant—"

"Benjamin," Jess interrupted. "Your grandmother."

"Mom . . ."

Sandy placed her hand on his shoulder. "You're such a good grand-son," she said, "taking care of your grandmother and producing a pod-cast at the same time. That's really cool."

Benjamin's cheeks flushed.

"We have to go," said Jess. "Sheriff Axel is expecting us."

Sandy offered Benjamin her hand, which he greedily accepted. "It was very nice meeting you," she said. "I can't wait to check out your podcast."

They left him there at the front door. As they walked to the car, Jess prayed silently that Sandy would say nothing about her son. That she would know better than to comment on anything in that moment. That while she was glad that Benjamin was taking responsibility, she wished he would do it on his own, or rather after she told him to, not because some hot, young production assistant told him to.

Thankfully, Sandy was good at reading the room.

CHAPTER THIRTY-FOUR

Jess Keeler

Present Day

Jess enjoyed researching at the sheriff's office. It beat suffering through the distractions readily available when she worked from home. Or at the library. When she set up shop in the Lake Castor Public Library, she would inevitably be stopped by someone who recognized her. People always wanted to tell her about how those murders affected them. Maybe they had a mother or an aunt who was a nurse at the hospital where the killer worked, or they remembered when the couple went missing. Jess was grateful that people felt any connection to her work, but she wasn't at the library for connection. She was there to research.

Working at the sheriff's office alleviated that problem. Sheriff Axel offered her and Sandy an empty interrogation room in which they could spread out their notes and the contents from the case file, then work until he clocked out for the day. No one ever bothered them, save for the sheriff's occasional visits—if any—to stop in and chitchat, see how the investigation was going. If they needed anything—clarification on some point or another, or some background on a name mentioned in the police reports—all they needed to do was cross the hall and knock on his door to ask.

Easy peasy.

That afternoon, they had made an appointment with Sheriff Axel to view the case files again, so they might research for an upcoming shoot that weekend. When they arrived, however, they found Sheriff Axel consulting with a pair of deputies.

"We found a body in the woods with advanced decomposition," Axel told Jess and Sandy.

"That's horrible," Jess said.

"It's inevitable," he sighed. "Only problem is we don't know if it's a homeless person or if it's a homicide. I'm needed to help coordinate the team, make sure all the i's are dotted and t's crossed."

"I understand."

"Do you mind if I postpone our conversation for another half hour or so?"

"Absolutely not," Jess told him. "We have plenty of things to work on in the meantime. Do you care if we run downstairs to the archives and grab the case file?"

"Perfect." He fished the ring of keys out of his pocket and handed them to her. "Head on down, and fetch what you need. I'll have this wrapped up as soon as I can."

Jess and Sandy took the steps down to the archive room two at a time. Once they let themselves in, Jess moved through the files with her fingertips, accessing the *F*s in search of FOSSKEY, J. En route, she glided over FONTENOT, DWIGHT, and paused.

"What is it?" Sandy asked.

"This name sounds familiar," Jess answered. "Where do I know it from?"

Sandy peeked over her shoulder. "Dwight Fontenot was the sniper's fourth victim. The gas station attendant."

Jess jerked her hand away from the box, as if it might be hot to the touch. "Oh." She quickly resumed her search for the FOSSKEY box. Behind her, Sandy didn't stir.

"You're going to tell me you aren't the least bit curious," Sandy asked.

"Me?" Jess shook her head. "It's not the job. Fosskey is the job."

"I know that's what Aaron said . . ."

"And Aaron was right." Jess's eyes ran up and down the file boxes. "We're considering putting my mother in a home. That's going to cost a lot of money. Money that Story Time Productions can help me make. What happened the other day was wrong. I was out of line."

Sandy didn't buy it. "The Jess Keeler I remember from *Something Bad Wrong* would want to know what's in that box," she said. "In fact, she'd *kill* to see what's in it."

Jess stopped her search. Something in Sandy's voice grabbed her by the soul and shook it. The young woman had a point.

"Maybe just a little peek . . ."

The file was thin, but the first item was a photograph of a man lying face down, half-in and half-out of a service station door. He was dressed as an attendant and had been shot in the back, between the shoulder blades.

The second item was the incident report, filled out by Officer L. M. Axel, which stated that at 15:06, he had answered a call that brought him to the Esso Station on Newton Street. The witnesses claimed Fontenot had been filling up a station wagon when he suddenly started walking toward the front door, where he collapsed. No one saw or heard anything.

The final item was the medical examiner's findings. According to him, the cause of death was a gunshot wound from a .308 round fired from an M40 rifle.

"Are we really doing this?" Sandy asked.

"Shh," Jess answered. "Get your phone."

Sandy reached for her phone and checked over her shoulder. Jess stood between Sandy and the door, blocking the view of anyone who might enter, while Sandy snapped a picture of each document. When she was finished, Jess carefully replaced the file where she had found it, then checked her notes before moving quickly to the *D* files. There, she retrieved the file for DAYE, RONNIE, who had been the sniper's first victim.

They read over each detail, preserving the information with the camera in Sandy's phone. Already, a narrative began to take shape in Jess's head, in a way that was much more dynamic than the Fosskey murders. She stuffed the papers back into the file, then began to retrieve the file for each of the sniper victims—one by one. All in all, there were six of them—five fatalities—and she found it fascinating that the first five shooting victims were nearly identical. All of them had been felled by an unseen assailant. Each of them had been ignored in the press. And all of them had been struck down by a .308 round from an M40 rifle.

"Whoa," breathed Sandy as she sifted through the pages of the last box.

"What is it?" Jess asked, already reaching for them.

"All those similarities end right here."

She was right. Harold "Hal" Broadstreet had been a white man, targeted inside his house. His murder was not ignored, but rather made front-page news and resulted in a citywide manhunt, which netted a suspect, Ricky Lee Patience, who was later convicted of the murders.

"That's not all," said Sandy. She pointed to a particular line in the incident report.

Jess read it. She read it again. She wiped her eyes and had yet another go at it.

It said that Broadstreet had been killed by a .50 round from an M82 rifle.

Jess dropped the papers into the box and stared at it. "If this information is accurate," she whispered, "then it means Broadstreet was killed with a different gun than the other victims."

"According to the articles in the paper," Sandy said, also whispering, "Ricky Lee Patience had never been linked to a single sniper rifle, not to mention *two*."

"You know what this means?"

Sandy answered by nodding silently, her eyes wide and full of understanding.

"We're not going to get any answers by asking Sheriff Axel or Ennis Worthy," Jess said.

"So what do we do?"

Jess considered the question for all of five seconds before she was back on her feet and fingering through the *P* section until she found the file marked PATIENCE, RICKY LEE.

They worked quickly and silently. Jess laid out each page, and Sandy snapped a quick pic of it. They didn't take the time to read because they could do that later. They made it through most of the documents before they heard pounding on the door.

"Hey, ladies," called Axel, through the door, "you have my keys. Could you please open the door?"

Jess quickly shoved the contents back into the file and replaced it. Sandy snatched the FOSSKEY file and jammed it under her arm, then raced to the door and, upon receiving the all clear from Jess, opened it.

"Sorry," Sandy said, "but this stuff is just so engrossing. We couldn't help but lose track of time. Has it already been a half hour?"

Axel glanced over her shoulder at the file cabinets, then said, "It's my fault. There's a lot going on today. Is there any way we can reschedule our interview? I'm needed at the DA's office for that mess over in Whitfill, and I can't get out of it."

"It's really no problem," Jess said. "We were just here looking for some color on the Vandals motorcycle club because there just doesn't seem to be much information anywhere on them. I'd like the script to touch on some of the details, but I've got nothing to go on."

"I tell you what," Axel said. "How about I hook y'all up with Deputy Tate Magaw? She's the detective in our unit who specializes in motorcycle-club activity. She's practically an encyclopedia."

"That would be great!"

Jess thanked him and followed him upstairs so he could set up the meeting between them and the deputy. However, her mind was far from anything concerning outlaw bikers. Instead, her every thought was consumed by the information they had just discovered.

If Harold Broadstreet had been killed with a different gun, that meant there could have been two different killers. The police had to have known this back in 1984, but they prosecuted Ricky Lee Patience anyway.

One look at Sandy and Jess didn't need to be a mind reader to tell she was thinking the exact same thing.

What if Ricky Lee Patience was actually innocent?

CHAPTER THIRTY-FIVE

JESS KEELER

Present Day

When Jess and Sandy returned to their car in the lot of the sheriff's office, the last thought in their minds was the meeting they had scheduled with Tate Magaw, or the info they would soon obtain about the Vandals motorcycle club. In fact, very little occupied their thinking other than how quickly they could get back to their car so they could read the files they'd photographed. It was all they could do to keep from breaking into a run.

"Why don't you drive?" Sandy handed Jess her keys. "That way I can read the files."

Jess cracked a smile. "No chance. Hand me your phone, and let me read them."

"What if I promise to read out loud?"

"I've got the better voice."

It was Sandy's turn to laugh. "How about if we wait until we get somewhere that we can both look at them?"

"How does the All-Niter sound?"

Sandy checked her watch and rolled her eyes. "It sounds like we don't have much choice at this time of day."

"You'll love their chess pie."

Fifteen minutes later they were in a booth at the diner. Sandy had forwarded the photos to Jess, so they sat across from each other in silence with their attentions fixed to their screens. As they scrolled, Jess occasionally jotted down a note on her pad, or Sandy typed into her Notes app. Jess was a regular, so the waitress knew better than to interrupt them and to keep their coffee cups filled.

Sandy finished reading first, but waited patiently for Jess to catch up. When she did, she set down her phone and stared at her yellow tablet for a moment, in order to let her thoughts congeal. The caffeine thrummed a nice hum in her head, but she felt like she could go harder. She'd need to if everything she'd uncovered turned out to be true.

"This is a lot to process," Jess said. "Tell me what you've got."

Sandy read from her Notes app. "Ricky Lee Patience was on the cops' radar before the snipings. We already knew from Wilhelmina Potts that he had been arrested before they picked him up for the shootings, but she didn't have much more detail than that. Now we have those details."

"It says here," Jess said, pointing at her yellow tablet, "that he was picked up for assault and impersonating a police officer. Those are pretty serious charges."

"But he wasn't convicted of them necessarily," said Sandy, "because he was found mentally unfit to stand trial, then was sent to Addams State Mental Hospital."

Jess swallowed her coffee in one gulp. "Right. What's odd, though, is the amount of time he spent there. Did you see that?"

"Yes." Sandy double-checked her notes. "Three weeks."

"Three weeks for an assault charge? For impersonating police?"

"That sounds pretty light, right?"

"When remanded to a state hospital, you are kept there until you are deemed fit to return to society, as opposed to being sentenced for time served in the state prison system. Still, I find it hard to believe that he was unfit enough to stand trial, but three weeks later would be released."

"You think something shady happened?"

Jess gave her a glance that answered that question in the affirmative.

Sandy scrolled through her notes, then the photographs of the files.

"What are you looking for?" Jess asked.

"Trying to find out which doctor was in charge of Ricky Lee's care at Addams."

"It was Dr. Jonas Stephens." Jess turned around her clipboard so Sandy could better see. "Maybe we should make an appointment."

Sandy was already typing into her phone. Jess motioned for a coffee refill. The waitress delivered it with a warm smile.

"How is your son, Dotty?" Jess asked her.

"Still a handful," answered the waitress. "How about your momma?"

"Don't get me started."

The waitress placed a hand on her shoulder. "You tell her I said hello, will you?"

"I will," she said.

After the waitress walked away, Sandy slapped the top of the table. "Of all the rotten luck."

"What is it?"

"There's plenty on the internet about Dr. Jonas Stephens . . ."

"That's good."

". . . including his obituary."

Jess sighed. "That's not."

Sandy showed the image on her phone of a smiling man with a snow-white beard wearing a lab coat. He was flanked on both sides by a squadron of about two dozen nurses.

"Maybe someone at the state hospital would have some more information about Ricky Lee's quick release," Jess offered.

"Maybe they would," said Sandy, "if the hospital hadn't been shuttered back in 2008."

Maybe it was the coffee, but Jess found it nearly impossible to sit still. No, she told herself, it wasn't the coffee. It was the *feeling*. She had it. She remembered it well from her previous investigation. That *feeling* when she knew she was on the right trail, following the right clues, inches away from something and not knowing exactly what it was.

They were getting close.

"How about," said Jess, pointing to the picture on Sandy's phone, "we ask one of *them*?"

Sandy turned the phone to look at it, then smiled. "You mean one of the nurses?"

Jess nodded.

"I'll start tracking them down as soon as I get home." Sandy set her phone down on the table for the first time since they'd arrived. She leaned back in her seat and took a breath. She looked around the room, as if seeing it for the first time, then settled her gaze back on Jess.

"What is it?" Jess asked.

"That was fun back there." The overhead lights twinkled in Sandy's eyes. "At the sheriff's office. You and me."

"It was," said Jess. "For a minute there, it was like having a . . ."

She stopped herself before she said anything more.

"A sister?" Sandy's smile grew wider. "I've never had one of those, but yeah, I guess that's what it might be like."

"I'm old enough to be your mother."

"I've had one of those." Sandy's smile twisted to one side of her face. "Trust me, you're nothing like her."

"I was going to say that it was like having a *partner*."

Sandy's face fell, and Jess knew what she was thinking. Everyone had heard what had happened to Jess's partner, Dan Decker, while investigating for the *Something Bad Wrong* podcast. Jess never talked about it publicly. She felt by not addressing it with Sandy, she might betray the bond they had just shared. She wanted, more than anything, to tell the girl *yes, my partner was killed. We were pursuing a suspect believed to have committed a double homicide years earlier, and during that pursuit, Dan Decker had been murdered. I survived to tell the story, and sometimes I feel guilty about that. It would serve us both well to remember that because this is dangerous work.*

Jess wanted to tell Sandy those things, but didn't. Instead, she reached across the table and squeezed her wrist.

"I like *sister* better," Jess told her. "I've never had one of those either."

CHAPTER THIRTY-SIX

HAL BROADSTREET

1984

Hal called around to the station, asked after Officer Lorne Axel. The dispatcher said he was on patrol. He asked which beat, and they asked who was inquiring. Hal identified himself, and the line promptly disengaged.

He spent the better part of the next hour cruising the streets of Lake Castor, dialed into his scanner, until he sniffed out a lead. Once he gathered coordinates, he stepped on the gas and gunned his El Camino into the east end of the Back Back.

That's where he found Lorne Axel and his partner. They had cordoned off the neighborhood's basketball court with crime scene tape and stood guard over the body of a young man who lay in a pool of his own blood just shy of the three-point line. They were the only white faces among a gathering crowd of angry citizens.

"Come on, man," shouted one man at the cops. "It's been over an hour. Y'all just going to leave him there?"

Shouted a concerned woman, "Why don't y'all put a sheet over him or something?"

"Man, fuck the police," muttered still another.

Hal gently elbowed his way through them, arriving just shy of the tape, and motioned to Axel. Axel cut eyes at his partner, an overweight, middle-aged cop named Stokes, then moseyed over to the reporter.

"What gives?" Hal asked him.

"According to witnesses," Axel said, "our victim was playing basketball with three other individuals when he collapsed onto the court, where you see him now. They rolled him over and found he had been shot in the chest."

Hal scanned the crowd and saw three taller gentlemen in gym clothes. "I reckon if they were guilty, they would be long gone by now."

"They didn't do it," said Axel, "but they ain't saying who did."

"Who's the victim?"

"His name is Quincy Williams. He's a local boy, but attends Central University down in Durham. Home for summer break."

"Let me guess: nobody saw nothing, nobody heard nothing."

Axel shrugged. "A couple folks heard a shot. A couple folks didn't. But yeah, nobody I've talked to has seen a shooter."

"Sounds familiar," Hal grumped. He was being cynical, but then realized it *should* sound familiar. "Same thing happened a few days back with Ronnie Daye. You hear about that? He was shot in broad daylight, and nobody saw anything."

Axel's partner, Tommy Stokes, approached them. "What happened to Ronnie Daye was a reckoning, a long time coming. Of course nobody saw nothing. They know what would happen if they did."

"Ease up, Stokes," Axel muttered.

"You act like it's an anomaly," said his partner. "They *never* see nothing. It's a tale as old as time. These animals detest law and order. You cross Sylvan Street, and all of a sudden, it's the rule of the jungle."

Hal motioned toward the body. "What's the holdup? Where are the detectives?"

"Who knows," said Axel. "We called in over an hour ago."

"If you ask me," said Stokes, "they heard the address and decided they ain't going to slap on any roller skates. Take their sweet time. Just another shooting in the Back Back."

Hal looked toward the body, then the crowd of people growing more impatient. The sun overhead climbed even higher. He thought of the condition of the body and the speed at which the summer heat would deteriorate it.

"If you ask me, I blame it on that new synthetic cocaine," said Stokes. "It's turning them against each other. You hear about that stuff? They actually found a way to make cocaine stronger and cheaper. The only problem is, it's fifty times more addictive, and it's turning them into animals."

"Shut up, Stokes," hissed Axel. "You want to get us killed?"

"I'm just reporting facts," Stokes argued. "It turns their women into hookers and their children into killers. They got mothers leaving their children, and we're supposed to act surprised when they—"

"*Goddammit*, shut the hell up." Axel tensed, standing straighter, trying to remain a stoic presence, but Hal could feel the panic wafting off him as he checked his watch and once again scanned the horizon for the detectives or the medical examiner.

"Hey, Lorne," said Hal, "I know this is probably a bad time, but I wanted to run something by you."

Axel cut eyes again toward his partner, whose face registered displeasure. Despite that (or maybe *because* of it), Axel stepped aside to confer with the reporter.

"What have you heard on the bikers?" Hal asked.

Axel's expression was flat. "What bikers?"

"The ones you pulled over after the murders at Fosskey's?"

"Dammit, Broadstreet." Axel threw up his hands. "You're still on about that? That was over a month ago. I don't know if you've noticed, but this summer has enjoyed no shortage of murders. One of which, in case you've forgotten, is your number one suspect for that shit that happened up at Fosskey's."

"Sure, Digger is dead. But those other two are out there. Aren't you even looking for them?"

"Me?" Axel liked to have split a gut laughing. "I can't even get the detectives to care about *this* murder. You think I'm going to get them to chase after two bikers they wouldn't be able to hold anyway?"

"I've got a witness."

Axel's eyes narrowed, seemed to take him in a little differently. "What do you mean you have a witness?"

"I mean there was someone else in Fosskey's apartment who saw the whole thing."

"How are they still alive?"

"They were hiding in a closet."

"Who was it?"

Hal shook his head. "I'll get him to testify once you bring Dickerson and Charlie Chains in for murder."

"Not going to happen." Axel's expression remained impassive. Behind them, a woman started to lead a chant demanding justice for the dead kid on the basketball court. "Nobody's looking for them."

Hal clicked his pen shut. He took a final look at the growing mob behind them and at the body of the poor son of a bitch on the basketball court.

"Thank you, Officer Axel," he said.

Axel was confused. "That's it?"

"You said you got nothing, so you got nothing." Hal turned and headed for his El Camino.

"It's not like you to give up so easy."

"My editor told me to get a quote from law enforcement," Hal called over his shoulder. "You gave me one."

CHAPTER THIRTY-SEVEN

JESS KEELER

Present Day

Jess had just driven across the Richmond city limits when her phone rang. The screen read AARON CAMERA. Her sigh was audible over her music, which she had cranked up loud. She activated her Bluetooth, so she could answer hands-free.

His voice filled the car. "Hey, Keeler, where are you?"

"I'm prepping for tomorrow's interview with Lawles County's biker-gang liaison, Deputy Tate Magaw," she lied. "If we want to get the best content out of her, we're going to need to have all the background we can muster on these outlaw motorcycle clubs. But don't worry . . . I'm on it."

"Is Sandy with you?"

"No . . ."

"Because she told me she was doing the exact same thing."

Jess thought quick. "She is. I'm researching the Vandals, and she's digging up everything she can on their rivals, the Rare Breed."

This, of course, was another lie. Jess and Sandy had tracked down every nurse in the photo with Dr. Jonas Stephens outside Addams State Mental Hospital. There were nineteen in total. Light internet research revealed that twelve of them had passed away. The remaining seven had retired and scattered across the state. Jess and Sandy had placed calls to each of them, but when there were no answers, their plan was to knock on doors and speak to them in person.

They'd split up the list. Sandy took the nurses on the coast, with stops in Virginia Beach, Newport News, and Mathews. Jess had two addresses in Richmond and one each in Fredericksburg and Charlottesville.

They had only one day.

"This is important," Aaron reminded her. "Felix and Friedrich have lined up a meeting with a top-tier streaming service, and they want to see footage. We need something that pops."

"Got it," Jess said, her eyes fixed on the road. *"Pops."*

"I'm serious, Keeler. Right now, we're far from a hundred percent. We need content that sings. When we sit down with this deputy tomorrow, I want her to give us information that buries these three suspects. I need her to say the words."

"And if she won't?"

"It's your job to ask the questions in a way that gives me their heads." Aaron cleared his throat without moving his mouth from the receiver. "They're dead anyway. What's it going to matter?"

Jess breathed in through her nose and held it while she followed her navigation system's directions toward the off-ramp.

"So stay on target tomorrow," Aaron said. "No detours, no zigzagging . . . nothing like what happened with Oliv—"

"Aaron," she said quickly, "I've got another line. I need to call you back."

That was not a lie. Her screen had flashed alive with an unknown number. The 540 area code betrayed it as coming from the Fredericksburg area, which Jess knew was home to one of the nurses on her list. She disengaged the call with Aaron and clicked on with the second call.

"Ms. Shapiro," she said, "this is Jess Keeler. Thank you so much for calling me back."

The voice on the speaker was quiet. Frail. "Well . . . you were quite persistent. You liked to have filled up my answering machine."

"I wouldn't bother you if it wasn't important," Jess said. "Listen, I'm pulling into Richmond now. I could be in Fredericksburg in an hour, hour and a half. Can we meet? I'd really like to—"

"What's all this about?"

"It's better if I tell you in person."

"It's not better for me."

Jess maneuvered off the highway. She came to a stop at a light. "Ms. Shapiro . . . May I call you Claudette?"

"Will you just tell me what you want?"

"I'm working on a story about Addams State Hospital," Jess said. "You worked there in the 1980s, am I right?"

"You are, but I don't see why that would—"

"Did you work with Dr. Jonas Stephens?"

There was silence on the other end of the line. Behind her, a car honked. Jess realized the light had long ago turned green. She moved through the intersection and found a paid parking lot.

"Claudette?" she said. "Ms. Shapiro, are you still there?"

The voice was thin and reedy. "I am."

"I was asking about Dr. Jonas Ste—"

"I really shouldn't be talking to you."

Jess was losing her. She spoke faster. "We can talk off the record, Ms. Shapiro. Your name doesn't have to be written down anywhere. I just want to ask a couple of questions about your time there."

"You said you were writing a *story*. What kind of story would anyone be writing about Dr. Stephens's work after all these years?"

"Ms. Shapiro, do you remember a patient named Ricky Lee Patience?"

The line went silent for so long, Jess thought the woman had hung up.

"Ms. Shapiro?"

"Please don't call me again."

That time, the line was disengaged. Jess leaned into the bag on the passenger seat and retrieved her clipboard. She crossed off the name CLAUDETTE SHAPIRO.

Jess knew better than to expect any different outcome. Her work on her podcast had required her to try and interview medical professionals. That experience revealed that doctors and nurses could be very tight lipped and not forthcoming when it came to discussing the sins of yesteryear. Jess had yet to determine whether they were afraid of shame or litigation, but knew they weren't easy to get talking.

When she slipped her car back into gear, she realized where she was. Across the street from the pay lot was a public park. The entrance was an archway, and at the top of the arch were the words **ADDAMS PARK**. She killed the engine and walked to the plaque standing right in front of it.

THIS PARK WAS DEDICATED BY ADDAMS STATE HOSPITAL TRUSTEES IN 2010.

"Two years after the hospital closed," she murmured to herself.

Jess was halfway back to her car when her phone rang. Her screen read SANDY NEWMAN.

"Where are you?" Sandy asked before Jess could say a word.

"Richmond," Jess answered. "The nurse in Fredericksburg is a bust, and I'm not getting any response from any of the Richmond nurses. I figure I can knock on one more door out here before heading out to Charlot—"

"Forget all that," Sandy said. "I've got something big."

"How big?"

"Texas big," she said. "Scratch that: Great Wall of China big."

"So spill it."

Jess could hear the playfulness in Sandy's voice. "Not a chance," she said. "You need to hear this in person."

"Where are you?"

"I'm driving in from the coast. There's a truck stop off the highway halfway between here and Richmond. I'll text you the address."

Jess had already started the car and headed for the highway.

CHAPTER THIRTY-EIGHT

Jess Keeler

Present Day

They met at a truck stop off a lazy Virginia highway between Richmond and the coast. Sandy found a table near the back while Jess wrangled them two cups of coffee. Traffic was light. Jess took one of the earbuds from Sandy's phone, and Sandy took the other. Sandy held her finger over the screen for a moment until Jess glanced up and they locked eyes.

Jess nodded.

"Play it."

[The camera brings the viewer closer to the front door of a neatly manicured home. Sandy's hand reaches into frame and knocks on the door. After a moment, it is answered, and we are looking at the kind face of KIM LIU, a small woman in her late sixties or early seventies.]

KIM LIU: Hello?

SANDY: Hi, Ms. Liu?

KIM: Yes?

SANDY: My name is Sandy Newman. I'm the reporter that reached out to you over the phone.

KIM: Oh, yes! Yes! Hi, I'm Kim.

SANDY: As I told you over the phone, I'm part of a team that is producing a program on the history of mental health treatment, how far we've come, where all we have left to go . . . all that . . . and we've been researching some of the top state hospitals and sanatoriums from the time.

KIM: That sounds like such an interesting project.

SANDY: It's a lot, believe me. The way we, like, view mental health as a culture, you know, has changed in many ways from the old days.

KIM: And, in many ways, it hasn't.

SANDY: Exactly! That's the kind of insight which will be invaluable to our research.

KIM: Would you like to come in? I can make us some tea.

SANDY: That would be amazing!

[Ms. Liu holds open the door and allows Sandy to enter. The home is modestly decorated. Sandy is led into a sitting room.]

KIM: I don't get many visitors these days. I was part of the Kiwanis Club for a—

Sandy rolls her eyes. "For the next—I don't know—fifteen minutes or so, she goes on and on about all the stuff she was into and all the local boards she sat on or chaired. This lady liked to keep busy."

"You lied to her about why you were interviewing her?" Jess asked.

"I got in the door," said Sandy defensively. "Besides, it was something I learned from you by listening to your podcast. Isn't that how you got the killer to speak with you in *Something Bad Wrong*?"

"That was different." Jess wasn't sure how, or if, that was even true. "Still, we shouldn't do that."

Sandy stifled a laugh. She scrolled through the video until she found what she was looking for.

"You got your seat belt fastened?"

She pressed play.

KIM: —managed to advance research into mental health, which was quite impressive, given our shortcomings.

SANDY: What do you mean by shortcomings?

KIM: *Oh, the usual. Lack of resources. Limited public understanding of mental health challenges. Bureaucratic inefficiencies which made rapid innovation next to impossible.*

SANDY: *During your time there, were there any particular physicians who you felt like were standouts in their field?*

KIM: *Oh, most certainly. While many of the top researchers ended up in the private sector or chasing more noteworthy positions overseas, Addams still managed to lure some extremely creative professionals.*

SANDY: *Like Dr. Jonas Stephens?*

[Ms. Liu answers by closing her mouth tightly. Her eyes don't blink.]

SANDY: *What is it, Ms. Liu? Was it something I said?*

KIM: *No, dear. It's just . . .*

SANDY: *Please . . . tell me about Dr. Stephens.*

KIM: *[A beat . . . then an audible sigh.]*

SANDY: *Dr. Stephens was employed by Addams between the years of . . . oh, give me one second . . . 1983 and 1985. That's not a very long time, is it?*

KIM: *No. It isn't.*

SANDY: *In fact, his tenure there was easily one of the shorter ones. Is it because he was chasing a more lucrative position elsewhere?*

[SILENCE]

SANDY: *Did something happen?*

KIM: *[EXHALES] Some of the medical professionals who passed through the doors at Addams had some controversial applications to what had been an unsolvable problem.*

SANDY: *Like what?*

KIM: *I really shouldn't be discussing any of this. I don't see how it would relate to your study.*

SANDY: *You know . . . he's long gone, Ms. Liu. I see he passed in 19—*

KIM: *I was raised to never speak ill of the dead.*

SANDY: *Is that what this is? Speaking ill? If he was pursuing what he thought was his own justified philosophy, then wouldn't you be defending him?*

[SILENT MOMENT]

KIM: Dr. Stephens was a proponent of electroconvulsive therapy. Are you familiar with it?

SANDY: Do you mean shock treatment?

KIM: I suppose, but that lends itself to what I was saying earlier about limited public understanding. Although the practice, at the time, was somewhat controversial—and it was very much brutal and barbaric—Dr. Stephens had decades of research and studies which argued for its efficacy.

SANDY: What sorts of mental illnesses did Dr. Stephens believe shock tre—er, electroconvulsive therapy could treat?

KIM: Oh, so many of them. Depression. Anxiety. Bipolar disorder. Schizophrenia. Dr. Stephens argued it was applicable for everything from psychopathic tendencies to the cessation of habits, such as smoking.

SANDY: Jesus . . .

[SILENCE]

SANDY: I'm gathering that you weren't exactly a fan of those treatments.

KIM: Like I said . . . barbaric.

SANDY: When a patient would be remanded to Addams by the courts, how long was a typical stay when they were under the care of Dr. Stephens and his controversial therapies?

KIM: It could vary. Sometimes they were kept there indefinitely. Sometimes, only months. As stated in sentencing, it was up to the discretion and judgment of the hospital.

SANDY: Could a patient who was sentenced there by the court be released after a mere three weeks?

KIM: That would be highly unusual. Typically the intake process would be very involved. We would need at least that much time for observation.

SANDY: But could it?

KIM: I suppose. It would depend.

SANDY: On what?

KIM: The level of treatment. You see, Dr. Stephens was a publishing doctor. He had several theories, and he was constantly testing them. If his

argument was that ECT could treat schizophrenia, then he would need a
fresh subject upon whom he might steadily increase the dosage.

SANDY: And then?

KIM: And then the dosage could run so high that the subject might no
longer be of value to him.

SANDY: Because he'd shocked them too much?

KIM: That's not how I would phrase it, but in a sense, yes.

SANDY: So the doctor was experimenting on patients who were sen-
tenced to Addams?

KIM: This practice was common in state hospitals across the nation, as
I'm sure you have discovered in your research on . . . What did you say your
study was about again?

SANDY: Let me see if I've got this right . . . these subjects had com-
mitted a crime and were found mentally unfit to stand trial. This would
be determined by a physician who testified for the state, like Dr. Stephens.
They would be sentenced to the care of a physician at Addams—like Dr.
Stephens—who would then experiment upon them to further his own stud-
ies. And then when that subject was of no more use to his experiments, Dr.
Stephens would simply release them back onto the streets?

KIM: Yes. Again, I would phrase it differently, but essentially, that's
exactly what happened.

SANDY: How the hell could he justify doing such a thing?

KIM: To make room for new subjects.

[SILENCE]

KIM: And, dear, there were always new subjects.

Sandy pressed stop.

Jess removed the earbud from her ear and turned her face to the
window.

Neither woman spoke a word for the next ten minutes. The silence
seemed more profound after it had been shattered.

"What do you think Aaron will say when he sees this?" Sandy
asked, seemingly breathless. "Or better yet, the Germans?"

Jess thought it over before she answered. "We can't tell them. Not yet."

"But this is much bigger now," said Sandy. "Bigger than us."

"Which is exactly why we can't go to them with it."

"I don't understand," Sandy said. "We just got documentation that Ricky Lee was brutalized by the psychiatric system. Even if he *did* commit the murders, which I question now more than ever, we can prove that he was far, far from his right mind when they happened."

Jess chose her words carefully. She felt like she was walking on unsure ground. Like any minute, the wrong word may send her through a trapdoor.

"Sandy," she said slowly, "if we go to the Germans with this, I fear they may bury it so deep that we'll never be able to uncover it. They want to paint Ricky Lee as some deranged serial killer. They could twist this information to support their narrative, and if that happens, we would never be able to get the wine back into the bottle. Right now, we have the truth. We need to protect and defend it."

"So what do you propose we do?"

Again, a long silence.

"We sit on it. For now." Jess felt the electricity crackle. "We'll keep working on the Fosskey case, like good little girls, but when the opportunity presents itself . . ."

Sandy was already feeling it.

". . . we jump."

CHAPTER THIRTY-NINE

HAL BROADSTREET

1984

Hal sat down at his desk in the *Times* office to write his exposé on the Vandals motorcycle club and their connection to the Fosskey murders. Once upon a time, the room would have been filled with the sound of the hammers smacking and clicking the ribbons, or the rings of the carriages, but now it was only him and his typewriter. To keep him company while he worked, he often turned on the police scanner. He'd half listen, filling the silence with the cadence of the dispatcher's calls. They would fall into a rhythm, and when finally he realized he'd heard something of interest, it was too late.

He grabbed the scanner and pulled it closer.

"What did you say?" he asked it, as if it could possibly repeat itself. It did.

"Repeat: Homicide victim on the 800 block of McCorkle. Victim ID: Moulton, Clarence. Negro. Approximately six—"

Hal was already dialing the phone. It rang once. Rang a second time. On the third—

"Lake Castor Police, how can we dir—"

"I just heard over the scanner that there's been a homicide near the intersection of Loftin and McCorkle," Hal shouted into the phone. "Can you—"

"Sir, I'm going to have to ask you to remain calm. Is this an emergency?"

"No, dammit. I'm trying to get information about a homicide. I just heard that—"

"Sir, I'm going to have to ask you to calm down and speak more slowly. Can you please rep—"

"My name is Hal Broadstreet, and I work for the *Lake Cas*—"

"Did you say *Broadstreet?*"

"Yes. I'm a reporter for the—"

The line disconnected.

Hal didn't wait to call back. Instead, he leaped behind the wheel of his El Camino and ripped across Lake Castor, picking up speed once he hit the Back Back. He careened down its potholed streets, remarking on how few people were populating them, until he arrived finally at Loftin and McCorkle. He tamped his speed, but not his urgency. Scanning the urban landscape for any sign of police activity, any sign of disturbance, keeping his eyes peeled until—

Aha.

He made out the red and blue lights oscillating across the face of a shuttered three-story building. Hal hit the brakes hard. He threw open his door and abandoned his vehicle in the street.

The medical examiner's technicians loaded the body into the back of a marked van. The only onlookers were two uniformed cops who noted Hal's panic with light amusement.

"Wait, stop!" Hal shouted at the technicians manning the gurney. "Let me see him."

They paused, and Hal caught up with them. "Sir, we have to ask you to—"

"I think this is a friend of mine," he said, out of breath. "Can you unzip the . . ." Hal couldn't finish the words.

"It's not necessary," the tech explained, with a soft smile. "He's already been identified. His niece was—"

"Please let me see him!"

Realizing how unhinged he appeared, Hal quickly took a breath and showed both hands, as a gesture of apology. The two uniformed officers appeared less bemused and more interested, with one of them placing a hand on the cuffs at his belt, the other speaking into his radio.

Hal unzipped the bag and caught a look at Clarence Moulton or, more intimately, Uncle Meaney, the man he had *known* as Uncle Meaney, the man who cooked the best hooch anyone in Lake Castor had ever tasted. Hell, Hal thought absently, as sort of a memoriam, Uncle Meaney could stand his worst corn against the best Kentucky had to offer and still hold his head pretty damned high.

But not anymore.

No longer, because it wasn't Uncle Meaney zipped into that bag, but rather, the remains of *Clarence Moulton.* Someone's son. Someone's uncle.

Someone's friend.

Hal found himself gripping the thick plastic of the bag with both his hands and wondered when all of it might stop. First Jem and the boys, now Uncle Meaney. Added to the loss of Ronnie Daye—although they had only a passing acquaintance in courtrooms as a journalist and a heroin dealer, respectively—and it would seem that someone was taking them all out . . .

. . . and no one could be bothered to give a rolling goddamn.

Hal spun on his heels and crossed the makeshift crime scene. His target: an elderly Black man watching the proceedings with limited interest. Hal braced him, stopping only inches from the elder man's nose.

"What happened?" Hal demanded.

The older man appeared to have no interest in Hal. He averted his eyes, focusing instead on something farther away.

"Hey, pal. I asked you a question." He had never spoken to someone like this in his life, but desperation crept in on him. "Tell me what the hell happened to him."

"I didn't see nothing," said the old man.

Hal laughed wryly. "Of *course*. You didn't see nothing. You didn't hear nothing. It's like it didn't happen, because none of you people see a goddamn thing."

The older man jerked, as if on a string, at the words *you people*. His eyes cut toward Hal and bled something like *hate* from them. Hal shifted some of that vitriol toward the cops.

"And *you*," he said, pointing a finger at one of the officers. "What the hell are you going to do to solve this?"

"Watch your tone, buddy," said the cop.

"What if I don't?" Hal spat. "Are you actually going to get off your ass and do something? I highly doubt that. Because if it's not rousting Blacks and la—"

The cops moved in, but were stalled by the appearance of another in their ranks. Lorne Axel had arrived on the scene, his patrol car spinning lights, his partner waiting in the shotgun seat.

"Hang on, guys," called Axel to the advancing patrolmen. "He's with me." He approached Hal. "What the hell is go—"

"Was it you?" Hal searched Axel's face for any clues. "Tell me the truth, Lorne. Was it you?"

"Was it me, what?"

"Did you tell them I had a witness? Did you tell them about Uncle Meaney?"

Axel's eyes went to the man in the gurney being loaded into the ME's van. "I didn't tell anybody anything, Hal."

"He was my witness," Hal said, trying to hold it together. "He was my friend."

"It wasn't me, Hal. I didn't even know."

"He was my *friend*."

"Maybe . . ." Axel searched for the words. "Maybe you told some-body else?"

Hal wanted to punch someone. He wanted to lash out and exact revenge for Jem, for Uncle Meaney, for everyone whose death was left uninvestigated. But he knew it would bring no one back.

Still, a pervasive thought festered in his mind.

He *had* told someone else.

Hal shoved past Axel and got into his car. He turned it around to drive out of the Back Back and toward the offices of the *Times*.

He had some questions he needed to ask his editor.

CHAPTER FORTY

HAL BROADSTREET

1984

Vince Fenelli lived in one of the last developments to be built in Lake Castor, before the mill shut down and all the real estate went belly up. The Trenholm Farms subdivision was intended to house the city's well-to-do but, in the end, remained only partially constructed. Vince and his family had been one of the first to move in.

Oddly enough, they had also been one of the last.

Hal waited for him on his front porch, sitting on a lawn chair and balancing a baseball bat in his lap. He'd been there quite a while before he heard the throaty growl of Vince's cherry red Camaro Z28 slipping into the driveway. It wasn't until he heard the engine quit its purr that he finally rose from the chair, just in time to catch Vince rounding the hedges with a sandwich in his mouth.

"Hal . . . What the—" Vince stopped short. His eyes cut from Hal to the bat, then back to Hal. "Is everything okay, buddy?"

"Was it you?"

Vince's face was the personification of a question mark. "What are you talking about?"

"Dammit, Vince." Hal grabbed the sandwich from his editor's mouth and threw it against the wall so hard that it rained down ham, cheese, and lettuce upon his sidewalk. "Answer me: Was. It. You?"

"Hal, I swear . . . I have no idea what you—"

"Did you hear about Clarence Moulton?"

"Who?"

"The man who was shot today in the Back Back."

Vince's face registered nothing.

"Today, Vince. A man was shot in the Back Back."

"I mean, Hal . . ." Vince tried a smile on for size. "That's *hardly* news."

"It is if he was the only witness to Lake Castor's bloodiest massacre."

Vince's confusion gave way to realization.

"Wait . . ." He got it. "So that was . . ."

"Uncle Meaney," said Hal. "My source."

"Oh, my . . ."

Vince looked for somewhere to sit. He would have to cross Hal and his baseball bat to reach the lawn chairs, but didn't appear to want to do that. Instead, he steadied himself by reaching his hand for the wall.

"So, Vince," said Hal. "Who did you tell?"

"I didn't tell anybody, Hal. You think I'm crazy? I wouldn't do that. This story is everything to you, and I know it. Hell, it's everything to the *paper*. I would nev—wait . . . Where are you going?"

Hal rested the bat on his shoulder and walked off the porch toward the driveway. Vince trailed after him. Hal stopped at the front of Vince's car and tapped the bat against the bumper.

"Hal . . ." Vince didn't like it. Not one bit. "Hal, what are you—"

Hal's swing was low and sweet, like Ryne Sandberg's, driving the wood into Vince's driver's side headlamp. Glass sprinkled the driveway, unheard due to Vince's hysterics.

"Hal, you motherfu—"

Hal crossed the front of the car, coming to rest before the passenger side. He cocked the bat again on his right shoulder and tested a couple of practice swings.

"Who did you tell, Vince?"

Vince's energy was frenetic, panicked. "Trust me, buddy. I would nev—"

His words were interrupted by the sound of bat against headlamp.

"Please stop!" Vince dropped to his knees, his eyes unable to part from his car. "Are you happy now? You've ruined her!"

"Not even close, Vince." Hal pointed the bat toward the windshield. "Batter up!"

"No! Wait!" Vince spoke quickly, before the assault could continue. "Dammit, Hal. I talked to Dorritt. Okay? I talked to Dorritt."

Hal rested the bat on his shoulder. "Captain Dorritt?"

"Yes. I told you I was going to get a quote from downtown. He asked what we had, and . . . well, he asked . . ."

"You told the captain of Crimes Against Persons my source?"

"I . . . uh . . ."

"Vince . . ."

"I had to, Hal."

"No, you didn't." Hal's grip tightened on the handle. "You absolutely didn't."

"I did. He—"

"What did they offer you?"

"*Offer me?*" Vince's eyes were wild. "Hey, look, buddy . . . I see you're upset, but what makes you think anybody offered me anything?"

"What did you trade them for Uncle Meaney's life, you fucking cockroach?"

"Hal, that's not what I—"

Hal drove the Louisville Slugger straight into the Camaro's windshield. It didn't break, so Hal struggled to free the bat from the safety glass. Once he did, however, he geared up for another swing.

"Goddammit, Hal." Vince was resigned. There was nothing left to fight for. "Fine. You know what? I get it now. I see why everyone hates you. Why no one can stand the sight of you. You operate on your own morality and weaponize it against the rest of the world. You claim these high standards of journalism, but you, yourself, don't even follow them, nor do you give one shit about playing in the same sandbox with everyone else. It's not you against the rest of the world, Hal. It's just you. The rest of the world is over it."

Hal barely listened. Those words, he reckoned, would register later.

"Hey, Vince," he said, "skip to the part where you sold me out."

"Where do you get off accusing me of anything?" Vince was gathering his oats. "Your brain is so wired with Dealey Plaza–style conspiracies that you can't see the forest for the trees. Okay, so I spilled your man's name to Dorritt. The guy turns up dead in the Back Back. One plus one does not always make two, Hal."

"No editor worth his salt would sell out his paper's journalist to the cops unless he was getting something good in return. So what was it?"

"We're not a *newspaper*." Vince grimaced, as if he might be sick to his stomach. "Not anymore, we aren't. We're a scandal sheet. A *tabloid*. And you're not a journalist. Maybe you used to be, but not anymore."

"Is that right?" Hal cocked the bat. "Tell me what I am then, Vince."

"Put that bat down, and I will."

"Say it."

Vince gave in. "You're a joke, Hal. Get it? You're a goddamn joke, so yeah. I told Dorritt. And in return, he's going to feed us daily commentary on the crime blotter and a daily column coming out of Crimes Against Persons. There's a turf war heating up between two biker gangs, and he's promised us insight on that."

"So you're going to promote propaganda?"

"Grow up, Hal. Not everything is Area 51. Some things just are what they are."

Hal hitched the bat. He wanted to smash the windshield, the side panel, every window. He didn't because he realized that would never be enough for him. He could set fire to Vince's Camaro, but even reducing it to a charred, smoking frame would never, ever deliver him the satisfaction he needed.

Instead, he dropped the bat.

"I'm not going to be your Walter Winchell."

"Hal, come on . . ."

Hal turned on his heel and left.

"Where are you going, Hal?"

Hal ignored him.

"What are you going to do?"

Hal didn't stop until he reached his El Camino. He slipped inside and fired up the engine. Gunned it until he was off Vince's street and out of Trenholm Farms. He didn't know if he could call himself a journalist, and furthermore, he didn't know if he cared. Instead, he centered all his focus on the single fact he did for sure know.

One way or another he was going to burn them all.

CHAPTER FORTY-ONE

Jess Keeler

Present Day

Sheriff Axel allowed the crew into the chamber reserved for press conferences. A long meeting table cut the room in half. Jess sat on one side. Behind her, Sandy fed questions into a microphone that relayed into a bud in Jess's ear. Buffy manned a shotgun mic. Aaron positioned two cameras at different angles.

Deputy Tate Magaw sat across from Jess. She was in her midforties and wore her brown uniform and badge. She appeared surprisingly assured. Jess's experience interviewing law enforcement officers taught her that it took them a good bit to relax in the presence of journalists. Magaw appeared confident from jump street.

"I hear you're the one to talk to about Lake Castor's biker gangs," said Jess.

"The preferred nomenclature is outlaw motorcycle *clubs*." Magaw tucked a blonde lock of hair behind her ear. "I'm certain there are more qualified than me, but I'm happy to answer whatever I can."

"We can start by asking why Sheriff Axel believes you might be the authority."

Magaw offered an aw-shucks smile. "I guess I'd have to blame my daddy."

"He was a cop?"

"No. He used to ride."

"Your father was in a motorcycle ga—er, *club*?"

Magaw nodded. "He sure was. When I was a little girl, he rode with a crew called the Regulators who used to go on runs with the Blood Ravens, who later became the Vandals. He wasn't so much into the drugs and stuff, or so he told me. Who can really be sure? But I became acquainted with some of those boys. Still am, as a matter of fact."

"They don't have a problem with your daddy's daughter wearing a badge?"

"Naw," she said. "They go about their own business and respect I got to go about mine. It's a big enough county for both of us."

"But they definitely know who you are?"

"I was sitting on a barstool, drinking a longneck at Crazy Eights last night," said Magaw. "That's a damn good way to make sure they keep things on the up-and-up, if you ask me."

Jess liked her. Magaw had the proper ratio of sass to confidence that could put people at ease.

"Most of these boys are legit now anyway," Magaw explained. "Nowadays, our local MCs have traded in their leather cuts for suits and ties. Most of their businesses are legitimate, like Crazy Eights, or the Public Hardware store downtown, or any number of other business holdings."

"So the outlaw clubs are hardly outlaws anymore?"

"Oh, I didn't say that," Magaw said. "They still get their fingers plenty dirty. They still have interests in internet gaming, human trafficking, and drugs. But they ain't near as rowdy as they used to be."

For the next ten minutes, Deputy Magaw spilled the tea on how things *used to be*. Jess tried to narrow her focus to the detailed tutorial of motorcycle clubs in the area, but her mind kept drifting back to what she and Sandy had discovered while hunting Addams nurses. She understood that linking the Fosskey murders to the Vandals was the job she was paid to do, but what stoked her passionate curiosity was trying to find out if Ricky Lee Patience had been conditioned in that hospital to kill, or if he had been framed, and why.

"Where are you, Jess?" whispered Sandy's voice through the earbud. "You're letting her ramble."

Jess snapped to suddenly and found Deputy Magaw was still talking.

". . . veterans came home from Korea and were still chasing the combat highs and camaraderie from the war. They killed both them birds by starting a motorcycle club more akin to the infamous Hells Angels. I'm not sure why they chose the name Blood Ravens. They formed alliances with some clubs, like my daddy's Regulators, but developed rivalries with other, more violent groups."

Jess got her head back in the game. "You're talking about the Rare Breed?"

"Yes," said Magaw. "They were an outfit from the coast. They were numerically superior, more armed, and better financed than the Blood Ravens, which is the reason why they heard offers to incorporate with more established clubs like the Hells Angels, Outlaws, and the Vandals. Those clubs were envious of the Ravens' position on highly lucrative drug routes between New York and Miami. So, in 1983, the Blood Ravens patched over with the Vandals, and what began as a group of motorcycle enthusiasts looking to have a good time turned overnight into a well-organized criminal enterprise."

"What can you tell us about the violence?"

The deputy shrugged. "Can you be more specific?"

"The murders at Jem Fosskey's garage?"

"There was chatter, for sure," said Magaw, "but never anything in public. If somebody did a murder, the last thing they would do is brag about it in front of anyone who might talk. These guys were dumb, but they weren't stupid."

Jess could feel Aaron growing impatient behind her. He wanted Magaw to point a line definitively from the Vandals to Fosskey, but she wasn't doing it. Jess decided to nudge a little harder.

"What about Digger Crowe?"

Deputy Magaw's eyes bugged. "My daddy always said Digger Crowe was a mean old cuss. Kind of like that guy in the Mafia movies, Luca Brasi. They said he wasn't somebody you wanted to mess around with, which makes sense that the Rare Breed would have taken him out first. They wanted the Vandals to know they were the ones who killed him, so they left a belt buckle next to his body and basically jump-started the 1984 war."

"War?" Jess glanced over her shoulder at Sandy, who nodded. She turned back to the deputy. "Tell us more about this war."

"It was bloody," said Magaw. "It was like a big old game of chess, where each side kept trying to take each other's pieces off the board. One day, a Rare Breed would turn up dead in a tobacco field; then a week later, a Vandal would be found with a couple extra holes in them."

"It seems like they got away with so much for so long," Jess said. "What straw was it that broke the camel's back and got the law involved?"

"There were a number of incidents during that war that mostly flew just under both law enforcement's and the public's radar. However, there was a shoot-out on the interstate that claimed the life of a civilian, and that's when folks decided they'd had enough. It was one thing to target criminals, but killing innocent people would bring the heat. After that, it was only a matter of time." Magaw smiled and shrugged. "Honestly, I could tell you all about the war, because those old men talk about it all the time down at Crazy Eights, but if you want to talk about Operation FIASCO—"

"What's that?"

"It's the initiative taken by a joint task force that involved several different agencies here in Virginia and North Carolina."

"Which law enforcement agencies were involved?"

Deputy Magaw shrugged. "A lot of them, I've heard. I can't tell you much about it, except what you can already find in newspapers, but if you wanted the nitty-gritty, it's best you hear from someone who was there."

"Like who?"

"There's an agent up in Richmond who participated in the bust," said Magaw. "Marty Jancowicz retired from Virginia's Bureau of Criminal Investigations, but he's still the go-to resource for anything we've ever needed while investigating MCs. The man is a legend. He's got more information in a single notebook of his than all the computers of law enforcement combined."

Jess fired a glance over her shoulder at Aaron. He peeked up from his viewfinder and nodded vigorously.

"Will he talk?"

"He's a retired lawman," said Magaw. "He'd *love* to talk."

CHAPTER FORTY-TWO

ENNIS WORTHY

1984

The door opened, and the whole of the restaurant drew quiet as the white policeman entered the room. Folks quit talking, quit eating; nobody moved except for Mac, who rounded the corner in his greasy apron, brandishing a rolling pin and fifty years of justified anger.

"Can I help you?" Mac asked the white policeman.

Deputy Ennis Worthy stood up from his table in the back of the room, where he'd been nursing a glass of sweet tea.

"He's with me," he said.

That seemed to do it for some people. Not Mac. He cut a look toward the white cop, then a second one toward Worthy, which seemed to say, *You have a lot of nerve, boy* . . . before heading back to the kitchen.

The room didn't immediately relax. One by one, they returned to their lunch plates as Officer Lorne Axel crossed the room to Worthy's table.

"Thank you for meeting me," said Axel.

Worthy said nothing. Axel motioned toward the empty chair across from Worthy. "May I?"

Worthy nodded. Axel took his seat, and Lou Belle, the waitress, arrived. Instead of a pen and ticket pad, she bore only great consternation.

Axel removed his patrol cap. "What's good here?"

Lou Belle answered him with nothing but a resentful expression.

"I'll have whatever he's having."

Worthy could read the meaning behind the look she shot him before she left for the kitchen. Same for what was going on behind Axel's eyes.

"What *are* you having?" he asked Worthy.

"Fish."

"I like fish."

"I'm having it fried," Worthy said, "which ought to rankle my girlfriend plenty. Shirley has dinner plans for us tonight with some of her law school friends. If she hears I ruined my appetite with some country-ass food, as she calls it, then she will be none too pleased. But I can't pass up a plate here. You'll thank me for it." Worthy unwrapped his cutlery from a paper napkin. "You know, we could have met over on your side of town."

Axel found the humor in that. "Oh, I don't think that would have been a good idea."

"There's a reporter at the *Times* who spoke very highly of you," said Worthy. "I told him about my situation, and he referred me your way."

"Hal Broadstreet." The look on Axel's face suggested he might be turned off his appetite. "Funny how he always manages to turn up."

"Like a bad penny?"

"More like a case of head lice."

Worthy hid a smile behind one hand while he stirred his straw with the other.

"Tell me what's going on."

Worthy laid out the bare details. He told the patrolman about Rosalie Patience and young Ricky Lee, how he'd stepped off the path early in life and how his mental health seemed to be deteriorating. Mostly, he communicated how helpless he felt.

"I don't know how I can help either, I'm afraid," said Axel. "I'm a patrolman and not one of my captain's favorites at that."

"I have the feeling that a call might be coming your way soon," said Worthy. "When that happens, it'd be much appreciated if the responding officer was sympathetic to the boy's situation." Worthy sipped from his drink. "I'd also appreciate a phone call."

Axel nodded once, then seemed to think it over a bit longer before nodding again. "I can do that," he said finally.

"Thank you," said Worthy. "Thank you very much."

"Unfortunately, that ain't the only problem I have cooking down in the Back Back."

"Oh?"

"People are getting shot, it seems."

Worthy nodded. "There's a lot of hard times up that way, I reckon."

"I agree," said Axel, "but this ain't just that."

Axel then proceeded to detail to his fellow lawman the calls he had answered down in the Back Back. Four shootings. Black victims. Random. Unseen assailant. Nobody saw anything.

"In each case," Axel told him, "there is a single gunshot. One clean shot through a vital organ or another. Pristine kill."

Worthy studied him. "You seem to have arrived at a theory."

"Not one that would be taken very seriously by my superiors," said Axel. "For one thing, I'm merely a patrolman."

"For another?"

"The Crimes Against Persons division doesn't seem to be investigating these murders."

Worthy opened his mouth to ask *Why not*, then closed it because he realized he already knew the answer. Worthy took stock of the man sitting across from him. They didn't appear to have that much difference in age. They'd grown up on different sides of the state line, and they worked in different agencies, but Worthy began to suspect they might have more in common than he originally thought.

"Do you know why I like working for the sheriff, as opposed to police?" Worthy asked. "A sheriff is one man. The people elect him, and he serves the people with the mandate they gave him. If he's a total bastard, as some are, then that's what the people of that county want, or else they vote him out. Everyone that works under that sheriff operates at his will, and if his will is for the good of the people . . ."

Worthy let the silence fill in the rest of the thought for him. When he was certain that Axel had filled in the gaps, he continued.

"Police, on the other hand . . . that corruption is institutional. You can't vote it out. You can't eradicate it by replacing one leader with another. All the hopes, dreams, and aspirations will never do anything to eliminate the cancer of hate and control from that system because it is built into it. It's the very foundation upon which it was constructed."

Axel swallowed and appeared to consider and reconsider several responses. Finally, he asked, "Do you have a solution?"

"I don't. Not yet." Worthy shrugged. "Maybe there isn't one. I don't know."

Axel took a breath, then met his colleague's gaze. "I believe the shooter fired from above and at a great distance."

"Why do you say that?"

"Something my partner said." Axel twisted a finger in the air, like he was writing in the sky. "You heard about that dirtbag in California this past week. San Ysidro? Walked into a McDonald's, armed to the teeth, and shot up the place."

Worthy shook his head. "I ain't never heard of nothing like it."

"Not since Charles Whitman in Austin. It's like all of America is going to the dogs."

"What about it?"

"He fired round after round, killing people for an improbable *seventy-seven* minutes." Axel shook his head at the thought of it. "He probably would have kept going, if it weren't for the police setting up a sniper across the street at an old post office. He got the guy in one shot."

"Praise Jesus."

The silence settled between them. Worthy could feel Axel's eyes on him until all the pieces fell into place.

"You think your shooter is a sniper?"

Axel nodded. "I do."

Worthy's eyebrows rose slightly. "Who has that kind of training around here?"

"Hell, any Joe Bob with a deer lease knows how to hit a buck at two hundred yards, but this guy . . ." Axel appeared to lose his train of thought for a moment as another one took hold of him.

"Officer Axel . . . ?"

"Huh?" Axel snapped out of it. "Oh, sorry. Nothing. Listen, thank you, Deputy. I was starting to wonder if I was going crazy. Seeing connections in places where maybe there weren't any. Even my partner, he wasn't . . ." Axel caught himself. He locked eyes with the deputy. "Like you said, *police*."

The waitress arrived. She set a fresh, steaming plate of thick-battered fish and salty fried potatoes in front of Worthy. In front of Axel, she dropped his food wrapped to go.

"That will be four dollars, sir."

Axel appeared to catch the drift. He fished five dollars from his wallet and offered it to her. He rose from the chair and collected his patrol cap.

Worthy stopped him. "Officer Axel?"

"Please. Call me Lorne."

"Lorne . . ." Worthy lifted his chin. "Thank you."

Axel tipped his patrol cap at him and winked. "Next time we'll get lunch at one of my places in town."

Worthy glanced at his fish. Already his mouth was watering. He kindly shook his head.

"Fat chance."

CHAPTER FORTY-THREE

HAL BROADSTREET

1984

Hal could not bring himself to drink the last of his corn liquor. He'd stashed two jars beneath his sink, next to the cleaning supplies, ever since a shortage in '81, brought about by a massive crackdown on Fosskey's bootlegging operations by Lake Castor's vice squad. He often joked to himself that he was either aging it or saving it to clean his drainpipes. He'd downed the first jar on the night that Uncle Meaney died. Since then, he'd limited his sadness to errant sips, until that sadness had become so complete that he found himself nearing the dregs at the bottom of his last jar. He set it down and stared at it. He knew that when it was finished, there would be no more.

Ever.

It was the last of the liquor stilled by Uncle Meaney. The last of the booze sold by Jem Fosskey. Once Hal killed that last swallow, all that was left of Fosskey's bootlegging crew would be erased from the earth.

The thought flooded him with the profound grief that he had been denying himself. He'd spent decades covering crime, translating the ripples from its wake to a ravenous readership. He could detail the injuries from a woman abused and forgotten, and still find a way to sleep like a baby. He could describe a child abandoned in a dumpster with only rats for company, then step out for a steak. He'd never had the patience for grief; his pen would be readying for the next story.

All this, he reckoned, was thanks to Jem Fosskey and Uncle Meaney's booze, and as he stared at the dwindling remnants of their efforts in the bottom of his jar, that grief slowly boiled into a rage. One that would not be sated by mere alcohol.

No.

He would need answers.

Hal took the back roads. He hit the farm-to-market road leading into Deeton, then cut off on the slim red clay drive that opened into a parking lot beneath a thick canopy of pine and poplar. Club 809 sat at the end of the lot. Hal parked his car and stared at the building, wishing he had more of Jem and Meaney's corn liquor.

The joint was much quieter than during his previous visit. The heavy metal music on the juke had given way to sad country songs. The long row of motorcycles was gone, leaving only twin Harleys on jiffy stands. Hal straightened himself before he entered the building.

The bar was near empty. A young kid waited on two biker women at the bar. Billiard balls clacked against one another in the adjoining room. Hal peeked in his head and found what he was looking for. One man lined up his shot, while big Billy Wayne Dickerson slept one off in a chair tucked into the corner.

One of the women from the bar recognized Hal. She broke from her friend and braced him. "What the hell are you doing here, Hal?" she asked.

Hal blinked her into focus. The last time he had seen Duchess was weeks earlier, shortly after the Fosskey murders. Then all he wanted from her was information on Digger Crowe. Now he wanted her to get the hell out of his way. She halted his advance upon the sleeping frame of Billy Wayne.

"As far as bad ideas go, Hal, that one's a blue-ribbon winner." Her eyes were pins, and she chewed the insides of her cheeks. "Especially tonight."

"Why tonight?"

"Because they've been celebrating for two days. He ain't got the mindset for anybody sticking their noses in his business."

Hal felt a cold sweat forming on the back of his neck. "What have they been celebrating?"

"Those two just got patched in."

"Patched in?"

"That means they're no longer prospects. They're full-fledged members of the club now."

Billy Wayne stirred in his sleep. The second man barely considered Hal as he plucked billiard balls from the pockets and dropped them into the triangle rack.

"They've been wasted for the past two days," Duchess explained. "The whole thing is some kind of reward for something they'd done for the club, and I think they may finally be com—"

"What kind of something?" Hal demanded.

Duchess appeared offended. "Do I look like I'm dumb enough to ask a question like that?"

The juke changed the record from one sad, shitty cowboy song to another. The biker finished racking the balls and chalked his cue. If he knew Hal and Duchess were there, he showed no sign of it.

"Hal," Duchess said, "you should go home."

Hal's focus on Billy Wayne was so intense that it seemed to nudge the sleeping giant to waking. Billy Wayne blinked the world into view, then scanned the room. He found his jacket on his body, his smokes in his pocket, his friend at the pool table, his beer warming on the seat next to him, and . . .

. . . Hal.

"I'm serious, Hal," Duchess whispered. "Those two are half out of their minds on quaaludes and Benzedrine. There's a war heating up right now, and I won't be able to save you if you don't—"

"Who's your friend, Duch?" Billy Wayne lumbered to his feet. His footing was unsure at first, but he quickly found his sea legs. He tossed his locks over his shoulder and squinted to better see the reporter.

Hal ignored Duchess's warning and moved closer, keeping the pool table between him and the two bikers.

"Did you hear me, Duchess?" Billy Wayne asked, slightly slurring his words. "I asked you who was your friend?"

"I don't have any friends," Hal answered for her. "I came here to talk to you."

Billy Wayne had alerted the second biker, who stepped to the side of the pool table. They had Hal from two different angles, if needed. The energy of the room prickled Hal, heightened his senses. Time slowed. He sobered.

Focused.

"Congratulations, Billy Wayne," said Hal. "I heard you got a big come up this week."

Billy Wayne cut eyes to Duchess. "Heard from where?"

"I'm a journalist." Hal picked up the cue ball from the billiard table and tested its weight. "It's my job to hear things."

"You suck at your job, then." Billy Wayne laughed. "Or else you would have heard it ain't such a good idea for you to be sticking your nose where it ain't wanted."

"I covered you once," said Hal. "Once, when I was just starting out at the *Times*, I caught a game with the old sports-desk writer Deke Graham. You remember him? We watched you play against Tucker. Great game."

Nothing moved behind Billy Wayne's heavy-lidded eyes. "Is that right?"

"It is. You went three for five, hitting for contact each time, and two sacrifice flies."

"Ancient history." Billy Wayne shrugged. "So you wrote a sports story. So what?"

"No, that's not when I covered you." Hal rolled the cue ball from one hand to the other. "I covered you when you came home from overseas. You remember that little parade? The mayor was there with your daddy and that other boy who came home. What was his name?"

"Kenny Gartland."

"That's right. Whatever happened to him?"

Billy Wayne turned down his eyes. Hal knew what had happened to Gartland. Two years after coming home, he shoved the barrel of a .38 into his mouth and ate a bullet. It was another of those things nobody talked about.

"How about you?" Hal asked. "How has it been for you since coming home?"

Billy Wayne's eyes came up slow. They focused again on Hal, and a slight smile crept upon his lips.

"You want to know what I did over there?" Billy Wayne asked.

Hal didn't. More than anything, he did not want to know.

"I was a shooter."

Billy Wayne mimed shouldering a rifle and aiming it at Hal's head.

"I was a sniper."

Hal felt the sweat break out on his forehead. The booze had left his system, as had any inkling that it had been a good idea that he come to the 809. He immediately realized how remote the area was. How long it might take for anyone to find him.

Duchess must have realized it too. She called over her shoulder to the boy behind the bar.

"Bubba, go get your daddy."

Billy Wayne's smile spread farther across his face. He reached for something in his jacket pocket. Hal readied the cue ball, knowing he had one shot with it and only one, wondering if that one shot should be spent firing into Billy Wayne's forehead and what might happen if he missed. Before he could decide, he felt a blow against his body as the second biker grabbed hold of him and shoved him out of the room, out the building, and into the parking lot.

"Do you want to die tonight, shitbird?" hissed the man who had accosted him. He wore a Vandals patch on his cut, same as Billy Wayne. He had long blond hair and an unkempt beard, and Hal could taste the beer on his breath. The biker's strength was deceiving, as he was small but able to hold Hal in place despite the struggles. Only when Hal gave in did he notice the name patch on the front of his cut.

CHAINS.

Charlie Chains.

"You're Charles Wilcox," Hal said.

"And you're a dead man if you keep poking that bear."

Hal wrested himself free of Chains's grip. "Do you know who I am?"

"You ain't listening, brother. I'm trying to save your damn life. But I ain't going to try for long."

"I know what you did," Hal said.

Chains didn't like that answer. He drew back and slapped Hal's face—*hard*—with the back of his hand. The sting brought tears to Hal's eyes, but he didn't want to be seen wiping them away. Instead, he doubled down his hateful stare.

"I know what you did," Hal repeated, "and I'm going to prove it."

Chains lowered his head and shook it. "Brother, I'm trying to keep you alive. Now you need to help me help you. Forget about all this.

There's plenty other things for the newspapers to write about. Do you hear me? Forgetting about all this might be the smartest thing you do."

As if to punctuate his point, Chains drove a fist into Hal's belly, which doubled him over. Hal lay there in the dirt at Chains's feet, spitting and gasping for air.

"Next time," Chains said, "it might be somebody else telling you. They might not be so nice."

CHAPTER FORTY-FOUR

JESS KEELER

Present Day

The local sheriff had offered his office as a favor to both Sheriff Axel and Martin Jancowicz, the agent who had worked the FIASCO operation that probed the Vandals in 1984. Janco, as he was known across several law enforcement agencies, had been invaluable to hundreds of inquiries into motorcycle clubs over the past forty years. For that reason, he'd endeared himself to many investigators, including Deputy Tate Magaw, who had set up the interview, and the sheriff who had loaned them his conference room. While Aaron fixed the lights and Buffy tested her audio equipment, Sandy and Jess prepared Jancowicz for the interview.

"Just make sure they can't make out that it's me," Jancowicz insisted. "Blur me, bleep me, whatever y'all do. This pretty face weren't made for television."

Jess's laugh came out nervous. His "pretty face" was anything but. He was in his early seventies, but those years had not been kind to him. The lines in his face were set deep. A scar ran from his ear to his chin, the result, he'd told them, of an operation gone wrong. His arms were cluttered with tattoos that had aged as poorly as he had. His scraggly beard had frosted completely white. He took comfort from even the dimmest of lights by slipping on a pair of sunglasses.

"We can't show a single shot of footage without your signed consent," Jess promised. "Nobody wants to deal with that kind of litigation."

"We'll shoot as normal," Aaron told him, "but add something that obscures you during post. We'll either pixelate your face or cast you in silhouette."

"What about my voice?" Janco asked. "It's pretty recognizable."

He was right, Jess thought. His voice sounded as if it had been dragged, kicking and screaming, across broken glass.

"That won't be a problem," Buffy told him. "I have all sorts of applications that can mask your voice. No one will know it's you."

"It's kind of sexy, actually," said Aaron. "The confidential-informant aspect adds a mysterious texture to the production."

"Most everybody from those days has either hung up their cuts, or rides the great highway in the sky," Jancowicz said, "but still I bet there's one or two still around who wouldn't mind getting their hands around the throat of someone who worked on Operation FIASCO."

"That's the operation that took down the Vandals?" Jess asked.

Jancowicz nodded. "The Vandals and a mess of other crews."

Aaron signaled that his camera was rolling. Sandy called the scene and slapped the slate. Buffy settled into position with the boom mic on her shoulder.

Jess leaned forward. "Can you tell us what your role was on Operation FIASCO?"

"Investigations," Jancowicz said. "Operations. I filled in wherever I was needed."

"That sounds kind of vague."

"Because it is." Jancowicz wiped his bearded cheek with a mottled hand. "It was a team effort. The largest of its kind here in Virginia. We had seven different law enforcement agencies cooperating on this one, which was unheard of at the time. Sheriffs' offices, police departments, the BCI, the FBI . . . everything from arresting officers to undercover agents, confidential informants, all the way to the accountants that signed off on invoices. Everyone involved in this thing made their career. They could choose where they wanted to go."

"How many arrests did FIASCO net?"

Jancowicz smiled, revealing a disastrous set of teeth. "We got a bunch of them. We obliterated the top ranks of the Vandals, netting their president, vice president, and sergeant at arms. Most of the big guns below them had already been taken off the board during their dustup with the Rare Breed."

"Like Digger Crowe?"

"I ain't—" Jancowicz's twisted face twisted even farther. "I haven't heard that name in quite some time."

"We don't know nearly enough about him," she said. "We know he was one of three suspects in the murders of—"

The door behind them opened, and a deputy in uniform filled the frame.

"Ms. Keeler," he said, "there's a call for you."

"I'm in the middle of an in—"

"It's urgent."

Jess felt her face flush. She couldn't imagine what kind of emergency would require her to abandon the interview. She turned and looked to Aaron, to Sandy.

"I don't . . . Who is it?"

"It's Sheriff Lorne Axel from Lawles County, ma'am," said the deputy. "He said to get you on the phone as quick as possible."

Jess set down her notes and apologized to the room. She followed the deputy to the front desk, where she picked up the phone.

"Jess," said Sheriff Axel through the line, "you weren't answering your phone."

"It's on silent," she said. "I'm in the middle of an interview."

"Your son has been trying to reach you for nearly an hour."

"My—Benjamin . . . Lorne, what's the matter?"

"He's okay," said the sheriff. "Benjamin is just fine. I promise. I've spoken to him myself."

Jess felt immediate relief. It was quickly replaced by something else.

"Jess, it's your mother." She could hear the sheriff take a breath through the line. "She's gone missing."

"Wait . . . *what?*"

"We've got men out looking for her, but at the moment, we can't find her anywhere."

A million thoughts went through Jess's head at once. Too many for her to pin down any single one. The words left her mouth before she could stop them.

"I'm on my way."

CHAPTER FORTY-FIVE

JESS KEELER

Present Day

Jess kept the speedometer at fourteen over the limit, slowing only when she drove through towns and rural burgs. It was a two-and-a-half-hour drive from Richmond to Lake Castor, but she was determined to make it in just under two. Normally during these drives, she enjoyed listening to music. This time, she would not so much as touch the radio.

Instead, she was on her phone.

She tried her mother for the tenth time since she'd jumped into the car over an hour ago. Again, it went to voice mail.

"Dammit, Mother," Jess snapped. However, she reminded herself not to waste all her anguish on her mom, when there was still plenty to go around. She tried her son again, only to catch his voice mail as well.

This time, she left a message.

"Benjamin, I swear . . ." Jess gripped the steering wheel tighter. "You better call me back on the double, or I . . ." It was all she could do not to scream. "Ben, why are you doing this to me?"

Panicked, and with no one else to call, she dialed her ex-husband. He picked up on the third ring.

"I wouldn't call if it wasn't an emergency, Philip," she said, "but I need your help. Mom's gone missing, and Ben was supposed to be watching her. I was in Richmond on an interview, and right now am racing back home, but I won't be there for another hour and a half, and I need someone to help me. Oh, Philip, please help me."

He was silent on the line for so long that Jess wondered if he'd ever picked up. Finally, she heard his trademark exasperated sigh.

"I don't know what you think I can do, J. . . ."

"You could help me find my mother." Jess could think of it in no simpler terms. "She couldn't have gone far. They said it's only been a couple of hours, but Ben won't call me back, so I can't—"

"I told you she shouldn't be living alone anyway, J.," said Philip. "She's all the way over in Lake Castor. With all that's going on with her, it makes perfect sense for her to move in with you."

"To my house in Deeton?" Jess kept an eye out for speed traps. "She hates that house, and besides, with Ben living there, we hardly have the room."

"About that . . ." Jess could hear her ex-husband drawing out his words like molasses. "I talked to Ben earlier, and he asked what it might be like if he came and lived with me for a little while."

Jess couldn't believe her ears. "You talked to Ben *when*? I can't get him to answer the phone right now, and besides, he's helping me watch Mom . . . or at least that's what he's *supposed* to do. We agreed if he wasn't going to stay in college, then he would help me out at the house while I work."

"He's almost twenty, J.," said Philip. "He's still a kid. He needs to live like one, not be forced into servitude."

"It's taking care of his *grandmother*," Jess spat. "Not *slavery*. And, yes, he's just a kid, so you're telling me he needs to live with you so that you can live out your frat-house fantasies?"

She was greeted with silence from the other end of the line.

Jess shook it off. "Can we talk about this later, Philip? Right now, my number one concern is my mother. Can you please drive over to her house in Lake Castor and cruise the streets? She could be wandering them, and I don't think—"

"Jess, I'd love to . . ."

"But?"

"But I'm not in town," he said. "I'm actually in the mountains with Kimber."

"Kimber?"

"I told you . . ." She could hear him inhale, but not exhale. "I've been seeing her and—"

That's right, Jess suddenly remembered. *The yoga instructor.*

She disengaged the call. Jess rode in silence a bit before breaking down and trying her son once more. Straight to voice mail. Same with the next call to her mother. She wanted to scream.

No one would ever claim she was close to her mother. When Jess was growing up, there seemed to have been a sort of screen between them, something where only the smallest amount of light could get through. When that was all a person had ever known, she reckoned she'd grown accustomed to it and forgotten it even existed. Still, she'd hoped there was still time to reconcile all this before . . .

The phone rang.

Jess nearly broke her fingers answering it. Then jammed the button on the console, and the car was filled with the voice of former Deeton sheriff Ennis Worthy.

"Jess, I just heard the news."

She hadn't heard his voice in so long, but immediately felt a warmth and security that she hadn't known was absent—for how long? Her chest felt as if someone had blown up a balloon inside it, and the pressure against her ribs threatened to pop it. She resisted that, because if she succumbed to sobs at seventy miles an hour, she'd likely wreck the car.

"I don't know what to do," she whispered.

"Don't worry about a thing," said Worthy. "I pulled some strings, and the new sheriff has sent a couple of his boys up to Lake Castor to help him find her. I'm on the ground here as well, in fact. We'll find her."

Jess was losing her battle against the tears. She struggled to squeeze out thanks, but couldn't manage the words without collapsing.

"Thank me when we find her," Worthy said, "which we will."

He hung up, and Jess felt lost. She thought about everything Lorne Axel and Ennis Worthy were doing to help her. She wondered where she would be without those two men. After all the bad press that law enforcement received from the media, these two men continually went above and beyond to help her with what she needed.

Which was why she felt so horrible. While they consoled her and scoured the county limits for her ailing mother, she had gone behind their backs to do the one thing they had explicitly asked her not to do. Axel had opened the books on the Fosskey murders in order to facilitate their true-crime documentary, and she had used the unprecedented access to look into the sniper killings. While Worthy cashed in favors to help her, she was testing the guilt of the very man he had put away for the murders.

She couldn't afford to think about that, she told herself. To distract herself, she dialed Sandy's number. She gave up after six rings. Worried that Sandy might be upset with her for bailing on the interview early, Jess next called Buffy.

Again, no answer.

Three minutes later, she received a text from Buffy.

Can't talk now. Will call back when finished with interview

Jess replayed the text three times, just to make sure she hadn't misheard. *Interview?* She wondered. *Interview with whom? Had they really continued the interview after she had left? Would they do that? Did it matter?*

Jess checked her watch. She still had thirty minutes to go before she reached her mother's Lake Castor neighborhood. Frantic, she dialed her mother again. Then her son.

He answered on the third ring.

"I'm sorry, Mom, don't be mad at me."

Jess didn't know if she wanted to hug him or strangle him. She could do neither for another half hour, so she took a deep breath and asked, "Where are you?"

"I'm at Grandma's," he said. "It's where I've been all day. I swear, I was in the kitchen on my phone when—"

"On your *phone*?" Jess reminded herself to keep calm. "Doing what?"

"I told you: my podcast."

Jess was losing her battle with sanity. She shelved any natural response and opted instead for the measured one.

"We'll talk about that later," she said, "but what's important right now is that we find your grandmother."

"The sheriff told me to stay here in case she comes home," said Benjamin. "So that's what I'm doing."

Something in his voice set Jess on edge. She wanted to ask what he was thinking. She wanted to remind him that he was nearly twenty years old and would need to grow up. Maybe, she thought for a fleeting moment, her ex-husband was right and Benjamin needed time to be a kid. All she could think about in that moment, however, was finding her mother.

A text flashed across the screen in her console from Buffy. It read,

Interview ended. Packing up. U good?

"I'm almost there, Ben," she said.

Twenty minutes later, she pulled into her mother's driveway. She raced up the walk and threw open the door to find Benjamin scrolling on his phone. She grabbed him and hugged him and squeezed him tight, forgetting all her frustrations with him for a moment. When they parted, she turned to see two county cruisers and Worthy's pickup truck on the street outside.

Jess raced out the door and was on the lawn when Worthy emerged from his truck, escorting her mother by the arm.

"Where was she?" Jess demanded, after hugging her mother for dear life. "Mom . . . What happened?"

"I don't know what's the big deal," her mother groused. "I was just going for a walk in the neighborhood, and next thing you know, there's a big fuss."

Jess looked over her mother at Worthy with eyes that asked a million questions.

"She was down by the civic center," Worthy said. "I found her on the playground."

Jess looked again at her mother. The knees of her pants were filthy.

"Mom . . . What were you doing?"

Her mother waved her off. "I don't want to hear it from you too. I'm going inside to take a bath. All of your histrionics have given me a headache. Can I go inside, Officer, or is that some kind of crime these days?"

Worthy nodded to her, and Jess waited until her mother was inside before she collapsed into his arms.

"Thank you so much, Ennis," she said. "I don't know where I'd be without you."

"Don't you mention it," Worthy said. "It's my job."

"Not anymore." Jess laughed. "You're retired."

"You don't get to retire from taking care of your people." He wiped a tear from her cheek with his finger. "Y'all are my people."

Suddenly, the guilt was too much to bear. Worthy had, at a moment's notice, dropped everything and crossed out of his former jurisdiction to help find her mother. His voice on the phone had offered her comfort when there had been none to offer. How had she thanked him for this and all his past generosities?

By going behind his back and investigating the sniper when he had asked her not to. By questioning his very role in the arrest of Ricky Lee Patience.

The weight of it all threatened to drop her to her knees. Worthy realized this and supported her weight with his shoulders.

"Come, Jess," he said softly. "Let's take a seat on the porch."

Worthy helped her to the patio, where they sat together on the stoop. His kindness hit her where it mattered. It was kindness she had not received from her ex-husband, or her mother, or even her son. Kindness that was absent, even, from her partner in the investigation, Sandy.

"Thank you, Ennis," she said. "You have no idea . . ."

Worthy slid his arm around her shoulder, like a loving grandfather. Her tears fell and would not stop.

"There, there . . ."

"Ennis," she said, slowly, "I have something to tell you."

And she did.

She told him everything.

CHAPTER FORTY-SIX

ENNIS WORTHY

1984

Deputy Ennis Worthy listened as Rosalie Patience detailed her son's latest outburst. She was infinitely more frantic than the last time he had stopped by her house in Lake Castor's Back Back neighborhood. More desperate. She had nowhere else to turn.

They stood in the living room that Ricky Lee had destroyed.

"I had to send little Wilhelmina to her auntie's house," said Ms. Patience through miserable tears. "I can't bear for her to see her brother like this. What happens if he turns his rage on her?"

"Where is he, Ms. Patience?" Worthy asked.

She shrugged. "When I begged for him to stop, he kept saying to me, 'Ricky Lee isn't here anymore.' He would say, 'If they can do it, then so can I.'"

"He can do what?"

"He never did say. He kept smashing my things." She turned her sad eyes to her living room. "They're just things. I can get new things. But what happens if he . . ."

She didn't bother to finish her sentence. She didn't need to.

Worthy put his hand on her shoulder. "When is the last time you saw him?"

"This morning," she said. "He slammed the door on his way out. Please, Deputy Worthy. I'm so scared for my daughter."

Worthy assured her as best as he could, then saw his way out of her house. As he walked down the sidewalk to his car, he was struck by how still the air was, how quiet things were. No one was on the street. He found the silence unsettling, and every hair on his body seemed to stand on end. There was an electricity to the afternoon.

An electricity that was shattered by the sound of a single gunshot in the distance, followed by screams.

Worthy broke into a run.

The man lay in the middle of a tight convenience store parking lot. Two sacks of groceries were spilled out, milk leaching into the man's blood on the asphalt. He shouted for help while clutching his arm to staunch the bleeding.

Worthy came in low, his eyes scanning the lot for danger. All he found was fear. A woman and her child cowering behind a car. Three people peeking out from the store windows. No one stepping out into the open to help the injured man. Not on their lives.

Worthy grabbed the man by the shoulders. Training dictated that he should not move the injured man, but instincts told him something else. He dragged the man—screaming now, in pain—to a space between the building and a parked car.

"Where is the shooter, son?" Worthy asked.

The man spoke through clenched teeth. "I didn't see anyone."

Worthy inspected the man's injury. Upper left arm, through and through. The man was bleeding rapidly. Worthy ripped off the right sleeve of his uniform and used it to fashion a tourniquet just above the wound. The man howled out in pain, but his eyes showed appreciation.

Worthy knew the shooter was still at large. But where? Something tickled the back of his mind, and it took the flash of a moment for him to realize it was the words of Lorne Axel.

"The police set up a sniper across the street . . . he got the guy in one shot . . ."

Worthy scanned the landscape. People ducked behind parked cars. Peeked out from between window blinds.

"You think your shooter is a sniper?"

"I do."

He lifted his gaze to a higher vantage. There were too few trees in the Back Back. The tops of the one-story storefronts were bare.

"Who has that kind of training around here?"

"Any Joe Bob with a deer lease knows how to hit a buck at two hundred yards, but this guy . . ."

Worthy's eyes settled on the grain elevator. Long unused, rusted, and forgotten.

And with a clear sight to their position.

"Keep pressure on this wound," Worthy instructed the injured man.

"Where are you going?"

Worthy didn't answer. Instead, he drew his weapon. He kept his figure low, making himself as small a target as possible, and raced in the direction of the grain elevator.

◆ ◆ ◆

No one alive could recall a day when the old grain elevator was not part of the skyline of the Back Back. Worthy's father would tell him of days when it was up and running, but those were long in the rearview, as he could summon no memory of it without its dulled patina of rust and decay. It loomed large over the community, as if it were a landmark of blight. It grew larger as Worthy ran nearer, his pace slowing as he approached, noticing the men standing in front of it.

There were three of them. Men of the community, although Worthy didn't recognize them. Their skin dark, their teeth bared as he approached, as if to warn him away without words. If their expressions didn't do it, then their armaments might. One held a baseball bat. Another a shovel. The third gripped a mattock with both hands. Their frames blocked the door of the grain elevator, which had been pried away and hung on a single rusted hinge.

"Turn around, cop," growled the one with the shovel. "You ain't got no business here."

"Someone's been hurt," Worthy said, nodding over his shoulder in the direction of the man he had left bleeding at the convenience store.

"Then maybe you best go see to him." The man with the bat gripped it tighter in his fists.

Worthy didn't raise his weapon, but he didn't holster it either.

"I'm the law," he said.

The one holding the shovel said, "Not around here, you ain't."

Above him, Worthy heard the sound of someone crying out in pain. Worthy's gaze darted up to the top of the tower. It was easily eight stories tall. The men guarding the door noticed. They tensed. Worthy knew everything could go sideways very easily, so he made a show of holstering his weapon.

"I'm going in there," he said to them. He was not confrontational, but firm. He inched forward, one slow step following another. As he reached the door, the big man with the mattock nodded at the other two. They parted before him like the sea.

Worthy entered. Inside, it was dark. Only slivers of sunlight slipped between the planks of plywood used to board up the windows. It was enough to see the cobwebs. The rotting furniture. The dust on the floor that had been disturbed in the direction of the rickety iron staircase. Somewhere above him, the sound of wings flapping.

Someone cried out again.

Worthy moved slow. Unsure. He reached the staircase. His foot tested its weight upon it. He climbed the first step. Then the next.

Halfway up the steps, he passed a Black man on a landing. Worthy knew by the way he was standing that the man had a weapon, but couldn't tell exactly what. A knife? A gun?

"Cut your eyes off me, cop," he hissed as Worthy continued his ascent.

With every step, Worthy could hear a man being beaten at the top of the stairs. With each blow, the man's cries grew more and more faint. As Worthy reached the top landing, blocking his view was a small Black man carrying a two-by-four. Two nails poked out the end of it. The man raised an eyebrow, then stepped aside.

The top landing was a small chamber with a boarded-up window on each of the four sides. One of the boards had been removed, which bathed the room in sunlight. Worthy did not need to look out the window to know it would provide a direct line of sight to the man lying in the parking lot with a bullet hole in his arm.

What he saw instead was a group of people—six men, two women, all Black—who stood over a bloody and beaten biker. A large man, long hair, beard. Eyes nearly beaten shut. A sniper rifle lay kicked out of reach in the corner of the chamber.

"What happened here?" Worthy asked.

But he knew.

"Peckerwood think we didn't notice him," one man answered, although he didn't take his eyes off the biker. "White man in a little white car, down here in the Back Back. Moving around like he thought he was invisible. All the while, people getting shot."

To punctuate his statement, he drove a boot into the biker's belly.

"I'll radio it in," Worthy said. "My cruiser is just down at—"

The small group of people collectively tensed. The man motioned for them to hold.

"You ain't calling nothing in, Deputy," he said. "Cops didn't want to do nothing when people were getting shot. That means they don't get to do anything when we catch the motherfucker who done it."

Worthy turned his attention to the biker, bleeding on the floor.

"What's your name, son?"

The biker spat a tooth and sent it skittering across the floor. "Eat shit."

"He ain't got no name," said one of the women. "All he got left is time, and all that's running out."

Worthy felt his mouth dry up. "You can't . . ."

"He killed four people that we know of," said another man. "It would have been five, but we stopped him."

Below them, the biker coughed something loose in his lungs. Worthy realized it was his laughter.

"It's going to be a lot more than that," the biker said. "And ain't no one going to care. You—*all of you*—are expendable. None of you matter. You are the *enemy*."

"Shut up," Worthy hissed.

The biker did not. "You are the enemy, and you want to know what I was trained by our nation to do with an enemy?"

Worthy could see glances pass between the group of vigilantes. They seemed to communicate without speaking something fluent between them. Worthy understood it too. They were making decisions. Ones that they wouldn't be able to undo.

Panic licked at his belly. "Shut up, dammit."

The biker laughed again.

"I'm taking him in," Worthy said. "He'll face justice for what he's done."

"Damn straight he will," said one of the women.

"He's going to face it right now," said another of the men.

The biker spat another tooth, then wiped his mouth with a broken hand. "Killing the enemy"—he coughed—"was all I was ever good at. And, brother, I'm good."

281

"Goddammit," Worthy spat, "do you *want* to die?"

Worthy could see the answer in the biker's eyes.

And in the eyes of the people surrounding him.

"Go downstairs, Deputy," said one of the men.

"No." Worthy settled in. Readied himself. "I won't let you."

Two men took him, one at each arm. Worthy wrested free from them.

"Deputy . . ."

"Go on." The biker laughed. "Leave me to these *animals*."

Worthy closed his eyes. There were eight of them. He would never win. And if he did, what would he have accomplished?

"I was meant to die in a jungle," said the biker. "And here I am."

The men escorted Worthy to the stairs. "Goodbye, Deputy."

Worthy descended.

"I'll kill them all." He laughed. "Eradicate the enemy, soldier!"

The man's laughter rose in pitch and volume. He laughed loud and long. It bounced off the iron walls, and as Worthy descended, he clamped both his hands over his ears to drown it out. It didn't work. By the time Worthy reached the bottom of the stairs, however, he realized it had long ago stopped and all he was hearing was the echo.

◆ ◆ ◆

Worthy sucked on a blade of grass and watched the men and women march past him one by one. No one bothered to avoid eye contact. They knew what they had done. They knew he was complicit. Unlike him, they were proud of it.

No one spoke a word.

The only acknowledgment he received was when one of them spat on the grass before his feet.

He couldn't blame a single one of them, he thought to himself as they reached the street, then scattered in their own different directions.

No one had bothered to save them, so they had saved themselves.

Worthy unfastened the walkie at his belt. He pressed the button with every intention of calling in the dead body up top of the grain elevator, then thought better of it. He repositioned his walkie on his belt.

Instead, he fished a quarter out of his pocket and scoured the Back Back for a pay phone that worked.

◆ ◆ ◆

"It was self-defense."

Officer Lorne Axel didn't appear to believe a word of it.

"Ennis, this man was tortured."

"He went for his gun, and I—"

Axel raised a hand and stopped him from further incriminating himself.

Worthy exhaled. "This man killed four people. It would have been five."

Axel knelt to the biker's body. Worthy watched him study the man's face.

"Did you know him?" Worthy asked.

Axel nodded. "His name is Billy Wayne Dickerson."

Worthy tensed.

"He was a good kid, once." Axel's voice was tinged with sadness. "Folks in this town knew him real well. They're going to . . ."

Axel's words trailed away.

"I'll stand for it," Worthy said. "Whatever happens, I'll stand for it."

Axel rose. He turned to face his friend.

"This is bad, Ennis. Real bad."

Worthy cut him a glance.

"If we take you in," Axel said, "then we're bringing in a Black man implicated in the merciless bludgeoning of a beloved member of our community."

"A biker who shot and murdered people?"

Axel shook his head. "That's not what they are going to see. They are going to see a Black vigilante, out of his jurisdiction, who tortured and executed a former ball player. Someone's son. Someone's brother. A war veteran."

Worthy shook his head, awash in rage and irony. *"Beloved . . ."*

"Once, sure." Axel nodded toward Worthy's chest. "That badge won't matter neither. Only the colors of your skins."

Worthy said nothing.

"I'm not saying it's fair or it's right," Axel continued. "I'm only telling you what I know. I hate every bit of it, but it's the way of things in Lake Castor. In America." Axel let that sink in, then continued. "But if we leave him . . ." Worthy glanced up and measured Axel's expression. He opened his mouth, but Axel held up a hand. "If we leave him . . . ," he continued, "and the community here finds out a white man was targeting Blacks, they're likely to rise up. Lake Castor can't afford that right now."

You have no idea, Worthy wanted to say, but kept his mouth sealed tight. He placed his hands on his hips.

"There is," Axel said slowly, "another option."

Worthy wasn't going to like it, no matter what Axel proposed. But the deputy told himself it didn't matter.

There was no way he was getting out of this with his soul intact.

CHAPTER FORTY-SEVEN

HAL BROADSTREET

1984

The sun was tucking itself behind the pines when Hal pulled his El Camino into the lot of the EZ GO. He parked near the pay phone and fumbled out a dime from his center console before remembering the cost of a call had been increased to a quarter. He ran inside to break a dollar, then returned to the phone booth. He closed the door and made the call.

Peg answered on the second ring. "*Lake Castor Times.* How may I direct your call?"

"Peg, I need you to do me a favor."

"Hal?" He heard her lower her voice, almost to a whisper. "Where the hell have you been?"

"I've been at the funeral all day."

"What funeral?"

"For Billy Wayne Dickerson."

"Oh." He could hear her clear her throat through the line. "I had no idea he was . . . that you and he . . ." She struggled to find her words, then simply said, "I'm sorry, Hal. It's horrible, but Vince has been—"

"Peg, be a sweetheart, and run some information for me. Will you do that?"

There was a small pause. He could hear paper rustling. "Hal," she said finally, "I think you should come in. I'm starting to worry about you."

"Not right now. Listen, Peg . . . I'm close. I can feel it. Did you hear Billy Wayne was found beaten to death?"

"I'm sorry, Hal."

"Yeah, well . . ."

The glass of the phone booth was blurry and smudged. Hal could barely see out, but that meant no one could see in. This both calmed and unsettled him.

"I need a line on the man they call Charlie Chains," Hal said. "I got a look at his bike at the funeral. I need you to run his plates for me and get me all the registration information. Can you do that?"

"Hang on, one second," she said. "I'm going to transfer this call and take it at your desk."

"No!" Hal surprised even himself at how abrupt he sounded. "Not my phone. I've been hearing clicks—"

"Clicks?"

"Yes. Like maybe someone is listening . . ." Hearing himself say the words made them sound even more ridiculous. "I think my phone may be tapped."

"Hal . . . you can't be—"

"No, it's good. It's good. It means I'm on to something. If they're going to all this trouble, it means I'm headed in the right direction."

"I really think I should get Vince. He can—"

"That's not a good idea."

An 18-wheeler rumbled down the highway, drowning out part of Peg's response.

". . . and he's been asking for you."

"I'll bet he has," Hal said. He flashed back to the memory of Vince's face as Hal smashed the windshield of his Camaro with a Louisville Slugger. "Peg, just get me the registration information on those plates. Get me anything you can on the owner of that motorcycle. Charles Wilcox."

"Sure, Hal."

Hal gave her the plate number. "You heard the old biker adage? 'Three can keep a secret if two are dead'?"

"Not really, but I don't—"

"Two are dead, Peg."

Hal hung up and climbed into his El Camino. The sun had disappeared behind the trees, casting the world in a darker hue. Hal flipped on his headlights and took FM 809 into town. His eyes were on the road, but his mind was on the story. He had the pieces. He could put together large swaths of the puzzle. Still, however, he felt like he needed to step back and see it better.

Fact: Jem Fosskey, Felton Loe, and Mel Kemble were murdered by three Vandals—Digger Crowe, Billy Wayne Dickerson, and Charlie Chains—as witnessed by Baby Doll McNaughton and Uncle Meaney.

Fact: Baby Doll, much like Digger's two ex-wives, mysteriously disappeared without a trace. Uncle Meaney was shot by an unknown assailant in the Back Back.

Fact: The three Vandals were arrested the morning of the murders, then subsequently released. The murders at Fosskey's garage had never been investigated.

Fact: Digger Crowe was found murdered in the back of a pickup truck. Although a belt buckle discovered with the body would indicate involvement with a known rival, the Rare Breed, the scene appeared staged.

Fact: Ronnie Daye and Uncle Meaney were two of five people gunned down in the Back Back by an unknown assailant, who appeared to shoot them from a high vantage point. Billy Wayne Dickerson served as a sniper in the marines during the Vietnam War.

Fact: Billy Wayne Dickerson's body was found, bloodied and beaten, in the grain elevator that overlooked all five crime scenes in the Back—

Hal glanced at the rearview mirror, again noticing two twin light beams that had been following him for the past five or six miles. At first, he'd thought they might belong to the headlights of a car or truck; however, as they appeared to weave one way and then the other on the two-lane blacktop, he realized they weren't the light beams of one vehicle, but two.

Motorcycles.

They appeared to be picking up speed and closing the distance between them. Hal's hands gripped the steering wheel tighter. His pulse rocketed. He had entered a two-lane stretch of highway that was practically a gauntlet in the dark, with nothing but forest for miles on either side. It would be another ten minutes before he reached a gas station, or any other sign of civilization.

Dammit.

Hal's thoughts turned to who might know where he was, or how long it would be before anyone realized he was missing.

One of the lights sped up, grew larger in his rearview, before Hal realized it was passing him. It's engine growled terribly as Hal watched it pass him on the driver's side; all he could make out in the dark were the tattoos climbing up the beefy man's arm.

This is how it will happen . . .

The second bike remained close behind at Hal's rear bumper while that first one slid into the lane in front of his El Camino, then softly applied its brake lights. Hal was forced to choose between ramming into the back of him or slowing down.

Never the one to opt for harm, Hal applied his brakes.

They were boxing him in.

Hal ran through his dwindling options. He could pull over, but he'd be in immediate peril. The night was too dark, and there were too few passersby. He'd be at the mercy of his captors. He could try and go around the bike, then outrun it, but he knew those Harleys were much faster than his El Camino and the riders were likely far too skilled. The other option was, of course, to use his vehicle as a weapon.

Lucky for Hal, he was never forced to choose. Just as he felt his back was firmly against the wall, up switched the cherry light on the dash of a four-door. Hal had never once in his life been grateful for the presence of police until that very moment. He yelped out loud and pounded the ceiling of his car in celebration as he watched the two motorcycles gun their engines and speed away.

The cops, however, did not pursue them. Instead, they rolled closer to Hal's rear bumper, filling his rearview with their lights. Hal slowed his car and pulled over to the side of the road.

On that dark, lonesome highway, he threw his gear into park. He watched through his side mirror as a plainclothes detective approached the driver's side window. Hal's first instinct upon recognizing the detective was relief.

"Smolinski," Hal said, "I never thought I'd be glad to—"

"Turn off your engine, Broadstreet."

"Sure, Jack." Hal did as he was told. "Sorry, I was—"

"Out of the vehicle."

"What's that, Jack?"

"I said, *step out of your vehicle.*"

Hal felt his stomach flip. "I don't understand. I was just—"

Sergeant Bravos appeared at the passenger side, ducked low enough to lean through the window. "Is there going to be a problem, Broadstreet?"

"No. No problem. Just . . ." Hal showed both his palms. He opened the door and stepped out into the summer's night. "Sorry. Just a little nervous because, as you saw, those bikers were—"

Smolinski spun him around and forced him hard against the car. The movement was so sudden and unexpected that the air was chased from his lungs. His arms were thrown against the hood with more force than necessary.

"Hey, what the hell?"

To answer, Smolinski shoved Hal's head hard enough against the hood to dent it. As Hal struggled to regain his senses, the cop took advantage of his disorientation to roughly frisk him.

Behind them, Hal heard footsteps. There were more. Several more. He realized how terribly alone he was on this dark highway.

"I've done nothing wrong," Hal said, spitting blood from his mouth. "Those two bikers . . . they were trying to intimidate me because of what I'm trying to write. If you're going to harass someone, don't you think it should be them?"

"*Harass you?*" The voice came from the men behind them, and Hal immediately recognized it. His stomach flipped, and his chest constricted. The realization hit him about the same time the cop slapped the handcuffs onto his wrists.

It was Kip Avondale.

"Y'all hear that?" Avondale laughed. "Newspaper boy thinks this is *harassment*."

"Come on, now," Hal said, barely able to choke the words from his throat. "Let's talk about this, guys."

"You want to know what *harassment* is?" Avondale stepped close enough that Hal could smell the beer on his breath. "Harassment is following someone day and night, digging through their trash, and printing stories about them in the local paper which slander their name."

"It's not slander if it's true."

Avondale showed teeth. Behind them, Hal heard the other men titter. He craned his neck to get a look at them, but the cruiser's headlights prevented him from seeing any more than silhouettes.

"I got an idea," Avondale said. "Why don't we show him what harassment really looks like?"

Hal thought he might be sick. He prayed for a car to pass, for someone to see, someone who might help.

Those prayers would remain unanswered.

CHAPTER FORTY-EIGHT

Jess Keeler

Present Day

Jess told Worthy.

Worthy raged at Sheriff Axel.

Axel spoke with Story Time Productions.

Each betrayal eclipsed the one previous. Worthy was angry that she had not heeded his mandate to abandon the sniper investigation. Axel did not relish the fact that she had abused her access to his files in order to investigate Ricky Lee Patience. The Germans resented her disclosing these truths, which therefore resulted in the rescinding of their access to the sheriff's resources.

By noon the following day, Jess's cell phone service had been terminated. She lost access to her Story Time email account an hour after that. That evening, a courier delivered a letter informing her that the production company had severed their relationship with her, and her services would no longer be needed.

Jess fell into a deep funk. She loved her mother, but could hardly bear to speak with her. Samantha had grown angry over temporarily moving into Jess's house in Deeton, which had been her childhood home. Benjamin sulked in his room as if he were a teenager. Jess had no opportunity to escape or any work to distract her.

Late that evening, the doorbell rang. Still in her pajamas, she grabbed a robe when she saw Buffy at the door.

"I thought we could commiserate," Buffy said, hoisting a bottle of bourbon. "Since neither of us have to work tomorrow."

"They fired you as well?"

"No." Buffy's grin spread wider. "I quit when I heard what they had done to you."

Jess opened the door wider and stepped aside. "Come on in, and mind the mess."

Buffy followed her into the kitchen, where Jess retrieved a pair of glasses. Buffy drank her whiskey neat, while Jess applied a handful of ice cubes. They sat across from each other at the small dining room table.

"After you left the interview with Jancowicz," Buffy said, "Sandy made her move. Aaron was disappointed that the interview would be cut short, but Sandy convinced him that she could get Jancowicz talking. She finished the interview for you."

"How was she?"

Buffy raised her eyebrows. "She was everything they wanted her to be."

Jess let that settle. She'd been coming to terms with how miserable the docuseries had made her life. While that style of journalism granted her a wider audience, her losing battle to keep control of the truth was killing her. However, now that the job had been taken from her, she felt as if she'd lost a limb and could still feel it twitching.

"They sent around a video yesterday before I quit," Buffy said. "It was an edited clip of Sandy's interview with Jancowicz. I downloaded it to my personal phone, so when they revoked my access, I still had it. If you even want to see it, that is."

"I do."

Buffy scrolled and clicked. A notification from Jess's new phone confirmed that it had been sent.

"They were already discussing replacing you when the call came," Buffy informed her. "Sandy's interview style was what they were looking for, and she had no problem leading her subjects toward the sound bites that Aaron wanted. All around, they said she was a team player, and when the idea was floated, she went hard at it. She brought up the fact that her social media presence brought a built-in audience and she was camera ready."

"Of course she did," Jess muttered. "She was hungry. She wanted it more than I did."

"She sold you out."

Jess shrugged. "It was bound to happen. Especially after I told Ennis that we had been secretly investigating the sniper."

"About that . . ." Buffy allowed a moment of decompression to slip between them. "When Sheriff Axel threatened to rescind cooperation from his office due to their investigation of Ricky Lee Patience, Sandy told the Germans to call his bluff."

"Why is that?"

"Her argument was that they no longer needed law enforcement cooperation."

Jess held her drink just shy of her mouth. "Because of what we uncovered?"

"That," said Buffy, "and apparently more. She implied that since Sheriff Worthy was the officer who arrested Ricky Lee, he might have been complicit in framing him. The Germans decided to back her play."

"Wait a second," said Jess, "you mean to tell me they are going to try and bury Worthy?"

Buffy nodded. "Apparently, they believe he has something to hide on the sniper, and that Lorne may not be disclosing everything in regards to the bootlegger murders."

"They can't do that . . ."

The expression Buffy leveled toward Jess said that they absolutely could and, most likely, *would*.

After Buffy left, Jess queued up the video. She forced herself to watch it. It was unedited, so Jancowicz's identity had yet to be obscured. Jess could see the deep lines in his face, the wrinkles crowding his eyes, the tattoos on the backs of his hands. Also unedited was Sandy's intense hunger. Jess watched with a sort of admiration at how confident and poised her former protégé seemed to appear in the chair across from him, how deftly she led him into answering the questions in the way Aaron would need for the so-called truth he planned to splice together.

She watched it twice more before the bourbon finally shuffled her off to sleep. She watched it again the next morning, still lying on the couch, which was where she was when the knock came at the door. Looking out the window, she recognized the Lawles County cruiser.

Sheriff Axel stood at the door when she opened it.

"How's your momma?" he asked her.

"She's fine, Sheriff," she said. "I can't thank you and your boys enough for what you did."

"Actually, it was Ennis who found her."

Jess sighed. "He's not answering my calls, so . . ."

"Mind if I come in?"

Jess held open the door. He entered like a cop, checking the corners of the house for would-be assailants. Finding none, he edged toward the couch, but did not sit. He glanced at thzze near-empty bottle of bourbon on the coffee table. Jess shrugged.

"You ever been fired, Lorne?"

"No," he said. "But I have left a job that wasn't right for me. It was the best thing I ever did."

Jess thought it best to let that sentiment sink in before polluting it with a comment.

"Those folks you got mixed up with have got all sorts of notions," Axel told her. "You should know that we've refused them all access to our records and resources."

"I've heard," she said. "I want you to know that all I was looking for was the truth. I was never out to hurt you or your agency."

"I know that."

"Does Ennis?"

Axel grimaced. "You'll have to ask him yourself."

"I don't think that's going to be possible."

"Not for a minute, no." Axel placed both his hands on his hips. "But give old Ennis a little bit of time to stew. He'll come around."

Jess's mind flashed to the trajectory of her friendship with Sandy. She understood. Betrayal was a slow burn.

"In the meantime," Axel said, "how are you keeping yourself busy?" He glanced at the video she'd transferred to her laptop. "What's this?"

"It's the interview they completed with your retired friend, Jancowicz," she said.

"Who?"

"The agent in Richmond who Deputy Magaw confided to be the best resource for motorcycle clubs."

"He's no friend of mine," Axel said. He lowered himself so he could better see the screen. "I've never met him. Magaw was our liaison. I believe she said he was involved in the operation which resulted in the arrests of several officers in the biker clubs? Did he say what role he served?"

"Not to me, but he may have explained it better to the crew after I was called away." She picked up the whiskey glasses and the bottle and headed for the sink. "One thing I really regret right now is that their story may place you and Ennis in their crosshairs. When I was involved, I could have contained the narrative. Now, even if I tried to do my own story, theirs would be more sensational and land nowhere near the truth, and probably to a bigger audience as well."

"What if I told you I could give you one piece of the puzzle that they couldn't possibly get?"

Jess stepped back into the living room. Axel had placed his spectacles on his face and was studying the screen of her laptop even closer.

"How so?"

Axel stood and looked over the tops of his glasses. "Remember how I told you I never forget a face?"

"I do."

"That man there," said Axel as he pointed to the image of Jancowicz on the screen, "is the man I pulled over with Digger Crowe and Billy Wayne Dickerson on the morning after the murders."

Charlie Chains.

PART THREE

CHAPTER FORTY-NINE

Martin Jancowicz

Present Day

"Hi, my name is Marty Jancowicz . . ."

Jancowicz drew a breath. He kept his gaze pinned to the floor. He hated these things. Forty years, and he still could look no one in the eye when he spoke at meetings. He had endured a great many ordeals—some of them brave, many of them not—but he could not abide the sight of people casting judgment upon him. It was the real reason he refused to remove his sunglasses indoors.

". . . and I'm an alcoholic."

The room replied in unison: "Hello, Marty."

He sat still a moment. The only sounds were the incessant hum of the air conditioner. The occasional gurgle from the coffee maker. A rattling cough from an old cigarette smoker. Beneath that silence, Jancowicz felt the words that he would never speak fighting their way to the surface. He wanted to tell them all his ghosts. How they'd lain dormant for years—decades—but recently had returned. That so much of his past that had been buried deep down inside him had resurfaced. That no matter how many times he turned the pages of *The Big Book*, or accepted higher powers, or talked with his sponsor, none of it was going away, and the worst thing possible would be to share any of this out loud.

How silence was his only friend.

Instead of saying all that, he merely mumbled, "I am sober today, and that's all that matters. Thank you for letting me share."

"Thank you, Marty," replied the room.

"Keep coming back," said an upbeat man near the front. "It works if you work it."

When the meeting ended, Jancowicz was the first out of his seat. He would have loved a cup of coffee, but a visit to the coffeepot could lead to small talk, and there were fewer things more dangerous than *small talk*.

Small talk.

Small talk dismantled him piece by piece. An innocent conversation about the weather or traffic could, in no time, lead to a discussion about life at home. Where you came from. What you did in life for money.

Those were topics of conversation that, over time, he'd found people believed to be normal. He'd found them best to avoid, which was why he'd walked out the door of the church house before anyone else could get out of their seats, happy to avoid any conversation with anyone, only to find that he was not to be so lucky. Waiting for him beside his car was a man he'd never expected to see again.

"Hello, Janco." The man would be in his eighties now, but he was no less severe than he had been the last time Jancowicz had seen him. Decades had passed, but the man required no cane. His eyes remained hawkish and alert, his shoulders and chest broad. "Why don't you take a walk with me?"

The first time Jancowicz had seen the man had been forty years earlier. Jancowicz had been a new recruit for the agency and was asked to assist on an undercover weapons deal. Another agent was the principal in an operation targeting the Vandals motorcycle club, and Jancowicz's only job had been to establish a position at the bar while the transaction occurred in another room. On the signal, Jancowicz, along with other operatives in plainclothes, would assist in the arrest of the suspect.

However the signal never came.

The operation had been aborted, and while debriefing back at the rendezvous, the man summoned Jancowicz in for a private discussion.

"After you established your position at the bar," the man had said, "you were approached by an individual. Tell me what happened."

Jancowicz was aware that he'd worn a recording device and anything he said could be verified. He didn't lie.

"An individual struck up a conversation with me," Jancowicz said, "based on the shirt I was wearing, which made reference to the US Marines. He asked if I served, and I told him I did."

"Did you?"

"No sir," said Jancowicz. "I received a deferment so that I could attend the academy. However, since I was technically undercover, I maintained that I had served. I let him talk a bit about his time over there, and we commiserated about friends we had lost. That much was true, sir, as there were several men from my hometown who didn't return."

"The man you established this rapport with is a prospect for the Vandals motorcycle club." The man waited to read a reaction from Jancowicz. "We see this as an opportunity."

"What kind of opportunity?"

"To infiltrate." The man had appeared pleased with himself. "Tell me, son, what was this prospect's name?"

"Billy Wayne Dickerson."

The man had been intimidating then, but even more so decades later, when he met Jancowicz outside the church house. They walked away from it, across the parking lot, taking slow steps at first. The afternoon was crisp, but still a bit hot for men of their age. The man, however, showed no sign of fatigue.

"You are in the program." The man nodded slightly behind him, toward the church house. "How is that going for you?"

"I've been in since the day you pulled me from deep cover and ordered me to clean up. Forty years now."

"You have forty years of sobriety?"

"God no sir." Jancowicz watched a blue jay chase away a smattering of sparrows. "I've managed two years and six months this go-around."

"Why do you suppose it is so difficult for you?"

"It's difficult for everyone, sir."

"Why did you relapse this last time? What did you say, two and a half years ago?"

"Same reason as always." The blue jay took to the skies. "Ghosts."

"What happens in those meetings? You confess your sins?"

"There are no confessions necessary."

"I thought that was one of the twelve steps."

"I believe you are thinking of *amends*."

"Ah."

Jancowicz turned his head from the sunlight. "It's where you atone for the things you did while you were using."

"I don't see the difference between that and confessing."

"Even still"—Jancowicz shrugged—"I always seem to relapse before that step comes along."

"Good for you."

They walked in silence toward a small churchyard, falling into step with each other as they passed between the gravestones.

"Do you remember the last time we spoke?" the man asked.

"I do."

"You were in a very bad place."

"It was a long time ago."

The man nodded.

"Eight months of deep cover with the Vandals," Jancowicz said. "I didn't know what I was doing. I had never been in a situation like that before."

"None of us had, son. What you did was unprecedented. It was unexpected. It was remarkable."

Jancowicz said nothing.

"I'm serious," said the man. "Because of what you did, a lot of very bad people were taken off the street."

"A bunch of them pleaded out or sold out their buddies for lesser sentences."

The man shrugged. "You saved a lot of lives."

"It's possible that I took more than I saved."

The man stopped walking. He turned to face Jancowicz. "None of that matters now."

"Because it happened so long ago?"

"Because everyone who knows about it is gone."

Except the two of us, Jancowicz thought, but did not say.

"You're familiar with the saying 'three can keep a secret if two are dead'?" asked the man.

"Of course."

"Of the three men who were there when that tragedy happened at the bootlegger's apartment, only you survived."

"That wasn't me," Jancowicz said. "That was my cover. That was Charlie Chains."

"Of course," said the man. "And he is dead too."

Years ago, when the man had come to him, Jancowicz was thirty pounds lighter, emaciated from amphetamine and alcohol, his mind stark raving mad.

"We're pulling you out," the man had said. "It's over."

Words that Jancowicz had waited every night for eight months to hear had filled him immediately with sadness. He feared it would be impossible to shed Charlie Chains's skin, to rid himself of his horrible secrets. That someone might find out, that someone would keep looking.

"They won't if he is dead," the man had offered. "No one will look for a murdered biker in the middle of a gang war."

So they had set about "killing" his cover. Captain Hank Dorritt had planted the stories of the discovery of Charles "Chains" Wilcox's body being discovered in a shallow grave. He reached out to the proper authorities in the jurisdiction where the body had supposedly been found. Charles Wilcox had come from nothing, and just as easily, he was returned to nothing.

Hank Dorritt died from cancer in the late 1980s.

Three can keep a secret if two are dead . . .

If his handler ever thought about these deaths that had haunted Jancowicz for so long, he kept it to himself. As they walked the old boneyard, Jancowicz wondered if he ever thought about them at all.

"You spoke with someone," said the man.

Jancowicz felt his insides turn cold. "I didn't tell them anything."

The man lifted an eyebrow.

"I didn't," he said. "It was some silly documentary about motorcycle gangs from the past. They asked questions about FIASCO. I gave them nothing more than they would find in old newspapers."

"You let them take pictures of you."

"They said they would distort them."

"Someone could recognize you."

"Who?" Jancowicz asked. "Everyone is dead."

"If you need to talk to someone, after all this time," said the man, "you could always pick up the phone."

"I don't need to talk to anyone."

The man's eyes cut toward the church house, where the other members of the group were leaving for their cars.

"People have begun to inquire about you," said the man.

"What people?"

"Does it matter? They are asking. There are things they want to know."

Panic seized Jancowicz's throat.

"This woman with the podcast," the man said, "she is no different than that reporter. The one from the scandal sheet."

"He was harmless."

"Only after you rendered him so."

Jancowicz felt a heaviness settle into his shoulders. "It's different. She doesn't know anything."

"If that were true," said the man, "then I wouldn't be here."

They left the graveyard. They crossed the parking lot, and before they spoke again, they were standing next to Jancowicz's car.

"We will need you to handle this situation," the man said.

"With all due respect, sir," said Jancowicz, "I'm retired."

"It's you or them," the man said, ignoring him. "Out of respect for what you did for FIASCO, I will let you make that decision. But make no mistake: it will be made."

The man placed his hand on the trunk of Jancowicz's car.

"You have all the tools you need to make it," he said. "Only it will need to be made soon, because, like the reporter, she is getting close. Much closer than we can afford her to be."

The man removed his hand from the trunk and touched Jancowicz's shoulder with genuine fatherly affection. Only when he removed it did Jancowicz realize how empty the gesture was. The man turned his back to Jancowicz and climbed into the passenger seat of a waiting car, which then drove away.

Jancowicz didn't need to open the trunk to know what he would find inside, but he did anyway. Laying his eyes upon it was like seeing a long-lost friend for the first time in ages.

It was an M82 sniper rifle.

Next to it was a Beretta.

Three can keep a secret . . .

CHAPTER FIFTY

HAL BROADSTREET

1984

The drugs wore off long before Hal awoke. Before his eyes fluttered open, he could hear the beep, beep and whir of the machinery in the room with him, the soft whispers of the duty nurse, the gentle calamity in the hallway. He was aware, more than anything, of the thickness in his belly, the pounding in his skull, the pain that seemed to overtake the whole of him.

He was in a hospital bed. A nurse attended to the instruments that were tethered to him.

"How long have I been out?" he asked her.

"You're awake." Her voice was chipper, upbeat. Pleasant.

"How long?"

"Just overnight," she said. "We moved you out of the ER and into a room only a couple of hours ago."

Hal blinked the room into focus. Random images crept into his consciousness. Billy Wayne's casket being lowered into the earth. Twin headlights on a dark highway. Kip Avondale taking him down to the asphalt.

"How did I end up in here?" he asked.

She smiled kindly. "The doctor will be in very shortly. It might be better if he—"

Hal drifted away before she could finish her thought.

When he returned, the sun had gone down. Vince Fenelli stood over him with an unidentifiable expression. He carried lilies with him.

"Peg said to bring you these." He set the flowers down on a chair reserved for visitors. He reached into his jacket for a pint bottle of whiskey. "I personally thought you might find this more useful."

Hal tried to smile. It sent shock waves of pain down the nerves of his spine.

"They found you on Highway 809," Hal said. "It looked like you had been in an accident."

Hal laughed.

Vince frowned. "The police say it was—"

"Police say." Hal tried the words on for size.

"You were lucky they were in the area. We all are, in fact. There have been a rash of hit-and-runs up and down that stretch of road. The police say that—"

"*Police say?*" Hal spat out the words like they were rancid meat. "Since when do we give a flying shit about what *police say*? We're journalists, Vince. At least, we *were*."

"Hal, I don't think—"

"I'm close, dammit." Hal raised his hand to make a point, but realized the IV restricted his movement. He cut eyes toward it as if it were the cause of all his woes, but saw the point moot. "I don't know how the police are tied to this, but that little incident on the highway just proves that they were."

"What little incident?" Vince said. "Hal, the police saved you."

"Jesus, Vince. You really are gullible."

"I'm worried about you, brother. I really am. Ever since Jem Fosskey, you haven't been yourself."

"I've been exactly myself. It's everyone else that's gone apeshit."

Vince unscrewed the cap from the pint bottle and took a pull for himself. He wiped his mouth with the back of his hand and offered it to Hal, who refused.

"There's a connection," Hal said. "I don't know what it is, but we can print what I know. That will rattle some cages and shake some bushes. What I want more than anything is Charlie Chains, scared shitless of me and my next story. I've got Peg running his motorcycle regis—"

"Oh, Hal . . ."

"What?"

"I have to tell you something."

Hal didn't like Vince's expression. He motioned with his hand for Vince to spit it out.

"Charles Wilcox is dead."

Hal didn't know what to say. The sedatives still cobwebbed his head. He had a general light-headedness that prevented him from full comprehension. He blinked a handful of times, then asked Vince to repeat himself.

"It's true," Vince said. "The story was in the *Herald* this morning."

"In the *Herald*?" Hal still had trouble with it. "Since when did they give a shit about—"

"He was found in a tobacco field. Shallow grave. It looks like an execution. Police say he was—"

"Police say?" Hal struggled against the IV again. "Vince, you better come off it with the *police say*. I want something better than an article from Liv Crane filled with *police say*. I want some hard evidence. I want to see this guy's body."

"Hal, you can't—"

"I'm on these guys, and I'm supposed to believe that he's dead just because *police say*?"

"You're drawing lines where there aren't any."

"She's their *shill*, Vince. The *Herald* thinks that printing 'police say' is the only confirmation they need."

"You'd rather quote a criminal?"

"What's the goddamn difference?" Hal threw up his hands. "They beat me up in the middle of the highway at night, Vince. They had Uncle Meaney killed. Just shot him in the street like he was a sick dog."

Vince looked upon him with an expression that was akin to pity. "You've got a vendetta, Hal. The *Times* can't be part of your revenge agenda."

"You pick now to be principled?" Hal couldn't suppress his laughter. "Last week you ran an article claiming JFK was living as a cyborg in southern Virginia. Last month, you printed an interview with a woman claiming she was abducted by lizard people living in the sewers beneath the Althiser housing development. Don't tell me now that you've decided to be *selective* when I produce some uncomfortable truths."

Vince took a step back. He spoke as if his mind were made up. "We're not running the piece," he said. "Not until you take a much-needed vacation."

"Who got to you, Vince?"

Vince ignored him. "Take some time off. Heal. See the coast. When's the last time you had a good meal at a nice restaurant?"

"You of all people . . ." Hal couldn't seem to get enough air to his lungs. "What did they offer you?"

"I'm going to pretend the only reason you're saying those things is because you're exhausted," said Vince.

Hal fired back, "And I'm going to pretend that you still have a backbone."

Vince nodded and backed slowly toward the door. "I'm putting you on leave, brother. As of this minute. You're off the story."

"You can't take me off the story," Hal said. "Because I don't write for you anymore."

"Hal, don't."

"If you won't print it," Hal said, pressing the button to summon his nurse for more drugs, "then I'll find someone who will."

CHAPTER FIFTY-ONE

Jess Keeler

Present Day

His name was Dan Madsen, but everybody only knew him as Cochise. He fixed bikes and rode bikes and bought and sold bikes, or did just about anything and everything that had something to do with bikes. Then, in the evenings, he'd stop by Crazy Eights for a game of pool, a couple of cans of beer, and a few rounds of shooting the shit.

That's exactly what Jess Keeler wanted to do. She warmed him up with a couple of games of nine ball, then sat with him at the bar while he tried to impress her with wild stories from his youth. He was in his sixties, but his lifestyle left him looking significantly older. Age had worn down the rough edges, however. He kept a playful twinkle in his eye, even when she retrieved her recorder from her purse and set it on the bar between them.

"Lady," he said, nodding at it, "if you pulled out one of them doohickeys back in my hooting-and-hollering days, I'd be liable to take it from you and do something with it that you wouldn't like."

"You old flirt." She swatted at his shoulder. "Don't tell me you're afraid of answering a couple questions for my podcast."

"Hell, you could probably talk me into just about anything."

"You said you rode with the Vandals back in the eighties?"

He gulped the last of the beer from his can, then motioned for the bartender to bring him another one. "On her tab," he said, motioning to Jess. "Yeah. I came on in, oh, about seventy-six, back when they were called the Blood Ravens. A lot of things changed over the years. Myself included, I reckon. I'm still here, though."

"A lot of people aren't."

"No ma'am, they ain't. We lost some good ones."

"Like Digger Crowe?"

Cochise laughed out the side of his mouth. "Missy, I don't know what you heard, but he weren't one of the good ones."

"I've heard a few things."

"If you heard them about ol' Digger, you might keep those things to yourself. I still don't like to talk about him, for fear that he might rise out of the grave and snatch out my tongue."

"That's a visual."

"I've seen it in my sleep."

Jess drank from her own beer. "What about Billy Wayne Dickerson?"

"It was a shame what happened to him."

"What happened to him?"

Cochise's expression tightened. "He got caught up in that mess between the Vandals and the Rare Breed. The way I heard it was that the Rare Breed caught him alone and hauled him up top of an old grain elevator down in the Back Back to torture him. That got every Vandal good and mad, and I reckon none of them would have stopped until every Rare Breed was dead and gone, but for those arrests putting an end to the war once and for all."

"You were friends with him?"

"Honey, everybody was friends with Billy Wayne. He was that sort of fellow." Cochise smiled, his eyes somewhere else. "He was a good kid. Served his country. Came home and got himself killed. That's the way of it, I reckon."

"I'm trying to find out more about a guy named Charlie Wilcox. I believe they called him Chains."

"Chains Wilcox?" Cochise twisted his face, scattering those deep wrinkles every which way. "Can't say I remember nobody named Chains."

"I'm getting a lot of that. It sure would help if I could find a picture of him."

"A picture for your podcast?"

Jess smiled. He was sharper than he let on. "The listeners would like to hear my impressions of him."

"Not sure if I have what you're looking for, but come with me." It took some doing for Cochise to dismount the barstool, but once he found his legs, he quickly crossed the room to a corner where framed photographs had been nailed to the wall. He traced his finger from one to another until he found what he was looking for.

"This here is Billy Wayne."

Jess leaned closer for a better look at the photograph. There were three men and a woman. The men wore leather vests with Vandals patches and colors. They stood in front of a white two-door car. Everyone was all smiles except for one.

"That sourpussed bastard right there," Cochise said, pointing to the man in the middle, "that's Digger Crowe. He weren't one to be messed with."

Jess focused on Digger. His eyes were dark, piercing. His lips twisted into a scowl. He wasn't the largest of the men in the different photographs, but she reckoned he more than made up for it with meanness.

"I bet he was great at parties." She pointed to the taller one. "Who's that?"

"Caleb McNaughton. Him and Billy Wayne were good pals. Almost inseparable until . . . well, they fell out."

"Why was that?"

Cochise shrugged. "Why do you think men fall out?"

Jess studied the picture of the woman. "She's pretty."

"Baby Doll was a pip, sure. She was married to McNaughton until he left the club. After that, she started running around with Digger."

"Is she still around?"

Cochise drank from his beer. "No, dear. Women who ran around with Digger didn't stick around very long."

"What happened?"

Cochise closed one eye to better see inside his beer can. "I think it's time I fetch another beer."

As he walked away, Jess pulled out her phone and snapped a picture of the photograph. Something about it triggered a memory, but before she allowed it to manifest, a call came through. She answered it.

It was Sheriff Axel. "I just got off the phone with the records department up in Richmond," he said. "I am not able to access any operational information without a federal court order."

"So we can't find out what Jancowicz's role was in FIASCO?"

"Not yet, we can't." She could hear the adrenaline in Axel's voice. She wondered how long it had been since he'd been this deep into an investigation. "I have friends in various departments at different agencies, but so far, everything I can access is strictly biographical."

"What does that tell you?"

"Nothing out of the ordinary. It says he graduated from State at the top of his class, then entered the academy. He joined investigations with the state police almost immediately. There's a huge gap in his activity between late 1983 and early 1985, after which he essentially remained in administrative roles."

Jess's stomach tightened, like she might have had too much caffeine. "Any explanation for that gap?"

"Not an official one."

"What about *unofficial*?"

"I don't need to tell you that those dates would encompass the Fosskey murders," Axel said. "What about you?"

"I'm not having any luck here either," she reported. "I can find no photographs or anyone who can positively ID Wilcox as Jancowicz."

She heard Axel sigh through the line. "I just don't get it."

"What?"

"Let's continue the argument for a moment. Jancowicz went undercover for Operation FIASCO and successfully infiltrated the Vandals. His death was fabricated in order to pull him out so they could try the bad actors."

"That's where the information is leading us." Jess saw Cochise waiting for her at the bar with two fresh beers. She lifted a finger to signal she'd be right over. "What specifically has you flummoxed?"

"To fake his death," said Axel, "would be a massive undertaking. We had police reports, autopsy reports, and several newspaper articles. How could all of these institutions conspire to cover it up and get away with it?"

Jess thought on it some. A thought presented itself rather quickly.

"I can't tell you for sure," she said, "but I can think of someone to ask."

CHAPTER FIFTY-TWO

Jess Keeler

Present Day

The hostess greeted Jess with a smile. "Nice to see you again so soon, Ms. Keeler."

"Thank you, Melissa," Jess said. "What's it been? Two weeks? Three? I suppose I'm becoming a regular."

"Ms. Crane is expecting you. Would you like me to show you to her table?"

"It's okay," Jess told her. "I know the way."

She did. This would be the third time she'd met Olivia Crane. All three times the former newswoman had insisted on meeting at the same steak house for lunch. All three times, she'd refused to speak after the food was served.

Only this time, Olivia told her she'd have to keep it short.

"My time is very limited today," Olivia said, checking her watch. "My lunch appointment will be here directly, and it's a very important meeting."

"Thank you for squeezing me in." Jess took a seat across from her at the table.

"I'll have you know that I really respected the work you did with *Something Bad Wrong*," Olivia said as she sipped her coffee. "But I was extremely disappointed with your line of questioning during your last visit."

"I apologize. I promise to keep my questions related to the Jem Fosskey murders."

Olivia frowned. "I heard you were no longer working with that television program."

"News still travels fast. Where did you hear that?"

"I never reveal my sources." Olivia coyly shrugged. "You know, I always imagined I could enjoy a second career in television. I watch these investigative formats and entertain some real notions. If we had the opportunities that you have back when I was in my heyday . . . let me tell you."

"It's true that I am no longer with Story Time Productions," said Jess. "I've struck out on my own. I'm podcasting again."

Olivia's eyes cut toward Jess's handbag. "Where is your little recorder?"

"I don't need it today."

Olivia looked somewhat disappointed. "Then what is it you want?"

"To ask you a couple of questions."

"No," said Olivia, folding her hands. "What is it you *want*? Why is it that you are doing this?"

"To get to the bottom of this story."

"You're not listening to me. I am asking you *why*. *Why* is it that you are putting yourself through all of this? Is it for the money? The fame?"

Jess tried and failed to stifle a laugh. "Those aren't exactly the trappings of a true-crime podcaster."

"Then *why*?"

"The truth."

Olivia shook her head. "The truth is the truth whether you know it or not. What do you really *want*?"

"I want to get the story right and get it out there."

Olivia rolled her eyes. "I need to get ready for my appointment. They will be here any moment, and I really should—"

"I want to look in the eyes of the victims' families and tell them what happened." Jess realized her voice carried a bit, but didn't care. "When I am sitting across from these people who have lost a loved one and nobody—no one at all—has seemed to care over all of these years . . . I get to be the person who tells them their loved one's story matters, and I can be the one to tell it. I can give it shape and purpose and put it in front of an audience so that they can see—truly *see*—these people and what they meant and what was taken from them. I can communicate their grief with the world and make it a *shared* grief, and if that gives someone peace or any sort of semblance of peace, then that's why I do it, because I did it while doing the one thing I'm good at: telling a story."

Olivia's eyes remained fixed on Jess, as if they were seeking out some cracks in the veneer. Finding none, she turned her attention briefly to her watch.

"You have three minutes," Olivia said.

Jess wasted no time. "Charlie Wilcox. He was one of the three bikers that Harold Broadstreet reported to have been arrested on the morning of the murders."

"Hal . . ."

"Yes. *Hal.* He reported extensively in the *Times* on these three men, all of whom died within two months."

Olivia met this information with a flat expression.

"Please . . ." Jess reached for her clipboard and produced a printout of an old *Herald* article. "Your paper reported on Wilcox's death. What proof did you have that he was dead?"

"Proof?"

"Yes. How did you know he was dead?"

"Because the police said he was."

"Police said?"

"Yes," said Olivia. "The police said it, so I reported it."

Jess nodded. "Okay. *Who* told you?"

"You mean specifically?"

Jess nodded again.

"You really expect me to remember? It was forty years ago."

"Yes," said Jess. "I do."

The only sounds were the scraping of forks against plates. The low din of lunchtime conversation. A soft tune from the restaurant's speakers.

"Please, Olivia," said Jess. "Hal died for this."

"*What?*" Olivia balled up her napkin. "How dare you—you listen to me just—"

"No, *you* listen to *me*. This is important. Everything—all of it—is tied together, and I don't know how. There are missing pieces, and I think you have some of them. You reported this bit of information, and I need to know how you got it. It's *important*."

Olivia measured the moment before saying, "Hank Dorritt told me."

"*Captain* Dorritt?" Jess asked. "He called you with this information?"

"No. He met me at Honey's. It was an all-night diner back in the old days, just after the mill closed. He handed it to me and told me to print it."

Jess tried not to look as shocked as she was. "He met you *in person?*"

"Yes, dear."

"Was that common? For the captain of the police department's Crimes Against Persons division to meet a reporter and hand them a story to be published?"

"Hank and I were close," Olivia said. "Once upon a time, I was married to a former colleague of his."

"But was it *common?*"

"No," Olivia conceded. "It was a touch unusual."

"Then you ran it?"

"You're holding it in your hand."

Jess leaned back in her seat. The math came at her too fast to properly calculate. "Did you check the information before you printed it?"

"It was a death notice," she said. "Why would I check it?"

"To see if it was true."

"I knew it was true."

"How could you know without checking?"

Olivia nearly laughed out loud. "Because police said it was."

"Police said." Jess realized her mouth was hanging open. "*Police said*, and you accepted that at face value?"

"That's usually all you need, sweetheart."

Their eyes met for a moment. During that moment, several things went unsaid. After it passed, Olivia averted her gaze, looking instead at the tabletop and the many distractions poised upon it.

"You sound like him, you know."

"Is that a compliment?" Jess asked.

Olivia smiled lightly. "No comment."

Jess reached across the table and placed her hand on Olivia's forearm. "Olivia, Hal died for this. I can't prove it yet, but I am going to. With or without anyone's help. Because if I don't, then the truth about why all those other people were murdered and why Ricky Lee Patience spent the last forty years in prison will die with him, and I can't let that happen."

Olivia opened her mouth to speak, but something prevented her from doing so. Jess couldn't suss out if it was shock or shame, but she realized she wasn't getting it from her today. She'd made her point.

"I should let you go," Jess whispered, letting go of Olivia's forearm. "I'd hate to keep you from your other appointment."

Jess excused herself. The entire walk through the restaurant to the front door, she felt rejuvenated, but that feeling was dashed upon sight of her former protégé at the hostess stand. Jess quickly ducked into a small alcove.

"My name is Sandra Newman," Jess could hear her telling the hostess, "and I'm here to meet Olivia Crane."

"She's already at her table," said the hostess. "Shall I lead you back?"

"My television crew will be joining us," Sandy told her. "If you will lead them back when they arrive, that would be great. In the meantime, could you direct me to the restroom?"

"Certainly. It's right this way."

Jess watched as Sandy disappeared into the women's room. Through the window, she could see Aaron instructing a young man how to assemble his lavalier mic packs. Jess realized she needed to move fast. As soon as the hostess returned to her position, Jess slipped into the women's room.

Sandy stood in front of the mirror, fussing over her hair. She froze a moment upon sight of Jess in the reflection, approaching her from behind, then resumed her preening.

"So it's Sandra now, is it?" Jess said to Sandy's back. "I like it. It sounds so professional. So much more mature than *Sandy*, which is absolutely the name of a social media influencer chasing likes and subscribes in her bikini."

"I thought this place would be out of the price range of an unemployed mommy blogger," said Sandy. "What brings you out to this part of town?"

"Same as you, I reckon."

"Aah . . . Olivia." Sandy primped a perfect lock of blonde hair. "I warned the Germans that we should have made you sign a noncompete clause."

"I have a feeling we'll be telling two different stories," Jess said. "Mine will smell a little bit less fabricated and more like the truth."

"Perhaps," said Sandy, turning off the water. "But it will be to a much smaller market share than ours. How many downloads did you get with your little podcast? One million? Two?" She shook her head. "How *cute*."

"Two million and one," Jess said, "if you would like to hear the exclusive scoop I've got lined up."

"That sounds like a nice story," said Sandy, "but our interview with Ricky Lee Patience should put us well over the top."

"You scored an interview with Ricky Lee?" Jess couldn't hide her shock. "How?"

Sandy dabbed at her mascara with the tip of her pinkie. "The Germans. Yes, you were quick to discount them, but it's nice working with people who have connections."

"The *Germans*? They said the sniper story was irrelevant. Why are they interested in Ricky Lee?"

"My research convinced them otherwise."

Jess realized she'd balled her hands into fists. "I think you mean *our* research."

Sandy shrugged. She wiped her fingers with a paper towel, then handed it to Jess. She did not take it. Instead, Sandy dropped it to the floor at Jess's feet.

"I meant what I said about you being an inspiration to me," said Sandy. "You still are, in fact." She ran her eyes down the length of Jess, then back up again. "I don't plan to make the same mistakes."

Sandy left Jess standing stock still, her anger preventing her from making any moves. To put down one foot would mean she'd have to put down another, and she didn't trust herself not to rush headlong into the restaurant and grab Sandy Newman or whatever her name was by the hair and slap some sense into her.

But Jess wasn't going to do that.

Instead, she decided she was going to play by their rules for a change.

"If they want to play dirty," said Jess, "then maybe we should all play dirty."

CHAPTER FIFTY-THREE

HAL BROADSTREET

1984

The kid at the plate smashed the baseball, sending it to the stratosphere, up over the center fielder's glove and into the stands. The crowd leaped to their feet, some in fury, others in jubilation, as the kid rounded the bases and headed for home.

Not Hal. He barely noticed. Instead, his eyes were on the guy wearing the Braves ball cap in the row in front of him. Hal had been studying him the entire game, and once he'd gathered the information he needed, he leaned forward and tapped him on the shoulder.

"The player in the on deck circle," Hal said. "He's your kid?"

The man beamed proudly. "He certainly is."

"He's doing pretty good, huh?"

"He's two for three this game," said the father. "Batting .410 for the season."

"Wow." Hal slapped his own forehead. "That's better than Teddy Ballgame, ain't it?"

The father laughed. "Not by much, but Ted Williams never had to face division-A pitchers."

"We all got to start somewhere. Am I right?"

The man nodded, then returned his attention to the game. Hal thought quick for something to say, then, falling short, pointed to the seat next to the man.

"Do you mind?"

The man, somewhat distracted, looked at the seat and shook his head. Hal climbed over the row and, after brushing aside some peanut shells with his hand, sat down next to the man.

"Any college plans?" Hal asked him.

The father's eyes went wide. "Some scouts came up from State last week when they played the Panthers. Rollie went four for four with a home run and five RBIs."

"If that don't get him a scholarship, then I don't know what will."

"We're working on his grades, though."

"State has been known to look the other way for the right player."

The father's demeanor darkened. "Not my boy," he said. "I have him study every night and limit his distractions. I tell him there'll be plenty time for girls once he goes to college."

"If he's anything like his old man . . . Right?"

The father smiled tightly, then watched as his son stepped up to the plate and took his practice swings.

"My name's Harold," said Hal.

"Frank." Frank shook his hand, but didn't take his eyes off the action in the field. "Which one is yours?"

"Oh, I don't have a kid. I just love the game."

Rollie let a ball pass high and away for a one-oh count. His father clapped and shouted, "Good eye, son!"

"What do you do, Frank?" Hal asked.

"I work for the county."

"Aah. That's a good gig. Secure, I bet. Even if another recession hits, it's pretty hard to fire somebody from the county."

"I'm elected," said Frank, "so it's a bit easier. So far, though, no one has run against me."

"Uncontested? You must be a Democrat."

Frank laughed, but shook his head. "I'm a coroner, so it's not a party position."

"Coroner? You been in that gig long?"

Frank paused while his son swung and missed. He balled his hands to fists and pounded both his knees once. "I've told him time and again not to swing at trash. What was he—" He caught himself, then, half-distracted, said, "The people have graced me with the position for going on ten years now, after my daddy retired. He'd been coroner of Iredell County for fifty-two years before me."

"Wow," said Hal. "Only two coroners for the county in over half a century. That's some power right there."

Frank threw a glance at Hal that might have been laced with suspicion, if it weren't for the ump calling the next pitch a strike.

Frank rose to his feet. "Get your eyes checked, Bruce! That was nowhere near the plate, and you know it!"

The umpire ignored him and settled in for the next pitch.

"I bet you have lots of stories, working as the coroner of a small county like this," said Hal. "I hear if there's anybody that can tell you how the sausage is made, it's probably you."

"Did you know," Frank said, "the only person in North Carolina who can arrest a sheriff is the coroner?"

"You don't say."

"It's true."

Rollie let another pitch go by, low and inside, for a two-two count. Frank leaned forward in his seat, both legs tapping. The tension dripped off him like fat off steak.

Hal felt it was now or never.

"Say, I heard about that biker y'all found," he said. "The one who was prematurely interred."

Frank quickly glanced at him, then back at the field. He said nothing.

"I read about it in the paper," Hal said. "It sounded like a real mess."

"Most of death is."

Another pitch. Three-two count. Rollie stepped out of the box to take some more practice swings. The pitcher consulted his rosin bag.

"Thing is," Hal said, "I went by your office and didn't see any report on it. I've checked around the funeral homes, and nobody ever reported picking up the body. The only thing I've seen anywhere is some article copying a press release from the Lake Castor police that this man was found buried in a shallow grave down here, but I can't find anything that will confirm it."

Frank turned to face Hal, taking him in completely for the first time. In doing so, he missed the payoff pitch, which was fouled behind the first-base line.

"Who the hell are you?" Frank asked. "And what are you doing bothering me at my kid's game?"

"I told you," said Hal. "My name's Harold. I'm just a guy asking the county coroner about a dead guy I heard about in the paper, but it seems everywhere else he's a mystery."

"So what?"

"So I happen to like mysteries."

Frank's eyes narrowed. He looked Hal up and down, as if searching for somewhere to land a punch. In doing so, he missed his son smacking the tar out of the baseball and starting to blaze the base paths.

"Listen here, buddy," Frank said through his teeth. "I don't know who you are or what you're up to, but you stay away from me, and you stay away from my family."

"Like I said, I stopped by your office, but your receptionist said you wouldn't see me."

"You're that tabloid writer from Lake Castor?"

"I've been called worse."

Frank stood up. He picked up what was left of his fountain soda and poured it down the front of Hal's shirt. Other spectators turned their attention from the game and pointed at the pair.

"Stay away from my family," said Frank. "People have ended up on my slab for less."

CHAPTER FIFTY-FOUR

HAL BROADSTREET

1984

Olivia Crane was halfway through her cheeseburger when Hal slid into the booth across from her. She set down her sandwich, struggled to finish chewing.

"You look like shit, Hal," she said. "When is the last time you slept?"

"I'll sleep when I'm dead." He shook some of the rain out of his hair and pointed at her fries. "Do you mind?"

She slid the plate closer to him. He grabbed one and stuffed it into his mouth. He grabbed another before he had swallowed the first.

"When is the last time you ate?" she asked him.

He ignored her. "I've got the mother of all stories, Liv."

"Can you put another record on, Hal?" she sighed. "This song is getting a little tired."

"This time I mean it."

Olivia swallowed her food. He snatched another fry. Over her shoulder, he saw a man in the corner booth glance up at him from his newspaper. The man quickly turned his attention back to the comics. "They're watching me."

Olivia rolled her eyes. "Come off it, Hal."

"They're not very subtle about it either."

"How hard did you hit your head in that accident on the highway?"

Hal saw his old rival in a new light. "The gulf between what you know and what you think you know is pretty far and wide." He glanced over his shoulder, finding no one there. "That was no accident on the highway."

"Oh yeah, that's right," she said. "The secret conspiracy to silence a tabloid journalist."

"Just because you're paranoid don't mean they aren't out to get you."

"I ran that by Hank, and you know what he said?"

"Dorritt?" Hal laughed. "I can only imagine."

"He said if it wasn't for his men coming along and finding you, that you would probably not have survived."

"Fantastic story, but I wouldn't pay three dollars to see it at the matinee."

Olivia reached for Hal's face, but he jerked it away. She tried again, and this time he let her. She brushed the wet locks from his eyes. He couldn't remember the last time someone had touched him with any amount of affection.

"Hal, have you talked to Vince?"

He shook his head. "I'm not going back to the office. They've gotten to him."

"Who got to him?"

Hal reached into the inside pocket of his overcoat. He came out with a file folder that had been folded in half. "I need you to take this."

She looked at it like it might give her the rickets. "What is it?"

"It's the article I've been working on." He set it down on the table in front of him and slid it toward her. "It blows everything wide open."

She slid it back across the table to him. "I think you should give it to Vince."

"This is bigger than Vince. It's bigger than the *Times*. It's bigger than you and me."

"But Vince is the one who will print it."

Hal glanced again at the man in the corner booth and attempted to suppress his smile.

"They're not even trying to hide what they're doing," he said. "He's holding the newspaper upside down."

"What on earth are you talking about, Hal?"

"They've tapped the phones at the *Times*, Liv."

"You're suggesting some big conspiracy?"

"I'm more than suggesting it."

Olivia didn't buy it. "You sound like a hack crime novelist."

"Look around, Liv." Hal waved his arm over the room, but sig-naled the entire world. "Everything, everywhere is a conspiracy. All of it. Redlining. Trickle-down economics. Who gets to sell what drugs and where, and who does or doesn't get arrested for it. All of it is designed by rich men with power, and the entire country looks the other way. Conspiracies are everywhere. This is small potatoes."

Olivia closed her eyes. "I'm worried about you, Hal."

"Don't be," he said. "It's how I know that I'm getting close."

"Hal, sweetie . . ."

"Don't *Hal, sweetie* me, Liv. I can see it in your eyes: you don't believe me. It doesn't matter now, but in time, you're going to see that I'm right." He pushed the folder closer to her. "Just read it. You'll see."

Olivia didn't budge. Instead, she held him in her gaze.

"Hal," she said, "do you remember what you said to me when I was first getting started on the crime desk?"

Hal forced a laugh. "Come on, Liv," he said. "We're dinosaurs. That was too long ago for a memory like mine."

"It was thirteen years ago. I had been writing articles in the Home Decor section, talking about home tips for housewives and hating every minute of it."

"You were the queen of venetian blinds, Liv. Your articles about what to do with throw rugs were revolutionary."

Olivia's smile was tight. "I would have done anything to get off that beat."

Hal heard something in her voice. Was it *regret? Pride?* Whatever it was, it left a stink on her words.

"The night I got my big break," she said. "Do you remember it?"

He did. "It was Christmas."

"Yes. Christmas." Her eyes went somewhere else . . . some*time* else. "Every man on the crime beat—and they were *all* men—was either home for the holidays or out piss-drunk. I was the only reporter in the building when the detectives came in that night."

"Hank Dorritt and Jack Powers."

"That's right." She rolled her eyes at the mention of her ex-husband, Powers. "If I'd have known then what I know now . . ." She regained her tone. "At any rate, they came in and wanted to get the word out about a couple who had gone missing. They were sure the kids had run off and eloped, but since it was the holidays, their families had grown concerned. Just in case, the detectives wanted to alert the public. I, on the other hand, was certain something bad had happened, which of course, we later found out it had. This was my first big break, and I didn't want to waste the opportunity. I wanted to report what my gut was telling me. You were the only colleague who took me seriously, and when I told you, do you remember what you said?"

"Like you said"—Hal smiled—"if we'd have known then . . ."

"You said to ignore my gut." Olivia sat back in the booth and crossed her arms. "You said the only thing that matters is what can be double or triple confirmed. Everything else, you told me, is conjecture."

Hal felt the weight of her words.

"Twelve years was a long time ago," he said. "A lot of things have happened since then. To the *Times*. To Lake Castor. To me . . ." The article felt like hot coals in his hand. He pushed it toward her again. "Take it, Liv. Read it."

This time, she did. Without so much as glancing at it, she shoved it into her handbag.

"Thank you."

She shook him off. "Get some sleep, Hal. I mean it."

Hal stood. As he did, he saw the man in the corner booth lay down his newspaper and signal to the waitress for his bill.

"You know," Hal said, "you may be the only friend I have left."

"If that's true," Olivia said without smiling, "then you are truly good and screwed."

CHAPTER FIFTY-FIVE

Ennis Worthy

1984

Ennis Worthy had been nodding off at the desk in the jailhouse for nearly half an hour when the news broke. He heard it first from his sheriff, Bobby McCoy, who walked in the door slow and casual. He alternated his gaze between Worthy's unopened lawbooks and the prisoner in cell 2.

"There's some boys up in Lake Castor asking for you," said the sheriff.

Worthy sat up straight and wiped the sleep from his eye. "Me?"

"Yup." McCoy picked at a mustard stain on his necktie. "There was a murder up that way a couple days ago, and they said you might know something about it. I reckon it's because you've spent so much time in the Back Back lately."

Worthy felt the tension take hold in his shoulders. So far as he knew, he and Officer Axel had covered up any trace of their involvement in the murder of Billy Wayne Dickerson. The day after it happened, Axel had "randomly" found the body while patrolling the area and called it in. The investigators tore the place apart in search of clues that they would never find. Both newspapers detailed the discovery, as

Billy Wayne had been a son—if not a *prodigal* one—of the community. Everyone chalked his murder up as another casualty in the ongoing tensions between biker clubs. By the next day, conversations had moved elsewhere.

"A murder?" Worthy asked. "What would I know about a murder in Lake Castor?"

"Turns out there's been some fella shooting folks over there," McCoy said. "Like some kind of *series killer* or some such. You heard of this?"

Worthy merely shrugged with his eyebrows.

"It hasn't been reported on much because, thankfully, this son-bitch has only been targeting Black folks." McCoy fingered open a half-empty bag of potato chips that Worthy had been snacking on. He peeked inside, then seemed to think better of it. "Only with his latest victim, their killer seems to have *escalated*."

Worthy blinked his eyes open wider. "What do you mean?"

"That's what they call it when a series killer breaks from his usual patterns." McCoy appeared pleased with himself. "They can't help themselves, it turns out. Folks think these maniacs are some kind of criminal masterminds, but most of the time, they ain't nothing but a bunch of—"

"No," Worthy said, his heartbeat kicking up a notch, "what do you mean by *his latest victim*?"

McCoy appeared bothered a moment before finally saying, "He finally killed himself a white man."

Worthy's mind raced. Nothing was making sense.

"And if that weren't bad enough," McCoy continued, "he didn't pick him just any old white man neither. No sir, he shot himself a *newspaper writer*. Hoo-boy, tell me that ain't going to open up a world of hurt for him."

Worthy's chest constricted. He tried to puzzle it together. All evidence pointed to Billy Wayne Dickerson as the man who'd been shooting folks in the Back Back. *Hell,* Worthy reasoned, *he'd admitted as much up in his own sniper's nest with the rifle practically in his hands.* He ran down every possible explanation, but still came up empty with any sound reasoning why there could still be someone shoo—

"This so-called sniper," McCoy was saying, "has really done it now. He's ratcheted himself up and now is going to get caught, which is what I read they're angling for in the first place. Deep down in their subconscious, that is. That's why he's progressed. Why he *escalated.* Instead of killing Darkies on the street, he done killed this Broadstreet fella in his own house, and that's going to—"

Worthy rose to his feet. "What did you just say?"

"I'm sorry, Ennis." McCoy snatched his hat off his head. "I mean, instead of shooting *Coloreds . . .*"

"No . . . Did you say *Broadstreet?*"

"Yeah. You know him?"

Worthy felt dizzy. Too many thoughts crashed into his brain at once. His synapses crackled.

"Anyway," McCoy said, "they say you know this whack job who's been doing all the shooting. He's in the wind, it seems, but they think you might be able to help bring him in."

"Me?" Worthy couldn't make sense of it. "How the hell could I—"

"It's some old boy," McCoy said, "named Ricky Lee Patience."

Worthy heard no other words from the sheriff. He snatched his keys off the desk and broke for the door.

◆ ◆ ◆

It was a twenty-five-minute drive from Deeton's jailhouse to downtown Lake Castor. That afternoon, Worthy made it in fifteen. He'd barreled through stoplights and stop signs, the cherry light on his county car spinning like a top, his siren screaming like a cranky toddler. He'd left his jurisdiction when he crossed the state line, but he'd heard that so many times inside his head and out that the concept had become white noise. It meant nothing.

Jurisdiction no longer mattered.

What he first noticed was how quiet downtown Lake Castor was for a Saturday afternoon. Since the mill closed, foot traffic had slowed considerably, but Worthy couldn't remember ever seeing the streets *empty*. The windows of storefronts *boarded*.

Shops were closed. The city pool was vacant. It was as if what remained of Lake Castor had dried up and blown away, leaving behind a ghost town.

This changed when Worthy steered his car into the streets of the Back Back. Suddenly the world came alive. One city cruiser zipped through an intersection. Moments later, another crept soundlessly down an alleyway. Here the shades were drawn. Here the windows were open.

It's not the shooter they fear down here, Worthy reasoned. *They know he's been neutralized.*

As Worthy turned onto Rosalie Patience's street, a black-and-white cruiser pulled up alongside him. The cop riding shotgun leaned out the window.

"You lost, Deputy?" he asked.

"I'm looking for that boy," Worthy hollered back.

"Good on you," said the city cop. "You find him, you make sure to radio us for backup. Don't keep him for yourself. I want to be sure to thank him for taking out that reporter."

His partner leaned across the seat. "When we're done with that, we want to put a few holes in him our own damn self."

"Captain Dorritt mandated twenty hours of target practice," cracked the first cop. "You think this will count?"

Worthy nodded. He slipped the car back into gear.

"Just don't forget what side you're on, Deputy," said the cop behind the wheel. "That badge means the only color you see is *blue*."

◆ ◆ ◆

Ricky Lee's mother had shed no tears for her son.

"The police have already been here," she told Worthy. "They turned his bedroom inside out. Every half hour they come back. They don't even knock. They just kick in the door. I told them he's not here. I tell them I hope he doesn't come back. It don't matter, though. They still kick in my door."

"Have they found anything?"

"They found a round from a rifle in his bedroom."

Worthy narrowed his eyes. "You told me he didn't have a rifle."

Rosalie Patience looked elsewhere around the room.

"This is important," Worthy said, his hands on her shoulders. "Did he own a rifle?"

"No."

"Did you tell the police this?"

Rosalie's eyes were pleading. "What do you want me to do, Deputy?"

Worthy removed his hands from her.

"Tell me." It was her turn to command his attention. "If you have the magic formula for saving my boy, then tell me, and I will do it. I swear it before my Maker and all of his creation. But there is a tidal wave coming, and I am just one woman. If I was alone, maybe I would be brave enough to face it, but I'm not alone. I got a baby girl. I have to think about her. Don't you understand?"

He did. He didn't want to admit it, but he did.

"It's too late for Ricky Lee," she said, "but it's not too late for my Willie."

Worthy backed away from her. "I can't give up on him."

Rosalie considered this, then said, "May God bless you for being a better person than I know to be."

She closed the door.

Worthy had returned to his car and jammed the key into the ignition when the news came over his radio.

They'd found Ricky Lee.

◆ ◆ ◆

They'd called the cavalry.

Nearly every single police officer had arrived at the Barclay Street Kwik-E-Mart in nearly every single police cruiser, carrying every conceivable piece of armament. The Lake Castor Police Department could have gone to war with a small country upon the cracked asphalt if the convenience store had been contested turf.

Lieutenant Avondale was the commanding officer on site. While several officers took cover behind the open doors of their squad cars, eyes focused upon the front door of the convenience store, Avondale briefed his men on the situation.

"At just after thirteen hundred hours," Avondale announced, "an armed suspect entered and took control of the premises. Three civilians escaped and gave a description of the man, which matches that of Ricky Lee Patience, who is the suspect in the Broadstreet shooting, among other incidents in the area. The subject is believed to be armed, but we can't confirm how many other civilians are in the store with him."

Worthy spoke up. "Did anyone witness him with a firearm?"

Avondale's eyes went from Worthy's face to his badge, then back to his face. His expression conveyed annoyance.

"Several accounts place the subject with a firearm," Avondale answered.

"A rifle?" Worthy asked.

Avondale's patience appeared to be wearing thin. "All reports indicate a .38, *Deputy*."

"But not a rifle?"

Avondale turned to his men in blue. "Captain Dorritt has been briefed on the situation. His orders are to neutralize the suspect before he causes any further harm to the community. *Theirs or ours.* Remember: it is not an official directive to use lethal force while subduing this suspect, but *unofficially* . . . let's just say there will be a special bonus for the man who teaches this boy what happens when the bullshit spills over into our streets."

Worthy raised his hand once again. "Sir . . . with all due respect . . ."

Every uniform turned to the deputy. Worthy could see Lorne Axel among them, narrowing his eyes to slits, shaking his head slowly, as if some sort of warning.

"I know this boy," Worthy said. "He didn't shoot anybody. He's not a killer. He's a—"

"We should all offer the kind deputy here a thanks for helping us identify our shooter," Avondale announced to his men. "Dorritt informs me that it's the deputy's diligence that brought our attention to Mr. Patience. However, he should be reminded where his jurisdiction ends and where ours begins, so that we might take things from here." Avondale turned to the armed patrolmen behind him. "Officer Axel, if you'd please escort the deputy back to his car."

Axel obeyed. As they neared the deputy's car, Worthy said, "It's not him, Lorne. You know it wasn't."

"Let it go, man."

"You *know* it wasn't." Behind them, the officers pointed their weapons toward the door of the convenience store. Avondale called for Ricky Lee to surrender through a bullhorn. He promised not to harm him. The salivating officers put off an energy that said otherwise. "That biker, Billy Wayne, is the one who shot those people, not Ricky Lee. You were there."

"Let it go, Ennis." Axel continued toward Worthy's car. "There's nothing we can do."

"We can tell them the truth."

"That won't do anyone any good."

"I'm sure Ricky Lee would argue that."

Axel kept his head down. "What we should be asking," he said, "is who did Broadstreet. If Billy Wayne was the shooter, and he's dead, then who—"

"I don't care about Billy Wayne or Hal Broadstreet right now," Worthy spat. "I'm trying to save that boy's life."

Axel stopped and looked Worthy dead in the eye. "You can't do nothing for him right now." Axel pointed at the scene behind them. "Three days ago, any one of those officers would have earned a promotion for putting a bullet in Broadstreet's skull, but now . . . right now, the last place we want to find ourselves is caught in the crossfire."

Worthy's eyes covered the distance between the officers and the door to the convenience store.

The crossfire.

His mind performed measurements. Axel watched him for a moment; then the realization settled over his face.

"Ennis," he murmured, "don't do it."

Worthy ignored him.

"Cover me, Lorne."

Worthy broke into a run.

◆ ◆ ◆

The distance to the door of the Kwik-E-Mart was thirty yards. Worthy had run track, but had not been allowed to join the football team for the recently integrated Deeton High. Despite the addition of years and extra pounds of equipment, Worthy doubted he had ever run faster, or felt more pressure, than in that moment. He threw himself through the door of the Kwik-E-Mart, dove straight for cover behind a magazine rack, and held his breath until he had assessed the situation.

The windows had been covered by advertisements. This was a practice common in the Back Back to keep prying eyes from the goings-on inside, mostly from police. However, in that moment, it made the room seem dark. It took a second for Worthy's eyes to adjust. He used that time to establish contact with Ricky Lee.

"It's only me, son," Worthy called into the store. "It's your friend, Ennis Worthy."

There was no answer, but Worthy could make out movement in the back of the store. He scanned the store for shoplifting mirrors, found one in the back corner.

"You remember me, don't you, son?" Worthy called. "I gave you my badge. Remember that?"

Still no response. Worthy needed to get closer to the mirror, so he stood and raised his hands to show he was unarmed.

"Hey, I was wrong about that Prince album," Worthy said. "That thing is explosive. Did you watch the movie? It was pretty good."

Worthy inched closer to the mirror, and his vision cleared. He could see Ricky Lee's reflection. The boy was cowered behind the chip aisle, holding tight to a revolver.

"Somebody told me you got hold of a gun, Ricky Lee. Is that right?"

"You got one too." The boy's voice contained a flat affect.

"I do, sure, but you and me are friends, so I don't need it. Would you like me to put it on the floor?"

Silence.

"How about I do that, Ricky Lee? I'm going to set it down. Since you and me are friends, I don't need it."

"What about your other friends?" Ricky Lee asked. "They got plenty of guns."

"They do," Worthy said gravely, "but they are not my friends."

"They want to see me dead."

"You're probably right, Ricky Lee," Worthy said, "but that's why I'm here. I'm going to make sure that don't happen."

"Don't nobody care," Ricky Lee said. "My momma don't care, so why do you?"

Worthy took another step toward the potato chip aisle, where Ricky Lee was hiding. He could see from the mirror that the boy held the gun with both hands, the barrel positioned against his own nose. He was scared. He was alone.

"I care," Worthy said, "because nobody else seems to."

"Why does she hate me?" asked the boy.

"She doesn't," Worthy said. "She just doesn't know what to do."

Worthy scanned the room. There were no hostages, no casualties. He knew if that information reached the men outside, they wouldn't hesitate to storm the building. In that case, Worthy would have lost all control of the situation.

If he ever had any.

"I didn't do what they said," Ricky Lee told him. "I didn't kill those people."

"I know you didn't."

"Do you?"

"Yes, son. I do."

"Why do they think I did it?"

"Because they need to blame someone." Worthy watched the boy through the mirror. "Here's what we're going to do, Ricky Lee. You and me are going to walk out that door together and explain that to them. We're going to tell them that you are innocent, and I'm going to tell them why."

Ricky Lee shook his head.

"We have to, son. The last thing we want is for those officers to come in here."

"They are going to kill me."

"Not if you are with me. Do you remember my badge?"

"Yes."

"It will protect you from the police."

Ricky Lee's voice grew childlike. "Like a force field?"

"Exactly like a force field." Worthy lifted his eyes to the ceiling, as if asking God to forgive him for the lie. "The police won't hurt anybody who wears a badge. It's in the rules."

"Police ain't got no rules."

"They do when it comes to the badge."

"Is that true?"

"Would you like to wear it?" Worthy asked. "To keep you safe from them?"

Silence.

"Put the badge on, son, and they can't hurt you."

"You promise?"

Worthy let out the breath he'd been holding.

"I promise I won't let them."

Ricky Lee stepped out from behind the potato chip aisle. Worthy's pulse raced. The muscles in the boy's face had gone slack. The pupils of his eyes were the size of saucers. Worthy recognized this affect from his own experiences with his uncle Charlie. An energy hummed off the boy that scared the hell out of Worthy, made worse by the gun in Ricky Lee's hands.

Worthy unpinned the shield from his chest. "I'll trade you," he said. "You keep my badge, and I'll take your weapon."

"That's hardly a fair trade."

"It's the one that's going to keep you alive, son."

Before walking him through the door of the Kwik-E-Mart, Worthy called out, "I've got the boy. He's unarmed. I'm bringing him out."

Through the glass, he watched the officers tighten their grips on their weapons. The barrels of their guns grew larger, darker.

"I repeat: Ricky Lee is *unarmed. Do not shoot!*"

Upon emergence, Worthy heard the sound of weapons being readied to fire. He raised his hands high and instructed Ricky Lee to do the same.

"Deputy Worthy," called Avondale through the bullhorn, "step away from the suspect."

There was no chance of Worthy complying. He knew that to do so, he might as well pull the trigger himself.

"I have relinquished him of his weapon," Worthy called. "He's coming in peacefully."

"I gave you an order, Deputy!" The voice belonged to Avondale. Worthy didn't like what he heard behind it. "You are to step away now."

Worthy knew that if he did, they would open fire. He began to wonder if they would even if he didn't.

"I'm afraid I can't do that, Detective," Worthy called. "This man is my prisoner, and I am taking him in."

"You have no jurisdiction here," Avondale called. "If you do not do as you are commanded, then you are in violation of the law and will be treated as such."

"What are you going to do, Avondale? Shoot me?"

"You are out of your jurisdiction!"

A voice called out, "But I'm not!"

Worthy turned to see Lorne Axel appearing alongside him. He'd drawn his weapon and held it at the ready to take on any of his fellow officers who might challenge him.

"We're taking him in."

CHAPTER FIFTY-SIX

Jess Keeler

Present Day

No one had ever asked for her to relinquish the Story Time Productions ID badge, so Jess had kept it. She had debated whether to throw it in the trash or burn it, but instead had chosen to keep it as a memento of her misfortune. It came in handy when she presented it to the guard at Stormgate Prison.

The guard consulted her clipboard before glancing back at Jess's badge. "The log says we are expecting a Sandra Newman."

"Such a silly mistake," Jess said with a smile. "Sandy is the intern at Story Time who arranged for my meeting on behalf of Felix and Friedrich Schafer. I am the correspondent. Jess Keeler. It should be my name on the log."

"I'm sorry," said the guard, shaking her head. "I have Sandra Newman written here, and that's who gets in to see the prisoner."

"Typical." Jess threw up her hands in mock exasperation. "The men who run the company—the two brothers, Felix and Friedrich—hired her, despite the fact that, between you and me, she's not very smart. Who has to pay for her incompetence? Not them, that's for sure. Want to know why they hired her?"

The guard frankly didn't appear to care.

Jess pulled up an image on the screen of her phone and showed it to the guard. "That's why," she said. "She was a social media model before working for Story Time, so . . ."

The picture she showed the guard was actually a screenshot, because Sandy—er . . . *Sandra*—had scrubbed her profiles of any bikini pics in order to appear more professional after she had taken Jess's spot as lead journalist and producer on Story Time's production team.

The guard looked at the picture and frowned. Still, she said nothing about it.

"Me, on the other hand . . ." Jess showed her a picture of herself presenting on behalf of her podcast, *Something Bad Wrong*. It was a professionally shot photo, and quite truthfully, her hair had looked great that day. "I'm at the mercy of their fragile male egos."

"You're also an hour early."

"Gotta get that worm." Jess winked at the guard. "Women have to work harder than the men do in order to get things done. But of course you know that."

The guard rolled her eyes. Confronted with the possibility of spending the next hour with Jess waiting in the lobby, the guard picked up the phone.

"We need to retrieve an inmate for visitation."

Jess smiled and checked her watch. Twenty minutes later, she sat on one side of a table in a small room, under the watchful eye of three prison guards. The door opened, and in walked Ricky Lee Patience.

There had been no photographs since that single grainy black-and-white picture printed when he was arrested, so Jess didn't know what to expect. It certainly wasn't the thin, bespectacled man standing before her. His prison jumpsuit was bleached bright white, with impeccably sharp creases throughout the fabric. He took time with his appearance. His hair had been carefully picked. His teeth were impossibly white.

The jailer released Ricky Lee from his handcuffs once he'd sat in the chair on the opposite side of the table from Jess. He removed his glasses and polished them with a square of fabric that he neatly folded and returned to his pocket.

"Thank you for seeing me," Jess said.

Ricky Lee responded with a tight smile, which promptly disappeared.

"What were you told about why this visit was requested?" she asked him.

"That you are a journalist who wants to do a story about the crimes for which I confessed to." His voice was clipped and mannered, as if he had spent time developing the sound of each syllable.

"That's essentially true," Jess said.

"Essentially?"

"I'm working on a pair of stories, actually. I have discovered they may be related."

"That sounds intriguing."

"It is."

"I assume I am involved in one of these stories, or else you wouldn't have gone to the trouble to pay this visit."

Jess nodded. She produced her recorder from her bag. She noted his immediate discomfort.

"It's only audio," she said. "I'm not recording any video."

"As you should have been instructed, I do not give my consent to be recorded."

Jess made a show of setting her recorder aside. "I have been speaking with your family. They are the ones who approached me."

"My family?"

"Yes. Your sister, Wilhelmina."

Ricky Lee's eyes turned to the wall. "Willie . . ."

"That's right. She—"

"I wouldn't know her if I saw her, Ms. Keeler." Ricky Lee turned to face her again. "We haven't spoken in quite some time."

"That's not her choice." Jess reached into her bag. "I brought you some photos and her—"

Ricky Lee turned away, refusing to look at the photographs.

"She has two children. They're grown. A daughter and a son."

Ricky Lee answered only with silence.

"You'd like her boy. He's a very handsome young man. His name is—"

Ricky Lee cleared his throat, indicating that he was not interested.

"Fine." Jess closed her bag and dropped it below the table. "Why don't we start with what you remember about her. Let's talk about when you were younger. Would you mind if I recorded a—"

"I do mind," Ricky Lee said. "I do not give my consent to be recorded."

Jess reached across the table to touch his arm. One of the guards stepped forward.

"Ma'am, there's no contact with the prisoner."

Jess retracted her arm and placed her hands in her lap. She let out a breath, then restarted.

"I want to tell your story, Ricky Lee. Don't you want people to know the truth?"

"The truth?" Ricky Lee's face twisted into a miserable smile. "What could you possibly know about the truth?"

"I know quite a bit. I've been very busy the past several months."

Ricky Lee folded his arms. "And what would other people knowing the truth gain me?"

"Your freedom."

A bemused look crossed his face.

"I have information that places a huge question mark on your involvement in those killings," Jess said. "I don't think you killed anyone. Certainly not Harold Broadstreet."

"Who is that?"

"The white man who was gunned down." Jess cocked her head. "You really don't know who he was?"

"I confessed to those killings."

"I've heard enough stories about how confessions were obtained by police back in those days."

Ricky Lee removed his glasses again and polished the lenses with the square of fabric. He couldn't seem to get them clean enough for his liking. He rubbed them harder. Finally satisfied, he returned the square to his pocket and the glasses to his face.

"Have they told you about my life in here?" he asked.

"No. Will you tell me on the record?"

"I do not give my consent to be recorded." His tone took an edge to it.

"Understood," she said. "Tell me."

"I run group-counseling meetings here now," he said. "When I was first admitted, I didn't want anything to do with group. People endlessly whining about their every day, refusing to make things better. I didn't want to work with the doctors on staff; I didn't want to be cooperative in any way. I was unwilling to change. That was the hardest lesson for me to learn. I had to be *willing* to change. And I was. Now I run group. Every day. I have for years."

"I know about Dr. Jonas Stephens," said Jess. "I know about your time at Addams State Hospital. I've spoken with a nurse. Do you remember Kim Liu?"

Ricky Lee's face remained impassive.

"She remembers you," Jess said. "She suggested that they weren't very nice to you while you were in the hospital. I was wondering if you could tell me more about that."

Something flashed behind his eyes. "I don't want to talk about my time in the hospital. I do not give you consent to record me."

"You don't have to," she said, "but you seem like a very smart man. Don't you want justice?"

"For whom?"

"The dead."

"Does justice really matter to them?"

"Their families, then."

Ricky Lee shrugged. "After forty years? If there's even still a scab, why would you want to pick at it?"

"Then how about for yourself?"

Ricky Lee leaned forward. "I used to read the newspapers in the library here. I could see what you people do to one another out there. I know how you treat the poor and the weak and the . . . *the sick*. I know what compassion you lack. I don't read those newspapers anymore. I don't like to have my heart broken again and again and again. I don't want the stink of your society on me any longer. When a new prisoner comes into group, that's the first thing we do, is wash your stink off him. We must disinfect them. You say you want to *free* me, Ms. Keeler. I tell you that in here, I have never been more free in my entire life. Here, I can receive treatment. Here, I am administered medication that I could never afford out there. Here, I am minded after. What do you think they would do for me *out there*? What would they do for me that my own mother would not?"

"There are programs, Ricky Lee," she said. "There are—"

The door opened, and two jailers flanked a very angry warden. The warden walked briskly to the table. He snapped his fingers at the jailers.

"Please return the inmate back to his cell." He turned his angry gaze to Jess. "And I want this woman removed from the property."

"Sir, can I—"

"Unless she would like us to find her more *permanent* accommodations."

Jess was escorted by two jailers from the room, down the hall, and back to the front lobby of the prison. There, she found Sandy Newman with her arms crossed over her chest and an expression of unadulterated rage.

"What's up, *sis*?" Jess smirked.

Once outside, Jess checked her phone and saw an email notification. She climbed into her car and opened her inbox. The message was from Olivia Crane. The subject heading read, **You talked me into it.**

Jess held her breath as she opened the email. There was an attachment. The text read:

> It may have been a great mistake not to have published this forty years ago. I fear the bigger mistake may be not publishing it today. I have no idea what the right thing is to do with this, but I am hoping handing it to you will absolve me.
>
> Go find your truth.

Jess opened the attachment and nearly dropped the phone. It was Hal Broadstreet's last, unpublished article.

CHAPTER FIFTY-SEVEN

HAL BROADSTREET

1984

LAKE CASTOR'S BLOOD RED SUMMER

(Part 3 of 5)

By Harold S. Broadstreet

The early-morning hours of June 4 would be otherwise unremarkable on the sleepy streets of Lake Castor, if it weren't for a routine traffic stop. Two third-shift officers, L. M. Axel and T. F. Stokes, witnessed a white Ford Pinto run a stop sign. They threw their lights and raised the siren. Seconds later, they had the vehicle pulled to the side of the road.

In a perfect world, this is the moment where everything would change for the people involved. As you will soon find out, Lake Castor is far from a perfect world.

Eryk Pruitt

In the previous installments of this series, we have detailed the rise of the outlaw-motorcycle-gang culture along the Atlantic Seaboard, as well as in the Lake Castor area. We have listed the lineages of our local clubs and their transition from the easy-riding Blood Ravens to the criminal intentions of the Vandals.

The Lake Castor Police Department would also have been aware of this organization, so when they found three members of the Vandals in that white Pinto, they were immediately given cause for suspicion.

William "Billy" Wayne Dickerson was behind the wheel. Riding shotgun was Edward "Digger" Crowe, and Charles "Chains" Wilcox rode in the back seat. Although they were pulled over for running a stop sign, the reason they were arrested was listed as "illegal possession of drugs, possession of illegal weapons, and possession of drug paraphernalia."

In other words, they were found to be in possession of methamphetamine, marijuana, a Bowie knife, a pair of brass knuckles, and a .38 handgun.

Officers Axel and Stokes remanded the three men to the Lake Castor jail, taking note of the bloodstains on their boots and clothes. The next afternoon, when they returned to their shift, the officers were shocked to discover that the three men had been released without posting bond, facing a judge, or being questioned.

354

It was simply as if they had never been booked at all.

What's most shocking is that between their arrest and subsequent release, the bodies of three bootleggers had been found—beaten, stabbed, and shot—only three blocks away from where the men had been arrested.

Still, they have not been called to question for these crimes.

It could be argued that there are three very solid reasons that the police never pursued this very crucial lead by questioning Crowe, Dickerson, and Wilcox for the murders of the bootleggers. The very glaring reason would be that since their arrest and subsequent release, all three have been unceremoniously slaughtered one by one. Digger Crowe was found two days after the Fosskey killings with a bullet in the back of his head. The body of Billy Wayne Dickerson was discovered beaten to death inside a grain elevator. Most recently, Charles "Chains" Wilcox was reported dead by Iredell County officials. All three believed to be victims of a gang war with the rival motorcycle club, Rare Breed, which has claimed a total of seven lives so far.

Law enforcement's complacency to interrogate them for the deaths of Fosskey, Felton, and Loe could be blamed on their disinterest in investigating crimes against criminals.

When asked about their failure to arrest Crowe, Dickerson, and Wilcox for the murders, Captain Hank Dorritt of the Crimes Against Persons division replied, "If those animals want to thin their own herd, then who am I to stand against progress?"

This lack of concern trickles down to the rank and file who serve beneath Captain Dorritt, including his lieutenant, Christopher "Kip" Avondale, whose misdeeds—evidence tampering, evidence planting, and forced confessions—have been tirelessly detailed by this reporter in the past. Currently, a spate of shootings terrorizes the citizenry of Lake Castor's Back Back community, murders which Lake Castor detectives also fail to acknowledge or investigate.

It is this writer's belief, however, that the most important reason for law enforcement's failure to investigate the bootlegger murders is because they were complicit in covering it up.

While Captain Dorritt may claim that "police are like any other bureaucracy" and that "mistakes get made," evidence appears to show more than passive participation in the clean getaway enjoyed by our primary suspects. First, they were released before they could be questioned. Second, further interrogation of the suspects was never pursued. Third, there was the elimination of the only witnesses.

The six players in the bootleggers' murders are all presumed dead. However, there were two individuals who could identify the killers and connect them to the deeds. Clarence "Uncle Meaney" Moulton detailed the crimes to this reporter (see part 4 of this series). Within weeks, he was found dead, having been felled by a single gunshot in the streets of the Back Back after his name was revealed to Captain Dorritt and his squad.

The only other witness was Delilah "Baby Doll" McNaughton, the lover of Digger Crowe and the ex-wife of former Vandal Caleb McNaughton, who also owned the white Pinto. When questioned, McNaughton insisted his innocence, as well as his ignorance of the whereabouts of his wife, who had gone missing shortly after the murders. Sadly, this is the fate of women who found themselves in the orbit of Digger Crowe. If Delilah is out there, we can only hope that she will come forward, but as is the case with two former wives of Digger Crowe, we can expect this to be unlikely.

Delilah McNaughton isn't the only death that has been unable to be confirmed. Of the eight people involved in the fatal dealings on that fateful night, she is the only one unaccounted for. However, there has been very little to detail the death of Charles "Chains" Wilcox besides a small article in the *Lake Castor Herald* and a mimeographed copy of an Iredell County medical examiner's report.

Most startling, however, is that there are far fewer records of Charlie Chains's life.

Who is Charlie Chains Wilcox?

More in part 4 of our installment about Lake Castor's Blood Red Summer.

CHAPTER FIFTY-EIGHT

EXCERPT FROM *BLOOD RED SUMMER*

EPISODE 5: "THE WHITE PINTO"

[The sound of birds chirping. Cars passing. A knock at a door.]

MALE VOICE: Hello?

JESS KEELER: Hi. I'm looking for Caleb McNaughton.

MCNAUGHTON: You found him.

KEELER: Oh. I'm sorry, but the Caleb McNaughton I'm looking for should be significantly older. What are you, midthirties?

MCNAUGHTON: A little older than that, but thank you. You may be looking for my father? I'm Caleb Jr. Everybody calls me Cal.

KEELER: That sounds about right. The man I'm looking for was born in 1961.

MCNAUGHTON: Yep. That would be Dad.

KEELER: Can you tell me how to reach him?

MCNAUGHTON: I hate to be the one to tell you, but Dad passed away about eight years ago.

KEELER: Oh my God, I'm so sorry. May I ask, How did he die?

MCNAUGHTON: Cancer. Lungs, then it spread from there.

KEELER: That is so horrible. I wanted to ask him some questions, but maybe you can help me. You see, my name is Jess Keeler, and I'm a producer for a podcast about a series of tragic events that occurred in 1984 that was known as the "Blood Red Summer." Would you mind if we talked inside?

[Their voices trail away as the BLOOD RED SUMMER *THEME plays in the background.]*

NARRATOR (KEELER): Cal McNaughton Jr. is a very nice man. About six foot two; broad shoulders; short, cropped hair he wears high in front. He's very receptive and open, generous with his time. But he—much like yourselves, I imagine—was very curious about what brought a true-crime podcaster to his living room on an early summer evening.

We know from a previous episode that, in the early-morning hours of June 4, 1984, then patrolman Lorne Axel pulled over a white Pinto for rolling through a stop sign. Inside, he found three men with known ties to the Vandals motorcycle club and, upon further inspection, discovered a set of brass knuckles, a knife containing evidence of blood, and small amounts of methamphetamine and marijuana. The men were arrested, booked, and placed in a holding cell.

When news of the murders of the bootleggers in Fosskey's garage broke, it would seem that a trio of likely suspects would be waiting to be interviewed. Only that was not the case.

SHERIFF AXEL: When I reported for duty, I asked the desk sergeant if the bikers I'd pulled over and arrested had been questioned. I was informed that they had been released.

KEELER: Did he say why they had been released?

AXEL: He said the evidence I collected had been lost and there was no reason to hold the men in overcrowded cells.

KEELER: Nobody thought maybe they should hold three bloodstained bikers when unknown assailants committed a massacre the night before?

AXEL: Everybody had it in their heads that the killings were the handiwork of a couple of escaped inmates that were all over the news. By the time cooler heads had prevailed, those men were in the wind. Nobody wanted to raise a fuss about it, and quite honestly, those kinds of bureaucratic mistakes weren't uncommon with Lake Castor police back in those days.

KEELER: And when you went to look up records on those men that you had arrested, what did you find?

AXEL: That they had been misplaced.

KEELER: They were missing?

AXEL: Misplaced *is the word that was used.*

KEELER: So all record of that traffic stop and arrest was lost to time?

AXEL: Not exactly.

NARRATOR: No. Not exactly. Patrolman Lorne Axel kept his notebooks from his short stint on the beat, and years later, as Sheriff Lorne Axel, he granted our team access to them.

There were three men in that Pinto when he pulled it over. According to their ID cards, their names were Edward Crowe, Billy Wayne Dickerson, and Charles Wilcox. However, the white Pinto was registered to none of them.

It was registered to a man named Caleb McNaughton.

JESS KEELER: Did you ever interview Mr. McNaughton and ask him why his car was being used in what we now believe to have been a horrible murder?

SHERIFF AXEL: I did not.

KEELER: Why?

AXEL: I was not in a position to choose my priorities at the time.

KEELER: To your knowledge, was Mr. McNaughton ever questioned by anyone in the police department?

AXEL: Not to my knowledge. No.

NARRATOR: But it turns out, he was *interviewed. The sheriff is right: it wasn't by anyone at the police department.*

Instead, he was interviewed by Harold Broadstreet of the Lake Castor Times.

[CUE THEME MUSIC]

NARRATOR: We've all heard the saying "Behind every good man, there is a great woman." But what if I told you that behind every bad man, you might also find an even worse old lady?

Now, before you go lobbing charges of sexism or ageism over my use of the term old lady, *let me explain to those of you who may be uninitiated. The term* old lady *is motorcycle-club parlance for a woman who is the primary companion of a patched-in member of the club.*

Perhaps companion *is a polite way of phrasing it.*

Property *is more accurate.*

VENUS: There ain't exactly much room for feminism in the club, if you know what I mean. When you first start coming around, you get kind of sucked in by how big and macho the men are, maybe you get turned on by the noise of the bikes and the power and all the danger. It's kind of sexy. You find out pretty quick, though, where your place is as a woman in the club.

NARRATOR: That's Venus. It's not her real name, but that should come as no surprise, because nobody—especially women—goes by their real name in a motorcycle club. Everyone is given a nickname. That nickname could stem from personal appearances, attributes, or some anecdotal reference to a significant moment in their early days in the club. Venus, as we're calling her, went by a different nickname, but we've changed it to protect her anonymity.

VENUS: When you start coming around, they call you a hang around. You belong to the club, not to nobody. For the most part, it's innocent. Everybody is drinking and drugging, so the moods can shift. One minute, you're playing pool. Then somebody might like the way you lean over the table to take aim at the cue ball, and next thing you know, you're pressed against the wall with some guy you haven't even met yet doing what he wants to you. It's not rape, so much. Nobody used words like that. If you didn't want it to happen, you could always speak up or fight back or whatever. The other men would make it stop. They fancy themselves gentlemen in that manner. But then maybe you ain't asked to hang around no more.

So for that reason, you just kind of put up with it.

So it wasn't uncommon for chicks to be passed around. But eventually, you curry favor with somebody, and if you did, you become their old lady. If you're somebody's old lady, that means hands off. Couldn't nobody else touch her or talk shit about her. She was the personal property of a member, and just like that, [SNAPS FINGERS] she was off limits to the rest of the boys. She was one head above the other skanks who came slagging around.

KEELER: *What happened if a woman wanted to leave a man for another one?*

VENUS: *[LAUGHS] Oh, that didn't happen.*

KEELER: *Ever?*

VENUS: *No.*

KEELER: *So an old lady stayed with the man who chose her, and that's that?*

VENUS: *Not exactly. An old lady could quit the club, but she didn't want to do that because people would come looking. Of course, a man could dump her and pick another old lady, which would return her to the pool. Or . . .*

KEELER: *Yes?*

VENUS: *If an old man quit the club . . .*

KEELER: *Did that happen often?*

VENUS: *Not often, but it happened.*

KEELER: *What happened then?*

VENUS: *The club didn't like it. First, they would strip the member of all his property. And I mean* all *his property. His bike, his patch, his cage—*

KEELER: *I'm sorry, his what?*

VENUS: *Cage. It's what they called a car. If he had a car, they would take it from him. They would take all his property.*

KEELER: *His woman?*

VENUS: *Like I said . . . all his property.*

KEELER: *Is that what happened to Delilah McNaughton?*

VENUS: *Who?*

KEELER: *I believe she was known back in the old days as Baby Doll?*

[SILENCE]

KEELER: *The way I heard the story is that when Caleb McNaughton left the club, they stripped him of his bike, his Ford Pinto, his patch, and even his wife, Baby Doll McNaughton. In fact, I heard that she became the property—I mean old lady—of one Edward Digger Cr—*

VENUS: *I don't have anything to say about that.*

KEELER: *Were you familiar with Baby Doll and Dig—*

VENUS: *I said I don't have anything to say about that because I don't know anything. Get this thing off me. How do I—*

[SOUND OF MICROPHONE FALLING OVER
CUE THEME MUSIC]

NARRATOR: *Based on what we've heard from former gang members, and added to what we have read in Harold Broadstreet's last, unpublished article, Caleb McNaughton became disillusioned with the direction of the motorcycle club after the Blood Ravens patched over with the Vandals. He left the club. For that reason, he was stripped of all of his property. His patch, his bike, his car . . . and his wife.*

His wife, Baby Doll, became the property of Digger Crowe. All reports indicate that the two of them "dated" for some time after Caleb left the Vandals. He also claimed Caleb's car as his own.

Caleb's white Pinto.

So what happened to Baby Doll?

SHERIFF AXEL: *She went missing during the summer of 1984. We never heard from her again.*

KEELER: *What happened to her?*

AXEL: *Honestly, we don't know.*

KEELER: *And if you had to speculate?*

AXEL: *If I had to speculate . . . when we investigated Digger Crowe, we found out he had been married to two women in Omaha before he moved to Lake Castor. Both of those women had gone missing, never to be seen again. We'd heard rumors that he got his name because he could effectively make people disappear. So when Delilah McNaughton went missing . . .*

KEELER: *You just assumed she met the same fate as Digger's other two companions.*

AXEL: *Women in that culture go missing. It's a hard fact.*

KEELER: *And you don't go looking for them?*

AXEL: *We've never had any luck finding them.*

NARRATOR: *Which brings us back to the front porch of Cal McNaughton Jr., the son of Caleb and Delilah, also known as Baby Doll. Cal's mother left him and his father before he'd turned two years old. He grew up without a mother, a hard fact that was difficult for him to reconcile. But, as we got to know him, he revealed something that absolutely threatened to blow apart everything we thought we knew about the murders of the Blood Red Summer.*

Namely, that one of Digger Crowe's victims was not dead.

MCNAUGHTON: *My mother is not dead. She is very much alive.*

CHAPTER FIFTY-NINE

Martin Jancowicz

Present Day

Jancowicz opened up the case. The aroma of gun oil invaded his nostrils. His eyes canvassed the wood grain of the stock. The steel barrel. The felt lining upon which it all rested. Every sensation returned him somewhere he'd long ago forgotten. Muscle memory.

The best kind of memory, in his opinion.

You're not so different from me.

"I'm not you, Billy Wayne. I'm nothing like you."

Over the years, Jancowicz would come to swear that he could hear Billy Wayne Dickerson's voice in his ear. *Was it guilt?* he often wondered. Guilt for not being there to protect him before his last trip up the grain elevator. Guilt because Jancowicz had begun to crack at the seams and pleaded endlessly with his handler to pull him from deep cover, leaving Billy Wayne alone when he was found by the rival motorcycle gang, or whoever decided to cash in his chips for him. Or was it guilt for standing idly by while Billy Wayne's demons consumed him? For not reaching out when Jancowicz could see how the killing might be affecting him.

You had an exit plan, Charlie Chains. There was only ever going to be one ending for me.

Or, more likely, was it Billy Wayne's ghost? His spirit, sent to torture Jancowicz for all the havoc he had wreaked. Jancowicz's mind and soul, its own haunted house.

Jancowicz tried to ignore him as he assembled the rifle. He was positioned on top of a parking garage that overlooked the All-Niter café, a small diner on the edge of downtown Lake Castor, fifteen miles and forty years from those moments with Billy Wayne on top of the grain elevator.

He fit the scope onto the rifle and adjusted it. He peered through the lens. Down below, at three hundred yards, the diner appeared close enough for him to reach out and touch it. It was three in the afternoon, so traffic was light. That would limit collateral damage.

Visibility?

Maximum. There wasn't a cloud in the sky.

Wind speed?

Almost nil.

Moisture?

Jancowicz licked his lips. He traced the parking lot with his scope. There were four vehicles on the premises, including the one belonging to the target. Glass windows lined the perimeter of the diner, which offered him a visual of everything inside. Two employees. Four patrons, including the target.

This is exciting, much like our first target. Do you remember that?

Jancowicz opened both eyes and lifted his head off the rifle. "Ronnie Daye."

Thunder told us that Negro was holding up progress. He controlled the Darkie drug trade, and with him out of the way, the Vandals could take over his traffic. They flooded his drug routes with their cocaine, and we got our patches. We take out one drug lord, and we become full-fledged Vandals.

"But why the second one, Billy Wayne? That kid had nothing to do with us."

What makes you think that was me?

"Don't bullshit me, brother. I knew it was you the second I heard about it. That had your hallmarks written all over it."

That was beyond my control.

Jancowicz couldn't hide a smile. "You really believe that?"

I do. Do you know how many kills I had in country? I took those to bed with me every damned night. Not the deed, but the fact of how little I cared that I had done it. I wrestled with it all the time. Was my country worth the price of my soul? Then, at Jem Fosskey's that night . . .

"I don't want to talk about that."

That night, at Jem's, it was like a scab had been picked off me. I didn't want to kill those men, but Digger made me. He forced me to do it, and after it was done, I didn't have to care anymore about what I had done or how I felt about it. I just had to do it.

"So you killed that kid?"

So I killed the kid.

Jancowicz turned from his weapon, half expecting to find Billy Wayne standing behind him. The voice had never been so clear, so present.

Below him, in the All-Niter parking lot, another car whipped into a spot. He did not let the movement distract him from his target.

You knew I killed that kid, and you used my hate to eliminate a target of your own.

"That man could have identified us. He saw everything."

You let him go.

"It was a mistake. I cleaned it up."

More like you had me clean it up.

"He could have ended it all."

Would that have been so bad?

368

Jancowicz took a breath. He became aware of everything moving in slow motion. A gentle wind lifting the leaves of the trees. The woman crossing the lot below to enter the diner. The cardinal and its song.

"Why did you keep killing after that?" Jancowicz asked the empty parking garage.

Why do you?

Jancowicz zeroed in on his target below. She sat alone in a booth, sipping coffee she had received three minutes earlier. She faced the window and offered him a clear view of her. Even from three hundred yards away, he could make out a pimple forming on her left cheek.

Jess Keeler.

When you killed the reporter, you felt what it was like to be me.

"That was different," Jancowicz insisted. "I didn't enjoy it like you did. I didn't crave it. It gave me nothing."

It gave you freedom. Freedom from atonement.

"I *have* atoned."

Is that what you are doing now? Atoning?

Jancowicz ignored him. He pressed his eye farther into the scope's lens. He moved the crosshairs up Jess Keeler's body, stopping at her chest, where her heart would be. Tracing the length of her throat, timing the rhythm of her breath, following the curve of her lips, slow like a lover. Up her nose, until finally settling in the spot between her eyes.

It's like riding a bicycle.

"This is the last time."

After you kill her, there will be another.

"I'm done."

There will always be another.

"It's not a clean shot," Jancowicz hissed. "I can't account for the window. Not at this distance. I'll take the shot as the target exits the location."

Take the shot now.

"There will be less collateral damage."

There is only ever collateral damage, Charlie Chains. You should know that by now.

Jancowicz exhaled half the breath. The world drew still.

Pull the trigger and end it.

Jancowicz rested his finger on the trigger.

One pound of pressure.

Two.

Movement in front of the crosshairs. The woman from the car had taken the seat directly across from the target. She turned as she placed her purse at her feet, allowing Jancowicz to see her face in full.

It can't be . . .

His breath stuttered. He lifted his finger off the trigger.

No . . .

It was her.

The woman joining Jess Keeler.

Baby Doll.

It was like seeing a ghost.

Jancowicz loaded the rifle back into its case.

You can't leave this unfinished. You must take the shot.

"Aborting the mission," Jancowicz said to the empty air around him. "The objective has been changed."

CHAPTER SIXTY

JESS KEELER

Present Day

Jess could not stop staring at the woman. She'd heard so much about her. She'd seen timeworn photographs and fingered through dusty knickknacks. She'd imagined what her voice might sound like, and pictured her mannerisms. Ever since Jess had heard the woman's name, the ghost of her had haunted Jess's investigation, but had never quite materialized.

Until she took the seat across from her in the booth at the All-Niter.

"You're younger than I thought you'd be," Delilah "Baby Doll" Dennis said as she looked Jess up and down.

"You'd be the first person to ever tell me that." Jess motioned for the waitress. "I can't believe I'm actually talking to you. It wasn't exactly easy to find you."

"That was by design." Delilah unwrapped her silverware from her napkin and laid it in her lap. Her manners were clipped. She was dressed smart. Her hair had been recently styled, and she wore it in a tight bun. According to Jess's research, Delilah would have been twenty years old when she went missing, which placed her at sixty. She didn't look it. "If it weren't for my son, I'd be fine if the whole world thought Delilah McNaughton was dead."

They might have, Jess thought to herself. It hadn't been easy to track her down. According to her son, she stopped using the name Delilah McNaughton long, long ago. The name written on the return addresses on the birthday and Christmas cards listed her as *Lila Dennis*, with an address in Emerald Isle, North Carolina.

"I stopped going by *Delilah* the morning I caught that first bus out of Lake Castor." Lila's eyes moved around the room, and Jess wondered for a moment what she might be remembering. "I got a job waitressing in a place very much like this one, and one night, I met George Dennis, who was a very lovely man. It's no exaggeration to say that he saved my life."

"What have you been doing for the past forty years?" Jess asked.

"I helped George raise two children from a previous marriage." She knotted the napkin in her lap with both hands. There was no hiding how nervous she was. "He lost his first wife to leukemia two years before we met. We spent many years arguing over which one of us was more lost before he walked into that diner. He helped me buy an antique store back home, and I spend my days with my customers."

"What does he know about your past?"

"Before my son called and said you were looking for me?" Lila's gaze took on an edge. "He knew nothing. We didn't talk about it. All he knew was that I was running from something and I never wanted to talk about it. George was a sweet, decent man, and I have never fooled myself into thinking I deserved him. I've worked hard for forty years to make sure he knows I'm grateful for everything he's done for me."

"How did you reconnect with your fam—" Jess caught herself. She tried again. "Your *old* family."

"You mean my son and his father?" Lila appeared amused for a moment. That expression, however, was quickly replaced with one signifying pain. "The news got back to me pretty quick that Digger, Billy

Wayne, and Charlie Chains were all dead. Even still, I looked over my shoulder every minute of every day. After a while, there would be more and more stretches where I would forget about it, until one day I couldn't remember the last time I'd thought about it. That was over ten years later. I saw in a newspaper that my little boy was playing high school basketball and they had a tournament nearby. It was the hardest thing I'd ever done, but I went."

"And you introduced yourself to him?"

"Not then, no. But the seed was planted. There wasn't a night when I didn't think about him and how well he had grown up. On his next birthday, I sent him a card. He wrote back almost immediately."

"How did Caleb—his father—take it?"

"Not well, initially." Lila's smile twisted scornfully. "He fought it, at first, but he had remarried. Moved on. His new wife saw things in a different light."

"I've met her," Jess said. "She's a good woman."

"A much better woman than I would have been."

The waitress arrived, and they ordered their food. Lila apologized for her lack of appetite, but asked for a slice of buttermilk pie. As soon as they were alone, Jess changed the trajectory of their conversation.

"Take me back to that night," she said. "Tell me how you ended up at Jem Fosskey's apartment."

Lila sighed. She seemed to have known this conversation was due. She composed herself like a woman who had known this moment was coming her entire life.

"I was partying with some of the other old ladies at the 809," she said, "when Digger came and told me we were going for a ride. He had Caleb's old car, and he loved driving me around in it. You know, to show off all the things he'd taken from Caleb."

Lila's expression turned inward, as if she might be disgusted with herself. Jess watched her, absolutely curious, noticing for the first time the edges of a tattoo peeking out from beneath Lila's shirtsleeve.

"Two other boys were in that car," Jess said. "Do you remember them?"

Lila nodded. "Billy Wayne and Charlie Chains."

"Where did Digger tell you they were going?"

"He said we were going to Jem's."

"Did he tell you why?"

Lila's hands kept kneading the paper napkin in her lap. "He said he wanted to score some hooch, but Jem wouldn't sell to him anymore. I don't remember why he said, and it wouldn't have mattered anyway. I was partying, and we were all cranked up in those days. Things just happened, and you got caught up in them. It was such a scene, and Digger was the guy on the scene, the one everyone was afraid of."

"Not you?"

"Oh, I was probably more afraid than anyone else," Lila said. "I heard about those women back in Omaha. I knew how he could be, and I knew that no one would do anything to him if he did it to me."

"But you stayed with him."

Lila's eyes were lasers. "You must think I'm trash."

"Quite the opposite," Jess said and meant it. "I think you're a very strong woman who has been forced to adapt during some unusual circumstances."

Something softened in Lila's gaze. All the while, her hands continued twisting the paper napkin.

Jess kept at it. "So you get in the car, and you all drive to Jem's. Tell me about what happened."

"I knew before we got there that they were up to no good," Lila said. "The air in the car . . . something wasn't right. I said something about it, and Digger kept telling me he just wanted to scare Jem, don't worry about it, everything was going to be fine. But I could tell by the way Billy Wayne and Charlie Chains were acting that Digger was lying."

The food arrived. Neither woman acknowledged it. Jess didn't bother to speak, for fear of breaking the spell of memory that Lila seemed to be under.

"When we got to the apartment," Lila said, "Digger told me to go up and knock on the door. To tell Jem I was shopping for some corn. Like I said, I had a funny feeling, so I asked him could I not. That's when he hit me."

"Digger hit you?"

Lila nodded. "It wasn't the first time, and I knew it wouldn't be the last. He got real serious, those dark eyes of his . . . he was a man without a soul. I know that now. I've been blessed to know a good man, and I doubt I would have recognized him if I hadn't already been with the Devil. Digger, he pulled me in real close and told me to get up those stairs and knock on the door and that all they were going to do was scare Jem, but I knew that wasn't all he was going to do. I knew in my bones what was going to happen, and I still climbed up those stairs and knocked on the door and told Jem to open up."

"It's not your fault," said Jess.

The napkin Lila had been working in her lap finally snapped. She held the two ends in both hands in front of her eyes and stared sadly at them, as if accepting that she could never put them together and make them whole again.

"What happened next?" asked Jess.

"What happened," Lila said, in a near whisper, "is the reason you are working on this story."

"Did you see it happen?"

Lila shook her head.

Jess asked, "How long were you on the premises after Jem opened the door?"

"Once Digger and the boys went inside," Lila said, "I was gone. I was down those stairs and up the street, and I never looked back. Not until yesterday when Caleb Jr. called me on the phone. I knew Caleb would never take me back, and if he did, that would be the first place they came looking. Digger or the cops, someone would come, and they'd never stop. I couldn't go to any of the other old ladies because there was never any doubt where their loyalties lay. No, I hauled ass across Lake Castor to the bus station and did what I had to do to afford a ticket that went all the way to the end of the line, which turned out to be the coast. This is the first time I've ever set foot back here, and to be honest, I still don't feel safe."

"You don't?" Jess asked. "Not even after forty years?"

Lila shook her head, then looked over her shoulder. Outside the window, traffic lazed past. The sun rose high over the parking garage across the street.

"I sure don't," Lila murmured. "I'll never shake the feeling that someone is watching me."

Jess reached into her bag and produced a file folder. "I'm going to show you a photograph. I want you to take a look at it."

"Okay."

"If you recognize the man in the photograph," Jess said, "I want you to tell me. It's very important."

Lila took a deep breath. "Hit me."

Jess opened the folder. On the top was the official eight-by-ten file photograph of former agent Martin Jancowicz. It was several years old, taken a few years before his retirement. Not much had changed between the moment the shot was snapped and when Jess met him at the sheriff's office near Richmond.

Lila leaned forward and studied the photograph. Jess could see sparks of recognition, but they seemed to be hampered by something that kept her from committing.

"There's something familiar about him," Lila said, "but I can't quite place it. Maybe it's the eyes . . . ? Anyway, I'm real sorry to disappoint you, but my memory these days . . ."

"It's okay," said Jess. "Perhaps if I showed you an older photograph."

Jess moved the photo to reveal another, smaller one behind it. This one was taken in 1987, shortly after the last trials from the FIASCO operation. Jancowicz was clean shaven, which revealed a ruddy network of acne scars and laugh lines. He'd cleaned up, for the most part, but the shadow of his former life still shrouded his complexion, which was what Lila recognized almost immediately.

"That's Charlie Chains," she said. "He looks different, but it's certainly him."

"You're positive?"

The expression on Lila's face caused Jess to flinch. It was as if the biker persona had returned after forty years to inhabit the older woman's body.

"I already answered you," Lila said. "Don't ask me again."

CHAPTER SIXTY-ONE

JESS KEELER

Present Day

Ennis Worthy sat in his chicken yard. He did not look up from his hens as Jess entered his periphery. Instead, he kept his eyes on the birds. His shoulders slouched, and for a moment, Jess thought he appeared defeated. She waited for him to acknowledge her, wondering what she might do if he didn't. In the meantime, she watched as a parade of chickens took turns pecking at a speckled hen.

When she could no longer stand the silence, she asked, "Why do those chickens pick on that one like that?"

"She's broody," Worthy answered.

"Broody?"

"Broody is when a chicken's instinct to mother takes her over," Worthy explained. "She feels like she needs to hatch the eggs into babies, only I ain't got a rooster, so there won't be no babies. She don't know that, though. It's just her instinct."

"That doesn't explain why the other chickens peck at her."

"They know it's her time. They can't abide that she ain't in the coop sitting on the eggs. It's her job."

"What if she doesn't want to?"

Worthy shook his head. "Ain't no *want to* about it. It's her instinct."

"It's bullying, is what it is."

"Like I said."

They watched in silence a moment as the chicken, tired of being harassed by the other hens, waddled off to the darkness of the coop.

"How is that any different than depression?" Jess asked.

Worthy turned his head and looked at her for the first time since she'd arrived.

"I can't say that it is."

Jess nodded and let that settle a bit. Then she said, "We're close, Ennis."

He had no reply to that, other than chewing on the insides of his cheeks.

"I don't know what Axel has told you," Jess continued, "but we're almost there. Everything has been falling into place for a long time. It's all coming together, but we're still missing a piece. A very big piece."

Worthy folded both hands on his stomach as he leaned back and scanned the landscape in front of him.

"Why, Ennis?" Jess asked him. "Why won't you tell me?"

His voice was hoarse and resonant. "Tell you what?"

"The truth?"

Worthy grimaced, as if he had asked a question and she had given him the incorrect answer.

"I found someone who can definitively ID Jancowicz as Charlie Chains Wilcox from the Vandals," she said. "It's him, and we know it. It's not enough to convict, but Axel believes it would be enough to get a grand jury who could unseal his records and expose him as working undercover inside the Vandals. Then our witness testifies that he was there the night of the murders, and we'll have him."

Worthy remained nonplussed, his attention seemingly elsewhere.

Jess tried again. "I have a good enough theory that Billy Wayne Dickerson shot the first five sniper victims. According to our sources, he was a sniper in the marines while in Vietnam. He was a *marksman*. His body was found at the old grain silo, which would have given him a vantage point over each of those victims."

Worthy's infamous poker face remained steadfast. He blinked in a slow, slow rhythm while sucking easily on the insides of his cheeks.

"A different rifle killed Hal Broadstreet." Jess was losing her patience. Anger singed her words. "The other five were shot with a .308 round, while Broadstreet was murdered with a .50. Broadstreet was killed after Billy Wayne's body was discovered and after Charlie Wilcox had been declared dead. Only now we know Wilcox wasn't really dead, that he was Jancowicz, and Hal was trying to expose that with his articles when he, himself, was murdered."

Worthy let out a long, heavy sigh. "Let's argue for a minute that you are right," he said. "What good will it do? You tie Jancowicz to the murders, and then what happens? All that work that was done to take down those criminal organizations with FIASCO will be called into question. There could be lawsuits. There could be sentencings over-turned. Is that what you want?"

"Are you justifying *murder*, Ennis?"

"I'm saying it happened forty years ago." It was the first time she had ever heard him raise his voice. "What wrongs do you plan to right with this information, Jess? Tell me that."

"It could free a man from prison," Jess said. "One who does not belong there."

Worthy turned on her, his face rattled with incredulity. "How could you possibly know that?"

"Because he was falsely accused!"

A gray chicken cozied up to Worthy's leg, which seemed to break the spell between him and Jess. He reached down to rub his fingers against her feathers. After a moment, the chicken strutted away, leaving him to wither alone beneath Jess's accusatory stare.

"I realize there's little point," he said, "in trying to convince you to do the right thing."

"This *is* the right thing, En—"

Worthy silenced her by holding up his weathered hand.

"Sometimes you think you are doing what's right," he said. "Sometimes you bend yourself over backward just to do what you think is good and, in doing so, you end up doing something you will forever regret."

She watched him with the chicken and felt the edges of a thought forming. She could picture a young Ennis Worthy in his county browns. However, where she used to imagine him confident and full of pride, she now saw him in a different light.

Jess's eyes narrowed. "What did you do, Ennis?"

Worthy stood, which took some effort at his age. He dusted his hands on his thighs. He started for his house.

"Ennis," Jess called after him. "What did you do?"

He answered by letting his back door slam shut behind him. Jess was left there with the echo of it mingling among her myriad unanswered questions.

CHAPTER SIXTY-TWO

ENNIS WORTHY

1984

Deputy Worthy had been separated from Ricky Lee Patience and led to an unused interrogation room. They left him there most of the day. He sat in one of the three chairs at the table on the side generally offered to suspects. Twice an officer ducked in his head to ask if Worthy needed anything. Both times, he declined. He'd made a note that if he were to be asked again, he would request to call Shirley.

He'd begun to wonder if they had forgotten about him when the door opened and Captain Hank Dorritt entered. He carried a manila file folder and a steaming cup of coffee with him. He placed the coffee in front of Worthy. Worthy approached it warily, uncertain if it was a gift that would come with strings.

"I trust my men have made every effort to keep you comfortable," Dorritt said.

"How is he?" Worthy asked.

"You're talking about Mr. Patience?"

"Ricky Lee. Yes."

"He's unhurt, if that's what you are asking."

"Has he seen a lawyer yet?"

Dorritt gave a quick shake of his head.

"He'll need a lawyer," said Worthy. "If you let me call my girlfriend, she can—"

"I was thinking perhaps you could have a word with him."

"Me? I'm not a lawyer yet. I still need to—"

Dorritt scraped the chair across the floor and sat in it. He set the file folder on the table and opened it, revealing a single typewritten page.

"I was thinking," Dorritt said, "that you might tell that boy it's in his best interest to sign this confession."

Worthy crossed his arms. "Why would I do that?"

"Because it's the best way out for everyone."

"Not for him."

Dorritt said nothing. He kept his gaze fixed on Worthy, as if trying to read him. Worthy gave him nothing.

Worthy said, "I made a promise to his mother."

"His mother," said Dorritt, "is prepared to testify against him, if this goes to trial."

"She . . ." Worthy couldn't complete the thought, much less the sentence.

"Right now," Dorritt continued, "she's ready to claim her son was on the grassy knoll if it means keeping him away from her daughter. She's recounted stories of him ranting and raving like a stark-mad lunatic back at home. She's prepared to testify that she's seen him with a rifle, and that the round my detective found in his home belonged to her son."

"That's a lie, and you know it."

"No, I don't, son. What I do know is that you are going to need to play ball. I've got a community too terrified to leave their houses and open their windows. A signed confession means they can go back to their happy, safe lives, content with the knowledge that Deputy Ennis Worthy and the Lake Castor Police Department have once again done their jobs."

"He didn't do it," Worthy growled.

"Then who did?"

Worthy ran the outcome of every possible scenario in his head.

"You can't know for certain that Mr. Patience didn't do it, so—"

"It was Billy Wayne Dickerson, sir." Worthy took a breath, then said, "Dickerson used the grain elevator as a sniper's nest and chose his victims at random."

"Mr. Dickerson was found beaten to death two weeks ago."

"Yes sir," said Worthy. "I was there when it happened."

Worthy told him everything. About how he'd arrived on the scene after Gary Mock had been shot, then determined the shooter's location. How he had discovered Billy Wayne Dickerson at the top of the silo, and how he had been detained by the mob of angry citizens. He recounted all of it to Dorritt, except for any names or descriptions of Dickerson's attackers, and without mentioning Lorne Axel's involvement.

He didn't have to.

Dorritt watched Worthy for a moment before nodding slowly, then rising from the chair. He walked to the door and opened it. Leaned his head outside and asked an officer to find Lorne Axel, then returned to his seat.

Worthy twisted in his chair. An eternity seemed to pass while they waited for Axel to arrive. When he did, Dorritt commanded him to close the door behind him.

Axel glanced from Dorritt, to Worthy, and then finally to the typed paper between them.

"Officer Axel," said Dorritt, "you were the one who discovered Billy Wayne Dickerson's body two weeks ago. Am I right?"

"Yes sir."

"Is there anything you failed to tell me?"

Worthy leaned forward. "Lorne wasn't involved, sir. I was the only one who—"

Dorritt silenced him by holding up his hand. "Officer Axel?"

"I was there, sir."

Dorritt turned his eyes to Worthy. He slid the confession closer toward him.

"I won't do it, sir," said Worthy. "I refuse to be a party to ruining that boy's life."

"And what about Officer Axel's life?" Dorritt asked.

Axel protested, "I'm a big boy, sir. I can take care of myself."

"What about the people in the Back Back?" asked Dorritt. "What about their lives?"

"I couldn't tell you their names even if I wanted to, sir," said Worthy. "What will you do? Arrest them all?"

Dorritt shrugged a single shoulder, as if he couldn't bother with the effort of the second one. "The directive," he said, "wouldn't be to arrest them."

"You wouldn't dare."

"It would hardly be the first time."

Worthy looked everywhere but at the paper in front of him.

"If it helps you any," Dorritt offered, "you wouldn't be ruining the boy's life. This might be the best thing for him. After he confesses, he would be a guest of the state, and I would personally see to it that he gets the care that he's been denied on the outside. Furthermore, he'd be away from his mother and sister, which would keep them safe."

Dorritt retrieved a pen from his shirt pocket and laid it atop the typed confession.

"Everybody wins, son."

Worthy could look neither of them in the eye.

"Justice isn't always pretty," said Dorritt. "It's rarely ever fair. But this is a win, or as close to a win as we're liable to get in Lake Castor."

Dorritt rose. He opened the door and signaled a dismissal to Axel. Axel left. Before Dorritt stepped out the door, he turned to Worthy and said, "You'd be wise to take it."

Worthy was left alone with the pen, the confession, and a sense of duty that he swore would be the end of him.

CHAPTER SIXTY-THREE

MARTIN JANCOWICZ

Present Day

Jancowicz made it a point to drive slow. To obey every traffic law. To not draw any attention to himself.

Remember what happened last time we ran a stop sign?

Everything had changed the moment he saw Baby Doll in that booth at the All-Niter. What had been a simple directive had shifted to a next-level clusterfuck. It was impossible, he had told himself, over and over. But there was no denying what he had seen through the lens of his sniper rifle's scope: Delilah McNaughton was back from the dead.

The last time he had seen her was on the landing outside Jem Fosskey's garage apartment. She had led them to the six-inch steel door and knocked, just as Digger instructed. When Jem had opened the door for her, Digger shoved her aside and advanced on the bootlegger, the giant blade of his Bowie knife glinting in the lamplight.

He'd made eye contact with her before entering the apartment. The world passed by in that moment. Had she been pleading with him? He stopped, there on the landing, and took her by the shoulders with both hands. Inside, he could hear Digger plunging that Bowie knife into Jem

Fosskey. The bedlam was deafening. Delilah was beginning to realize what she had done.

"Run," he told her. "Run, and don't look back."

When it was all over, Jancowicz pleaded to any god who might listen that Baby Doll would not be waiting for them. He endured Digger's manic tirade as he searched for her, comforted only that he wouldn't find her.

She was gone, so he hoped. He begged that she would stay gone.

Later, as the three of them lay low in a safe house out of town, Digger insisted on riding back to Lake Castor to search for her, leaving Billy Wayne and Jancowicz behind to fret. They knew Digger was scoring more crank, keeping his wires frayed while the two of them were forced to dry out cold turkey. Digger's paranoia had gone off the charts. He couldn't relax knowing that Baby Doll was out there somewhere, could possibly be snitching to the cops about what had happened at Fosskey's or, worse, informing the club. If the Vandals leadership found out what they had done, they would be angry at the three of them for acting out of sanction, drawing undue attention to the club. That couldn't happen. They couldn't find out.

Three can keep a secret if two are dead.

Jancowicz knew that it could be any moment that Digger returned from his search for Baby Doll with a wild hair and killed them all. Something had to be done if they wanted to stay alive.

So you tricked me into killing him.

"It wasn't a trick." Jancowicz parked his car in the driveway of the home he had lived in for the past forty years. It was this house where he had dried out after FIASCO, locked down upon orders by his handler. The neighbor lady next door waved as she watered her garden. Jancowicz waved back.

"Nobody tricked anyone." Jancowicz glared at the empty back seat through his rearview mirror. No one was there. "It was either him or us."

That's what you kept saying.

"And it was true. Neither of us would be here right now if we hadn't taken him off the board."

One of us isn't here right now.

Jancowicz killed the engine and climbed out of his car. Another neighbor jogged past and hollered salutations.

They have no idea, do they? You are that good of a liar.

The night they killed Digger, Jancowicz had spent the entire day trying to convince Billy Wayne of what they had to do. Billy Wayne hadn't been so sure. What sealed it for him were the first words out of Digger's mouth when he returned, cranked out of his skull on amphetamine.

"I found Baby Doll," he said, "and I silenced her for good."

He was lying.

"We know that now."

Jancowicz entered his house through the front door and immediately knew that something was wrong.

There was no one thing that set him off—just a *feeling*—but it was a strong one, and his instincts had yet to let him down. He couldn't put his finger on it, but the sanctity of his home was not intact. The air flowed different. The electricity rode another current.

He moved quick through the living room. He crossed the kitchen directly to the whatnot drawer. Slid it open. Stared stupid into it at an assortment of soy sauce packets, take-out menus, and plasticware.

"Are you looking for this?"

Jancowicz spun around. His handler stood at the opposite end of the room. In his hand was Jancowicz's nine-millimeter Beretta.

"Any chance of you handing that back to me?" Jancowicz asked.

"You won't need it."

The man was at a comfortable distance. He would have time to squeeze off two, maybe three shots before Jancowicz could cross the room. The man watched him do the math as a smile slithered upon his face.

"Janco," he purred, "you and I have been through so much together. In the past, you trusted me implicitly. You would land yourself in a fix, and every time it would be me who got you out of it."

"I wouldn't be in those fixes if it wasn't for you."

The man shook his head. "You act as if you had no choice."

Jancowicz raised his eyebrows, but said nothing.

"You always had a choice," the man said. "Every moment of your life, you had a choice. You could have left the agency. You could have refused the detail. No one held a gun to your head and told you to become an addict."

"I did what it took to survive."

"But it was a choice. Every moment of your life, you had a choice." The man crossed one hand over his gun hand. "Until now."

Jancowicz felt his stomach drop.

"Please," said the man, "come with me."

He led Jancowicz through the house, down the hallway, and into the back bedroom that Jancowicz used for a study. The man directed him to take a seat behind the desk. In doing so, Jancowicz noticed for the first time a sheet of paper lying neatly in the middle of the desk. He inspected it without picking it up.

"This is my handwriting," he said.

"It is," said the man.

"I don't remember writing it."

The man shrugged one shoulder.

Jancowicz shrank back from it. "It's a suicide letter."

"Why didn't you silence that woman?" asked the man.

Jancowicz pointed at the letter. "I didn't write this."

"You had orders to eliminate Jess Keeler. You didn't do it."

"Don't you see?" Jancowicz's voice raised an octave. "She's got it. She's got it all. She found the girl. Baby Doll. She'll tell her everything, and they can tie me to the murders. All of them. They're going to blow it all open."

"What's one more death, when you add it all up?"

There will always be another.

Jancowicz could no longer hear Billy Wayne in his head. Only the memory of his words. If they ever were his words.

Even the ghost of Billy Wayne had abandoned him.

Jancowicz was alone.

"This thing," Jancowicz said, his mouth turning dry, "it's bigger than Keeler now. Killing her won't stop anything. We're done."

"There's nothing that ties you to us," said the man.

Jancowicz looked at the letter again and laughed. "So that's your answer? I kill myself, and it stops with me?"

"It would be the honorable thing."

Jancowicz laughed harder at the word. "Three can keep a secret . . ."

"Only if two are dead."

"I'm not doing it." Jancowicz shook his head. "I'm not going to kill myself."

"Okay." The man pointed to something behind him. "Then how will you explain that?"

"Explain what?"

Jancowicz turned his head. He realized his mistake as soon as he made it. He heard the man advance. He smelled his cheap cologne. He felt the cold barrel of the Beretta against his temple.

He had just enough time to close his eyes before—

CHAPTER SIXTY-FOUR

ENNIS WORTHY

1984

Lorne Axel wasn't wearing his patrolman's uniform. That did nothing to abate the angry and suspicious glances from the woman behind the cash register at the tiny Back Back fry joint. The cook with the grease-spattered apron. The customers at the tables up front.

Axel slowly approached the table and didn't appear the slightest bit offended when Worthy did not stand to receive him. He should have expected no less.

"Afternoon, Ennis," Axel said. "I reckoned I might find you here. I saw you were at the courthouse."

"They found him guilty," Worthy said.

Axel nodded, seemingly aware. He kicked out the chair opposite Worthy and took a seat. Not long after, the waitress arrived. She held no pen or paper in her hand.

"I'll have what he's having," Axel said. "If you'd box it up for me, I'd be app—"

She left before he could finish his sentence.

"You're in plainclothes," Worthy noted. "They finally moved you off patrol and into that big case detail? I hope you're not undercover because those threads ain't fooling anyone."

The two men did not look each other in the eye. Worthy wondered how much time would pass before they ever could again.

"I'm wearing this suit," he said, "because I'm looking for a new job."

"You're what?"

"That's right." Axel nodded. "I can't do it anymore. There's something rotten in that department, and I can't let it get its hooks into me."

Worthy hadn't expected that. "I thought you said law enforcement was in your blood?"

"It is," Axel said, "but there's got to be another way. I was thinking about what you told me was the difference between police and sheriff's. The man in charge of Lake Castor is a good man. Not a *good old boy*, but a good man. I'd like to see if there's a way I can make a difference over there."

"The only problem," Worthy noted, "is they elect someone else every four years. What if the next guy ain't so good? The difference between sheriffs can mean the difference between working cases and jailhouse duty."

"Then we don't let him get elected."

Worthy arched an eyebrow, but didn't say a word.

"What about you?" Axel asked. "I remember hearing you say you weren't long for Deeton. Aren't you headed up to DC to practice law with your woman?"

Worthy shook his head. "She left last week."

Axel finally turned his eyes to Worthy. "I don't understand."

"My home is here," Worthy said. "I have a responsibility to the people here. It's where I can make a difference. If I can't help someone here, then what the hell am I going to do in Washington, DC?"

The waitress arrived with Axel's sack of food. She dropped it in front of him and slapped the bill on the table. Axel couldn't help but crack a smile.

They were silent a moment, the two lawmen. Something passed between them, but it wasn't peace. There wasn't enough of that to go around.

When finally they spoke, it was Axel who said, "I know we done bad, Ennis. You don't have to tell me because I know it already. It's the first thing I think of when I wake up in the morning, and it's the last thought in my head when I lie down to sleep at night."

Worthy thought on that a moment. "It's true," he said. "For all I know, we may burn in hell for what we done. All we can do is try and work to atone for it."

"Do you think we can?"

Worthy nodded. "We can try."

CHAPTER SIXTY-FIVE

Jess Keeler

Present Day

Jess parked in the spot farthest from the prison. Still, she could see the horde of reporters and journalists preparing their live feeds, all in anticipation of the big moment when Ricky Lee Patience would be released. She waited a moment before killing the engine, wondering if she shouldn't turn the car around and head back the way she came. She might have, if it weren't for the two passengers in the car with her.

"That's a lot of newspeople," said her son, Benjamin, in the back seat. "That's like all the stations, isn't it?"

Her mother, Samantha, riding shotgun, pointed through the windshield. "That's my daughter down there. We should go say hi."

"That's not your daughter, Mother," said Jess. "That's Sandy Newman from Story Time."

Samantha's expression knotted up, the way it often did when she grew confused. That had been happening more and more lately.

Jess watched Sandy, her former protégé, as she preened for the camera on Aaron's shoulder. Beside her were Wilhelmina Potts and her son, Martin, both seemingly excited about the release of her long-estranged brother for a crime for which he had been recently exonerated. Their faces had been aired on nearly every morning news program for the past two weeks as the big day loomed before them.

"You should be down there too," Benjamin said.

Jess had yet to remove her hands from the steering wheel. "This is as close as I plan to get."

So far, Jess had refused to watch the first three episodes that had been released on a popular streaming network. No matter how hard she tried, however, she couldn't ignore the marketing blitz. Trailers, interviews on the radio and local television stations, even a billboard on the interstate . . . all of it had been building to this moment that, she had no doubt, the Germans would be reserving as the climax to the series.

A knock at her window.

Jess turned to find Ennis Worthy. She patted her mother on the arm, then climbed out of the car.

"I'm surprised you came," she told him. "I thought this would be the last place we'd find you."

"I was here the day he went in," Worthy said, "so I reckon it's only right that I'm here on the day he comes out."

"Will you speak with him?"

"No ma'am," Worthy said. "You?"

"It's complicated."

Worthy nodded.

Jess needed no further explanation offered or given. Everything had moved so fast after she'd found Delilah "Baby Doll" McNaughton that she'd honestly believed she'd managed some sort of control over the events. She became convinced that her podcast was a necessary contribution, something that could be used to right wrongs and free an innocent man from prison and restore his name. She had busied herself by planning the trap she would spring to trick Martin Jancowicz into confessing his complicity in the death of Hal Broadstreet and Jem Fosskey's crew, when she'd gotten a phone call from Lorne Axel.

"I've got good news and bad news," Axel had told her on that day, weeks earlier.

"Give me the good news first," Jess answered.

"Jancowicz confessed to shooting Hal Broadstreet in 1984," Axel said. "Apparently he feared how close Broadstreet was getting to discovering the cover story of Charles Wilcox's faked death, and he panicked. He claimed to be afraid of his identity as an undercover operative being outed and retribution from the club."

"That means we got him," Jess said. "Between Baby Doll's testimony and his confession, we could get him for an unsolved case and overturn the conviction of an innocent man. This is huge."

"Yes ma'am, it is."

But Jess was reluctant to celebrate. "You said there was bad news?"

"This confession," Axel had said, "was delivered in a suicide letter."

Over the next couple of days, she was able to piece together details as they were revealed. A neighbor called the police to report an unresponsive male in Jancowicz's home. They found him sitting at his desk with his Beretta in his hand, single shot to his temple. On the desk in front of him was his blood-spattered confession.

His personnel files, which had previously been withheld from Sheriff Axel, were miraculously available shortly after. They confirmed Jess's theories. He had been an undercover agent in Operation FIASCO, the joint task force intended to infiltrate motorcycle clubs. Inside this new information, Jess discovered reprimands for drug use that stemmed from his deep-cover experience in the club. Also, that he had been a marksman.

After that, the wind had quickly left her sails. She couldn't explain why she mourned for Martin Jancowicz. He was a cop who turned killer. A man responsible for so much death and chaos over such a small period of time. Perhaps because it was once again a killer that she had pursued who had eluded justice. Or that it was because so many answers would be taken with him to the grave.

"There are still several things that bother me," Worthy said.

Jess watched the scene at the prison doors. Sandy prepped Wilhelmina Potts on what to say and do in the moments leading up to Ricky Lee's release. Willie had long expressed a desire to see her story played out on television and appeared to soak up every bit of the attention. *She's a natural,* Jess thought sardonically.

"Those records that were withheld until his death," Worthy continued. "That was awfully convenient."

Jess nodded. She had already puzzled over that.

"Do you think there might have been some institutional cover-up?" he asked.

"Most likely."

"Do you reckon that to be your next investigation?"

Jess shook her head. "No."

"Why not?"

Jess turned her head and caught sight of her mother in the front seat of her car. Ben in the back, showing her something on his phone. She thought again of someone high up in some law enforcement organization. Someone with the power to make bad things disappear, to make people forget, to make people go away. Someone who could make the deaths of so many people seem insignificant over time, could imprison an innocent man. What other lengths might they go to in order to preserve their little secrets?

She thought again of Olivia Crane's prophetic words: *You're not chasing some eighty-year-old doctor. The men who pulled the trigger may very well be dead, but the organization they belonged to is very much alive and has no interest in being talked about in public.*

"I'm done, Ennis," she said.

Worthy said nothing else, as if he understood all too well. And she knew he did. They shared the silence a moment, and she thought perhaps she finally understood Ennis Worthy, a man who had previously seemed so enigmatic.

Her phone rumbled in her pocket. She checked the screen and found a text from Sandy.

You showed your face. Trying to steal my thunder again?

Jess scanned the crowd and saw Sandy staring back at her. Jess thumbed out a reply.

The limelight is all yours, sister. Congratulations

Jess believed she could see Sandy roll her eyes. The young reporter started to type something back, but it remained three dots on Jess's screen because the prison gates began to open and the cameras clicked in unison.

Ricky Lee Patience emerged. He stood there, alone and frail, as the hubbub around him reached a fever pitch. The throng of reporters moved in a single mass, urging forward, microphones probing as their questions formed an indecipherable collective roar.

Without saying a word, Worthy tipped his hat at Jess. He turned and walked away. Jess didn't stop him. She, too, would leave if she could.

But she couldn't. She'd already damned herself to watching it all.

Willie Potts emerged from the crowd and stood before her older brother, whom she hadn't seen in over forty years. The media pool had been stunned into silence, anticipating anything they could steal for broadcast. Two strangers reunited. She held out her arms to receive him, but he did not seem to know how to react.

It was in that moment when Jess realized Worthy had been right. She had done everything she could to help release Ricky Lee Patience, but never until just then had she ever questioned if it was the right thing to do for him. The weight of her comprehension bore down heavy upon her. She climbed back into her car, heartbroken.

Benjamin watched a live feed of the proceedings on his phone. A breathless reporter whispered the reactions to Willie and Ricky Lee's long-awaited meeting.

"Are you okay, Mom?" Benjamin asked.

"Will you turn that off?" she said as she started the engine.

Leaving so soon?

Before Jess could turn off her screen, another text pinged.

Not sticking around for the end of the story?

Jess slipped the car into reverse.

Maybe you don't have what it takes to make it in this business after all, jess keeler

Jess threw the car into park. She tried to think of a different reply—any at all—but there was only one answer that was the truth. All others would be a lie.

I think you may be right

ACKNOWLEDGMENTS

So many things had to happen in order for this book to exist, and none of them would have happened without my agent, Josh Getzler, believing in me to get them done. I'm eternally grateful to him, Jon Cobb, and the entire staff at HG Literary, for everything they've done to get me here, including all the things I don't even know about.

Speaking of teams: I shudder to think what I might sound like if not for the diligent efforts of the Thomas & Mercer team. Thank you to Jessica Tribble Wells for providing her vast resources so that I might try new things, knowing that her folks would have my back. Charlotte Herscher, Sarah Shaw, Miranda Gardner, Alicia, Mindi Machart, and so many more that I will probably never know the names of . . . thank you so much.

I would never have had the time to meet my deadlines if it weren't for my two sisters from other misters, Alexis and Jackie. For real, y'all.

Thank you to my father, Charles, and my sister, Natalie, for all your unending support.

I also thank my writer friends who have helped keep my spirits up, whether it's fielding a phone call or reading with me at a Noir at the Bar or having drinks with me . . . this is a much lonelier adventure without S. A. Cosby, Rob Hart, Todd Robinson, Nick Kolakowski, Nik Korpon, David Swinson, James Grady, Jamie Mason, Katy Munger, Mike McCrary, Dana (and Corky) King, E. A. Aymar, Brooke Cain, Dale Edwards, Rob

Creekmore, Josh Pachter, Wes Browne, Meagan Lucas, Melissa Bourbon, Dianne Kelly, and so, so many more. Thank you.

A huge thank-you to Major Tim Horne (retired) and attorneys Sam Coleman and Russell Johnson for fact-checking me.

Where would I be without the folks out YONDER who cheered me on, attended readings, and supported me while I chase my dreams? Among the scores of them, I want to thank Sean, Kenny and Jada, DJ and Larry, Mary and David, Steve and Diane, all the Sara(h)s—Smith, LaFone, Timmel, Zaleta, and Young—Claudia, Maree, Paige and Eddie, Mattie Reames, Robert and Meghan, Wyatt and Jessie, Josh and Bethany, John and Doreen and Kelsey, Heather W., Bob J., Bob B. and Tracey, Elizabeth and Jason, WHUP FM, WCHL FM, Jeffrey and Michael, Amanda Boyd, Mayor Jenn, Victoria, Dr. Lunchbox, Kiah, Jesse, Dan Morrison, Lance and Becky, and Lupe from the very bottom of my dark heart. Thank you, thank you, thank you.

Also, a huge thank-you for the support from Purple Crow Books in Hillsborough, the Regulator Bookshop in Durham, and Pete Mock at McIntyre's in Pittsboro. Y'all are all so amazing.

And a huge thank-you to Lana Pierce, whom I am still trying to impress after all these years.

ABOUT THE AUTHOR

Photo © 2016 Alex Maness

Eryk Pruitt is a filmmaker, novelist, and screenwriter living in Hillsborough, North Carolina. His films have earned top prizes at film festivals around the world, and his novel *What We Reckon* was a finalist for the Anthony Award. His latest novel, *Something Bad Wrong*, is available wherever you buy books. He can be found either at his desk, hard at work on another story, or mixing drinks at his bar, Yonder.